THE LIFE CYCLE OF
THE COMMON OCTOPUS

The

LIFE CYCLE

of the

COMMON OCTOPUS

EMMA KNIGHT

Pamela Dorman Books • *Viking*

VIKING
An imprint of Penguin Random House LLC
penguinrandomhouse.com

A Pamela Dorman Book/Viking

LIBRARY OF CONGRESS CATALOGING-IN-PUBLICATION DATA
Names: Knight, Emma (Emma L.) author.
Title: The life cycle of the common octopus : a novel / Emma Knight.
Description: New York : Pamela Dorman Books/Viking, 2025.
Identifiers: LCCN 2024042645 (print) | LCCN 2024042646 (ebook) |
ISBN 9780593830451 (hardcover) | ISBN 9780593830468 (ebook) |
ISBN 9798217059324 (international edition)
Subjects: LCGFT: Novels.
Classification: LCC PR9199.4.K5768 L54 2025 (print) |
LCC PR9199.4.K5768 (ebook) | DDC 813/.6—dc23/eng/20240920
LC record available at https://lccn.loc.gov/2024042645
LC ebook record available at https://lccn.loc.gov/2024042646

Printed in the United States of America
1   3   5   7   9   10   8   6   4   2

DESIGNED BY MEIGHAN CAVANAUGH

for my grandmother Shirley Margaret Daynard,

formerly Flood, née Gardiner

If you took the monsters' point of view, everything they did made perfect sense. The trick was learning to think like a monster.

—Sy Montgomery, *The Soul of an Octopus*

Now

I know there are exceptions—pregnant male seahorses with their brood pouches and so on—but mostly, it's females who carry the future. It can be deadly work. In some corners of nature, children gain strength by eating their mothers alive. Among humans such theatrics are frowned upon. Rare is the mother who forgets the Goldfish crackers and is cannibalized in her minivan. More common is the one who devours herself.

It disturbs me, looking at your soft belly, to think of you growing into a woman. I lay you down on the white bedspread to towel you off after the bath. I sneak my finger into the crevice between your chin and chest to make you smile. You follow me with your trusting eyes, dark as the North Sea, forgiving me in advance, or so it seems, for the many ways in which I will fail you.

You are smooth and pink, and I pretend that we are still one. But even as I think this, I know it isn't true. I'm alone in my body again, and you're alone in yours.

I lower you into your crib. You murmur and turn onto your side, caressing the plush octopus she sent us, going somewhere I will never be able to follow. I watch you lying there, heavy with milk and sleep, and think: *We carry the past, too.*

I am thirty-one years old. From here I can see my own mother, far better than before. I can't see my grandmothers, but I can feel them. The choices they did not have. Their warm, mutilated hearts. Their capable fingers, finally at rest.

Within each of us is an inky bottom-place where fallen corpses and old skins feed new life. Flashes rise, unbidden, from the deep. What surfaces now, as I guard your sleep, is the age of leaving. The age of maturity, or so we thought at the time. In fact we were tender and exposed, in need of every trick instinct and evolution could bestow.

As nights smudge into looping days, I return to that year. I remember who we were, and what we thought we knew. I turn it over in my mind deciding what to let sink, and what to preserve for a future that I can hardly presume to imagine, because it will be yours.

Pollock Halls of Residence
The University of Edinburgh

September 13th, 2006

Dear Lord Lennox,

My desire to reach you has overridden my Canadian obedience, and
I am writing care of your literary agent, against the reasonable
advice of both receptionists at your publisher's. I want to assure you
that this is not a crazed fan letter.

   I believe you went to school with my dad, Edward (Ted) Winters.
He is not the most forthcoming of conversationalists, as you may
know, but I have pieced together some clues over the years, and they
all lead to you.

   I have recently moved to Edinburgh to begin a degree, and I
wondered if there might be an opportunity to meet you. I can travel
anywhere; this matter is as critical to my education as any.

                    With apologies for the intrusion and many thanks,
                    Penelope Elliot Winters

P.S. Though not crazed, I am a fan—and ever impressed by
Paquin's ability to solve a murder three drinks in!!

Talmòrach

Sept. 23rd

Dear Penelope,

*Delighted to receive your letter—glad you made it past the guards.
Fond memories of your father. Hope he's well? Come east. Must show
you the vistas and ruins of the Mearns, though perhaps not all at
once. Saturday next? The train will take you as far as Stonehaven.
Send your landing time and we'll send a good man with a good
mustache by the name of Hector (the man, that is).*

Yours,
Elliot Lennox

Ps. The first two never count.

Fall

1

If you were to interview a handful of students as they emerged, static-haired and blinking, from their rooms in Pollock Halls, some smelling inexplicably of horses and others more explicably of charred cheese, you would learn that breakfast at the John McIntyre Centre was not widely viewed as an inspiring meal. But Pen, who was ravenous in the mornings, looked forward to it.

It was a Tuesday, the third in the term. Pen arrived at the green and brown building in the middle of the residence compound at five minutes to eight. Cold, wet air was reaching under the collar of her raincoat. She stopped into the convenience store for a newspaper. At the last second, her heart thudding its disapproval, she also requested a ten-pack of cigarettes and a box of matches. The man behind the counter didn't even glance at her. She was back under the portico, folding newsprint against the wind to scan the headlines and thinking about the letter she had just read when Jo arrived with Alice trailing behind.

Her friends stood out. Jo Scarlett Moore because she looked so whole-some, with her pale hair wound in a braid across her forehead, that it did not seem possible for her to belong to this century of internet porn and ocean trash, and Alice Diamond because Alice stood out every-where.

"Morning, Stinky," Jo said, touching her lips to Pen's cheeks.

Alice, who had not yet shaken her national reflexes, bent down to hug Pen. As had become their custom since Jo had "discovered" Alice on the dance floor of the Opal Lounge (or had it been the other way around?) during the five-day game of chicken with mononucleosis known as Freshers' Week, the three went in to breakfast together.

By the time of their arrival in Edinburgh, Pen and Alice had been fix-tures in one another's lives for over a decade. Throughout high school, afternoons had found them sprawled on Pen's white duvet, their legs up the wall in a pose that Alice insisted was good for thinking deep thoughts, their bare feet brushing the Polaroids and ticket stubs on Pen's bulletin board, awaiting the beginning of life.

Although they shared many common circumstances—both had been raised on prosperous, tree-lined Toronto streets by loving parents who believed they hid their unhappiness well—Pen and Alice had no short-age of points of difference to find fascinating in one another. Alice had grown early into a tall and striking young woman with the coloring and survival instinct of a lioness, while Pen, a late bloomer, had usually been the smallest and quickest in their class, with the glow-in-the-dark eyes and skittish flinch of a black house cat.

Each had learned much of what her parents preferred not to talk about from books, but while Alice devoured anything that contained either an ambitious hero's dogged pursuit of his true destiny or technical descriptions of sex—and these she underlined for future reference—Pen became devoted, around her fourteenth birthday, to plowing through her mother's entire collection of thin-paged, densely typed nineteenth-century novels. At that age, their truths reached her only in the way one might catch a whiff, from across the fence, of a neighbor's dinner cooking on the barbecue. Alone in her room, she ran her eyes along the surfaces of their sentences, trying to convince herself that the enduring and transformative love they so often described must be observable somewhere in the real world.

Pen later learned that many of her favorites had been written by women for whom marital bliss had remained, for one reason or another, forever out of reach. She was able to conclude, then, with the relief that can accompany the death of hope, that these stories were mere fantasy, and that the conjugal disharmony of real life alone could be taken as fact.

Facts were of considerable importance to Pen. She had learned early to mistrust both the Pascal's wager Protestantism of the Winters branch and the residue of Catholicism that clung like incense to her mother. In the absence of religion, she found facts reassuring.

Alice was the only person to whom Pen freely related her many theories and discoveries without fear of being either mocked or fully believed. After eleven years of friendship, each had become adept at anticipating the other's thoughts. This, like their mutual (but independently made) decision to go to Scotland for university, struck them as both wonderful and dangerous. The comforting prospect of being together on a new continent was clouded by a shared awareness that they might, by relying too much on that comfort, prevent one another from achieving the state of self-sufficiency that both so achingly sought. They had thus made a vague but solemn promise, several months before the start of their first term, not to get in each other's way in Edinburgh.

. . .

The neon buffet featured scrambled eggs too puffy to be true, baked beans with a faint aftertaste of ash, pliable triangles of potato bread, and something darkly sausage-like. Avoiding the scrum of weather-dampened elbows, Pen ladled hot porridge into one bowl and filled another to the brim with sugary muesli. Her tray received a nod from the ladies who check that you're not overdoing it, and she poured a cup of coffee while she waited for Alice and Jo to catch up.

At this hour it was easy to find a table in the center of the action. Jo's twin brother was the first to join them. Fergus Scarlett Moore was tall and almost comically regal in his bearing, with neatly combed blond hair and an air of studied melancholy that reminded Pen of photos of F. Scott Fitzgerald. When he did not know he was being watched, she thought she could see a depth of humanity in his downturned gray eyes that was at odds with much of what he said. This, and his strange sense of humor, made her like Fergus more than she sometimes wanted to.

"How are we this morning?" he asked, lowering himself into the seat beside Pen's. She could see the film of rain on his royal blue sweater. Fergus belonged to a subset of English boys who never seemed to wear a coat. "What do the Trots have to say for themselves today, I wonder," he said, shaking open her newspaper.

Hugo Holloway arrived next, hiding an extra plate of sausage under his tray. Before meeting Hugo, Pen had harbored a secret tenderness for him. Not from physical attraction—Hugo was square-shaped, with ruddy cheeks and a high laugh—but because he looked forty. She'd spun a story involving a lonely struggle and the grit to start over, until Jo had pointed him out as Fergus's roommate from boarding school—actual age: nineteen—the third son in a family of sailing enthusiasts with homes in various tax havens, and a solid enough character, provided you kept your expectations in check.

"Do you know what I've realized?" Fergus said, laying down the newspaper.

"What?" asked Pen when no one else volunteered. She had discreetly picked all the sugar-coated raisins out of her muesli and placed them on a napkin in the corner of her tray. Fergus glanced at the pile and met her eyes.

"I must befriend a medic," he said.

"Must you?" asked Charlie, who was just sitting down. "Why?"

Charlie Watson lived above Alice in Baird House and had fallen into step with her during the Baird House Orientation Pub Crawl. Alice had felt a quick, energetic pull between them, but later noticed that everyone Charlie spoke with seemed to stumble away, dizzy and flushed from his attention. The next morning he'd sat at their table as if he and Alice were old friends, and three weeks later they more or less were.

Charlie had an even-planed face that filled with warmth when he was listening, and eyes that smiled under thick lashes. He dressed more tidily than the average student, except for a pair of filthy, paint-splattered canvas sneakers. It was hard to get him talking about himself, but Alice had managed to learn that he hailed from Dumfries, that he knew every bouncer at every nightclub by name, and that he was studying History of Art with the goal of one day opening his own gallery.

"We all must," Fergus said with greater urgency. "And soon. Rubens and epistemology are fine for a dinner party, but one never knows when one will get a gammy leg."

"Is your leg gammy?" asked Jo.

"No, and thank you for your concern," said Fergus. "But I believe in preparedness."

"Maybe you should switch to medicine. That way you can prepare your own poultices when the day comes," suggested Alice, who was emptying a packet of artificial sweetener into her mug.

"Soundly reasoned, Snow Yank," said Fergus. "But I'm shy of insides."

He picked up a raisin from the pile on Pen's tray, examined it, and tossed it at a red-haired girl at the next table. It left a puff of white sugar on her dark sweater, just below her ponytail. Fergus looked gratified and tossed another. The girl did not turn around.

Hugo, who had wiped his first plate clean, surfaced. "I'm doing biology, in case you'd forgotten," he said in his game-for-anything voice. "I might go in for medicine after. I'd be happy to practice operating on you, Ferg."

Hugo's tanned forearms were hairy where he had rolled up his shirtsleeves. His fingers had meaty pads that Pen found it difficult to imagine manipulating the tools of surgery.

"I won't forget your kindness," said Fergus.

"What'll you girls do after uni," Hugo asked brightly, spearing a sausage. "Move to London and get preggers?"

"Yes," said Alice. "That's the general plan. Assuming we can find someone to knock us all up." She looked Hugo up and down while he chewed. "A nice fertile medic, perhaps."

"Fuck off, Hugo," said Jo, who was more direct. Jo shared her brother's anachronistic accent, but while he emphasized his, she played hers down. Her voice had a pleasant rasp, and she swore often and with relish. "Alice is going to take the West End by storm. She'll become hideously famous and surround herself with backup dancers who feed her cheese toasties dipped in ketchup. Stinky here is going to spirit to the top of a news magazine of great editorial distinction, hiring lightweights like you and Ferg to fetch her coffee just so she can sexually harass you in the workplace. And I'm going to be a dissolute public intellectual who whips my female students into frenzies of desire, like Abelard, only harder to castrate."

Hugo chortled. He may not have known who Abelard was, but the idea of Jo whipping female students into frenzies appeared to make him a bit lightheaded.

Fergus turned to Pen and nodded thoughtfully. He picked up another raisin and took aim. This time it hit the back of the girl's head. She spun around, ponytail swinging.

"Fergus," she said in a plaintive voice, patting her scalp, "why are you throwing sultanas at us?"

"Raisins," he said, in a voice that suggested this would clarify matters. "What?"

"Sultanas are the yellow ones. It's an installation, Floss. 'Dusting the Duchess.' Muesli on . . ." He reached across to pet the fabric of her sweater. "Mohair."

Flossie glowered prettily up at him, using the full power of her pale blue eyes and heart-shaped face, and then returned to her breakfast.

"Right, I'm off." Charlie stood up. "Anyone fancy a lift?"

Charlie and Hugo were among the rare students who had cars, and both were generous with rides.

"Thanks, Charlie, we'll walk," said Jo. "The Canadians and I like to start our day with invigorating exercise. Take my brother, will you? He's delicate."

On the way out, Pen saw Fergus stop behind Flossie. He tossed a final raisin at her back at close range, watched it fall to the ground, and carefully wiped the dust from her sweater with his sleeve.

2

With gardens at its center whose sodden grass was deserted for most of the school year, except for the weeks before spring exams when it was possible to acquire a sunburn in the time it took to roll a cigarette, George Square was the academic nucleus of the university. A twenty-minute walk from Pollock Halls, it stood between Old Town to the north and the Meadows to the south. Half of the Georgian terraced houses rimming the square now sheltered the erratically heated faculty offices and tutorial rooms of the university's least lucrative departments. The rest had been razed in the 1960s to make way for taller, blockier buildings like the Main Library and the David Hume Tower.

The George Square Theatre was their destination, and its main lecture hall was nearly full when they arrived. Pen spotted three seats in the back row and they bumped past denim-clad knees to claim them. She slid out of her coat and opened her notebook, then glanced around at her classmates. She pictured her dad and Lennox among them. Nineteen and awash in glandular secretions. The image filled her with a particular kind of dread. The kind that urged her, when she spotted a motionless clump by the side of the road, to let her eyes linger, to see for herself the fur or feathers matted with blood, to confirm that yes, this had once been a life. "He's just sleeping," her dad had told her the day she'd tugged him toward a deflated raccoon on their street. It had been the first time she'd known for sure that he was lying.

That her father had a secret going bad inside of him had become known to Pen in grade four. Mr. Quinn, an unpredictable giant who brought his lunch in a rinsed-out ice cream container, had been reading aloud to them that morning while they practiced their cursive. Pen listened while savoring the loops in her name, like the upside-down swings of a roller coaster.

Alice was bent low over her desk in concentration. She had abandoned the handwriting task and was doodling instead. A girl with stringy hair, baggy jeans, and a flat chest stood grimacing under the word BEFORE, beside a smugly buxom AFTER in a tuxedo jacket, matching shorts, and knee-high boots.

Pen felt something humid on her neck and recoiled. Conor Minnow was peering at her column of identical signatures.

"Your middle name is Elliot?" he hissed. His breath smelled of Dunkaroos.

Conor Minnow had recently proposed to Pen, standing on a bench in the gym during indoor recess. She had said she'd have to think about it.

Pen turned. "So?"

"Is it your mom's last name or something?" he demanded.

"No."

"Well, it's a boy's name. It's ugly for a girl."

Alice whipped around in her chair and looked at Conor like she might punch him in the face. Which would not have been unprecedented.

"Watch your stupid mouth, Minnow," she said.

Mr. Quinn was looming over them now, his bushy eyebrows squished together like caterpillars.

"Stand up. Siddown," he barked.

Conor and Alice, who were accustomed to this form of punishment, bounced to their feet and returned to their chairs. Pen, who had never so much as elicited a raised voice from a teacher, was temporarily unable to make her legs comply.

"Can you hear me? Stand at the back of the room!" Mr. Quinn's voice boomed close to Pen's face, making her eardrum vibrate.

Pen stood with her back to the wall, erect as a tin soldier. She dug her nails into the soft flesh of her palms. Alice turned to look back at her, widening her eyes in sympathetic indignation and mouthing the word "dipshit."

It *was* strange, Pen was thinking. Elliot wasn't a family name. Her paternal grandfather had been called Edward, like her dad. Her mom's father figure, who had died before Pen was born, had been a Gregory. There were no Elliots, as far as she knew. When the bell rang, she waited for the class to clear out before leaving the room. Alice stayed behind. She stooped to link her arm through Pen's, forcing her to unclench her fists, and the two walked out to the playground together.

After dinner, when Pen's dad was in his chair at the kitchen table, a glass of wine before him, she climbed into his lap. Narrow but solid, with fading copper hair, her father looked to Pen like a weathered sea captain.

"Why do I have a boy's name?" she asked, rubbing her cheek against his, breathing in his smell, like a stack of warm printer paper.

"Penelope's not a boy's name," he said in the playful voice he'd used with her in those days. "Penelope was the daughter of Icarius, a Spartan king. He didn't want her to get married because he didn't want to lose her. But then Odysseus, the hero of Homer's poem, beat her poor old dad in a race, and he had no choice but to let her go."

"My middle name," she persisted.

"Penelope Elliot is melodic," he said, stroking her hair absently.

"Who was Elliot, Daddy?" The top button of his collar was done up. She stared at the imprisoned knob of his Adam's apple.

"Well, there's T. S. Eliot. And George Eliot, though of course her real name was Mary Ann."

"Dad."

He looked into his glass of red wine for what seemed like a long time. "Elliot was a close friend of mine," he finally said. "We were at school together. He's a writer now. He lives in Scotland." The words came out quietly, as if he were speaking to himself. Then he tilted her from his lap, depositing her socked feet on the floor, and took his glass upstairs to his study.

Pen sensed in these words the answer to a fundamental question that she didn't yet know how to ask. She repeated them to herself later as she was falling asleep, surrounded by her menagerie of stuffed animals, until they became a kind of incantation. He must have thought she was too young to remember. But children remember everything. It's adults who forget.

There wasn't enough air in the lecture theater. On Alice's left, Pen was in one of her trances, transcribing every word like a court stenographer. On her right, Jo looked down at the stage through half-closed eyes. Alice crossed her arms over her waist and managed to pull off her sweater without elbowing either of her friends in the face. Her T-shirt came up with it, briefly exposing her turquoise bra to the hundred or so assembled, but Alice didn't care. She was an actor; she was used to being seen.

She peeled the cotton away from the staticky wool and smoothed it back down over herself. Then she raked her hands through her mass of hair, twisted it into a knot, and exhaled.

"Better?" Pen asked. Pen was always cold, and she liked to make fun of Alice's tendency to strip the minute she got anywhere.

"Much." Alice opened her bent spiral notebook to a blank page and turned her attention to the man speaking at the front of the room.

It wasn't the same professor from the previous week, Peter something. Today's lecturer was younger, about forty, with wavy dark hair, a Roman nose, and serious eyes set deeply in a pale face. He wore a suit that fit him well. He was holding on to the podium with both hands, as if to steady himself, and talking about the German philosopher Immanuel Kant. He pronounced it *can't*, the corners of his mouth pulling apart. Kant, he was saying, tried to decouple (that was the word he used: "decouple") morality from religion. He wanted to prove that morality was a constant by grounding it in logic, because logic is irrefutable. Kant wanted to make morality irrefutable, too.

"According to Kant," he said, "'good' is synonymous with the will to do good."

Alice glanced at Pen to see her reaction. Even as a child, Pen had been preoccupied with the will to do good. She was always looking for something to feel guilty about. But Pen's chin-length dark brown hair had fallen out from behind her ear, and her face was hidden. Alice nudged her gently in the ribs.

"What?" Pen looked up from her notes and fixed Alice with her intense green stare.

Alice made her eyes big and gestured toward the stage. "Who's that?"

"Julian Sachs," said Pen in a low voice. "Our tutor."

Pen turned to the back of her notebook and pulled a schedule from the pocket. Alice, who had skipped the previous week's tutorial, nodded.

"What are you two nattering about?" Jo asked, leaning over Alice.

"Alice has discovered a latent interest in German idealism," said Pen.

"Aha," said Jo. "We wondered how long it would take you to warm to your outside subject."

At the end of the hour, Alice watched Julian Sachs fold his lecture notes in half and put them in his briefcase. Pen and Jo were standing in the aisle, waiting. In front of the lecture theater's revolving doors, Alice stopped to put on her layers, forcing the stream of exiting students to flow around her before dispersing across George Square.

From the south side of the square, Fergus was striding toward them. "The Pen is mightier than the sword!" he called out with Shakespearean emphasis, projecting over the wind. Several heads turned. He looked pleased with himself.

"Mightier than yours," replied Pen in an unconcerned voice that was just as clear.

A passerby offered an appreciative whistle. Alice smiled. Pen's habitual primness made her bold side more effective, when unleashed.

Fergus gave a formal bow, acknowledging defeat. Alice detached herself from the group, ascending the steps to the library. She contemplated a third coffee, knowing it would make her heart race.

"Hello," said a voice from behind her. She knew without looking who it was. She felt her chest tighten.

"Hi," she said.

"Hi," he repeated. They both stopped beside the entrance. "I wondered if I'd meet the elusive Alice Diamond."

Alice removed a strand of hair that was stuck to her lip. "How did you know my name?"

"I saw you arrive with your friends. They made excuses for your truancy last week. Said you were auditioning for a play." He said this as if it were a surprising thing, like she was trying out for the circus.

"I was," she said.

"Did you get the part?"

"I did."

"Will I see you this afternoon then?"

She nodded. He smiled again, his eyes crinkling.

"What's the play, if I may ask?"

"*Arcadia*. I'm Thomasina."

"*Et in Arcadia ego*," Julian said. He held the door open for her. "Even in Arcadia, here am I," he added more quietly, as she passed under his arm.

Alice forgot that she had wanted a coffee. She rummaged in her bag until she found her student card and all but ran into the library. McAvoy. That was the previous lecturer's name. Where was Peter McAvoy when she needed him?

3

"You should have heard our Alice," Jo told the others at the Crags that evening. They were squeezed together in the middle of a long picnic table on the pub's terrace. "You'd have thought Bernard Williams himself was speaking through her."

Sandwiched between Charlie and Fergus, Pen felt pleasantly hidden. She hadn't yet had a moment alone with Alice to tell her about the letter from Elliot Lennox, and she was having trouble thinking about anything else.

"Don't make fun," said Alice. "We can't all be as intellectual as you and Pen."

"I'm being serious," said Jo. "Your dramatic retelling of the thought experiment about hapless tourist Jim was spot on."

Alice knew her performance in that afternoon's tutorial had been decent. She had enjoyed having Julian as her audience.

"Good," said Alice.

"The greatest good," said Jo.

"Enough shop talk," Fergus said, drumming his fingers on the gummy tabletop. "Who's coming to Buttons this weekend? Mummy said to be six, and she specifically requested that Josephine bring her Canadians. Perhaps you remind her of our imperial glory—I can't think why else she'd have taken such a shine to you."

Buttons was the name of Jo and Fergus's family house in the Borders, where they had all spent the previous weekend swishing through grass so green it looked spray-painted, being lectured by Fergus on the ecological necessity of culling deer, and then warming up by the fire with mugs of hot port. It had been Pen and Alice's first experience of the Scottish countryside, and they had found it thoroughly enchanting.

"Flattering," said Alice. "I'm in."

"Same," said Hugo.

"Excellent, a chauffeur," said Fergus.

"Two," said Charlie. "For the way out, anyhow. I'll pop home Sunday."

Fergus raised his eyebrows at Pen.

"Thanks, Fergus. I'd love to, but I can't this weekend," she said.

"What?" His face fell into a pout. "You've been here less than a month. Who in Merlin's name is dragging you home?"

Pen glanced sideways at Alice, who seemed both surprised by Pen's answer and amused by Fergus's pique.

"Damned colonial! Don't be coy with me. Who is it?" Fergus demanded.

Pen's cheeks turned pink. "Elliot Lennox," she said.

"*Lord* Lennox, the writer?" asked Charlie, sounding impressed.

"Bloody hell," said Hugo.

"As in, brother of Margot Lennox?" asked Jo, looking between Alice and Pen.

The surname Lennox, already old and storied, was given its contemporary luster not only by Lord Elliot Lennox—the author of a bestselling detective series whose bedraggled hero, Inspector Robert Paquin, was beloved around the world—but also by his younger sister, Margot. Margot Lennox was a fashion designer who, by Alice's telling, had instigated the shift from women dressing for "the male gaze" to dressing for themselves and for each other. Margot had founded her eponymous label at age twenty-three, showing first in London and then in Paris, where she had situated her atelier in the 20th arrondissement and famously offered every one of her workers a living wage, shares in the company, and free on-site childcare. Her clothes were extremely tasteful, extremely expensive, and worn by several of Alice's favorite female actors, many of whom Margot dressed personally. Alice, who had been reading fashion magazines since the fourth grade, worshipped her.

"Why?" protested Fergus, still petulant. "What have they got to do with anything?"

"He's an old friend of my dad's," said Pen. "But they don't talk anymore," she added quickly.

Fergus drained his pint glass and put it down. "I'll ask Flossie then. Unless she's got a date with Sir Arthur Conan Doyle." He got up. "Another round?"

"I think my brother fancies Penelope," Jo announced to the table once he had gone.

"What gives you that impression?" Hugo asked, mock serious.

"Well, Doctor, it's something in his countenance—"

"Shush, both of you," said Pen. She was still embarrassed by the way she had dropped Lennox's name.

"He just doesn't like to be told no," said Jo, patting Pen's hand. "Hasn't happened to him much."

"I'll help Ferg with the drinks," Charlie said, standing up.

An unlikely bond had formed in the first weeks of term between Charlie and Fergus. Or unlikely to the Canadian Gullivers, who had noticed a certain frostiness between students like Charlie, who pronounced and sometimes rolled their r's and those like Fergus, who ignored r's that did exist, invented ones that didn't, and stretched their vowels out like a yawn. However, Charlie appeared to accept everyone on his or her merits. And Fergus, Jo had tried to explain to Pen and Alice, was not nearly as much of a snob as he pretended to be. "Actually, that's a lie, he's a hideous snob," she'd corrected herself. "But not about the things he professes to care about. He mostly has good taste in people. He finds himself odious, for example."

"Bring chips!" called Alice to Charlie's receding back. "Sorry, crisps."

Charlie turned around. "Thai chili chicken or prawn cocktail?"

"Gross. Both," said Alice. "Fergus can make fun of Canada all he wants, but at least our chips come in civilized flavors. Like ketchup."

"I know, angel," said Jo.

The table fell silent. Alice turned to Pen expectantly.

"He answered," she told Alice, not hiding her excitement. "I've never actually met him," she added for Jo and Hugo's benefit. "He and my dad went here together in the seventies."

"Where does he live?" Jo asked.

"Near Stonehaven. A man named Hector will meet me at the train," Pen said. "Why are you all looking at me like that? I got here from Toronto, didn't I? I can manage a train ride."

"Without Alice?" Hugo asked. "I didn't know you two could survive on your own."

"We'll write," said Pen, looking at Alice.

Alice did not reply right away. She was bristling at the suggestion that she and Pen were dependent on one another.

In order to convince her parents to let her go all the way to Scotland for university, where international student fees were exorbitant, Alice had needed to empty her entire savings account into tuition. Fortunately, she had amassed a considerable pile of cash over five years of photoshoots and TV commercials, during each of which a hoard of strangers had groped and prodded at her, all the while talking about her as if she couldn't hear them, the way people sometimes do with the very old or with non-native English speakers.

It had been worth it. Her parents, both of the "get a real job" mindset, had slammed the door on theater school, but she had formed a plan that could, if she did everything right, yield similar results. She would propel herself from the University of Edinburgh's Bedlam Theatre to the city's Fringe Festival in August, arguably the theater world's most important annual discovery vehicle, and from there to London's West End.

The alternative had been to follow the advice of her former talent agent, Richard, who had tried to convince her to join the rest of Canada's unblemished, camera-trained youths in decamping to LA with a suitcase full of headshots, no US visa, and a prayer. She had considered it. The problem was that Alice wanted to be judged by her talent, not by whether a group of strangers deemed her face and body sufficiently desirable.

Pen, meanwhile, had been bound for one of those blue-chip American universities with branded teddy bears, but had done a 180 and chosen Edinburgh. Their school's guidance counselor had been inconsolable, so she had needed to come up with a plausible explanation. There was the family history, of course. Pen's dad had been sent to boarding school in England as a teenager and gone on to Edinburgh. For anyone who found this excuse insufficient, Pen had a box of facts at the ready. Did they know that the University of Edinburgh had played a central role in the Scottish Enlightenment? That Adam Smith had taught there, or that Charles Darwin and Robert Louis Stevenson were alumni?

Alice alone knew what Pen was really looking for. Ever since she had discovered that her dad and Lennox had once been close, Pen had been nurturing a theory that there was a link between that aborted friendship and the slow-motion implosion of her parents' marriage in grade eight. It was almost as if Pen was hoping to find proof that divorce was a rare thing that required a special cause beyond human attraction stretching out of shape and fading into contempt, like a nice pair of underwear turned saggy and dishwater gray.

Alice was glad to be near Pen, and glad that her friend, who had a gift for absorbing other people's pain, had put an ocean between herself and Ted and Anna's waspishly repressed sadness. But she was not sure about the sanity of sneaking around trying to retrace her dad's steps, looking for whatever it was he might have dropped or buried. Privately, she thought it was a bit unhinged.

Alice drank the melted ice in her glass and reminded herself that she and Pen were different. If curiosity for Alice was like a stone in her shoe, Pen felt missing information like an axe in her big toe. For all her rule following, when she wanted to know something, or if she couldn't fig-ure out the answer to some problem, she'd sooner walk through a wall than give up on it. That was why she got such stupidly high marks.

And then—Alice felt a bit sick thinking it—given what Pen had been through with her mom, it did make sense that she would still be fixated on understanding what had gone wrong.

"I think it's great," Alice said finally. "He's going to love you. I just hope he lets us have you back."

4

The train that took Pen toward her dad's erstwhile friend's house smelled of wet socks, "man"-scented shower gel, and beer in a can. She was glad of her window seat, with the slate-gray Firth of Forth blanketed out beside her, wrinkled by the wind. The spiky-haired boys sitting opposite her were drinking steadily, though it was early. They had heaped their outerwear—damp sweaters, a nylon windbreaker with an orange zip—on the seat next to hers. A pop song burbled from one of their phones, muddying their voices and making it hard to eavesdrop.

The food trolley bumped up the aisle. Pen bought a bottle of water and something called a flapjack. It was delicious, like a dense, gluey oatmeal cookie. As neatly combed fields of dull gold rolled into view, the boys tucked into another round, filling the car with hoppy gas. She picked flapjack crumbs from the ridges of her corduroys and placed them in the wrapper.

Now that she was so close, her courage was failing her. The gulf between the dauntless version of herself who existed in her mind—the one who had moved halfway across the world to set this scheme in motion—and the easily crushed body hurtling toward the eastern edge of Scotland had never felt wider.

Four years after the Conor Minnow incident, on one of the last school days before Christmas, Pen had been sitting on a stool at the kitchen island, eating a bowl of Shreddies over the Arts section, when she'd first seen the name Elliot Lennox. Pen was thirteen by then, but while Alice and the rest of their friends were transforming into bra-wearing tampon purchasers who pored over glossy magazines, Pen remained boy-like and was training herself to read the newspaper from cover to cover each morning.

The article said that the ninth installment in the "criminally addictive" Inspector Paquin series, by Scottish author Elliot Lennox, was "another propulsive, grizzly delight," and that Lennox, nicknamed "the Peerless Peer," had been thrilling connoisseurs of the genre since the mid-eighties from his home on the east coast of Scotland.

Pen, who for all her hunger for information was not exactly a born detective, did not put it together right away. She merely clipped the article, sponging a drop of milk from the page with her sleeve before carefully tearing around the column of text, because she thought the first book from the series might make a good present for her dad. Inspector Robert Paquin of the Lothian and Borders Police sounded like the perfect distraction from what promised to be a gloomy Christmas.

The mood in their house had changed that fall and winter, but the mood everywhere had changed. It was 2001.

"You don't want to read those." Ted, appearing behind her left shoulder, startled her. She'd thought he'd already left for work. It was almost light out. These days he was usually gone well before she set out on the ten-minute walk to school.

"I don't?" she asked. "I thought I did."

"Nah," he said in the tone that ended conversations. He extracted the front section from the newspaper stack. "You won't like them."

At thirteen, Pen already knew her father wasn't going to win any awards for consistency. But this statement, delivered with such false detachment, was far enough out of character for her to turn around on her stool and examine him. Pen's parents had always made a point of letting her read whatever she wanted. Her dad would not meet her eyes and his jaw looked clenched as he leaned against the island, speed-reading the day's news.

Theirs had never been a boisterous household. There were only three of them. But the silent ease that had once lubricated their movements around one another had been replaced with something thick and heavy. The physical comfort that Pen had felt with her parents only a year or two before no longer came as naturally. Her parents, she now noticed, didn't touch very often. She began to feel self-conscious about her own shows of affection.

Family dinners had been a reliable feature of her childhood, but Pen's mother Anna seldom ate with them anymore. She came home from teaching her lectures and seminars and put herself straight to bed. In the mornings she emerged, tiny-looking in her robe, a fading shadow of her former self, to make sure Pen was dressed warmly enough and to wish her a good day.

Ted had begun leaving for the office earlier and coming home later, often just in time to find Pen charring a frozen lasagna. Twice a week, Pen's paternal grandmother collected her from school in her wide, leathery car and brought her to the austere house of Ted's youth for a dinner involving multiple forks and overcooked peas. Her grandmother's house had previously been a place for Pen to practice being a more grown-up version of herself, but lately Tilda's lessons in decorum—she was forever correcting Pen's posture, commenting on the length of her skirt, and reminding her not to air dirty laundry, even to Alice—were making Pen angry. The world was in chaos, Ted and Anna were behaving like aliens pretending to be human, and she wanted to shake them all awake.

Pen was well aware that something had gone permanently wrong between her parents. And watching her father's face, she knew that whatever it was had risen to the surface just now. She looked back down at the column she had clipped, and this time the name stood out to her. Elliot. A writer. Who lived in Scotland.

"So you've read them?" she asked her dad. Ted tried to look like he hadn't heard her. "The Elliot Lennox books," Pen clarified.

The name appeared to singe the inside of his ear. This was definitely the nerve. But why? Her brain was on fire with questions it would be useless to ask. Her father was an expert at answering her without answering at all.

"I've read a lot of things, Penny." He turned to face her. She could see for one reality-shifting moment the effort he was making to hide his fear. To make the world appear safe, even though it obviously was not. She was overwhelmed with gratitude and worry. How could he stand to exert such self-control all the time? How could anyone?

Ted drew in a breath, ran a palm across his face, downshifted his tone from warning to jocular. "What's on your Christmas list? And don't say a chestnut mare again. I'm all for it, as you know, it's just the matter of where she would sleep."

"Horses can sleep standing up," Pen said, relieved to find lightness restored. She would find out the rest on her own. "So she won't need much space. Stairs are a problem though. Maybe in the dining room?"

As soon as her dad went up to bed that night, Pen searched his study. Standing on the back of the sofa, reaching behind a row of double-parked military histories, she found what she was looking for. The whole Inspector Paquin series, all in hardcover. She picked up the first one and opened it to the inside cover. But there was no handwritten note made out to her dad, nothing that proved they had known each other. Just a typed dedication, *for Christina.*

She turned to the back flap. Elliot Lennox looked out through rimless glasses. His hair flopped across his forehead. His eyes held light and humor, like he was just pretending to be serious. The blurb beneath the photo made no mention of his being a peerless peer, whatever that meant. *Elliot Lennox studied English and Scottish literature at the University of Edinburgh. He lives in Scotland with his family* was all it said. She put the book aside and moved the military histories back into place, covering up the gap.

Still burning with curiosity, desperate for solid proof that this man was her namesake, she started in on her father's desk. In a drawer full of used printer cartridges and stray paper clips, she found a black-and-white snapshot. She did not immediately understand that one of the two young men in the photo was her dad. He looked different; his hair was longer and his frame leaner, but it wasn't just that. It was the smile of pure, unguarded joy that made him unrecognizable. Pen had never seen him look at anyone the way he was looking at whoever was holding the camera. In the picture he was standing on a hill beside Elliot Lennox.

The only other surprising thing she found was a half-empty pack of cigarettes. She smelled one and put it in her pocket.

It was nearly noon when Pen stepped down from the train onto the outdoor platform of Stonehaven station. The air was crisp and had a freshly washed quality. Pen followed a walkway edged with a low white fence toward a sign marked WAY OUT. Just as she was wondering if she would recognize Hector, and whether he would even really come, a compact man in a flat cap and green overcoat with a straight-bottomed salt-and-pepper mustache appeared before her.

"Penelope, is it?" he said, offering her a rough hand. He had friendly ridges around his eyes. "Hector Matthews."

Taking the overnight bag from her shoulder, Hector led Pen down a flight of stairs, under the tracks, and through the station to the parking lot, where he helped her into a high vehicle.

"All right?" Hector asked.

Pen nodded, settling onto the roomy front bench that could have seated a family of six. Satisfied, he took his place in the driver's seat and moved the flagpole-like gear shift into reverse.

Pen watched the stone houses on the outskirts of the coastal town, with brightly colored doors and front gardens still blooming with dusty pink roses, black-eyed Susans, and hydrangeas, fade into expanses of brown and green, and worried about the wheel of cheese in her overnight bag. Lennox's Inspector Paquin loved to eat Lanark Blue from a special shop on Frederick Street with oatcakes and whisky. She had assembled these items as an offering, which had seemed clever at the time but now was giving the air in the car a moldy fug that didn't mix well with her nerves. She looked at Hector, hoping he couldn't smell it. *What kind of person invites herself to a stranger's house and turns up with a bag full of stinky cheese?* she thought, and suppressed a smile. She found the hand crank and rolled down her window to let in an inch of fresh air. Hector glanced her way but made no attempt at small talk, and Pen was relieved.

How often would her dad have made this same trip as a student, she wondered, and what gift would he have brought? As an adult, Ted was good at giving gifts. Except when he wasn't. Pen remembered how that same dismal Christmas, her mother had opened a velvet box containing a pair of dangling, teardrop-shaped earrings encrusted with diamonds. Anna, who had been wearing the same small silver hoops for Pen's whole life, had looked confused, as if she had opened a gift intended for someone else. Pen had made a joke of it—"These are nice, but they won't match Mum's tiara"—and the three had set out together on Boxing Day to exchange them. Pen remembered her cautious excitement about a family errand, the stifling hush of the jewelry store, and the saleswoman who presented her mother with a note for store credit on a polished tray. The problem, Pen had worked out much later, was not the earrings themselves, but how much they had cost. Anna would have understood this gift, given at a time when she and Ted spent almost no time together, to mean that Ted had stopped seeing her. Ted would not have intended it this way—he would have been carrying out a duty with characteristic generosity, and likely with the help of his assistant—but Pen's mother would have taken the costly earrings to mean that to the man she had married, she was no longer herself, Anna; she was a Wife. And Wives could be bought. This view of herself, and of him, would have disgusted her. Anna had said nothing at the store, nothing in the underground parking lot afterward. In the car she had said just one word: "Stop." And then she had stepped out into the middle lane of traffic, narrowly missing being hit by a Canada Post truck.

She'd come back to the house an hour later with hands white from the cold and a scary blankness in her eyes. Pen, who had been on the couch pretending to read, had rubbed her mother's fingers between her palms, trying to get the color back into them. When her dad had come down dressed for work, as if it were a perfectly normal thing to go to the office at dusk on Boxing Day, Pen had gone up to her room, climbed under the covers with her book, and put her earphones in. Just after eleven, Pen had watched through a crack in the door as her dad made up a bed on the couch in his study. Her parents' third-floor bedroom had once been the safest place she'd known. He would never sleep there again.

"Here we are," said Hector. They had turned off the main road onto a narrower one that was lined on both sides with mature trees. Some leaves had begun to turn golden, but the palette was subdued compared with the exhibitionism of fall in Ontario. They continued slowly along what she now recognized as a driveway curving through forested grounds.

In a clearing up ahead appeared an elegant stone wall with an archway carved out of it. Small upper-story windows framed with shutters revealed it to be not a wall but a building. Broad ground-floor doorways and a familiar smell led Pen to suspect stables.

"Bryce," Hector said with gruff pride. Pen nodded sagely, having no idea what he meant.

On the other side of the archway, across a farther distance of driveway, stood a turreted stone construction that Pen could only describe to herself (though the word seemed to cheapen it a bit) as a castle. It was enormous—she couldn't see the whole thing without turning her head from side to side—and appeared to be made of several distinct sections that had been adjoined, like a child's creation with blocks. The ivy that climbed its central and most ancient-looking octagonal tower was tinged with red.

The effect of this building on Pen's imagination was immediate and chaotic. Several stories shook open in her mind, causing her to briefly lose track of who and when she was.

"Roberts. Unusual in these parts," said Hector, driving slowly across the beige gravel that surrounded the house, once again assuming a minimum base of architectural knowledge far beyond that which she possessed.

"When was it built?" Pen asked, trying to keep the awed ignorance out of her voice.

"Fifteenth century, the original tower. The rest was finished in the nineteenth, with improvements"—he sounded unconvinced—"through the twentieth. Just the house, mind. The estate dates to the Bronze Age." He yanked the gear shifter into park, fetched her bag from the back seat. "All right from here? No need to knock. Go right up the stairs. You'll find Lady Lennox in her kitchen."

"Perfect," she said, taking the hand he offered and then her overnight bag. "Thank you."

Hector turned the car back toward the stables, and Pen crunched along the gravel until she came to the front door. She reached for the heavy cast-iron knocker and lifted it before remembering what Hector had said. It took most of her body weight to push the door open, but it gave with a click. She slipped inside and pulled it closed behind her.

5

She found herself in a high-ceilinged entrance hall with an elaborately tiled floor. It was the kind of dim, mostly empty space in which organ music would have sounded natural. There were no shoes or boots left anywhere, so Pen kept hers on.

"Hello?" she called tentatively. Her voice echoed in the cavernous hall. "Hello?" she repeated. She went up a flight of steps, toward a pool of light.

The next stage of the house's interior was warmer. A round skylight several stories up brought weak sun onto the well-worn parquet and faded burgundy rug of a sweeping central stairwell that seemed to climb forever.

"Hello?" Pen called again, feeling like a voyeur, or a criminal. Looking for the kitchen, she continued past the foot of the stairs to where an open double doorway revealed an octagonal sitting room with big windows looking out onto the grounds. On the walls, paintings hung one above the other and looked like they had been in place for so long that the real color of the walls would be visible only if you moved them. A fire crackled in the grate and there was an ill-folded stack of newspapers at the foot of an upholstered armchair. Pen was about to turn around when she heard a smooth English voice behind her.

"Penelope! Is that you?" A woman in a dove-gray pullover walked into the room. She had the kind of unassuming, watercolor beauty that called birch trees to mind. "I suppose Hector left you on the doorstep like a parcel. We are brutes. How was your journey? I'm Christina." She kissed Pen on both cheeks. Her hair was a mix of blonde and gray and pulled into a low ponytail. Her radiant, tanned face was open in a smile.

"Thank you for having me," Pen said, hating how she sounded. Like a child arriving at a sleepover. She was mortified to have been caught barging into the living room.

"Nonsense! You must be famished. Come into the kitchen. Lunch is nearly on." Lady Lennox took Pen's shoulder bag and then met her eyes and squeezed her forearm briefly. "We're delighted you've come," she said.

Pen smiled, still feeling shy, and followed her back down the hallway and into a brightly lit kitchen.

"You can freshen up here. I'll show you to your room straight after lunch," Lady Lennox said, walking Pen to a door hidden in the wall at the back of the kitchen. Pen, who had had to pee for the last twenty minutes, was grateful to her host for saving her the embarrassment of having to ask. At Fergus and Jo's house, when she'd quietly asked for directions to a bathroom, Mrs. Scarlett Moore, a woman of ample voice, had pretended not to understand. "A bawth? At this hour?" she'd bellowed. "Americans aww queer."

Pen washed her hands and looked at herself in the mirror. Her lips were chapped and the purple ink spills beneath her eyes had come out from under the concealer she'd applied that morning. She dried her hands with a soft towel and slid the door open.

Lady Lennox was pulling jars and bottles out of the refrigerator. "I expect the boys will be back any moment. They're out with the horses. This will keep us from evaporating," she said to Pen, pouring them each a glass of cold sparkling water.

Heat rose to Pen's cheeks at the mention of "boys." It had not occurred to her that she might find either of the Lennox sons at home. She was aware, thanks to Hugo and Jo, that there were two of them. Hugo seemed to know the younger one, whom he'd called "a legend" and heard was in South America on his gap year, while Jo had said that the elder son, Sasha, was in his final year at St Andrews, where he belonged to a set of royal and quasi-royal people who were frequently mentioned in the tabloids. Pen was embarrassed all over again for imposing herself on this family that had no real reason to know her.

Lady Lennox opened an enameled oven. The scent of baking bread and melting cheese rushed out. "I had such a yen for pizza," she said, peering inside and pulling out a baking sheet. "Actually, they look rather good."

Pen agreed too vociferously and took a swallow of water to tamp down her desire to please. She was suppressing the effects of carbonation when the creak of a swinging door brought a man's voice and a scurrying spaniel into the kitchen. "Lady L! What sorcery are you conjuring in here?" The dog rushed toward Lady Lennox, who hastened to close the oven before patting its flank.

Two older boys entered, bringing with them a musk of hay and horse sweat. The one who had spoken was of medium build, handsome, and athletic-looking. His accent was public school, and his shirt was pushed up at the wrists, revealing a bracelet of red and blue embroidery thread. When he turned his head Pen noticed that his black hair was tied up in a curiously attractive bun.

"Hello," he said with the self-assurance of a head boy, offering a vigorous handshake while considering her with dark, round eyes. "I'm Chet Mehta."

The other boy was tall and willowy in worn black jeans and a moss-colored pullover. His brown hair was mussed sideways, as if by a strong wind. This, evidently, was Sasha Lennox. He had his mother's birch tree beauty, a shy person's slightly hunched posture, and a faint sunburn along the bridge of his nose. His hazel eyes met Pen's, sending a current through her.

"Hello," he said in a voice that seemed to come from somewhere in her own body. "I'm Sasha." The spaniel rushed to his knees, and he scooped it up. "And this is Nellie." Pen held her hand for Nellie to smell and then stroked her silky ears. When she looked up, Sasha's eyes were back on her face. They contained humor, like Lord Lennox's had in the photos, and were flecked with green and gold. Pen did not trust herself to speak.

"Didn't I tell you Penelope was coming?" said Lady Lennox. "She's come all the way from Toronto for uni, so do try to make a good impression. Her father's an old friend, though we haven't seen him in an age. Would you open these for me, darling?"

Pen noticed the use of "we" as Lady Lennox handed a jar of olives and a decorative bowl to Sasha, and then a large green salad to Chet. Picking up the trays of pizza, Lady Lennox sent the procession through the swinging door—blocking Nellie with her calf—into a dining room with a high, molded ceiling, where a table big enough for twenty was set for six.

This room seemed to belong to a different century than the kitchen, which must have been the site of some of the improvements to which Hector had referred. Lady Lennox pulled a lever on the wall that was half-hidden between a small framed painting of the sea, endless-looking and wind-torn, and the doorway.

Chet caught Pen noticing the painting.

"A Turner, I think," he said, seeming pleased to impart this tidbit. Then, gesturing toward the bronze-handled lever, "Summoning Lord L. He works down in the old servants' hall. Begins at daybreak and usually surfaces for lunch. But not always."

"He's rather in the thick of things at the moment. And poor George is recovering from a wretched night, so we won't wait," said Lady Lennox, sinking into one of the heavy chairs and dropping a worn linen napkin onto her lap. Pen wondered if George was the younger son, home early from his travels. But hadn't Hugo said the brother's name was Freddie?

"So, Pen, what are you studying?" Chet asked, arranging a heap of mixed lettuce leaves on her plate.

"English and French," she said.

"What for?" he asked, neither kindly nor unkindly.

"What do you mean?"

"What do you plan to do? Teach? Translate? Marry a Frenchman?" he asked, looking at her from under his eyelids. His blunt questions eased her nerves. Alice was the same way—direct with everyone, even complete strangers—and it was a quality that drew Pen out.

"Journalism, ideally. How about you?"

"Hm." Chet looked skeptical. "Odd to come all the way to Scotland. You're not on the run from the law, are you?"

"No. Just from the lawyers," she said, her natural voice returning.

"Your parents are lawyers?" asked Sasha.

"Clients," she said.

Sasha laughed. It was a brief, genuine sound. Lady Lennox glanced at Pen as if surprised by this answer.

Chet's smile was complicit and very white. "Ah, now I understand. My sympathies."

"Is that why you left New Delhi, Chet? Legal trouble?" Lady Lennox asked. "I've often wondered."

"No, I came for the weather," said Chet. "And stayed to keep my eye on this one. Make sure he doesn't fall asleep on the bus and wind up a cult leader on the Isle of Skye, that sort of thing."

"Good of you," said Lady Lennox. "Such a comfort."

Sasha, saying nothing in his own defense, ate an olive.

"We're just up the road from you, at St Andrews," Chet said to Pen. "In our fourth and, God help us, final year. I'm reading economics. And Sasha here, who wants no hand in the collapse of our diabolical civilization, is focusing on even more fiendish ones that have already bitten the dust." He looked at his friend, who shook his head.

"History," Sasha translated.

"He's very good at it, or so they say, but he'll never get a job with a degree like that," Chet continued. "Lady L will have to spend her dotage caring for him."

Pen looked at Sasha again. He was smiling gamely at Chet, whom Lady Lennox had just swatted with her napkin. She wished she could take a photo of him so she could keep looking at his face without it being weird. She took a sip of water and tried to concentrate on bending the large salad leaves into her mouth as daintily as possible.

"Lady Lennox," Pen said later, after she had finished helping with the dishes. She had retrieved her overnight bag and was pulling a heavy brown paper package from it.

"Christina, please."

"Christina," she said, although the name felt wrong in her mouth. The smell of moldy cheese hit them both. "A little something from Edinburgh. I so appreciate the chance to . . ." Pen trailed off.

"Oh—! Elliot will be pleased. And what's this?" Christina unwrapped the bottle. "This is terribly kind and terribly unnecessary. Thank you, darling." Pen felt the softness of Christina's sweater against her face as she was pulled into an unexpected embrace. "Sasha my love, why don't you boys help Pen get settled in the green bedroom and then take her for a walk so she can get her bearings?"

Sasha and Chet both smiled at Pen. Sasha took her overnight bag from her hand, brushing her knuckles with his fingers, and she reminded herself to breathe as she followed them toward the main staircase.

6

Pen was deep in a claw-footed tub. A wooden ledge ran across it widthwise holding a bar of soap and her book. The bathroom had its own fireplace, in which a fire was built but not lit. She had considered lighting it but that had seemed presumptuous, somehow.

She lay back so she was submerged to her chin. Despite its cold, stone enormity, the house was suffused with Christina's straightforward charm. She seemed to effortlessly intuit the needs of each person under its roof while drawing a firm boundary around her own privacy. *We* haven't seen him in an age, she had said.

Pen let the warm water thaw her to the core. Sasha and Chet had taken her for a long walk after lunch. Once they had gained enough distance from the house, passing not by the stables but in the other direction, beyond the sweeping terrace that looked over artful flower gardens and across the park, until they crossed into fields, Pen had felt herself relax. Being in nature shrank her self-consciousness into irrelevance so she forgot all about it.

Pen asked about the name of the place, which she had seen on Lord Lennox's notepaper but had not yet heard spoken aloud. Sasha pronounced it *tal-MOR-ack* and said it came from the Gaelic words *talamh*, meaning "land" or "ground," and *mor*, meaning "large" or "high." The estate had come into their branch of the family when a cousin of his great-grandfather's had died without a male heir, he said, as if to distance himself from this unusual living situation, or at least in acknowledgment of its strangeness.

He directed her gaze back toward the long drive, showing her where the village of Talmòrach stood, on the other side of the farmers' fields. Chet, pointing toward the ivy-covered tower, explained that it had been built around the central fortified tower, or "keep." "That's where Sasha's room is," he'd said with a grin. "It's the safest place on the property. Provided you trust Sasha."

Ignoring this, and remembering how Hector had tossed off names, Pen asked about the style of the house. Tucking his wild hair behind his ears, which stuck out a bit in a way that she found problematically endearing, Sasha said that the structure had been rebuilt and added to so many times, with each new layer done in whatever style had been popular in that time, from Palladian to Gothic Revival, that the building was an architectural dog's breakfast.

When they left the back fields and entered the forest, Chet began naming each species of tree they passed. Sasha pointed out that you can identify the Scots pines by their twisted needles and missing lower branches, the noble firs by their towering stature, and the Sitka spruce by their papery cones. Pen had been so enraptured by their company, and so intent upon disguising the thrill that went through her body each time Sasha leaned in to tell her something, that she had not noticed the dropping temperature. She was used to cold weather, as nearly everyone she met in Scotland liked to point out. But in Toronto the cold was mostly dry. It burned your ears and froze your eyelashes together in a clump, but it didn't get trapped inside your bones. Here on the edge of the North Sea, where no one wore Gore-Tex, it felt possible to freeze from the inside out.

She heard the clanking of pipes somewhere overhead and caught herself imagining Sasha's bedroom, up in the keep. *Stop it*, she told herself firmly; *you will not get distracted.*

The walls of the guest bedroom were papered in a leafy dark green, and with the mahogany furniture and worn, rust-colored rug covering creaking polished floorboards, it felt like an extension of the old-growth forest. Large windows looked west over the park, and she could see the saturated orange of the nearly set sun trying to break through the clouds.

While she was dressing, goose bumps rising along her still-warm skin in the cold air, there was a knock at the door. She hastily buttoned her blouse, toweled off her hair, and pulled open the heavy bedroom door to find Sasha on the threshold.

"Thought you might like a gin and tonic." He held out a tall glass that was frosted with condensation, a wedge of lime suspended above the layer of ice. His eyes flicked to her collarbone, and then returned to her face with something in them she could not read. He turned abruptly down the hall.

Pen looked at her white blouse, fearing a stain, and saw that she had missed a button. She sat on the upholstered bench at the foot of the four-poster bed and took a big icy sip, willing her heart rate to slow.

Elliot Lennox would have to come down for dinner.

Eventually, Pen ventured out of the green bedroom. She turned the wrong way. Her navigational instincts were seldom to be trusted, but she usually followed them for a few paces anyway, just to see where they took her.

The number of closed doors, spaced well apart, was baffling, she thought, tiptoeing to the very end of the hall, where a narrow spiral staircase promised more rooms to explore both above and below. But she felt like enough of an interloper already and was about to turn back when she heard something from behind the very last door. A crying baby. There was no mistaking the sound. She approached the door.

"Sssshhhh," came the voice of a woman, not quite irritated but not thrilled either. "You're all right."

Softly, the voice began to sing. The crying stopped. The door opened. A young woman emerged from the bedroom and, finding herself face-to-face with Pen, jumped. Pen was surprised, too. She hadn't known the Lennoxes had a daughter. She had inquisitive eyes and her curls glinted bronze in the warm light.

"Hello," she whispered, recovering herself. She listened at the door for a moment and then closed it gently and led Pen a few paces up the hall. "I'm George. Who are you?"

"Sorry for—I heard—I'm Pen." She extended the hand without a smudged highball glass in it.

George leaned in to kiss her on both cheeks. She took the glass Pen was holding and put it by the door. "Friend of Sasha's?" she asked.

"No," Pen said. "I'm visiting from Edinburgh for the weekend. My dad knows—used to know—Lord Lennox."

"You're American," observed George.

"Yes. Well, Canadian," said Pen. She never knew whether people meant North American or from the United States of America when they said that.

"Pleased to meet you. Sorry for the wailing. I didn't realize anyone was on this side. He's teething. Putting him down is a nightmare these days. God I could use a ciggy. You don't have one, do you?"

Pen smiled. She returned to her room and retrieved two from the pack she had brought with her. George was wearing tailored trousers, black lace-up boots, and an oversized wool sweater rolled up at the sleeves. She steered Pen into one of the rooms along the hallway. It was a vast, dark library. George led her out a pair of French doors and onto a small terrace.

"I've quit, obviously," George said, taking the cigarette Pen handed her and holding it to her mouth while Pen lit it. "Don't worry, I didn't smoke while I was pregnant—I'm not a monster," she added, blowing out a mouthful of smoke. "But now that he's six months, from time to time . . . well, you'll see. Maybe."

"Are you Sasha's sister?" Pen asked. George raised an eyebrow at her.

"Cousin. My mother is Lennox's sister, Margot," George said. "I was born here. I live in London, but I come up as often as I can. It's good for Danny. London gets a bit . . . claustrophobic with a pram."

"Mmm," said Pen, who had hardly heard the last part because she was still processing the news that this was the daughter of Margot Lennox. Pen wished, not for the first time, that she had somehow contrived to bring Alice with her for the weekend.

Pen didn't know what to say next, whether to acknowledge that she knew who George's mother was, or how to ask what she herself did for work. Presumably she wasn't working so soon after having had a baby, especially if she lived part-time in the Scottish countryside, but Pen didn't know for sure and couldn't come up with a way to ask that wasn't rude or clumsy. The world of baby-rearing was alien to her. They smoked in silence.

"We'd better go down," said George, looking at a black leather watch with a small gold face. "Lennox will be up by now and I'm famished. Have you met him yet?"

"No," said Pen.

"He'll love you," said George.

Pen had no idea what she meant or whether it was intended as a compliment, but she put out her cigarette in a sardine tin left there for that purpose and followed George back through the hall and down the main staircase.

7

Elliot Lennox had his back to them when they entered the octagonal sitting room that Pen had wandered into earlier. He stood very straight, facing the fireplace, prodding a log with a medieval-looking implement. Menacing opera music was playing, giving Pen the feeling that she was walking into a scene from one of his books. In gilt frames all around him hung handsome, regal bald men, disapproving women with tartan sashes, and a great many spaniels.

He turned as though sensing their approach, observing first George and then Pen with undisguised interest. He cut a trim figure in an old-fashioned three-piece suit. He had the same disorderly hair as his son, but his was more gray than brown and cut shorter. He looked exactly as she had imagined him, only more so. When he finally spoke, his voice had a smile in it, though he kept his features grave.

"Georgie, did you check her bag for weapons? Blunt instruments? Anthrax? One never knows of what today's crazed fans are capable."

George tipped forward onto her toes and kissed Lord Lennox on the cheek. "That'll do for now," she said.

"Lord Lennox," Pen said. Her voice came out watery. She took a breath to make it more substantial. "It's a pleasure to meet you."

Lennox put his hand to his ear. "What was that? Young Wolfgang is making a racket."

"Thank you for having me," said Pen more loudly.

"We're delighted you've come," he said, taking her hand, and bringing it to his lips. "And please, just Lennox. As Christina will tell you I have enough of a god complex as it is without being called Lord to my face. What can I offer you, Penelope? Whisky? Absinthe? Irn-Bru? Champagne? My sister keeps us well furnished in that department, for all her flaws. Aha, champagne it is."

His attention shifted to the doorway through which Sasha and Chet were now entering. Pen felt a buzzing in her chest at the sight of Sasha, who held a dark green bottle in one hand and glasses in the other. He went over to a hidden stereo and dimmed the surging Mozart.

"What are we celebrating?" Chet asked.

Sasha eased out the cork and poured five glasses.

"Our dangerous new arrival," Lennox said, looking closely at Pen again and raising his glass toward hers.

"Not as dangerous as all that," said Pen, overcoming her nerves and meeting his eyes. She touched glasses with George, who gave her a look that said, *Told you.*

When Pen looked away, she saw Christina in the doorway with an apron tied around her waist.

"It's time," she said.

.   .   .

Christina, Pen now realized, had been cooking all afternoon. She had made a carrot and coriander soup so comforting that Pen ate it in blissful silence, followed by roasted pheasant with honeyed parsnips and rosemary potatoes that were fluffy on the inside and crispy on the outside, and a salad of bitter greens and edible flowers that she had grown herself. The meal drew raptures from Chet that became more effusive with each bite. The wine was velvety, and by the time the pheasant was served Pen was conscious that the tips of her ears were hot. She tried to hide them behind her hair.

"Duck fat. The trick is to boil them first and then shake them in the pan to get the edges to crisp up," Christina was telling Chet at one end of the table. Sasha, who was perpendicular to Pen, appeared to be looking right at her. She tried to concentrate on her food and made a screeching sound with her knife on the plate. "Sorry," she said. Chet flashed her a mock-stern look.

Lennox, meanwhile, had begun lobbing questions at Pen—about Canada's withdrawal from the Kyoto accord, about her views on whether Scottish nationalism could be compared to Quebec separatism, about the evolution of Canada's national identity over the course of the twentieth century and its contributions and losses in the two world wars—and Pen, who had not yet found an opening to ask any questions of her own, and whose wine glass kept mysteriously being emptied and refilled, was answering him with increasing boldness. She found herself, midway through the salad, giving a short but impassioned speech about Canada's role in the battle of Vimy Ridge, and Lennox, much to her surprise, looked delighted. She did not dare look back in Sasha's direction.

"There is another important subject to discuss this evening," Lennox said, laying down his knife and fork and looking at Pen with his twinkling eyes.

Pen held her breath. She had been arguing with herself about whether and how to move the conversation toward more personal territory. She would have much preferred to speak privately with Lennox, or maybe with Lennox and Christina together, since they had evidently both known her dad. But she could not be certain that she would get such an opportunity.

"Enlighten us if you would, Penelope," Lennox continued after refilling his own glass and hers. "I believe I speak for the table when I say that we are woefully unknowledgeable when it comes to Canadian letters. I'll bet these young people don't even know their Davies from their Ondaatje. Where would you have us start?"

Feeling at least as much relief as disappointment, Pen exhaled. She asked Lennox what he'd read by Margaret Atwood or Alice Munro. When he said nothing yet, she could not quite keep the dismay from her face. As she advised him on where to begin, she noticed that Sasha's eyes were on her again. He was biting the inside of his cheek the way Alice did when trying not to make the sort of joke that no one else would understand. When she met his eyes, he gave her a conspiratorial smile that made her insides flip.

When Christina began clearing the table, Chet jumped up to help. Nobody else seemed to notice, and Pen, cemented in her seat by the wine she had drunk, did not think it wise to stand.

"I suppose you look like your mum," Lennox said to Pen, in a voice very different from the booming one he had been using to entertain the whole table. She glanced around. George and Sasha were engaged in a separate conversation and Christina and Chet had carried the plates through the swinging door to the kitchen.

She looked right at him. "Do you think so?"

"I don't know," he said. "I haven't met her. But I have reason to believe she's someone quite special indeed."

Pen tried to guess what he might have been implying with this statement, but it was difficult.

"Are they happy? Your mum and dad," he continued casually.

She laughed, not knowing whether he was joking. "God no. They can't even be in the same room. I think marrying each other is the regret of their lives," she said, as if it were normal to speak like this to a person she'd just met.

"I'm sorry," Lennox said, bowing his head. Pen was on the verge of asking, *Why? What do you know that I don't?* when the smell of sweaty sneakers hit her in the face. Christina reentered with the cheese plate, which she had arranged beautifully with figs and jams. As she leaned over him to place the plate on the table, Lennox reached an arm around her and brought her close to him. "My darling, that was spectacular. Possibly the best meal I've had in my life. Thank you," he said.

"You say that every time, my love. But it did turn out rather well, didn't it," said Christina, yielding to his embrace. "I'll let you guess which of these was a special delivery from Edinburgh." She handed her husband the cheese knife.

"Aha, so you did bring a weapon after all. Very good," said Lennox to Pen, using his public voice once more, but surveying her with something like fatherly pride. He scooped a large slice of Lanark Blue onto an oatcake. "Funny," he added just for Pen. "Your dad used to bring Mum the very same thing, once upon a time."

8

Pen awoke with a hangover. Her scalp was too tight, and her tongue was dry. She hadn't fully closed the curtains the night before, and autumn light was spilling across the bed. She patted the bedside table for the bottle of water she had bought on the train and finished it in one gulp.

After Lennox and Christina had gone upstairs, the "children," as Christina called them, had moved into the living room. Sasha had opened more wine and Chet had kept Pen's glass full until the early morning. More than what they had talked about, she remembered feeling a kind of warm rightness. A few times she had remembered herself and watched her body pretend to fit there, between Sasha and Chet on the long sofa before the fire, with George presiding from the armchair. But mostly, unusually for Pen, she had been there with them, telling stories about God-knew-what and laughing so hard her stomach muscles felt sore. Was it her imagination or had Sasha begun in the far corner of the sofa and moved closer to Pen as the night wore on? Just before they'd gone to bed, his right leg had been nearly up against her left, their thighs and shins centimeters from touching.

She made herself into a starfish and buried her face in the cool side of the pillow. The cotton soothed her too-sensitive nerve endings. She wanted to stay there forever. But in spite of the brief conversation with Lennox about her parents, the only new facts in her possession were that Lennox and Christina had both known her dad; that Lennox had never met her mother but thought her "special indeed"; and that he had not been aware of her parents' divorce. His mention of her mother and of their marriage increased her certainty that there was a link between the two ruptures. She got up and looked out the window. Outside her nest of blankets, the air was frigid. The grounds gleamed beneath a cobalt sky.

She picked up her phone: 7:42 a.m. There was a text from Alice, sent the night before: "Everything OK? Not murdered?"

She wrote back: "Alive and kicking. How are things at Buttons? Did you sew one on?"

She couldn't hear any sounds in the house except for the clanking and creaking of its systems at work, so she splashed her face, scrubbed at her dull tongue, drank some water straight from the tap, and ran a hot bath. She brought her book into the tub and luxuriated until she felt close to herself again. Only an ache in her eyelids and a powerful need to eat something remained of her hangover. She dressed quickly against the cold, towel-dried her hair, and slipped into the hall. She hesitated and then turned the right way and went downstairs.

No one was in the living room. Their wine glasses and ashtrays were still where they had left them, and the cushions were depressed where they had been sitting just a few hours before. Breathing through her mouth, Pen brought the full ashtrays, dirty glasses, and empty bottles through the dining room, where the picked-over cheese board sat out uncovered and the tablecloth was splotched with wine and wax, and into the kitchen.

The kitchen was eerily clean despite last night's feast, and someone had placed a bag of crumpets, a butter dish, and a jar of Marmite beside the toaster. Pen emptied the ashtrays and washed them along with the glasses in the trough-like sink. She rinsed the empty bottles and lined them up beside the bin. She considered doing something about the cheese board, but thought better of it, having no idea whether it would be considered garbage or lunch.

Next to the electric kettle were a teapot and a worn tin labeled TEA. On the sun-speckled kitchen table, beneath picture windows that looked over green lawns, there was a box of Weetabix and a selection of plates, bowls, butter knives, and spoons. Pen was reading the back of the Marmite jar when Hector came in through the back door, trailing an excited Nellie.

"Alright?" he asked, dropping a stack of Sunday papers on the table. The spaniel jumped at Pen, wagging her tail.

"Great—you?" she said awkwardly, stroking the dog's head.

Hector gestured toward the blue sky. "Never better." He looked at the untouched breakfast things. "You're an early riser for this house. They're not riding out till eleven. Be joining them, will you?"

Pen said she would love to, and Hector nodded and went back out, followed by the dog. She watched them cross the grass toward the stables. The kitchen clock said 9:15. Feeling like a thief even though she knew the breakfast things had been laid out for a reason, she fixed herself a bowl of Weetabix and some tea. She ate her cereal at the kitchen table, and then carried her mug of tea and one of the papers back into the living room. She fluffed up the couch and built a fire in the grate, like her dad had taught her long ago. She shuffled through the sections and selected Sport as kindling, figuring it was the least likely to be missed. Then she settled in with *The Sunday Times*.

· · ·

An hour or so later, Christina entered the room looking polished and efficient in slacks and a cream-colored turtleneck, as if she had already been to London and back that morning.

"Good God," she said, "Penelope, you've transformed the place. Do come every weekend."

Pen tried to thank her for dinner, but Christina waved her compliments away. "Did you unearth some breakfast? Hector tells me you'll be riding. What's your boot size?"

She glanced at Pen's feet.

"I have a ladies' size five—will that do?"

Pen, trying to remember how UK shoe sizes worked, followed her down the kitchen stairs to the boot room, where rows of cubbies and hooks housed boots, oiled jackets, felt hats, and riding helmets in every size.

Pen sat down and tried on the boots while Christina lowered a dusty velvet helmet onto her head. "You've ridden before?"

"I took lessons as a kid, but it's been years," said Pen, doing up the chin strap and shaking her head from side to side.

"Good." Christina tightened the laces at the back of the helmet. "We'll put you on Kevin. He's about as energetic as a stoned woolly mammoth. But on a day like this even he might be frisky; best to take precautions. Are there many places to ride in Toronto?"

"Not really. I learned at a farm outside the city. My dad used to take me on Sundays," said Pen.

She glanced up at Christina, who looked as though she was remembering something. "Were you at Edinburgh, too?" she asked.

"I was," Christina said in a tone that did not invite further questions.

"What did you study?" persisted Pen.

"Classics."

"Same as my dad." Pen was excited by this development.

"Yes." She handed Pen a riding crop. "You might need this for Kevin. Cup of tea?"

Christina had been to the early church service in the village that morning and her head was filled with the concerns of her neighbors. From Gail Hewitt, whose mother had been the late Lady Lennox's cook and whose son Kieran worked at the village store, Christina had learned that the best teacher at the village primary school had been offered a higher salary at a private girls' college in Aberdeen. From Betsy Farquharson, who ran the village tearoom, she had learned that Norbert Kelly, an old playmate of Elliot's who had inherited the Rose and Lion from his parents in the seventies and knew exactly whom to refuse after exactly how many, had been hastily summoned to Dundee to visit his ailing sister, leaving his son Ralph, a timid soul and no match for the village's rowdier drinkers, in charge. This had led to a handful of rows the previous evening and contributed to a gruesome incident involving Henry Ashton's left foot. The worries of Talmòrach were many and constant, and Christina, who had several calls to pay that afternoon and would need to enlist Hector's help in cleaning out the eaves before the next day's expected rainfall if they were to avoid another flood, was not, just then, able to offer her young guest her full attention. And so she would do what she always did under such circumstances and put the kettle on for tea.

They came up the stairs to find Sasha and Chet sitting at the kitchen table. Chet was devouring a crumpet spread thickly with butter and Marmite. Sasha looked up at Pen and smiled. She suddenly didn't know what to do with her arms. The riding crop felt strange in her hand.

"I'll go and see how George and Danny are getting on. Please bring our guest back in one piece," said Christina, slipping out of the room.

It wasn't much colder outdoors than it had been in the house when, after breakfast, they set out past the kitchen garden toward the stables. Chet walked beside Pen, continuing the previous day's running commentary about the types of plants they were passing, but now reciting each of their Latin names as well as their English ones. Pen was impressed.

"He's making those up," said Sasha, looking at her sidelong.

This is going to be fine, Pen told herself, breathing in and out. Why wouldn't it be?

9

Nellie barked a greeting when they entered the dim stables, and rubbed against Sasha's ankles like a cat. Kevin, who was dark brown with white markings—and the size of a transport truck—was tacked up and waiting. Hector led him out into the courtyard and took the crop from Pen's hand while she mounted. He offered her a leg up, but she placed a foot in the stirrup and levered herself onto his broad back—smoothly, she thought. Maybe the smell of manure had jogged her muscle memory.

"Like an armchair, he is," said Hector, handing her back the crop. "You'll need this to keep up with those two." He tightened the girth and Kevin turned to nip at him.

Chet threw himself onto a dapple gray called Brahms and led the way across the field at a trot. Sasha came up beside Pen on a mare named Cindy. Her glossy coat was the same sun-washed brown as his hair. "Her full name is Cinderella. I named her," he confessed to Pen as they walked in step. "But my brother gets full credit for Kevin."

"Who chose the name Nellie?" asked Pen, trying to recover whatever courage had possessed her the night before. "Let me guess. Your dad, for Nellie Bly." He just looked at her. "You know, the journalist. *Ten Days in a Mad-House*?"

"A mad house?" repeated Sasha. "This is nothing. Wait until you meet my aunt Margot. And you're lucky, you only have to stay for two," he added, smiling. Cindy whipped Kevin with her tail. Kevin stamped an enormous foot. "Don't worry," Sasha said. "Kevin fancies Cindy and she knows it, so she likes to tease him. But they get along. Does he feel okay?"

"Great." Pen tested out her legs as they walked, reminding herself how to use the gas and brakes. "A bit rusty, but good."

"Ready to trot?"

"Sure." She squeezed her calves. Nothing happened.

"He's stubborn," said Sasha. "Try a nudge with your ankle."

Kevin continued to lumber forward at a walk until Sasha brought Cindy in front of him. Then he broke into a jouncing, teeth-rattling trot to catch up. Pen rose in her saddle when Kevin's left leg was forward and sat down when it was back. It felt like she was riding a washing machine, so she bore down in the saddle for two beats to change diagonals, amazed that she still knew how to do this. The last time she'd ridden a horse she had been twelve years old.

Moving through the cool air with Kevin's heat beneath her felt so good that once they'd cleared the fields and entered the canopy of the woods, with the wide trail unfurling ahead, she followed an impulse. She could see Chet cantering up ahead on Brahms, and so she applied firm, even pressure with her calves, guiding Kevin from his bouncing trot into a smooth canter. It felt like slow motion, even though they covered twice the ground in half the time. The soft thump of the ground beneath Kevin's hooves, the trustworthy swoop of his stride, and the way the light filtered in drops between the leaves lulled Pen into a state of peace.

This pleasant illusion of control evaporated when the sound of a gun-shot crackled through the trees, followed by the frenzied flapping of wings. Kevin, spooked, pinned his ears back and threw his considerable weight into a gallop. Pen lost one stirrup and then the other. Leather and metal flailed against her legs as the enormous horse barreled forward. She clung to his belly with her thighs and leaned back on the reins. She knew there was an emergency stop method that had to do with yanking one arm up while the other stayed down, but she couldn't remember it, and she didn't want to hurt Kevin's mouth. She stayed on, trying to slow him down until Kevin veered from the path. As the branches rushed forward, she ducked low and flung herself from the horse's back, as if rolling from a moving car.

Kevin darted into the woods and Chet sped after him, hovering close to Brahms's neck to keep his head attached.

"Pen!" Sasha was sliding from Cindy's back, crouching beside her, his face contorted with anger and concern. He gently lay a hand on her arm. His touch cut through her shock. "Those bloody lunatics. Are you all right?"

Pen's wrists felt loose from hitting the ground and her spine had a jerked-sideways feel, but she'd landed well. She had always been good at falling. Although of course she had not fallen; she had jumped. Shame rose in her chest and pricked at her eyes. She blinked it away and sat up in the underbrush.

Chet returned before long, still mounted, and pulling along a heaving, wild-eyed Kevin.

"I'm so sorry. He could have been killed," Pen said, reaching out to touch Kevin's sweat-darkened neck. Standing now, she was at the level of Sasha's jaw.

"*You* could have been killed," he said, carefully removing a leaf from her hair, sending a tingle from her scalp down through her whole body. "If anything, the excitement will have added years to Kev's life," he added.

He passed her Kevin's reins. For a defeated moment, she thought he was going to suggest they walk the horses back. But he held the stirrup in place for her. She planted her left foot on the rubber tread and cast herself up.

Lightly, he loosened the rubber handle of the crop from her fingers—she hadn't realized how tightly she was clutching it—and tucked it beneath her leg under the saddle. They rode back the way they had come at a leisurely walk. Sasha glanced repeatedly at Pen, as if to make sure she was still there, while Chet explained the attraction of shooting pheasant and black grouse, and mocked Sasha for not participating.

"My aversion to blood sport does nothing for the family's reputation," he told Pen. "Mum lets our neighbors use the land, within reason. But clearly reason's boundaries are ill-defined."

After returning the horses to the stables, they entered the house through the side door and took off their mucky boots. Pen felt like a toy that had been put back together too quickly, with some of the parts screwed in wrong.

Sasha lifted another leaf from her hair and, as if not quite knowing what to do with it, put it in his pocket. "You sure you're all right?" Pen nodded.

In the kitchen, they found Christina half inside the dishwasher.

"Going somewhere?" asked Chet, kneeling behind her.

She backed out holding a shard of broken glass between rubber-gloved fingers.

"This was jamming up the spinning widget," she said triumphantly. "Pen, what time do you need to be back in Edinburgh?"

"I was thinking I'd take the 3:06 train," Pen said, rubbing soap into the dirt-encrusted lines of her palms.

"Nonsense," said Christina. "Sasha and Chet are driving down after lunch. You'll give Pen a lift, won't you?"

"If she promises to stay in the car," said Chet.

Christina did not seem to hear him. "Go get tidied up and then come and make yourselves useful," she said.

Sasha kissed his mother on the cheek and held the door for Pen and Chet.

At the top of the main staircase, Sasha and Chet veered left into a part of the house Pen had not yet seen. So endless were its painting-lined halls, and so distant its component parts from one another, Pen would not have been surprised if it contained several people she had not yet met. A beloved former nanny in the attic, maybe, or a mad first wife. A poltergeist at the very least.

Pen wanted to believe in ghosts. She found it reassuring to imagine that the dead might have something like selective omniscience. No heaven or hell, no naked cherubs or horned demons with whips, but the option of toggling between a dreamless sleep and a roving lens on the living, with all their tempests and teapots. Her experience of death was limited. The sudden silencing of the golf channel in her grandparents' house had been her first good look at its permanence. She had never pictured Edward Senior watching over her—she had known better than to think that the life of a nine-year-old could hold much interest for a man who had lost two brothers in the war—but she liked to think that his eternal spirit might have a good view of the putting green at the Masters Tournament, for example.

When Tilda Winters had been killed by a heart attack in her sleep seven years later, a tidy death of which she would have approved, Pen had acquired the habit of believing that her grandmother, who had been an important if domineering presence in her life, might look in, now and then. She hoped Tilda would be satisfied with what she saw. In Toronto, such superstitions were mostly reserved for the religious. Here, the idea that souls lingered seemed to be widely accepted. Maybe it was the old buildings with centuries of dead inhabitants. Or maybe the population-to-land ratio of Scotland relative to Canada just made for a greater density of spirits.

As she changed for lunch, Pen found herself thinking about Sasha's bedroom. Did it have gray goo on the walls where posters of Jimi Hendrix had been peeled off? Did he have a bedside drawer filled with condoms and dry, half-smoked joints, or with trading cards and a Tamagotchi he had starved to death? She was pretty sure Sasha could not have been interested in her—he was too much older, and too attractive; there might have been something happening between him and Chet for all she knew—so she forced herself to stop thinking about the shiver that had gone through her when he'd touched her arm, and to focus instead on applying eyeliner and mascara, as Alice had taught her.

10

In the dining room, Lennox and Christina were already at the table with George, who was holding a wriggling, curly-haired baby in her arms. They had before them steaming bowls of soup. Lennox was helping himself to a fat slice of crusty bread and a dollop of very yellow butter. George was trying to keep the baby from sticking his hands in her soup.

"Penelope, you're better than a rabbit's foot, and you smell nicer, too," said Lennox, setting down his bread. He was boyish in the daylight, and in the casual clothes of Sunday afternoon. Even more like his son. "I put the first draft of my new book to bed this morning, a mere twelve days behind schedule." Christina shot her husband a look that contained both affection and reprimand.

"Lucky draft," George said. She was slumped in her chair looking wild-haired and depleted.

"Oh darling, let me take him," said Christina, holding out her arms for the baby. "As soon as you've eaten something, have a siesta. Danny will come with me on my calls, won't you," she told him, nuzzling his neck. He giggled. "He's cutting teeth, poor thing," Christina said to Pen.

Chet and Sasha came in with three bowls of soup from the kitchen and took their usual seats. Sasha carefully set one down before Pen, and she smiled up at him in thanks.

"Afternoon Lady Georgina," Chet said. "Did you have a lie-in? It was the perfect day for a ride. Or a skydive for that matter. Wasn't it, Pen?"

George rolled her eyes. "I was woken up six times by a howling dictator, and the only way to shut him up was to bring him into my bed and shove my nipple into his mouth. I probably won't ride again until he leaves for school."

"Uh-oh," said Chet, helping himself to a piece of bread. "Not much I can say to that without getting smacked. Can someone rescue me please?"

"Has anyone seen the Sport section of *The Times*? I've been looking for it everywhere," said Lennox. "Hector says he's sure the paper was whole when it arrived."

Pen felt blood rush to her cheeks. "It was me," she said quickly to get it over with. "I used it to light a fire this morning. I'm sorry."

Sasha caught her eye and suppressed a laugh.

"Penelope! Did you sweep out the chimneys, too? Good lord," said Lennox.

Christina gave her husband another look, this one a shade darker. She bounced the baby on her knee.

"I saw Imogen at church this morning, and she told me a dreadful story. It seems Jane Ashton has stuck a kitchen knife into Henry," she said.

"Oh dear," replied Lennox with some alarm, turning to his wife. "A kitchen knife?"

"Yes, a chef's knife. Terribly sharp," said Christina. "Dropped it into his foot. Quite accidentally, of course."

"Oh dear," Lennox said again. He looked at his wife with a mixture of curiosity and foreboding, waiting for her to continue.

"Following what I gather was rather a long afternoon at the pub, Henry invited a party back to theirs for supper. Jane wasn't given a moment's warning, and they were all ravenous of course, but Imogen said she managed quite well, under the circumstances. Afterward, there were six of them playing Scrabble. Henry asked Jane if there wasn't another bottle handy, and if she couldn't scrounge up a shard of fruit or a biscuit for their guests, as her supper had been on the skimpy side. She replied that by all means he was most welcome to take a look. He went into the kitchen, bustled about for a few minutes, and then called for her. She went in after him, and they all heard a sort of high-pitched yelp."

Lennox winced. Sasha and George traded a glance.

"How unfortunate," said George.

"The odd bit," Christina continued, looking directly into her husband's eyes, "was that afterward, Jane came back in without a word and played her turn. Must have been in shock, the poor thing. She'd been playing quite well, apparently."

The table fell silent. Pen wondered whether Christina was offering this story as material, or as a warning. From the look on Lennox's face, she guessed both.

"Is Henry all right?" he eventually asked.

"Oh yes, a few stitches set him right. Dr. Morley came straightaway. Henry's a robust sort. And thankfully he doesn't use his feet a great deal. I do feel for Jane though." Christina lifted Danny up and blew a raspberry on his cheek. He giggled.

She turned to Chet and Sasha. "Boys, why don't you redeem yourselves for the near uselessness of your sex by fetching the pudding and making some coffee?"

Christina was satisfied that Elliot had understood her meaning. She liked her work on the estate and in the village, and she had chosen it. But she did not like for her husband to forget how it was that all his material and immaterial needs were consistently met, and that this great precarious pile of his family's was still standing. Nor did she like it when he donned the mantle of oblivious artist and failed to do his comparatively minor part. He had irritated her, this weekend, by spending more time shut away in his burrow than was altogether fair, given that he was the one who had invited the child. Christina was relieved that he had finished his draft, which was well over twelve days past due—Elliot often lost track of the date while writing. Still, she could not allow him to become complacent in the way that Henry Ashton was complacent. It was not much wonder that Jane had reached the end of her tether.

After an interval, Chet brought bowls of sticky toffee pudding from the kitchen and Sasha followed. Pen tensed when, standing behind her chair, he placed a cup of coffee beside her. Without turning she cupped the hot porcelain and let the smell steady her. Across the table, George yawned and stood.

"You're sure you don't mind taking him?" she asked Christina, who dismissed the question with a wave. "Goodbye," George said. "No, don't stand," she told Pen, who was already standing. George kissed her on both cheeks. "Hope to see you here again," she said, squeezing Pen's upper arm.

Danny followed George out of the room with his eyes and cried out. He lurched in Christina's arms, reaching for her glass and making a growling sound. Lennox brought his chair closer to Christina's and began playing peekaboo with his napkin. Danny forgot his agitation and shrieked with excitement, showing off the white glimmers of two bottom teeth poised to break through the gums.

Pen, in the vastness of her inexperience, was surprised to see that someone like George, who last night had held court on a dozen subjects, could be so diminished by a being so tiny. She wondered where Danny's father was. All she knew of him was that his name was Rosh, and that he worked "in the City," which Pen took to mean London. She did not know that it meant a specific part of London where vast quantities of human intelligence were trained day and night on computer monitors in the service of finance. At eighteen, Pen had never gone without the type of security Danny's father was striving, by working twelve-hour days seven days a week, to acquire. Nor was she familiar with the torpor that could threaten to submerge a person—from which Christina sprang each morning with a cold shower and brisk walk to the village, rituals that never failed to snap her back into the present tense—when a life that had looked so broad and open-ended at one time narrowed to a single corridor cluttered with promises.

While Pen had not gathered more than a handful of disjointed clues about the Lennoxes and her parents, neither did she, as she bid Elliot and Christina goodbye after lunch, consider the trip a failure. Beyond the tautness of her nerves as she took her place behind Sasha in his small car, she was aware of having witnessed, however briefly, if not transformative and enduring love, then at least a functioning partnership. Which was not nothing.

11

"You're in love," Alice accused. They were debriefing in Pen's room over a convenience store supper of marble cheese and melba toast.

"With Sasha?" Pen had wanted to say his name.

"With all of them." Alice sat on Pen's bed, her legs outstretched, her feet bare. Her toenails needed trimming and were half-painted with cracked coral polish. Her heels were white with dead skin. Alice was not fastidious about such things. Her socks were balled on the floor beside her purse, which was open, its insides exposed to reveal a long receipt, a nearly empty plastic bottle of warm Diet Coke, a hairbrush with strands streaming from its bristles, and a crushed pack of Camel Lights.

These private territories stood in contrast with the rest of Alice, who, at eighteen, inhabited the type of body that women's magazines extolled their readers to attempt to emulate, surely expecting most to fail. She had a long, elegantly curved figure and a wide, lovely, serene face. Her masses of corkscrewed hair and warm skin stored sunshine, and her wry mouth, often painted red, was capable of subtle miracles of entrapment.

Dark brows framed the attribute she best knew how to wield, thanks to years of acting classes: her maternal grandmother's rebellious eyes, in a startling shade of Mediterranean blue.

Pen, who had loved Alice since they had been too young to realize that strangers would one day judge them on their random genetic allocations, was aware of Alice's looks. It was hard to ignore the model scouts who followed them around shopping malls. Asking ten-year-old Pen if she knew her best friend was beautiful, however, would have been like asking her if she knew the walls of her parents' kitchen were pale yellow. Of course she knew, but it wasn't the point. The thing Pen paid attention to was not her face itself but the way it worked with her voice, and the frequent mad laughter they called forth.

Later, as they edged out of childhood, Pen would witness the ugliness her friend's beauty brought out in certain people. She would notice how they were prepared to be dismissive, threatened, even hateful—and watch as Alice learned to spare them the trouble with a well-placed joke.

Alice's mother, an interior designer who spent a good deal of time shuttling Alice's younger brother between hockey arenas, and her father, a dangerously likable anesthesiologist, had met at McGill. They lived in a big, comfortable, densely decorated house in the middle of Toronto where everyone drove everywhere even though they didn't need to, and her mom made a point of holding mandatory Friday night dinners, even though she hated to cook. Alice's parents were neither thrilled by her ambition to be an actor nor up to the job of stopping her. Toronto was a popular enough place to shoot TV commercials and teen dramedies that by age thirteen Alice was going to three or four auditions a week.

Her "youth talent agent," Richard, wore a suede vest, had a scraggly white ponytail, and seemed to derive great pleasure from pinching her hips to make sure she hadn't gained any weight. Her acting teacher, a mid-fifties beanpole named Stephen, hosted workshops in his industrial loft near the

Don River, and tried several times to convince her to accept his tongue in her mouth "while in character." Alice liked to say that because she had known since puberty what a shark looked like—meaning, how sad and coffee-breathed they were by daylight—she would never fall victim to one.

Both Pen and Alice found it freeing that no one in Edinburgh seemed able to picture where they came from. And they had, or so they thought, mostly managed to avoid being typecast by their clothes. They dressed experimentally, finding improbable and not always successful combinations at thrift stores.

Alice, who just then was wearing a pair of white denim overalls over a red and purple Toronto Raptors sweatshirt, peeled a slab of cheese from its sweaty-smelling plastic casing, placed it between two melba toasts, and took a bite. Pen tried not to wince at the crumbs that sprayed onto her bedspread.

"It's not just Sasha, though I know you think it is," said Alice, munching on the toast. "It's Sasha in his context. The way you describe him, he doesn't sound like he's going to set the world on fire, no offense. Imagine him in khakis and a polo shirt, drinking Labatt Blue and calling cigarettes 'darts.' Would you look twice at him? But in a castle in the countryside with horses and famous authors and a mysterious cousin whose mother is Margot effing Lennox . . . come on."

Alice wasn't trying to be mean. Pen, in recounting the weekend, had downplayed the chemical effect Sasha had had on her, and focused instead on his professional-grade charm. She hadn't told Alice, for example, about how Sasha's voice hit her in the solar plexus, or about his way of stooping a bit to get closer to Pen's height when he was talking to her, or about his disturbingly beautiful hands. Nor had she told her about how difficult she had found it to breathe during the car ride back to Edinburgh on Sunday. Thank goodness for Chet, who, upon learning that she didn't know what a WAG was, had taken the opportunity to fill her in on the past ten years of UK reality television/tabloid/football culture, which had segued smoothly into a rundown of the relative merits of every football club in the nation, and then the rules of cricket. When Sasha had walked her to the door of Lee House, she had leaned in to hug him and he'd gone in for a cheek kiss, resulting in an awkward moment during which he had held her close to him, their cheeks pressed together. He'd stroked her back once and emitted a shy half-laugh before letting go. She had replayed this four-second interaction in her mind approximately once a minute since her return. She hadn't wanted Alice to know the extent of her infatuation, because she planned to do with it what she considered to be the only reasonable thing, which was absolutely nothing.

Pen had told Alice about George with some reluctance, feeling guilty about her newfound proximity to Alice's idol. In high school, Alice, who could never remember when the math exam was, had always known the exact day when the French and British issues of *Vogue* would appear. She would carry them back to her messy room, close the door, and start to flip through the thick pages, pausing only to look at the risqué photoshoots involving bare nipples (in the French issue), until she found a society picture of Margot Lennox. And Margot would always be there. Sometimes posing for the camera at a glamorous soirée, dressed in an understated suit of her own design, and sometimes staring accusingly at the camera from her atelier in Paris, wearing a pair of tailored pants with a cuffed white shirt.

"Tomorrow's your first rehearsal," Pen said, changing the subject. "What's Thomasina going to wear?"

Alice's eyes brightened and she moved to Pen's closet. This was one of the many things they had in common: they never tired of transformation.

12

Alice slowed down, texting Pen as she walked. **Meet us at the wrap place at 1.** She snapped her phone shut and dropped it back into her coat pocket. Jo linked her arm through Alice's. Their sides collided every few steps as they ambled across George Square toward the restaurants on Chapel Street.

Jo was tactile. She rubbed shoulders, kissed cheeks properly rather than just grazing them with hers, and sometimes reached out to remove a strand of hair from Alice's sweater. Alice liked this about her, the quick warmth and assumed intimacy. It had taken Pen years not to tense up when Alice hugged her. Trying to get Pen to skinny-dip with the rest of their cabin at summer camp had been like trying to convince a nun to try group sex.

Knowing Pen's parents as well as she did allowed Alice a certain amount of insight into reflexes that other friends sometimes found affronting. The values of Victorian England had been preserved in Pen's paternal grandmother like an insect in amber. Ted had been groomed from childhood to take over the packaging business started by his great-grandfather. He'd spent his childhood summers cleaning urinals and waxing floors at the Winter Corp factory, learning every facet of every job that would someday be his to oversee. When he finally took the helm, he made such a success of things that his father—under whom the business had shrunk somewhat—had never forgiven him. Ted was a bundle of contradictions: by turns openhanded and stingy, broad-minded and prim, hardworking and decadent. Pen loved him and took his advice as something close to gospel, even though she had known from a young age that his relationship with the truth was complicated.

Pen's mother, Anna, meanwhile, came from a small town near the Manitoba border. She had been raised by an oldish Catholic couple who had taken her in as a child, whether because her birth mother had given her up or because Anna had been removed from her, Alice had never been quite sure. Anna had made it to the University of Toronto, where she was now a professor, on her own steam. She bought into exactly none of the Winters family's mythmaking, always voting as far left as she could lean without falling over and instilling in Pen a throbbing awareness of her privilege, and of the people it left behind. As a result of these dueling forces Pen often behaved as if someone were watching her and grading her on her manners, or her empathy, or both. Alice knew this because she did watch her. Once, on an evening when they had both been tipsy, Pen had left the bathroom door ajar. Alice had seen her take exactly two squares of toilet paper, fold them piously, and perch, straight-backed, on the edge of the toilet seat, peeing as silently as was humanly possible.

Aside from her green eyes, whose shade ranged from olive to radioactive depending on her mood, Pen's was the type of beauty that could be hidden, and Pen was practiced at hiding it. She had a boyish figure and legs that were accustomed to running fast. Her elfin face had a straight nose. All through school she had worn her hair long, often pulled into a braid that hung down her back, but in the first week of Edinburgh she and Alice had gone to a salon in New Town and asked to have it shorn to her chin, which made her look older. Her skin was pale and prone to changing color. In the summer her forearms and the bridge of her nose were brushed with freckles, and a flush often crept up her neck and across her cheeks, brought on either by vigorous exercise or by the vigorous self-chastisement that came from worrying too much what other people thought.

Jo and especially Fergus were fascinated by her. Fergus had been pursuing Pen since their first encounter, but also seemed to think it was his duty to make them both aware of their subservience to Mother England. He spoke of the Queen as a beloved relative and had, on more than one occasion while walking home from the pub, felt moved to offer a spirited and apparently unironic (though it was hard to tell, with Fergus) rendition of "Rule, Britannia."

> *Rule, Britannia! Britannia, rule the waves!*
> *Britons never, never, never will be slaves.*

Jo laughed at this side of her brother, just as she had learned to laugh at many things she could not control.

Alice and Jo shared a cigarette in front of the wrap place and then went in without waiting for Pen. The narrow café was crowded with students taking advantage of the hour-long break in lectures and tutorials. The front half let in some light from the street, but not much, and was lined on one side with small tables, all of them occupied.

Alice and Jo held their bags tightly under their armpits and slid sideways in between the tables and the crush of students lined up at the service counter. The queue was nearly ten people deep, and the chances of eating more than two bites before her next lecture were slim at best, but

Alice, as usual, was willing to suspend disbelief for the sake of a social interaction.

Pen arrived and, after a tidy string of excuse-mes, tried to take her place at the very back of the queue. Alice could not allow this. Now that they had put five thousand kilometers between themselves and the Winters family, she saw it as one of her jobs, as Pen's best friend, to save her from herself.

Alice turned to face the four students between them in line with a smile. "Our friend here has come a bit late; would you mind very much if she cut in front of you to join us?" she asked. Of course they wouldn't. Alice pulled Pen forward and they parted to let her through.

"Tell us every single detail," Jo said, kissing Pen on both cheeks. But Jo's eyes were distracted by a group perched around two tables pushed together in the front window. She clutched Alice and Pen each by the forearm, digging her fingernails into their skin, and whispered, her breath tickling Alice's ear: "See the girl with the Barbour and the fringe? That's her." Jo's face betrayed almost nothing, except for a dent between her blonde eyebrows.

The Saturday after Freshers' Week, exhausted from five nights out in clubs, the three of them had sat under Jo's floral duvet to drink four-pound wine and eat an ungodly number of Haribo gummies. Jo had divulged that the first girl she had ever loved was here at Edinburgh. She'd spotted her at Cabaret Voltaire on Thursday night. Her name was Sylvia Clarke.

Jo and Fergus had grown up between London and Buttons. At fifteen, they had been sent to a coed boarding school near the Cotswolds that Pen couldn't help picturing as Hailsham. In the first term of her second year there, Jo's housemistress had surprised her and Sylvia in the laundry room. The housemistress had informed the head of the school, who had summoned their parents and expelled both girls.

"Maybe it's why I avoid doing my washing until it's truly dire to this day," Jo had joked. Pen and Alice could sense the effort it took for her to tell this as an old story with no power to wound her in the present. Jo's mother, she said, had tried to defend her, but only to the point of asserting that the housemistress was plainly mistaken. She had refused to hear Jo's avowal that there had been no mistake, telling her briskly that she would change her mind when she met the right man. Jo's father had avoided looking her in the eye ever since. Only Fergus's behavior toward her had remained exactly the same. He had stayed at the school, grudgingly, but had signed himself out every weekend to visit his sister in London, where she'd been transferred to a day school and had, eventually, made some new friends. His solidity, she said, had made it possible for her to refuse to lie about who she was from that point forward. Because of that, and because he was her brother, Jo would defend him always.

Alice found Jo's hand. "Have you said hi to her yet?"

"Absolutely fucking not," said Jo, carefully keeping her back to Sylvia's table. "Ancient history. From what I've heard, she's straight now."

When they reached the front of the line, Jo and Pen entered a battle of politeness, each trying to make the other order first. Pen lost. She tried to order a wrap using North American words—*lettuce, zucchini, eggplant, tomay-to*—and the owner spread a piece of flatbread with hummus and then looked back up at Pen as if awaiting further instruction. Putting on Jo's accent like a piece of clothing, Alice placed the exact same order using their friend's vocabulary and intonation. "Salad, courgette, aubergine, tomahto, and fet*ter,* please. Actually, three like that and three Diet Cokes," she said.

Relieved by this small efficiency, the woman made the wraps in record time. Jo laughed. "That'll go over well at Bedlam tonight. This look is very Thomasina, by the way."

Alice was wearing one of Pen's schoolgirlish tunics, which were short on Pen and very short indeed on Alice, with black tights, loafers, a white collared shirt, a red toque, and a manly trench over her arm.

They brought their paper bags to the back room. The prime spot—a couch covered in colorful, patterned scarves with a view of the whole room—was just being vacated.

"How was your weekend at home?" Pen asked as they sat down. Jo brushed the nicety away.

"I won't share a shred about how Ferg pined for you the entire time, driving Flossie to a supersonic pitch of jealousy, until you tell us every-thing about the Lennoxes and their haunted house," she said.

"Alice thinks I'm in love with all of them," said Pen. "It was very Brideshead."

"God that's cool," said Jo. "And Alice tells me Margot's daughter was there. Georgina, she's called, or is it Georgiana? I remember seeing her in *Tatler* when I was in school." She looked around the café and saw that it had emptied out. "What time is it?"

Alice looked at her watch. "Three minutes to two."

"Shit, we're late! Bundle that up and come along," she said, pulling Alice by the wrist. "Sorry to abandon you, Stinky—you'll tell us the rest at the pub later, won't you?"

"Bye!" said Pen to their backs. Alice turned and engulfed her friend's rib cage in a tight squeeze. When she glanced back from the door, Alice saw that Pen had moved over to a smaller table, even though the café was now nearly empty, and pulled out a novel. This was one of the most fun-damental differences between them, Alice thought: Pen had been trained to breathe less air than everyone else, whereas Alice had never once in her life felt the need to apologize for taking up space.

13

Pen was at the desk in her room wearing a sweatshirt over her warmest pajamas and taking notes from a library book when her laptop made a pinging sound, and then another. She lifted its screen. *Chethan Mehta would like to add you to Chat*, said the first notification. She clicked "Accept" and closed the window. *Sasha Lennox would like to add you to Chat*, said the window behind it. She smiled, a warm feeling spreading inside her chest, as if she had drunk something hot. She accepted. Their names appeared in bold on her contact list with dots beside them showing that they were online. She tried to think of something witty to say. Nothing came.

She tilted her laptop screen back down and returned to the book. When researching for an essay, her method was to write out a full bibliography entry and, beneath it, to transcribe passages that might be useful for her argument with their page numbers. Her own comments were always in a different color. This was to keep her from plagiarizing accidentally, the mere thought of which made her feel like throwing up. And yet, no matter how many precautions she took, whenever a teacher lectured a room full of students about an incident of academic theft, Pen felt about as clear of conscience as Lady Macbeth.

The friendly bleep of an incoming message came from her laptop. She opened it, expecting to see Chet's name.

SASHA: I still can't believe you incinerated Dad's racing news.

Pen felt herself smile self-consciously. Fingers poised over the keyboard, she tried to think up a reply.

Sasha Lennox is typing, read the text at the bottom of the dialogue box.

SASHA: What will you burn next, his Jilly Cooper box set?

She hesitated again, and then started to type, hating every second that he could see she was working on an answer.

PEN: Who or what is Jilly Cooper?

SASHA: Is that a joke?

He was typing again, so she waited.

SASHA: And here I thought you seemed well-read.

PEN: Now you're torturing me.

She opened a web browser and typed "Jilly Cooper" into the search field. The results included images of a woman with snowy white hair and a gap between her teeth and books with names like *Riders* and *Polo*. One cover featured a red high heel stepping on a hand with a prominent signet ring on the pinky.

SASHA: Look her up in the library. I'd be curious to know whether they stock the good stuff over at Edinburgh.

PEN: It's required reading at St Andrews?

SASHA: Let's call it recommended. Start with Riders. If you can't find any copies, I'll loan you mine.

Pen realized that she had been holding her breath. She let it out. There was no reason to get all excited. St Andrews was a tiny golf course town in which, it was said, there was so little to do that everyone had sex with everyone else before their four years were through. There was probably a naked girl curled around Sasha at that very moment. Or naked except for red high heels. He was not about to get into his car and drive for one hour and twenty-three minutes (according to MapQuest) until he reached Pollock Halls, and then make his way to Lee House, where the corridors always smelled bad because her neighbors kept drunkenly falling asleep while trying to make grilled cheese in the communal pantry's toaster oven, to knock on the door with the PEN WINTERS name tag that made her look twelve, and stand in the doorway with a book under his arm, waiting for her to invite him in. For all she knew he had a girlfriend. Or a boyfriend. Or several of each.

Another bleep announced a new dialogue box, this one with Chet's name at the top.

CHETHAN: I have something difficult to tell you. I don't want you to take it the wrong way.

Pen felt a stab of dread. What had she done? Had she offended him somehow? Chet was typing.

CHETHAN: You're not a very good rider. I think you need private lessons.

Relief. And then annoyance. Her computer pinged and she silenced it.

CHETHAN: You're lucky. I've got just the man.

The other window popped up again.

SASHA: Or I could try tying it to Hedwig's leg. Assuming you know who that is.

Pen smiled again, appreciating his open dorkiness.

PEN: I'm not a total philistine.

SASHA: Thank God.

PEN: Pigeon would be more traditional in these parts though, wouldn't it?

SASHA: Ah. You know your messenger birds. Well, that could be arranged. We do have a doocot you know.

A what? He was typing again, giving her time to imagine Sasha and Chet sitting together at the kitchen table in their shared apartment, a bottle of something between them, messing with her. If that turned out to be the case, she would not mind; she was enjoying this.

SASHA: Did you know that during both wars the Allies used pigeons to send intelligence across enemy lines? Heroic creatures. Mind you, these days the Americans probably use eagles.

PEN: What on earth is a doocot?

SASHA: Next time you come to the house I'll show you.

She let the words reverberate through her. And then quashed the feeling.

PEN: Regular eagles or bald?

SASHA: Whatever Cheney can get his hands on, I reckon.

He was typing another message. Pen waited.

SASHA: Why do you ask? Are you a baldist, Pen?

Pen let out a startled laugh.

PEN: Certainly not.

He did not reply right away.

PEN: I love bald people! Montaigne was bald, and I have a bit of a crush on him. I just don't trust bald eagles. They're sinister.

There was no evidence of typing, and no reply. She opened the web browser again and called up some photos of bald eagles. They were sinister. The yellow eyes, the yellow beak like a coat hanger. She searched for an image of Montaigne to make sure she had been right. Yes, there he was, bald and bearded in his ruff and doublet. Suddenly, she remembered the paintings of the Lennox ancestors. Regret hit her sharply in the stomach. She stared at the screen, hating herself for being so insensitive. Boys had insecurities, too. Of course they did. Finally, he began typing.

SASHA: That's a relief. Important to get these things out in the open. Night Pen. X

His little blue dot disappeared, and his name dropped down to the bottom of her contact list. Pen was flushed. Why had she felt the need to bring up bald eagles, of all things? And she shouldn't have mentioned Montaigne. That had been very undergraduate of her. But then, she was an undergraduate. And so was he.

Chet's window popped up.

CHETHAN: You still there? His price is reasonable, I assure you.

Pen looked at the clock on her screen. It was nearly eleven, and she hadn't done a speck of work on her essay.

PEN: I'm not entering any derbies this week, but I'll keep it in mind. Time to do some work. Good night!

CHETHAN: Night night 😌 xxxx

Just as Pen returned to her book feeling truly determined to make a start on the essay before she closed her eyes, her cell phone started vibrating. "Mom," said the caller ID window. It was early evening in Toronto. Pen's mother was probably making dinner. She let it buzz itself back to silence. "1 New Voicemail," read the screen.

Pen felt connected to her mom. Not in the girlfriend-y way that some of her friends were close with their mothers—they didn't go to get their hair done together, and her mom had never taught her to wear lipstick or anything like that—but in a more private way. After the bad period, in their five subsequent years of living just the two of them (plus their dog, Olive, a border collie mix), she felt they had developed a kind of wordless understanding. It was because of this understanding that Pen had allowed herself to go to Edinburgh. She knew she no longer had to worry. Still, she played the voicemail to reassure herself.

"Hi, love, it's Mom at about, oh, sixish. Just thought I'd give you a call and see how you're doing. It's probably a bit late there . . . quite late, actually. No doubt you're in bed already, responsible citizen that you are. Give me a call any time you get a sec, no rush. Love you."

She let herself be comforted by her mother's voice and pressed nine to save the message. If she called back the next day her mom wouldn't ask about the weekend, and she wouldn't have to lie. Not directly, anyway.

14

At Pollock Halls on Tuesday morning, early risers trickled from their bedrooms and pooled in the courtyard, where the wind and rain cleansed their skin of the night's excesses. A malty gust hit Pen in the face when she pushed through the door of Lee House. When the wind blew in a certain direction it smelled of Marmite. An olfactory by-product, or so she'd been told, of the breweries and distilleries rimming the city.

Pen wasn't on her way to the JMC this morning. For the first hour of the day, she planned to park herself in the back corner of her secret Scandinavian bakery in the Meadows with a strong black coffee, a cardamom bun, and a stack of library photocopies on which, in minuscule font, were reproduced select essays by Michel de Montaigne.

Without Alice and Jo clutching her elbows and beseeching her to slow down, Pen could make it from Halls to the Meadows in fifteen minutes. Waiting at a red light, she tilted her face upward to receive the full tonic benefit of the horizontal spray that was neither rain nor mist, but some

Scottish hybrid. She had hoped the walk would help her organize her thoughts, but as usual they did as they pleased. She would have liked to have divided them into folders, the way she organized her coursework. The convenient thing about folders was that you could put them away. Instead, her thoughts had a habit of imposing themselves, exploding through her various lobes at will.

A large part of her wished she could stop caring about whatever it was that had come between her dad and Lennox. Why this fixation on a past that wasn't even hers? But she knew why. She could see how easy it would be to relive her parents' lives without quite choosing to, the way a toboggan finds its way into the pre-compressed path of whoever went before. She wanted to better understand the route they had taken, so she didn't fall into it by mistake.

Pharmaceuticals, with their ability to change a person, make her unreachable for a time, or loosen her grip on reality, scared Pen. But now that her social life involved spending several nights each week at clubs with names like Why Not?, she found herself watching the "pills" contingent with curiosity. She could appreciate that it must be nice to pull a fast one on your neural pathways, scrambling them up a bit, just to see where you landed.

The only mind-altering drug she relied on at this stage in her life (besides caffeine; and nicotine, she supposed, which gave her such a head rush that she sometimes had to sit down) was alcohol. She had been raised to view moderate drinking as no less natural than eating dinner, and she liked the role it could play in slowing, or perhaps just dimming, her thoughts. Especially the ones that were forever replaying stupid things she had said and done from different angles, like the slow-motion close-ups in a televised tennis match.

The bakery was empty, or nearly. In the back corner that she'd begun to think of as hers (Alice didn't like cardamom anyway; she said it made everything taste like curry), she blew on the steam coming from her coffee and took a sip. It burned the back of her throat just as she'd hoped it would. Warmth spread through her. She took a bite of the knot of dough and licked sugar from the corner of her mouth. She took another swallow of coffee.

She was halfway through the essay on Montaigne's friendship with Étienne de La Boétie when a shadow appeared over her stapled booklet.

"You read French, do you?" said Julian Sachs. He was wearing a wool overcoat with droplets of moisture on the sleeves and holding a paper coffee cup in one hand and a briefcase in the other. To see him outside of the classroom or lecture theater was unnerving, and she felt herself straightening her spine.

"When provoked," she said.

"It's your subject, I mean," he said, picking up the reading list from her open folder.

"Yes, French and English."

"You came to Scotland to study Canada's two national languages?"

Pen found it surprising how many people made this observation. Even the immigration officer at Heathrow had laughed about it. It interested her that they knew anything at all about Canada. What else did they know? she wondered.

"I guess I did," she said.

"Avoiding someone?" he asked.

She looked up at him, curious as to why he was still talking to her. "The studentry."

"No—by crossing the Atlantic."

"Can't I have come for the scenery?"

"Sure, if you'd like."

Pen suddenly understood why Julian was lingering, and the knowledge contributed to her irritation at being disturbed.

Pen was not especially noticeable. She liked it that way. If more eyes were settling on her of late, she told herself it was only nature's way of trying to auction off her reproductive powers at their peak; she did not expect it to last. Those who did notice her were almost invariably kind. They did calculus for fun and said cryptic things about William Carlos Williams. They may have been good at an obscure or solitary sport, speed skating or the 400-meter race, but they did not usually shinny or scrimmage. Nor were they arrogant philosophy tutors twenty years her senior. When a man like that flirted with her, Pen knew she was one of several routes he was pursuing in hopes of reaching Alice.

The landline in Pen's room had rung late the previous night, waking her from a deep sleep. Pen, who somewhere in her body was always expecting the call that would confirm her deepest fear, grabbed at the phone on her bedside table with panic in her ears. When it was only Alice, Pen was so relieved she nearly laughed. She let the images that had flooded her with cold terror disappear as quickly as they had arrived.

Alice told Pen that she had just seen Julian. Or she thought she had. A familiar, dark-suited figure had been leaning against the statue of Greyfriars Bobby, staring at the big red doors of the Bedlam Theatre, as if waiting for her to come out of her rehearsal. At her approach, he had disappeared into the shadows down Candlemaker Row.

"You're being paranoid," Pen said, both for Alice's benefit and for her own, as the dregs of fear left her body. "Isn't there a pub right there? It could have been anyone having a cigarette. It's just the adrenaline from your rehearsal. Try to sleep."

Pen had thought, hanging up, that it had been a tiny bit conceited of Alice to assume that just because a guy was leaning on a statue outside of a pub, it meant their tutor was following her around. But now she wasn't so sure.

"You're not Scottish either, are you?" she asked Julian, who was still hovering.

"I'm not," he said. He didn't offer where he was from.

"Why Edinburgh for you then?" she asked.

"David Hume."

"Right. Same year?"

"Ha-ha." Julian touched his hair. "I didn't matriculate at eleven, but I did come as a fresher. Stayed on for postgrad, and they offered me money to do a PhD. I've been here ever since, teaching and writing. Mostly teaching if I'm honest."

"What are you writing about?"

"Virtue."

"Right. And are you . . . avoiding someone?"

He looked her in the eyes as if pleased by the question. "My young wife."

She gave him a look that should have told him he had been charming a moment ago, but now he was being a jerk.

"That was a joke," he said.

"Which part?"

Julian flashed her a slanted smile.

"Enjoy your mountain," he said, tapping her pages. The door made a jingling sound as he left.

Now Pen found it hard to concentrate on the friendship of two men in the 1500s. Julian's closeness had affected her, but he was one of those men who operate their own magnetic fields, so that wasn't so strange. She wondered if he really was married. Did people still marry before the drive to procreate backed them into a corner? She supposed they did. Optimistic people did, anyway. He didn't seem like a Pollyanna type.

But then, she didn't know him. She drank more coffee, finished her pastry, and stared at a painting of a blue triangle that hung on the wall.

Pen thought most people who cheated were either vain or cowardly or both, trying to put another body between themselves and death. Alice held a more nuanced view. She and her younger brother, Eli, had known their dad was sleeping with his junior residents (it did not appear to matter which one) for years. Their mother knew, too, but pretended not to see it, and buffered herself against seeing it by purchasing an ever-growing collection of decorative throw pillows. This, for Alice, was the more infuriating of the two crimes.

Pen finished her coffee and returned to Montaigne, who—whatever his faults—had almost definitely kept it in his pants.

15

Alice had thought about Julian while getting dressed, hoping that he would be lecturing again, and knowing that she would see him in the afternoon tutorial regardless. She wore a tight cream-colored sweater with black jean shorts and thin black tights. She'd used one of her patent leather loafers to itch her calf and created a run in her tights that now laddered up to mid-thigh. This had annoyed her at first, but now she thought it was kind of sexy.

There was a slide projected onto the white screen hanging behind Julian's head, but Alice wasn't paying attention. She had once again succumbed to the nervous excitement that had kept her up for most of the night. She was sure it had been Julian outside of her rehearsal. But why had he disappeared as soon as she'd seen him? Maybe he'd hoped to find her alone.

It had been nearly midnight by the time they'd finished the table read and Neville, the gregarious second year playing her character's tutor, had offered to drive her home. Neville had taken Alice's hand and led her directly over to the place where the suited figure had been standing just a moment before. Stopping in front of the statue of Greyfriars Bobby, he began to tell her about the loyal terrier and the haunted Greyfriars Kirkyard—until, noticing her spooked face under the lamplight, he'd laughed and led her to the safety of his Mini, parked a few feet away.

It was not lost on Alice that Thomasina Coverley, the precocious young woman from the early Romantic period she would play onstage in the spring, felt something more than intellectual admiration for her tutor, Septimus Hodge. Neither had she failed to understand that Thomasina would be consumed by the flames of her desire on the eve of her seventeenth birthday, after a single waltz with Septimus. But Alice was eighteen. And this was not her first waltz.

She watched Julian lean over his notes. The top two buttons of his shirt were undone. No tie. He clearly believed in dressing for the part. They had that in common.

When the lecture was over, he looked out at the students. Alice told Pen and Jo that she'd catch up with them later and walked as slowly as she could down the stairs toward the stage, where he was answering the questions of each of his—largely female, Alice noticed—keeners in turn.

"Hi," she said when the others had all gone.

Julian pretended that he hadn't watched her approach out of the corner of his eye. "Alice Diamond," he said slowly.

"Great lecture," she said. It came out sarcastically, which was not what she had intended. She wasn't used to sucking up, and she was not good at it.

Julian reached into the hollow in the lectern and took out his briefcase. He tucked his lecture notes inside and stepped down from the stage.

"That wasn't very convincing. I'd expect better from an actress," he said. She liked how he pronounced the word.

"Actor," she corrected.

"All right," he said. "Actor."

She had planned to ask him outright whether he had been waiting outside of her rehearsal, but she found that she could not. This was how people with stage fright must feel, she thought. How stupid.

"I saw you," she managed finally. "By the dog."

"The dog?" he asked. He looked genuinely confused. "I'm afraid I don't know what you mean," he said.

"Greyfriars Bobby," she said. "The statue. Last night. I was leaving Bedlam, and I saw you."

"Must've been someone else," he said, giving her a curious look.

She couldn't tell if he was lying. They were the last ones in the lecture theater, and some students were starting to stream in for the next course. She followed him out.

"How are rehearsals going then," he asked. Before she had time to respond he added, "Are you pleased with your Septimus?" His voice was edged with suggestion.

She caught his eye. There was something taunting in the way he looked at her.

"Extremely," she said, her sangfroid returning. "It'll be easy to fall in love with him."

The look on his face confirmed it. She was more convinced than ever that he had been there, that he had seen her with Neville. Had it been a coincidence, though, or had he really been waiting for her?

"I'd like to discuss last week's essay with you," he said once they were outside. "Could you come to my office during the lunch break?"

"All right," she said.

"I'm in the David Hume Tower, 1203. Half one?" He was veering away from her already, as if in a rush to get somewhere.

"See you then," she said. She turned for the library, although she knew that no new information that entered her mind in the succeeding three and a half hours would stick.

Between 1:00 and 2:00 p.m. the David Hume Tower felt like a downtown subway stop after rush hour: empty, with the lingering thrum of freshly vanished bodies. Alice took the elevator. It was slow, which was what she needed. She was on her own, which was also what she needed. It lurched to a stop at the twelfth floor. She checked her teeth in the mirror, ran her fingers through her hair to make sure it wasn't too flat on her head, and stepped out onto the landing. Down the hall from their tutorial room, she found the door with a small placard marked with his name. She knocked.

"Come in," came his voice, faint through the heavy door. Julian was seated behind a large desk. The room was filled with books. They covered every wall and stood in stacks on every available surface, the floor included. A tall floor lamp stooped over his desk like a friendly old man. It was a stylish room for a tutor, far from the dusty supply closet she'd expected.

She closed the door softly behind her. Her face felt strangely tight, and her palms were already damp. She pressed them against her shorts.

Without greeting her, he gestured to the chair in front of his desk. She shifted a pile of books from its seat and sat down. She had to fight to keep her knees from shaking.

Julian riffled through the papers in front of him and pulled out the foolscap that she recognized as her essay. He'd stapled the pages together. He handed them to her. There was a 61 scrawled on the first page and circled with what looked like green pencil crayon. She felt rage and humiliation rocket through her.

"Don't look like that, Alice," he said softly. "Perfectly respectable for a first paper."

Julian was pleased to have Alice Diamond sitting across from him in his office. He knew what the number was doing to her. He had chosen it for that reason. It was easy to tell that she was the type who did well when she tried, and that she did not always try.

He liked how she was dressed: cutoff black jean shorts that cupped her perky bum; black tights with a ladder up the inside thigh; a soft, tight sweater that revealed the contours of upturned breasts. Had he known she would wear that today, he might have found it in his heart to give her a 65. But it was her first year, and it was just coursework; these grades didn't matter, except to her ego. And for his purposes, it would help if her ego were a bit bruised.

"I guess you asked me here to help me understand how to do better next time," Alice said. It was not a question. There was something hard in her demeanor that he hadn't sensed before. Was she uncomfortable to be so near to him, in a closed room, when she could surely sense his attraction? No. She must have been used to that, by now. A girl like Alice knew how to handle herself. Uncomfortable to be grade-grubbing, was it? But she wasn't. She wouldn't; she'd sooner fail.

"That's right," he said, looking at the handwritten pages as if rereading her words. "Plenty of potential here, no reason to get discouraged. Let's go through it." He gestured for her to bring the chair in closer. With a look that he couldn't quite place—defiance?—she moved the chair toward him until there was only half a foot between them. He could smell her sweat, now. See her thigh muscles quivering under the tights.

It was hot in his office. He did not intend to slide open the small window that gave onto George Square well below. He watched her face begin to glisten and wondered where else on her body sweat was collecting. Between the shoulder blades, maybe, dripping slowly down the small of her back.

Finally, somewhere around the fourth paragraph, she'd had enough. Arching her spine, she yanked the hot sweater over her head, bringing her filmy white T-shirt up with it. She pulled it back down, but it was too late. She'd caught him looking at her.

"What," she said, with surprising insolence.

Alice would have preferred to have danced around it for longer. To have punished him for his idiotic tactics, for this naked attempt to de-stabilize her. But that was impossible, now. She leaned across her stupid essay and kissed him first.

Talmòrach

Oct. 10th

Prudent Penelope,

Lovely letter. God you're well brought up. You will come back, won't you? I was too deep in my scribblings to pay proper attention to you last time. Christina said I was boorish, and I never question her judgment. I still want to give you a tour. Remember: the first two don't count. No need to bring cheese this time—! Give Christina the signal once booked.

Yours,

Lennox

Ps. Painfully good, your compatriots. Much obliged. But how can you have failed to mention The Penelopiad?

16

Since her first conversation with Sasha on messenger, Pen had begun to log on every night, telling herself she was only checking to see if he was there. The internet in Lee House, delivered through a blue ethernet cable, was slow enough to give her whole body a chance to fill up with adrenaline before her contact list had loaded.

Often, she was disappointed. Sometimes, though, just as the thousands of balloons that had expanded inside her were deflating in unison, his name would turn to bold and glide to the top of her list. Soon after, a message would appear. She did not allow herself to believe this was more than a coincidence, even after it had begun to happen regularly.

Their conversations skirted around the concrete. They did not talk about how they spent their days, although Pen had conjured detailed mental renderings of his room, of the apartment he shared with Chet, and of his life in St Andrews. Instead, they tested one another's appetite for the outlandish and played a kind of game where the goal was not to conquer but to prolong.

On a Wednesday evening, Alice, Jo, and Pen were in Pen's room, their backs against the wall and their feet dangling off the edge of her bed, waiting for it to be sufficiently late to line up in the cold for a terrible nightclub, when a message from Sasha popped up. Pen closed it, changed her status to offline, and toggled back to the movie they were watching on her laptop.

"How often do you talk to him?" Alice asked after a few minutes.

Pen busied herself with opening the bottle of Spanish red wine Jo had brought from the JMC convenience store. She sliced through the foil wrapper with the pointed tip of the corkscrew, balanced the edge of the utensil on the lip of the bottle, and speared the plastic cork.

"Not too often," she said, twisting and levering. It was true in a sense. She would have liked to talk to him every night, and it was closer to every other night—not nearly often enough.

Alice was not fooled. She leaned forward to look at Pen, who was sitting on the other side of Jo, and took the open bottle from her hands.

"I just don't see the point in falling in love with a fourth year," she said, taking a swig. "It's like adopting an elderly dog."

Jo shook her head. "He's not going to *die* when he graduates, Alice. At least, probably not. He'll just move to London."

Pen could not help but smile at the analogy, which she could tell Alice had been saving for the right moment. An easy reply occurred to her, but she held her tongue. She knew Alice was trying to help her avoid getting her heart broken.

Pen was already familiar with the other complaints Alice had with Sasha. They included his degree of poshness ("The titled ones never go for foreigners. I'm not even sure it's allowed"); his being at St Andrews ("Everyone there has at least one STD; there's nothing else to *do*"); and, apparently most damning of all, the fact that Sasha had not, according to her sources, had a proper girlfriend in three years.

"It means he's almost definitely pining for someone, or he's a confirmed man-slut—neither of which are any good for your purposes," Alice had said, as if certain of this being the final word.

Pen, who had no rational basis for being as drawn to Sasha as she was and could not explain why her desire to talk to him felt more like a necessary impulse than a choice, did not know how to convince her otherwise. So instead she kept the intensity of her feelings to herself.

She took the bottle back from Alice and poured herself a measure in the polka-dot mug she used for tea. Alice's meddling was beginning to annoy her. She, of all people, should have understood. Alice had been following her every pheromonal whim to its bitter end since the first stirrings of puberty, and her middle school crushes and high school dalliances, however ill-advised, had each required from Pen the same degree of straight-faced piousness about the inviolability of true love—couldn't she spare a few drops of benevolence in this case?

Something else was grating on Pen's nerves, too. She had been assiduously avoiding the subject of Julian because she could see, from the way Alice deflected any mention of him and from the strange way she acted after tutorials, that Alice wanted to keep whatever was going on between them to herself. Maybe secrecy was part of the thrill, or maybe she was embarrassed by how clichéd it was for a first year to be seduced by her tutor (although she was pretty sure Alice was doing at least an equal portion of the seducing). Whatever the reason, why should Alice be allowed to do as she pleased, while Pen's first and only choice was subject to such unkind scrutiny?

"I thought you wanted me to lower my standards," Pen said.

It was true: for years Alice had been trying to convince Pen to let her guard down and fall for someone—anyone.

"Not *him*," Alice protested. She turned to Jo for backup. "She needs a Stanley Kowalski type, someone who will rip her clothes off and awaken her id. Sasha sounds flimsy. There's no way he'd be able to pry off her inhibitions."

"Alice," Pen warned, coloring. She did not like where this was going. She gritted her teeth and worked hard to keep her tone light. "I'm not a jar of pickles. It's not like I'm just sitting around waiting for someone with a firm grip."

"No?" Alice asked. There was mischief in her smile.

Jo tactfully changed the subject, launching into a story about a dentistry student called Quentin whom she'd met on a school trip, and who had helpfully taught her, with a "firm grip" on her bottom and a tongue that seemed to be checking whether her wisdom teeth wanted removing, that she was not even a little bit intrigued by the offerings of the male anatomy. "So I recuse myself," she concluded.

The tangent put an end to Alice's dangerous mood. Pen felt her heart rate return to normal. Alice was the only person who knew the full extent of her sexual inexperience, and while Pen had never explicitly asked her to keep it a secret, she thought Alice understood that it was private. This was the closest Alice had ever come to mentioning it.

Pen was beginning to trust Jo—and in that moment her gratitude toward her was immense—but still, she was a new friend. And she had a twin. Pen would have had difficulty imagining a deeper source of horror than her virginity becoming a running joke between Fergus and Hugo. She hated what it would suggest about her—that she was frigid, probably. Or worse, naïve. When in fact she had nothing at all against sex. She just had not gotten around to having it yet.

Later, when Alice and Jo left for the club, Pen stayed behind and logged back on. Sasha messaged her almost right away.

SASHA: Hey, you evaporated.

PEN: Yes, it keeps happening. Must be the lightbulbs.

SASHA: Well I'm glad you've rematerialized because there's something I want to ask you.

Pen's heart galloped forward as she watched the dialogue box, her mind churning through things he might ask, none of them logical or probable. Finally, his next message appeared.

SASHA: Might you consider taking the train out to Stonehaven on Saturday morning? I have a polo match first thing, but I'm planning to drive up straigth after.

She spotted the typo and considered what it might mean. Had he typed too fast and pressed send before giving himself time to reflect? Was he drunk? He was typing again.

SASHA: *straight after. It's meant to be one of the last warmish weekends.

She smiled. Did he really think she would need climatic inducement?

PEN: Oh, well in that case. Sure.

Polo, for God's sake, she thought as, afraid she would lose her nerve if she hesitated, she went directly onto the ScotRail website and booked a ticket for Saturday morning, with a flexible return.

Sasha did not come online the next evening, or the following one. Pen was too excited to let this trouble her.

On Saturday, she made her way to Waverley station. She found a seat on the train, rested her eyes on the sweep of sea out the window, and fantasized about Sasha for a full two hours and thirty-two minutes, not even registering the clouds that had begun to crowd the sky or the rain that had started sliding down the windows, until the conductor called out, "Stonehaven."

17

It was Christina who met Pen at the station, wearing rubber boots and a raincoat, with the news that Sasha was held up. The polo match had been delayed by the change in weather, she reported, her hazel eyes, so much like Sasha's, shining apologetically. The other team, having traveled quite a distance with their horses the night before, had decided to remain in St Andrews for the morning in hopes that it might clear. In the meantime, would Pen very much mind a trip into town?

Pen's disappointment was softened by the prospect of spending time alone with Christina. Over the past three weeks, she had loomed almost as large in Pen's imagination as Sasha himself. Alice was right, she was a bit in love with all of them, but she was drawn to Christina in the special way a young person can be drawn to an elder who embodies qualities she hopes to cultivate in herself. In the case of Christina, chief among these qualities was a kind of self-containment that Pen found captivating. She had the impression, as they ran through the train station parking lot and into the shelter of the big car, that Christina did not need to look outside of herself very often for proof that she was living in the right way. But she displayed none of the smug self-satisfaction that one might expect to accompany this apparent peace of mind.

Manners, Pen had lately decided, could be separated into two categories. In the first she placed all those social protocols whose true purpose was to delineate between people who had been taught them and people who had not. She thought of her grandmother Tilda and her multitudes of seafood-specific utensils, each of which took as much practice to manipulate as a musical instrument. These were false manners, in Pen's taxonomy; what she thought of as real manners were behaviors undertaken to increase the comfort of another person. These were far less finicky and easier to guess at, provided one was able to imagine oneself in the place of another. Christina, Pen noticed, had little patience for the first type, and a natural capacity for the second.

As was often true of Pen's theories, however, she had missed something. She had not yet noticed that consistently putting others at ease must at times demand the skillful concealment of any inconvenience—a headache, a sleepless night, Gregor Samsa scuttling around his room—that might stand in the way of one's own comfort.

Stonehaven was no longer the nearest place to the house to shop for groceries, Christina explained to Pen on the short drive to the center of town, from which the sea was visible in a gap between buildings. In the village of Talmòrach they now had "quite a good little co-op," she said with what sounded like pride, as well as Betsy's Tearoom, a doctor's office, a pub, and a mobile post office that visited twice weekly. But Stonehaven, half an hour from the village by car, was still the nearest place for what she smilingly called "posh groceries"—foreign cheeses, fancy olives, Nellie's "by appointment of Her Majesty's corgis" kibble, and so on—and it was a charming old fishing town with a lovely beach, well worth seeing. Pen smiled back.

Christina parked in the Market Square and unearthed from the trunk a spare raincoat for Pen, who had packed too optimistically but was at least wearing waterproof boots. Hoods drawn, they made their way through a series of shops, picking out glossy green olives, slabs of aged Manchego, and a bag of dog food that really did bear the royal stamp. In each shop, Pen observed eyes lingering on Christina, who refused to notice.

After depositing the groceries in the car, Christina took Pen for a wet walk along the seaweed-strewn pebbled beach, in the direction of the harbor. Christina was seemingly as oblivious to the worsening weather as she had been to the neighborly attention. She pointed in the direction of the ruins of Dunnottar Castle, calling over the shushing of surf that this former stronghold up on a high green cliff was where the Honours of Scotland had been hidden from Oliver Cromwell, having been smuggled from "Scoone" in sacks of wool, and that some distant "Covenanter" ancestors had been jailed there. Pen, mortified by her ignorance, hoped she would go on. But further conversation was made impractical by the churn of wind and surf and the screeching of gulls, and she breathed in the mineral smell of the sea, watching wave after wave smash into white foam along the pebbles. This, she decided, was the vista depicted in the dining room watercolor.

On the way back to the house, Christina asked Pen if they might "nip into the village." The Kirkton of Talmòrach, as it was called, was tiny, charming, and extremely well maintained. It consisted of a single, gently sloping main street of reddish stone houses with slanted roofs down which the rain was sliding. At the top end, where they parked the car, St. Helen's Church presided over the main street from a grassy rise, with an ancient kirkyard sprawling down the hill behind it. The church was built from uneven stones held together with generous lashings of mortar, like the whipped cream in a wafer cake. Christina guided Pen around one side, past a blackened wall where she said the church had been damaged by a fire in the 1820s. They passed a communal vegetable garden and arrived at the village primary school, a pretty building with large windows and a blue door. With evident pleasure, Christina pointed out a new play structure just behind it.

They descended the rain-slick cobbles of the main street, which was dotted with lampposts. There was even a red phone booth. A functioning relic, Christina said, of a time before mobile phones. At the base of the street, where the ground flattened out, stood the pub and the village green, where football matches and the annual Hogmanay festival were held.

If Christina had been an object of interest in Stonehaven, here in "the village" she was greeted by each person they encountered with familial warmth. Christina glided through the narrow aisles of the grocery co-op with the speed and hand-eye coordination of a regular, adding packages of PG Tips, Alpen cereal, Fairy liquid, and Nurofen Rapid Relief tablets to her basket while carrying on a conversation with the stout, aproned young man stocking shelves, whom she introduced as her godson, Kieran Hewitt. No credit card was swiped, and no money changed hands at the register; Kieran made a note in a ledger and piled the provisions into a cardboard box from under the counter. Across the street at Betsy's Tearoom, which sold scones the size of baseballs, Christina bought two loaves of bread and a jar of blackberry jam from another godchild, a pretty, freckled girl she called Eliza, who likewise merely wrote down the amount owed and sent them on their way.

"You seem to have a lot of godchildren," Pen could not help but remark as they loaded the car.

"I'm a prolific godmother," agreed Christina, smiling inscrutably. "So much less painful to come by than one's own children." As if in reply, the church's enormous bell tolled the half hour, sending a flock of birds flapping out of the way. "Easier to manage, too," she added, looking up at the clouds and getting into the driver's seat.

Very soon after they left the village, Christina made a sharp left, and Pen recognized the winding road to the house. It was even more majestic looming against the unfriendly sky, and the ivy climbing the central tower was now a deep crimson. Sasha's car was not in its spot near the stables. They carried the boxes and bags up through the boot room to the kitchen, where George, who had been sitting on the floor playing with Danny, jumped up to greet Pen with kisses on each cheek, and then helped them put away the groceries.

They lunched in the kitchen on runny scrambled eggs laced with the cheese they had just bought and thick, buttered slices of the freshly baked bread. "Nursery food," Christina called it, and it was delicious. Danny was chubbier and more animated than Pen remembered; she was surprised to notice what a big difference just a few weeks had made. After cannily resisting their efforts to stuff him into his new high chair (the assembly of which, George joked, had caused nearly irreparable damage to her relationship with her uncle), he settled triumphantly into his mother's lap. He grabbed at handfuls of egg from her plate, pressing some into his mouth, which now featured two prominent nubs of teeth, tossing others on the floor, and making it almost impossible for any food to reach George's lips.

Pen devoured her lunch—she had been too jittery to eat a proper breakfast on the train, and everything tasted so good—and then managed to coax Danny into releasing his death grip on his mother. She took him onto her knees so George could eat. He smelled of milk and soap, and his weight was a comfort against the chill. In spite of Christina's kindness, Pen could not suppress the feeling that she was imposing.

Christina and Elliot had each, she tried reminding herself, written asking her to come again, and even George had texted with a vague entreaty not to stay away long—but the invitation she had taken up, the one that had specified a date and time, had come from Sasha. And Sasha remained absent. She had no reason to doubt the polo story, and was able to calm herself, somewhat, with the knowledge that she had not yet given him her phone number. Maybe there was a message waiting on her computer, which she had left on her desk in Lee House. She tried hard to rest on that thought.

Just as the last dishes had been washed and dried, the sound of a jingling cell phone caused Pen to lunge irrationally toward her bag. It was not her ringtone, she realized too late. Christina dried her hands and pulled a silver flip phone from her jeans pocket. In a gesture that made Pen feel both a rush of affection for her and a twinge of homesickness, she pulled up the antenna before answering with a melodic "Christina Lennox." After a pause she said, "So good of you to ring me back. Yes, it is. I'll just find a quiet spot; give me half a sec?" She looked closely at the keypad, as if searching for the hold button, and then covered the mouthpiece with her hand and said to Pen, "I'm sorry, darling. You're in the green bedroom again. Elliot will be through with his work shortly, and in the meantime perhaps Georgie could show you—"

Danny, whom George had placed in the enormous sink to de-egg, chose that moment to start wailing. Christina, the phone to her ear, backed out through the swinging door to the dining room. George gave Pen a regretful look, and Pen assured her with waving hands and words unheard above Danny's crying that she remembered the way.

And she was confident, as she climbed the central staircase with its elastic floorboards, that she did remember the way. But on this overcast day, with almost no sun coming in through the skylight, and with none of the sconces in the hallway lit, Pen found once she got to the top of the stairs that she was completely turned around. Her intuition told her the bedroom was down the hall to the right; aware of the faultiness of her orientational instincts, she went left instead. Although it was too dark to see their faces very well, there were oil paintings of ancestors, just as there had been before, and closed doors spaced well apart from one another— it all looked probable enough. After walking for what she feared was too long along this particular corridor, she doubled back and stopped in front of a door that she thought she recognized. Slowly, nervously, she twisted the handle.

The room was dark, its curtains closed, and she knew from the smell— a fug of sweat and grass—that it was not the green bedroom. A flicker of curiosity twitched in her chest. Instead of closing the door and turning around, she took a tentative step inside. She stood there, shocked by her brazenness, waiting for her eyes to adjust. The first thing that came into view was a clothes cupboard standing open, with stacks of T-shirts and sweaters spilled onto their sides as if someone had just ransacked it. On the back of its door hung a wooden hanger weighted down with belts and ties. An overstuffed army duffel bag, still zipped, and a large canvas knapsack were sprawled nearby. Pen was trying to make sense of this when she heard a low groan, a rustling of sheets, and then the creaking of an old bed frame. Horrified, she turned for the door, but it was too late. A single bed in the far corner contained the lump of a human figure, which was now emerging from the blankets. Tousled hair half covered the face, and a bare, concave chest gleamed in the dim.

"Who the wandering fuck are you?" asked the sleep-grogged voice of a skinny, squinting boy.

18

It is sometimes said that a mother is only ever as happy as her least happy child. In the case of Christina Lennox, this was not strictly true. Her children, both of them, seemed in general to be far more contented than they had any right to be, under the circumstances, and it was this fact that was making her unhappy.

Christina was, at eight thirty on Saturday morning, inside the white cloud of a duvet cover, grasping for two ties that should have been in the corners. Gladys had alerted her to the existence of these ties, whose clever purpose was to fix the insides in place, making the whole confection less prone to bunching, but she could not find them. Likely the ancient clothes washer had torn them loose and swallowed them. There was nothing to be done but stick the untetherable corners in place, shake the thing out, and hope for the best.

The freshly made bed, once pressed smooth, filled her with the satisfaction she had sought in setting herself the task. Christina loved this bedroom, with its green Petrouchka walls and carriage-like bed. The motions required to prepare it were helping to put her in the necessary frame of mind to meet the day. It was not, after all, Pen's fault that she was arriving at the worst possible time.

On Wednesday evening, when Sasha had messaged to say that he had asked Pen for the weekend, she had been glad. Apart from a brief attachment to Charlotte Rutherford, about whom Christina had enough reservations to fill a small hotel, it had been a long time since Sasha had invited a young woman home. Sasha had been painfully shy as a child. While Freddie had easily fallen in with whoever was at hand, Sasha had had trouble making friends. He had spent most of his time coming up with elaborate imaginary games in the woods, and, later, drawing made-up worlds on other planets and reading comic books. Even if he had learned, while away at school, how to give every outward sign of being comfortable in a group setting, and had even made a true friend in Chet, Christina knew that there were not many people he let in. Pen had drawn something out in him. Christina had felt real affection for her on her first visit, and in spite of the unease one always feels when one knows more than one ought to, she had been looking forward to seeing her again.

After the events of Thursday and Friday, however, Christina had not wanted visitors. She'd rung Sasha soon after the first shock, not only to ask that he put off his guest, but also because he listened well and was capable of sound judgment. Sasha had taken the news soberly and had agreed that Pen's visit must be postponed. And so it had come as another unpleasant surprise when Christina's phone had convulsed on the bedside table at seven o'clock that morning with a series of texts from Sasha explaining about his match and imploring her to collect Pen—whom he had forgotten to put off—at the station later that morning, and to please take good care of her until his arrival, with many apologies and much love.

Christina was often grateful, and certainly today she was grateful, that she no longer lived in a house full of eyes. When she had first come to Talmòrach, she had tiptoed through corridors policed by expressionless footmen and been all but barred from entering the basement kitchen, whence a procession of oversauced courses had risen twice daily, to be served on the right and cleared from the left by gloved hands, while the diners sat captive, saying nothing that risked interesting anyone at all, themselves included. It had been like living with a Greek chorus. Pronouncements on her every movement would filter through the village, becoming as mangled as the family's threadbare linens in the indestructible (but hugely destructive) clothes washer that was now her cross to bear. Yes, her domestic responsibilities were a delight by comparison. She loved to cook and took pleasure in doing most of it herself in her updated, aboveground kitchen with its large windows and swinging door to the dining room. The old kitchen and servants' hall had proven an optimal burrow for Elliot, who had set up a desk in the butler's pantry and liked to pace about the warren of rooms down there, muttering to himself while he worked.

Christina still employed a small team for the upkeep of the house and grounds, but they bore little resemblance to the old guard beyond being, for the most part, their direct descendants. Monday through Friday from eight until four she worked with them, dusting, scrubbing, de-cobwebbing, vacuuming, mopping, mowing, weeding, and generally rendering the house and its environs as inhospitable as possible to molds, moths, rodent families, and other gobblers of aged homes and their contents, all the while endeavoring to maintain a sufficient standard of human habitability—not leaving two-thirds of its rooms under dust sheets, for example, as she had initially suggested—so that a portion of the house could remain open to the visiting public two days out of each week (four during the summer months). When the boys had gone away for school, she had also begun letting it for weddings and film shoots, usually while Elliot was off promoting a book.

These were important revenue streams that Christina had established in recent years: it took all her ingenuity and more to keep up with the eye-watering sums required to prevent the ceilings from caving in, the cottages from falling down around their tenants, the village in a fit state for its residents, and the antediluvian St. Helen's Church from returning to nature.

Unless they were expecting a large party (and with the exception of Hector, who could not be stopped), Christina preferred not to have anyone working at the house in the evening or over the weekend. This was in part to buy her family some periods of relative privacy, and in part because she mostly employed women, like Gladys and Lily and Rebecca, who had school-aged children. Children whom Christina had known since they were born; whose christenings she had attended, sometimes as godmother, and who she knew had a stronger claim on their mothers' evenings and weekends than she did.

This "idiosyncratic" schedule for household staff, like her insistence on being called by her first name and the fact that she wore gardening clogs or wellies most of the time, had for years made Christina an object of ridicule, not only in the village but throughout the surrounding region. The old guard, whose stranglehold on public opinion was thank heavens fading, had looked on in despair when she had first taken over. But with time, her strange methods had come to be ignored by the neighborhood elders, which was perhaps as near to acceptance as she could hope for from that cohort. Members of the younger generation, meanwhile—those who had come of age with Elliot and Margot or later—had understood her updates far more readily, and many had become dear friends, nearly family members. Certainly she felt closer to Gail Hewitt and Betsy Farquharson than she felt to her own brothers, or to her parents, who scoffed at her life here, just as they had scoffed at her short-lived career.

Christina's father, Sir William Campbell, the third son of a landowning family from Gloucestershire, had (as he never let his own children forget) not inherited but earned his place in the world, thanks to two elder brothers who had, in his words, "proven stubbornly impervious to wars, shooting accidents, and useful calamities of all descriptions." He had distinguished himself while serving in the signal corps during the war and had gone to work in signals intelligence before becoming a member of the Diplomatic Service and, eventually, Her Majesty's Ambassador to Jordan and Egypt. Christina and her two older brothers, James and Philip, had been born in London but had spent a good portion of their youth in the various cities in which their father had served. He had been awarded a knighthood when Christina was in sixth form and had thereafter worn the name Sir William with the same off-handedness and yet insistence that one might wear a floor-length quilted velvet dressing gown (Sir William owned three). He had declared it a sorrowful fact when neither of his sons had taken up the diplomatic torch—James had become a solicitor and Philip worked for a company that sold agricultural chemicals—but it had not soothed him when his youngest child had shown an interest in this type of work.

"It is impossible to be a good ambassador without a good wife, Teensy" had been his standard line on the subject. This was not intended as praise for Christina's mother, whose good wifedom was taken for granted by all in the family, herself included. When "Teensy" (even now they did not call her Christina) had been offered a position in the Government Communications Headquarters, the same government agency where William had started out after the war, instead of helping her, her father had laughed at her. He had instructed her mother to post Elliot the recipe for her famous "Devils on Horseback." When Christina had given the thing up to care for her mother-in-law, it had been viewed by her father neither as a surprise nor as a disappointment. It had, however, left the post of Sir William's successor open to a future family member. And so it had been an important moment in the Campbell family when James's eldest son, Hugh, had received his first from Oxford and his offer of employment on GCHQ letterhead the previous summer.

Christina's idea of what constituted a "good wife" differed considerably from that of her mother, Lady Julia Campbell. Perhaps the most important distinction was that whereas her mother had long ago relinquished any claim on agency or fulfillment, Christina required both. When she had chosen to make her life with Elliot, she had gladly left the frustration and jockeying of her old role behind and taken on a new one that, as it turned out, better suited her desire to make tangible progress and her need for autonomy. And yes, it also allowed her to share a bed with the man she loved and, later, to mother on her own terms. Christina was grateful every day for this. She looked forward, as she fell asleep each night, to the sounds and smells of morning, to her cold shower (a habit born of impatience; the hot water took ages to arrive, and now she craved the rush), to her walk through this land that she adored. The beauty of Talmòrach still filled her with wonder. When she was taking a few days off to wander through the streets and galleries of London, her longing for the place was physical. *Talamh* meant "land" but also "earth" or "soil." This soil was a part of her, and she would one day become a part of it.

Once she had grown accustomed to the inquiring gaze of those neighbors who still viewed her as an odd duck, Christina found that she did not much mind being labeled as an eccentric. She was aware, however, that her family remained a regular source of gossip in the village, not all of it innocuous. She understood how quickly the bafflement they inspired could turn back to contempt.

Like the house itself, Christina felt her brain could be in order one moment and thrown into perfect chaos the next, when a heavy rainfall or an errant bird in a chimney sent everything teetering sideways. She labored alongside her team not only because it was necessary—there was more than enough work to go around, and there were never quite enough funds for all her plans—but also because she enjoyed setting things to rights. When she was visibly improving something—making a bedroom, a flower bed, the school, the kirkyard cleaner, brighter, more welcoming, more resilient—she could usually nudge off the self-criticism that tugged at the corners of her mind.

Christina was conscious of finding Sasha easier to blame than his brother. Perhaps it was because he was her eldest, but more likely it was because he took after her more directly than Freddie did, and so she sometimes fell into the unfair habit of judging him as an extension of herself. She was annoyed with him, this morning, for so blithely expecting her to stand in for him. He might at the very least have rung the poor girl himself. But to indulge too much in that annoyance would be wrong. Sasha was not the child pressing on her soul at the moment, the way they had each, at one time, pressed on her diaphragm and crowded her lungs, making it difficult to breathe.

Driving into town, Christina thought about how she might occupy her young charge away from the house for what remained of the morning, while keeping her own worries contained. Her solution was to whisk this assiduously unobtrusive daughter of Ted Winters along on a series of invented errands. She watched Pen's green eyes—clear as polished sea glass, so unlike her father's, although they bore his shrewd expression—study her carefully and, blessedly, miss much. While she guided Pen first through Stonehaven's shops and then, in a brief fit of tour guide's compunction, along its rain-washed boardwalk, Christina tried to work out her next course of action.

She could not look to her own mother as an example. For all her model wifedom, Lady Julia had deftly offloaded whatever concerns with which her children might have threatened to burden her onto the better-built (for that purpose) shoulders of a string of nurses, governesses, and tutors. Anything else, in that time, would have been viewed as not only overly indulgent but dim-witted. Many of the old conventions were awful to Christina, unthinkable, but there were moments when she thought she could do with a few hours' worth of the maternal absenteeism that had come naturally to her mother, and of which some—like Margot—continued to avail themselves. Holding herself accountable for every irresponsible thing her sons did was exhausting.

It had often been observed that Freddie had a touch of the Margot about him. It was not only his dark hair and his owl-like eyes that called his aunt to mind; he, like her, was capable of a degree of self-absorption that annihilated common sense, the common good, common anything. And as was the case with Margot, when frisked for scruples, as he regularly was by his mother (and Margot by George), Freddie held out empty pockets and offered a roguish smile.

Christina ought to have taken him out of that school at the first sign of trouble. She hadn't grasped, at the time, the full extent of the persecution he had suffered at the hands of Cousin Hugh. It was only in recent years that her sons had divulged the degree of cruelty exercised by this member of her own family. It was profoundly shaming to her that she had not prevented it. What folly to let either of them have as guides in the mucky business of male adolescence not their parents but mildewed tutors, permanently bewildered house masters, and, worst of all, their peers. Thrown together day and night, a clot of boys in uniform had all the dignity of a cackle of hyenas. It had been all right for Sasha, who had been the sort of child who could sit alone for hours with a pad of paper and box of colored pencils. It had even been all right for Elliot and Ted, and (perhaps less conclusively) for her brothers, once upon a time. But Freddie, who had found his greatest happiness amid a tumbling heap of boys on a playing field, had made friends with an amorphous pack of the sort that prized their own entertainment, and their talent for entertaining one another, above all else.

Had it not been for the severity of its potential consequences this latest jam of Freddie's might have been a tiny bit amusing. However, having spoken directly with the officials who controlled her son's future, Christina was not laughing. Neither was Elliot, although his reaction, as was often true when it came to real-life matters, was to throw his hands up and retreat to his books. He did not even possess a mobile telephone. This, like much else, was Christina's problem to solve. And so on Thursday she had, after receiving the call, marshaled every resource she could think of to have Freddie and his equally foolish friend escorted onto the next flight out of Lima. She was still endeavoring, by relying on those relationships left to her from her former life, to ensure that their delinquency was viewed in the most understanding light possible and—critically—to keep the story private. If it became a tabloid scandal, her contacts had warned her, there would be nothing they could do.

19

"S orry. Wrong door," Pen said, turning to leave.

"Wait," said the boy, yawning ostentatiously and groping at the side table. He found and put on a pair of glasses and switched on the bedside lamp, pooling himself in yellow light. "I know who you are. You're the Canadian." He blinked behind the black frames. "Dad did say something about a member of the Mounted Police ferreting around. Not sure why, but I pictured a minger. Mutton chops and a raccoon-tail hat. Or no—beaver pelt!" He grinned and held out his hand. "Freddie Lennox."

Pen was frozen in place, caught between laughter and anger. So this was Freddie Lennox, the "legend." How had neither George nor Christina seen fit to mention that he was not at all in South America, but was in fact asleep in a child's bed one floor above their heads? And had Lennox really said that she was "ferreting around"?

"You've gone quite pale," Freddie said. "Don't be afraid. I'm not dead or anything. Just keeping a low profile. A persona non grata. More Banksy than Banquo."

"Why?" asked Pen, beginning to recover herself. "What happened?"

Instead of answering, he leaned out of the bed, exposing a small heraldic rose tattoo above his hip, and reached for his discarded clothes on the floor. He wriggled into a black Libertines T-shirt. From the pocket of a pair of jeans he recovered a half-smoked joint and an orange plastic lighter. He put the joint between his lips, which were very red like Sasha's, although the rest of his face was wider and more expressive than his brother's. He flicked at the wheel of the lighter until it took. He pulled in hard and then coughed.

"Did you try to bring drugs across a border or something?" she persisted.

His cough turned into a laugh, then back into a cough. "Do I look like an amateur to you?"

He continued coughing, and the skunky smoke made its way toward her. "Sort of," she said, not to be unkind, but because it was true. She took a step backward, away from the smell. He grinned at her, revealing small teeth with gaps between them, like baby teeth.

"No, nothing like that. This"—he held up the joint—"is a family heirloom. I found it in the drawer of that bureau over there. I believe it once belonged to my grandfather, judging by its freshness. On Dad's side, of course, though God knows Sir Willy could use some. Those of us in the clink must find what diversions we can."

"Why are you being kept up here?" she tried again.

He looked thoughtful for a moment, and then licked his fingers and put out the spark. "I'd love to tell you, Nancy Drew. Really, I would. But then Mum would have to murder me." His face turned solemn. "She doesn't want anyone to know I'm back. At least until she's figured out what to do with me."

Pen, who was still processing all this, did not immediately turn to leave. As if in response to her hesitation, an impish light came into his eyes. "Since we're already keeping secrets, if you want this to be a conjugal visit, I'm up for it." He patted the bedspread beside him. This was enough; Pen waved and was gone.

It was Elliot Lennox who came upon her reading in the octagonal sitting room some time later, with an eager Nellie circling his feet.

"Oh lord, not the infernal Charles Swann," he announced, causing her to drop her book. He bent to pick it up and handed it back to her. "Hello, Penelope. Lovely to see you again. Join me on my afternoon constitutional, won't you?"

Nellie leaped up onto the sofa beside Pen, and she stroked the dog's warm fur. Lennox was dressed for the outdoors, in faded tweeds and a flat cap. The ensemble looked natural enough in this vast, ageless room, with its cavernous fireplace (which she had left unlit this time, although she was cold) and overly upholstered, straight-backed furniture. It was only in contrast with Freddie, whose confinement in his bedroom was casting his parents in a different light, that it began to look like a costume.

The rain was on the verge of freezing, and as soon as they stepped out the boot room door, Lennox having kitted Pen out in a pair of tall galoshes and a heavy waxed canvas coat, it began pelting their faces. Like Christina, Lennox evidently refused to view the inclement weather as a deterrent to outdoor exercise.

With Nellie leaping ahead, he began a guided tour of the grounds that was very clearly, Pen thought, a well-worn performance. It made sense to her that a famous author who had inherited a castle would be called upon, with some regularity, to show visitors around. She did not fault Lennox for having this canned act at the ready, or for relying on it now, while one son was AWOL and the other stashed in his bedroom like a prisoner awaiting trial. Still, as he talked about a king reviving an old title for his mistress, and about battles won and lost, Pen, who ordinarily loved a history lesson, found her mind wandering. The speech seemed to be molded around the requirement of drawing breath, like a hymn or a national anthem. He continued talking in one solid stream, even as the demands of the terrain made their breathing grow heavier. They hiked through a wooded area, across a rickety footbridge, and up a rocky incline to the highest point of the property. On a fine day, Lennox assured her, the view would extend to the North Sea. "We can't see much today, of course," he said by way of conclusion. "But it will clear."

"You think so?" Pen asked, seeing only gray, and not at all convinced.

Lennox looked at her strangely for a moment. "It was high time I gave you a tour of our ill-gotten gains, as my eldest son would have it," he said eventually.

The famous author persona had receded somewhat; this seemed to be the private Lennox speaking. Nellie led them back down the hillside by a different path. "Ill-gotten debts, in point of fact," he continued. "My father used to say the land doesn't belong to us, we belong to it. He meant to suggest, I think, that it is our duty to maintain it, that we are custodians for future generations—not that it would eventually bury us. Of course, the second interpretation turned out to be much more accurate." Lennox pointed down the hill, toward an ancient-looking chapel Pen had not seen before, with a small graveyard behind it. "He's buried right over there. I believe he intended to live by his word. Perhaps he even let himself believe he was. Astonishing, the worlds our fathers create for themselves to live in, isn't it?" He looked back at Pen, his rimless glasses dotted with rain.

Pen could feel her pulse in her throat. She knew this was her chance to pierce his chain mail, and that she might not get another.

"What kind of world are you creating?" she asked.

He stopped walking and looked at her again. "Ah yes, very good. I'm just as guilty, of course," he said. "But I do at least try to own that it's fiction. And to keep it in the books as best I can. Now look here. Do you know what used to live in this fourteenth-century eyesore?"

He had stopped in front of a beehive-shaped hut of irregular stone bricks covered with lichen and moss. It had a row of holes toward the bottom, like miniature windows, and was topped with a little stone pagoda-like structure. Pen felt a thud of disappointment as she realized what it was. A dovecote, or "doocot": the home for carrier pigeons that Sasha had claimed to want to show her. The sting of this memory made it easier to press on, and she did not weigh her words before letting them out of her mouth. "I don't mean the world you've created for your characters. I understand that world well enough; I've read each of your books at least three times. I mean the one you're creating here. The one where you pretend it isn't raining—that it's normal to live in a castle—and that one of your sons is in South America when he's upstairs in his room. And you're incredibly kind and welcoming, more so than I've ever had any right to imagine or expect, but you don't let me get anywhere near the subject that you must know I've been trying to ask you about this whole time, ever since my first letter. Why?"

Pen's voice sounded hoarse in her own ears. The tips of her fingers were turning numb. She tucked her hands, which had been active during this interrogation, into the pockets of the jacket that was not hers. She felt a tissue inside of one and began twisting it while waiting for a reaction from Lennox. He had tilted his chin to his right shoulder and his left ear toward her, as if to show that he was listening, but he was looking off into the distance.

Finally he brushed some dead leaves from a fallen log just beside the path and sat down. He gestured for her to sit beside him. She sat.

"Let's begin with the rain," he said. "This is Scotland. If we let a bit of rain stop us, we wouldn't go out at all."

He took off his wet glasses and used a handkerchief from his pocket to clean them, as if to illustrate his point. "As for living in a castle, you're right. It's appallingly impractical. Sasha is quite of the same mind. But allow me to ask you, Penelope. Are you familiar with the ancient Greek concept of xenia?"

Dear God, thought Pen. She had to tense her eyelids to keep her eyes from rolling, which probably made her look like an axe murderer. Lennox had sounded exactly like her dad. Was this what they had learned at public school: how to avoid answering direct questions by leading all conversations back to antiquity? It made sense, given the number of prime ministers the school where her father and Lennox had first met had turned out.

"I think so," she said. "Isn't that why Odysseus was always getting rubbed with olive oil?"

"Quite right." Lennox's eyes, visible again behind their polished frames, had regained their expression of complicity. "Xenia was the reciprocal understanding that unknown visitors must be welcomed as friends—bathed, clothed, fed, and offered safe passage to their next destination—and, in return, that travelers must not threaten their hosts, but must instead bring them fresh conversation, and news of the outside world."

Pen, conscious of her borrowed outerwear and understanding this as a condemnation of her line of questioning, reddened. But she had come this far; she could not capitulate so easily. "What about Penelope?" she asked. "Don't you think she took xenia a bit far, letting the suitors have the run of the house? Look how badly it turned out for them. A lot of people could have avoided being disemboweled if Penelope had shown a bit more spine."

He stood and brushed himself off. He held out a hand to her. She didn't need help getting up, but she took it anyway. "True enough," he said. "One mustn't take it too far. Neither must one forget, however, how dangerous the world becomes in the absence of such a principle. I don't suppose the Massacre at Glencoe ever came up in your history lessons?"

Pen shook her head.

"No, I suppose it would not have," he said. And then he outlined, with his usual penchant for grisly details, how high a price the MacDonald clan had paid in 1692 for their hospitality toward soldiers from clan Campbell. "My in-laws, as luck would have it," he said, shaking his head. "Terrible business."

He stopped to look straight into her face, addressing her, it felt to Pen, as an equal. "Christina and I, in our fumbling way, are trying to be friends to you, Penelope. I've been aware since your first letter that you were a kindred spirit, and that you would come here with questions, not all of which I would be in a position to answer. I ask for your patience. It *will* clear. As for Freddie." His eyes grew weary. "The unexpected homecoming of our younger son, I hope you will understand, is a subject that I do not wish at present to discuss. Now. We must get you back to the house to dry off before you become one of the ghosts malingering about the place."

As they approached the house, Pen saw Sasha's car parked by the stables, which triggered a riot of activity in her body. Nellie's reaction was similar, only she didn't try to hide it.

"If you'll excuse me, I've some business to attend to with Hector," said Lennox. "You go in and wring yourself out." He lay his hand on Pen's shoulder, and then turned for the stables.

Pen came up from the boot room to find Sasha and Christina at the kitchen table with steaming cups of tea.

"Hello," Sasha said, standing. He was taller than she remembered, and sturdier, not flimsy at all. He was wearing black jeans and a black sweater—not polo clothes, as far as she knew. There was something like an apology in his posture. Nellie jumped all over him with muddy paws and Christina went to find a towel.

As Pen got closer, she saw that the sunburn on his nose had faded. His face looked wan, and there was a bright red pimple on his chin. They were alone in the kitchen, and she entertained a fleeting but powerful hope that he would wrap his arms around her. Instead, without making eye contact, he kissed her lightly on each cheek, the way one might greet a second cousin, and quickly, so that by the time she'd regained command over her limbs, he was already several feet away from her.

"You'll never guess what I just saw," she said in a voice that came out unnaturally bright. She saw him pause, still without meeting her eyes, and realized, with a stab of dread, that his body language was that of someone at a party who doesn't want to get stuck in a conversation with you.

"What?" he asked.

Pen recognized the stiffness, the blank look, the withholding of connection. This was how her parents had treated one another toward the end. She couldn't answer him. She just shook her head as if to say, "Never mind," and slipped away to change before Christina returned to the kitchen.

Upstairs, in the hottest bath to which she had ever subjected herself, Pen hardened herself against him. Whatever had brought about this change, it proved that Alice was right. The Sasha Lennox she had been carrying in her mind since September was a figment. The real one was nothing special. She comforted herself with the knowledge that she had a flexible train ticket. She would make herself useful tonight, pay off as much of her xenia debt as she could, and leave in the morning.

Pen was in the kitchen helping with dinner. Christina had shown her how to cook duck breast, demonstrating the importance of searing the meat first to seal in the juice, and then "nipped" upstairs. Pen had made up her mind not to tell Christina about her run-in with Freddie. She had begun to see how many plates her host was spinning, her own presence in the house included. In her final hours at Talmòrach, Pen wanted only to alleviate some of that pressure. Although she had never shown any aptitude for cooking, Pen was very glad to have a sizzling pan on which to focus her attention when Sasha came in, greeted her with a subdued "Hi," and sat down at the table. He began riffling through the stack of Saturday newspapers.

Lennox appeared next, in slacks and a button-down, his damp hair brushed back off his forehead.

"You look like one of my autopsy scenes," he said to his son. "Long night?"

Sasha nodded but did not volunteer any details.

"Lucky the match was called off," Lennox continued.

Pen dropped the duck breast she was holding into the pan too quickly and was rewarded with a spray of hot fat on her hand. She went over to the sink and turned on the cold faucet.

"Tell me what you make of this, Penelope," said Lennox. "Sasha here, my eldest son and heir, is writing a dissertation on the Highland Clearances. It is his belief that we should relinquish our claim on Talmòrach and turn it over to the 'people,' as it were. Now, does it not strike you as inconsistent that a son like that, with such a principled, if somewhat idealistic, head on his shoulders, should also play *polo*, the sport of princes and pet food magnates?"

"Dad—" said Sasha, in a flattened voice. "Please."

"It was wrong to eject Highlanders to raise sheep, but it's perfectly all right, if I may misquote one of your Canadian songstresses, Penelope, to pave paradise and put up a polo pitch?"

The playful look in Lennox's eyes was, Pen thought, out of step with the effect this speech was having on his son. In spite of her decision not to expect anything more from Sasha, and even with the painful confirmation that the match had been canceled, and so he could, in all likelihood, have turned up earlier, Pen was more annoyed in that moment with the father than with the son. She'd had enough with Lennox's performances, and she resented being made the audience for this dig. Their earlier conversation had emboldened her. She'd seen in his eyes that he appreciated her directness, even if he had not answered in kind. And since she planned to leave in the morning and never come back, she didn't have anything to lose.

"Maybe," she said, looking at Lennox. "But polo is not something you just pick up by mistake. Someone must have taught him to ride. Sent him to the kind of school where polo is no weirder than wearing tails to class. He might play at least in part to have more in common with whoever that was. Even if that person is sometimes willing to use his supposed inconsistencies of character to avoid other subjects."

Lennox smiled. He said to Sasha in a stage whisper, "Not to hurry you, my boy, but that's the sort you keep around."

Mortified by this proclamation, and not wanting to see Sasha's reaction, Pen returned to her pan, where the nicely browned duck breast wanted turning.

Christina pushed through the swinging kitchen door with Danny in her arms. "He hasn't napped all day, the wicked elf, and George is at her wit's end," she said by way of explanation. "I'll bring her some supper later on."

Pen was glad to surrender the stove to Christina and hold Danny instead. This time he willingly accepted to be taken into her arms and began at once to play with the polar bear pendant on her necklace. Her mom had given her the necklace that awful Christmas, and Pen thought of it as conferring some kind of power, if only the power to endure. She was glad to be wearing it now.

"We're a jolly bunch," said Christina, checking Pen's handiwork with a nod of approval. "Perhaps the rain has finally gotten to us. Sasha my love, lay the table in here, will you? It's more cheerful. And Elliot, see if you can't dig up a particularly good bottle of Burgundy."

While Lennox opened the wine and Sasha set the kitchen table, Christina, unaware that she was being watched, placed not one but two plates of dinner onto a tray to bring upstairs.

20

On Sunday morning, Pen bathed and dressed, shivering in the stone bathroom, and went quietly out into the hall. She could hear Danny babbling away in George's room and knocked gently. "Mind if I take him for a walk?" she asked George, who looked like she could use about three days of extra sleep.

"I'll come with you," George offered blearily.

"No, you stay," said Pen, taking her cue from Christina. "I was given the grand tour yesterday; we won't get lost."

George smiled gratefully at Pen, dressed Danny in warm clothes, and gave instructions about his pram.

The rain had stopped, although there was no sun to speak of, and the air was bracing. Pen had slept deeply in the cold room under the heavy duvet, and she felt much calmer now. Twigs snapped satisfyingly under the wheels of Danny's stroller, and he leaned forward against the restraining straps that it had taken Pen ten minutes to figure out, pointing at everything he saw.

Pen took the driveway to its end and then followed signs to the village. Her plan was to go to the tearoom to pick up some baked goods to leave behind as a final offering, before making a hasty retreat to Edinburgh.

As she pushed the stroller through the church parking lot, which had been half-empty the morning before, she noticed that every spot was taken. *Of course*, she thought; *it's Sunday.* She found the church grounds alive with activity. Young children in carefully pressed clothes were darting around, making full use of the new play structure. The men wore suits, and some of the women wore hats. The church's double doors stood wide open, and a slow-moving crowd was funneling in.

Aware that these people very likely all knew one another and possibly Danny, too, Pen felt conspicuous. She smiled without meeting anyone's eyes and continued straight ahead until she had reached the main street.

Betsy's Tearoom was bustling. Passing the sweet-smelling doorway, Pen took her place at the end of the line. The two women ahead of her were deep in conversation, their hats touching. She couldn't see their faces, but she could hear the one with dark curls pinned into a tight bun say, in a voice full of righteous dismay, "—Peru. Imagine. They say the loon's done it this time. A right mess. If it'd been my Bobby, I'd have his hide."

"Aye," agreed the other, in a silver hat that matched her hair. "What can you expect. Not his fault if he was spoiled rotten, is it?"

The woman who was speaking turned to glance behind her. Pen saw her small mouth pinch shut. The woman forced the expression into a smile. "Dear wean," she said. "How old is he?"

"Eight months," Pen said, and tucked him up tightly under his blanket, hoping they would not recognize Danny.

All happy babies are alike, she thought, smiling inwardly. Pen had never believed in "happy families" as such, and so it had been easy enough, as she lay in bed the previous night, to release the Lennox family back into the confounded mass of general humanity. But in the same way that the zit on Sasha's chin and his rumpled exhaustion had had the effect of underlining his humanity and thus increasing, rather than diminishing, her physical attraction to him, she found all of them, and especially Christina, more affecting for being mortal.

Pen came into the kitchen with the rosy bundle that was Danny and a box of still-warm scones. Sasha was at the table. He stood as he had done the day before. There was color in his face again. His eyes had regained their brightness and were filled with something that looked like regret. Or maybe she was inventing it. She was careful to keep what she felt out of her smile.

"Can I make you a cup of tea? Some toast?" he asked.

"Do you have any coffee?" Pen had had more than enough tea, and she was pleased to hear the assertiveness in her voice. He set about making it while she found some of Danny's toys stacked under his high chair and sat with him on the floor to play.

"Pen," he said in a quiet voice that risked melting her wall of ice. He sat down beside her and placed the cup beside her outstretched leg. Her breathing responded to his nearness against her will. "I'm sorry I was on such bad form yesterday," he said, holding her eyes with his. "Something unexpected came up that—"

Christina breezed in through the swinging door looking as fresh and efficient as ever, with Nellie on her heels. Pen picked up her cup just in time to save it from Nellie's wagging tail.

"Pen! You angel," she said crouching down to wrap both of them in one of her spontaneous hugs. Contact with Sasha's body made Pen's go rigid. His neck smelled like soap. She wanted it to stop, but she also wanted to dissolve into him. "I looked in on George, and she said you'd kidnapped Danny for a walk," Christina continued. "And what are these? Betsy's scones, from this morning? You are an absolute dream." Was it wishful thinking, or did Sasha stay closer to her than he needed to, even after Christina had stood up? She pulled herself away and asked Christina for the phone number of a taxi company.

"At least stay for lunch," Christina entreated convincingly, although Pen knew it was out of habit not desire. "There aren't many direct trains on a Sunday; the journey will take longer than it needs to if you leave now. Sasha can take you back down when he goes."

Sasha was nodding, but Pen could not risk spending any time in a car with him.

"Thank you, that's thoughtful, but I have a fixed ticket," she fibbed in her newfound voice of authority. She did not care how long she would have to wait, or how many times the train would stop. What she needed now, more than anything, was to be alone.

21

The train was getting busier as they neared Edinburgh. A few stops south of Stonehaven, a burly man stood in the aisle next to where Pen was sitting, eyeing the empty seat beside her. Looking around at the increasingly crowded car, she saw that she had no choice. She moved to the window and gave him the aisle. Her book was already out, and she held it close to her face.

"Afternoon," said the man once he had sprawled into his seat and commandeered the middle armrest. He wore a tight long-sleeved T-shirt and the spotless Nikes of someone who owns multiple pairs. "Have you had a nice weekend?"

He posed the question affably. But there was no polite way to answer him without asking about his weekend in return. And she had no desire to do that while hemmed in by a stranger who looked strong enough to crush her by accident. Under the sleeves of his T-shirt, his biceps resembled baking potatoes.

She nodded in his direction, smiling tightly, and returned to her book.

"Is it true that the old sod doesn't even get out of bed for the first hundred pages?" the man asked, pointing to the cover. She was reading the first volume of Proust for one of her classes. He was leaning in close to her and had the vinegary after-smell of beer on his breath.

"Mm," Pen said in a "leave me alone" sort of way.

"Lazy bastard." The man chuckled. Pen made no reply. She was beginning to feel a disproportionate degree of antipathy toward this man.

"You must like it, though," he persisted. "You keep sticking your nose back in it, don't you?"

"It's schoolwork. So if you wouldn't mind, I have to concentrate," Pen said with what she hoped was calm finality. She pulled her iPod from her pocket and stuck the earphones into her ears. She flicked through the songs, looking for something noisy enough to carry her beyond his reach.

"This isn't the quiet carriage, love," he said loudly. Pen glanced across the aisle. The conversation in the seats nearby appeared to have dimmed, but no one turned around. She had a vision of punching him in the face. Would there be blood? Would her knuckles hurt afterward? She had never punched anyone. It wasn't a good idea. He could probably strangle her with one hand.

"I reckon you like it in bed, too, don't you," he added in a wet whisper. "You're no beauty, but I'll bet you'd be a decent lay." He was so close to her now she could see the flakes of dandruff on his shoulder. Pen remembered a self-defense lesson from high school. First, they had been reminded about the girl from their school who had been followed home, raped, and murdered a few years before. And then they had taken turns sticking their fingers into the eye sockets of life-sized dummy dolls. "Go for the sensitive parts," the teacher had instructed. "Eyes, nose, crotch." Would she have the courage to jam her fingers into this man's pink-tinged eyeballs if she needed to? Pen wondered. She knew Alice would. Instead she picked up her bag and edged past his body into the aisle. "Cunt," he hissed, pressing against her bum on purpose with his knees.

Just after Pen crossed into the next car, a bend in the tracks sent her careening into the legs of another passenger. It was an older man wearing shorts and high white sport socks, even though the weekend had not been "warmish" at all, but wet and freezing. "Whoops-a-daisy," the man said, smiling at her with such frank kindness that she felt her throat burn.

"Are you all right, hen?" the white-haired woman beside him asked as Pen picked herself up and apologized. She nodded and, knowing only forward motion could keep her from crying, continued on to the café car.

With her purchases—a miniature bottle of red wine and a bag of extremely overpriced salted cashews—Pen claimed a new spot at the opposite end of the train. She dragged her bag onto the blessedly empty seat beside her and took a sip of the refrigerated red liquid.

Clearly, Potato Arms had been right about one thing: she was "no beauty." Sasha had never been attracted to her; she could see that now. Flirting with her had been a diversion. He had not meant for her to actually get on the train to visit him. She was not worthy of his notice. That was what Alice had been trying to tell her, in a gentler way, she realized. The idea that Alice had foreseen this compounded her humiliation. On top of the twist of mortified pride in her lower abdomen, she was furious with herself for having been such an easy mark.

Pen had worked hard to acquire her protective coating, and she did not like to feel it crack. After her father had moved out and her mother had confirmed what Pen already knew, while they were packing her childhood illusions into boxes along with the contents of the house, Pen had decided that organized religion was not for her. She still believed in something, but it was not her grandmother's God. She had abruptly stopped praying. Going to church with Tilda had furnished her with a lifelong respect for the power of stories, and a physical response to certain hymns when sung by a choir, but it was time to stop asking imaginary forces for favors and start functioning as a self-contained unit, at least emotionally.

And, as she had reminded herself frequently enough since then that it had become almost a tic, who was she to ask that her family be a priority in the eyes of this God? She knew very well that their share of unhappiness was so minute as to be invisible. In a city like Toronto, they say you're never more than six steps from a rat; Pen knew that the same was true for misery. Even in a neighborhood of single-family homes and SCHOOL SAFETY ZONE signs depicting the outline of a mother holding her daughter's hand to cross the street, suffering was everywhere. It was in the eyes of the man with the dog outside the pharmacy who always thanked her for the smile, but who had nowhere warm to spend the night, even when it was thirty degrees below zero, because shelters did not allow pets. It was in the defiantly scrunched shoulders of the squeegee kids who ran into the busy intersection when the light turned red, dousing the windshield in suds before the driver had a chance to shoo them away (if her grandmother) or slide down the window to hand them all the loonies and toonies in the cupholder (if her mother). "They're children," her mom had said once, looking out the window with tears in her eyes.

Pen had never needed to go far to find suffering. She could feel it in the driver's seat of the car, across from her at the kitchen table, or a story above her in the silent house. She hadn't known what it was when she was young. She'd thought her mom got sick often—colds, headaches, the flu—because that was what her dad and grandmother had told her. "Your mother has a weak immune system," they said. "She just needs rest." It wasn't until afterward that she realized the phrase "your mother" was a bad sign.

She tried to look out the window, but night had fallen, and she saw only her reflection in the glass. The next station was Leuchars–St Andrews. The name seemed to jeer at her. Thinking of the longing it had inspired just the day before made the thin skin on the insides of Pen's wrists itch. *Not much of a leuchar, are you,* she told herself. It was a feeble joke, but it made her feel better.

A vibrating sound was coming from beside her. It took her a moment to understand that it wasn't the train but her cell phone. She fished it from the inside pocket of her bag. There were two missed calls from an unknown number. It vibrated again in her hand, "UNKNOWN" flashing on the call display. She knew only two people who blocked their numbers. She answered in a hopeful whisper.

"Alice?"

"Penny!"

"Dad?! Everything okay?"

"I've been trying to reach you." His voice on the other end was clear and booming, like he was speaking into a microphone at a company event. Pen worried that the whole car could hear him.

"Hi Dad—I'm on the train," she said, keeping her voice as low as she could. The train was slowing down. "In the quiet car. I'll be back in under an hour. Can I call you then?"

"Wonderful! Where are you coming from?" he asked.

"St Andrews," she said.

"Great. Talk to you soon," he said, and clicked off.

Lying to her father was a new feeling. It was not as difficult as she might have expected. Outside the window, a lit-up platform was coming into view. Here was Leuchars–St Andrews, earning the oversized spot it occupied on her mental map of the world.

22

Disembarking at Edinburgh Waverley forty minutes later, Pen cursed herself for having snubbed the limp sandwiches from the café car. She did not have the courage to face the JMC that evening and wondered whether Alice would have food in her room. The platform was chilly, and she strode quickly, her bag thumping against her thigh with every step. A figure in a familiar overcoat standing at the mouth of the station waved. Pen's body seemed to know who it was before her brain did. She ran at her father, leaping into his arms like a little girl.

"DAD!" She nuzzled her cheek against his smooth face. He smelled of leather and butterscotch. "What on EARTH are you doing here?"

Ted Winters held his daughter to his chest and stroked her hair. She had cut it. It had been two months since he and Nicola Diamond had stood together outside the restaurant where they had had their farewell lunch, watching their girls stride up the hill, and he had waved at Pen's receding back, proud and excluded.

Nicola—a tall and vital, if slightly overwrought, woman whom he privately thought Isaac undervalued, although he tried not to make a habit of speculating about his friends' marriages—had ushered him back inside and ordered two dry gin martinis at the bar. Later, on the plane, they'd both watched *The Pianist* on their miniature screens as an excuse to cry.

Ted took his daughter's weekend bag from her and guided her to the taxi rank.

"Corner of Thistle and Frederick, please," he told the driver through the partition, settling into the backward flip-down seat so he could face his child. Her hair was loose and grazed her chin. Her clothes were more feminine, a high lace collar under an unfamiliar sweater, a skirt made of velvet. Her face was different, too. It was narrower and more set. A woman's face. Her mother's face. He'd tried not to think it, but the thought had come anyway.

The distance between them had been restored by the presence of the driver, and Pen sat straight-backed, hands in her lap and ankles crossed. She turned to the window and felt something like the pride of ownership as they rode down the wide, sloping streets of New Town, even though it was one of only two and a half neighborhoods with which she was at all familiar.

She looked at her dad and smiled, taking in his weatherproof overcoat and thick sweater. He had not forgotten how to dress for Edinburgh. These streets had once belonged to him, too, she reminded herself.

"How long can you stay?"

"Just until morning. I had some business in London, and thought it was a good opportunity to have Sunday dinner with my favorite girl."

"I would never have gone away for the weekend if I'd known you were coming."

"Nonsense, I'm glad you're having fun. How was your time in St Andrews?"

"Good. Short." She hoped that she wouldn't have to say more. Lying to her father's face was a different story.

"And how are the Lennoxes?" He posed the question conversationally, his expression inscrutable in the cab's dark interior.

In the space of seconds Pen felt caught, angry, and then betrayed. It had to have been Christina, she thought. Lennox, a proud Luddite, left all the logistics of his life that could not be handled on paper to his wife. Christina, with whom she had just spent intimate hours unpacking groceries and washing dishes, on whom she had begun to model parts of her adult self, had called or emailed Ted. Christina and her dad had talked about her. The idea hurt Pen, but it also brought a bitter calm. She was too upset to answer him.

The restaurant shone invitingly on the street corner. Ted had a Royal Bank of Scotland note at the ready. He opened the door for his daughter, moved aside the heavy curtain that kept the cold out, and let it fall closed behind her. Here was Jean-Marc with his hands outstretched, and here was the familiar candlelit room with its chessboard floor and wood-paneled mirrors. He loved this room. The glass was blurry with age (*Me too*, he thought) and the sturdy tables and chairs were spaced well enough apart for relative privacy.

The maître d' greeted Pen's dad like an old friend. Ted had a way of convincing people who worked in restaurants that they knew him on sight, giving him the air of a well-liked local celebrity. With an admirable economy of movement, the man freed them from their possessions and led them to a corner table by the window. Gauzy white fabric obscured the street; the dining room was its own universe. He pulled a heavy lighter from his pocket and flicked the silver wheel, lighting the single votive on the table. Pen tried not to think about the pack of cigarettes that had just crossed the room in her coat pocket. She would not show weakness. Besides, she was not addicted, she told herself. She just liked the rush.

"Do you remember the nice little white we had last time? We'll start with a bottle of that," said Ted.

Pen looked up at the man, thinking that there was no way he could possibly remember the exact wine.

She could not have known that Jean-Marc, whose job it was to re-member, had set two bottles of the Meursault to chill that afternoon when M. Winters had rung, just in case.

Nor could she have guessed that Ted did not think of himself as a no-ticeable or memorable person, any more than his daughter did. He had merely learned, in his fifty-one years on the planet, that a warm inter-action was pleasanter than a cold one. He tasted the wine and nodded. Their glasses turned cloudy as Jean-Marc filled them.

"To your first term," he said. His daughter had not answered his question, and he did not force it. He knew how to wield silence. She was too young, still, to know how not to fill it.

Ted had indeed had some business in London. At the café in Notting Hill he had at first seen only her coat. Tapestries and broken pottery and ancient coins coexisted in its fabric, entire civilizations now dead and buried. She sat down beside him. He wanted to look at her and regretted having chosen a table that placed them side by side, facing the morning activity on the street. She wore her hair tied back at her nape. She tilted toward him to look down at the menu. Her part had gray in it and smelled exactly like it used to. It took a lifetime of discipline to avoid putting his hand at the place where the scalp was visible.

Later, he'd walked alone to the station. It had been years since he'd last taken the tube. It took him a few tries to buy a pass at the automated kiosk. *The world is your oyster,* he thought as the machine spat out a blue plastic card. It had been, back then. Finally, he pushed through the gates and went down the steep escalator, his hot palm hovering over the handrail. Notting Hill had been scrubbed clean; here, at least, the grime was intact.

He had forgotten how deep in the ground the tracks were buried. It was a relief to descend, to put stories between them. He felt calm when he reached the bottom of the moving staircase and found himself closer to the core of the Earth.

"Change here for the District and Circle lines," sang a female voice from somewhere above him. It was bright and impersonal, the soul of British efficiency. A voice unmoved by private sorrows. This was a city that had withstood Hitler's worst. Homes and shops, hospitals and schools pummeled from the sky, bones and belongings scattered. Londoners, civilians, had sheltered in these very tunnels. They had gone out each day and cleared the rubble. They had refused to submit. How arbitrary, that it was the men who had done battle: his father, his uncles; and the women who had stayed to make sure there was a future to come back to. If they came back. Neither was more heroic, he thought. The going or the staying.

Ted lowered his fingers onto the blue moquette of the seat and remembered across decades the thick fabric of her sheets, the grain of the linen against his outstretched feet. People were crowding up against him. He remembered the heat of her body in the galley kitchen where they'd collided like charged particles while making toast. The foil-lined broiler above the stove full of blackened failures, the smoke clinging to their clothes. Bitter coffee on her precarious balcony. The day she'd told him *no,* firmly, irrefutably. The way she'd looked at him sadly, as if disappointed in him. She had been wearing a light blue dress that day; it had been early summer; he remembered the small flowers.

"This is Queensway. Please mind the gap between the train and the platform," sang the voice. An elderly woman was glaring at him from under a puff of white hair. The skin on her neck was like a too-loose garment. She might have survived the Luftwaffe, Ted thought as he stood to offer his seat. *Living bodies decay, too,* he thought, gripping a loop that hung from the ceiling. *And here we are, already underground.*

"How did you know I went to see them?" Pen asked finally, breaking into Ted's memories.

She took a sip of the cool, crisp white wine in her glass. The red from the train was swirling in her near-empty stomach. Her dad, who had been silent a long time, smiled.

"I wasn't certain," he said. "Until just now, when you confirmed it."

She rolled her eyes at her dad's old trick and wondered what, exactly, Christina had reported.

"I won't dwell on this, but there is something I feel you should know before we move on to other subjects," he said.

She held her breath.

"You've read Elliot Lennox's books."

"Yes."

A waiter arrived to take their order. Her father made pleasantries, asking for his tuna to be served walking, and if he might have extra greens instead of the roasted potatoes, no need for a starter. Pen ordered the steak frites. She usually chose the vegetarian main, but tonight she needed blood. Her dad pretended, for a moment, that he had forgotten what they were talking about. And then he continued.

"Is it fair to say Elliot Lennox is pretty good at creating sly characters with complicated motives?"

"He writes detective fiction, Dad. Isn't that his job?"

"They don't come from nowhere, characters like that. They come from a certain kind of mind." His voice was gentle.

"Are you trying to tell me that Lennox has a twisted mind? That he's dangerous?"

"Of course not. Just don't put too much stock in him. That's all. I don't want to see you disappointed."

She thought of Freddie. And then of Sasha. Her dad reached for her hands across the small table. She let him. The silver fork was cool against the flesh of her forearm. She wanted to trust him. She had trusted him. She tried subtracting the years from his face, smoothing the lines from between his brows, taking the white out of his hair and restoring it to the strawberry blond it had once been. She pictured him sitting across from Christina, in this very restaurant, maybe, thirty years before. Asking her to trust him, to choose him. She imagined what would have happened to his face when she'd chosen his best friend instead. The slackening of surprise mixed with pain, like someone sucker punched. He would have recovered himself quickly, and forced (she knew how, too) what was soft to become hard, what was loose to be fixed, frozen.

Two waiters descended on them simultaneously. Pen let go of her dad's hand to make space for the wood-handled steak knife and the white plate, hot to the touch. The fries were thick the way she liked them, none of that fussy matchstick crap. A miniature casserole dish of steamed spinach was placed between them. Her dad ate a fry off of her plate and ordered her a glass of Bordeaux to go with her steak. "We're in your hands."

They ate in silence. Once the food had anchored her and another glass of wine obliterated her inhibitions, she turned his trick back on him.

"How long were you and Christina together?"

He laughed. Not the too-hearty bark he used to make people feel good, a real laugh. The waiter brought a crème brûlée they hadn't ordered.

"Where did you get that idea?"

He handed Pen her silver dessert spoon and picked up his own. By silent agreement they counted to three and tapped the crust. It broke with a snap. She remembered how she had loved walking around the perimeter of the schoolyard on November mornings, cracking frozen puddles with her toe.

"It was a shame in some ways, of course, although it's not my place to say."

Pen lay down her spoon. Her father was seldom willing to discuss the lives of others. He had trained her to view gossip as the lowest form of conversation, a mark of shallowness and stupidity, a step worse, even, than discussing one's own life.

"Christina could have been anything. She was brighter than the two of us put together," he continued.

He looked weary, and his eyes were a bit red, whether from alcohol or jet lag, she did not know.

"She finished with a first-class degree, while Lennox barely squeaked by with a 2:2. There were almost as many recruiters chasing her as there were men. After we graduated, I went home to start working at the business, and they moved to London. She'd chosen a gig in intelligence, like her father had done. I met him once, Sir William Campbell. He'd been an ambassador. An insufferable man, to tell the truth.

"But then Elliot's mother got sick, and his father couldn't manage. Elliot, being the eldest, went up to take care of things. When it became clear that his mother's situation would not improve, and that the estate's affairs were not in a good way either, Christina left her job and joined him. They had a small wedding with Lord and Lady Lennox present. I flew back for it. A beautiful ceremony if a bit sad. Within a year, his parents had both passed on and Elliot had inherited the land, the house, the debt, the whole albatross.

"In the meantime, he had started on a book; it seemed a long shot, but it was his best and only idea. He locked himself in his room for days at a time while Christina took on managing the property: looking after the tenants, turning the estate around. Of course, they'd known he would inherit one day. But they could not have anticipated what a shambles it would be in. She assumed the role that was required of her, and by all accounts she's done as brilliant a job at that as she would have done at anything else."

"Why did you lose touch?" Pen asked.

"There was no one thing," he said, rolling the dregs of espresso around inside his cup. "The years came between us, that's all. We were still close when I came back over for graduate school, although they couldn't get down to London much, and I only made it up there a few times."

He grew quiet, thinking again of his time in London.

"Then, of course, I married your mother," he continued in a brisker tone. "I had my work cut out for me at the company. We were busy and far apart. I remember writing a few times, but by then Elliot's first book had made him a celebrity; my letters would have been lost in a sea of adulation. It's hard to get in touch with famous people, even for an old friend."

"But you named me after him," Pen said. She bore her eyes into his, pleading for a real answer.

Ted smiled. He saw so much of Anna in her. He closed his eyes, hoping to God (not believing there was one) that she wouldn't suffer as her mother had.

He still couldn't explain why, exactly, he had resurrected the name he'd picked out years before, except that it represented to him something that was important. Perhaps the most important. Of all of them, he thought, Elliot alone had done exactly what he wanted to do with his life.

"Did I?" He reached over to smooth a lock of hair behind her ear. "Well, it's a lovely name."

He had been there with her for a moment, but now he'd closed himself off again. Pen dug her nails into her palms.

Ted left a big tip. They walked, arm in arm, over to Hanover Street and up through St Andrew Square to his hotel. Pen remembered the handful of times, before the age of twelve, when she had accompanied her dad on his business trips. Listening to him sing while he shaved, having warm croissants and ice-cold orange juice on a tray.

Her dad signaled for the doorman to find her a taxi. Sinking into her dad's embrace, she felt the years slide away until she was small again, a child enveloped in the safety of a stable world. She pulled back and climbed into the waiting taxi.

"Pollock Halls, please," she told the driver. She waved out the window at her receding father on the hotel steps, and left it open, letting the cold air splash her face as they sped up North Bridge toward the Royal Mile.

Winter

23

The mating rituals of university students in the first decade of the twenty-first century were embarrassing, Pen thought as she walked along Pleasance toward the student union building, her hands stuffed in her pockets. She felt a cringe climb through her body as she remembered the attempts she had made, the night before, to make herself look appealing. How she had hopped around to a trashy song, and how she had cheered—they had all cheered—the second time that song had come on in the space of just a few hours. Recognizing the tune had made them feel like they were doing the right thing. Like they did, in fact, belong in this dungeon-like club that smelled of chemical cologne and alcohol, and of the sweat and hormones they were intended to mask, on a cold Monday night in December.

Pen liked dancing when the music was good—and she knew it made sense for young people to examine one another's wits and shapes under the cover of noise and semidarkness—but she wished her generation had the waltz, or even just some kind of coordinated hop, in which to dress their hunger for acceptance, and for each other's bodies. A live band and agreed-upon footwork would have lent dignity to their yearnings. Gyrating without skill to music from a compressed digital file made the business of continuing the species uglier than it needed to be.

The trick, Alice had told her many times, was not to think. Alice did not possess natural rhythm, and she did not care. As a result, she still managed to look cool while dancing.

"Just turn off your brain," Alice would admonish. They both knew this was something Pen could never do, no matter how much vodka she drank.

It was in part her attraction to the promise of form, and in part pure curiosity, that had drawn Pen to write her name down on a sign-up sheet for the university's Reeling Society. Fergus and Jo, who had learned to reel at school, were amused by Pen's interest, and had also put their names down. The others had not taken much persuading.

Now Pen and Fergus were chairing the committee that was planning the Reeling Society's Yuletide Ball, which was to take place in three weeks, on the final night of term. It was to be an abbreviated version of a traditional reeling ball, meaning it would include a sit-down dinner but would not go straight through the night or serve breakfast the next morning. They had used ticket sales and student union funds to rent out the ballroom of a swanky members' club in New Town. For this one night, instead of off-brand vodka, they would drink prosecco with elderflower cordial, and instead of sneakers and jeans, the dress code would require floor-length gowns for women and kilts or tails for men. Each guest would receive a dance card on thick paper stock with a tiny blue pencil attached by a string.

Pen lit a cigarette in front of the sports union complex and texted Alice. A damp-haired pair of students with water bottles pushed through the doors and glared at her. She felt a pang of guilt for having chosen artificial stimulants while others worked up honest endorphins on elliptical machines. After a few autumn jogs along the base of Arthur's Seat and through Holyrood Park, she had stopped putting on her running shoes. It got dark too early, and she didn't have the energy. But she missed the way she used to feel afterward. When she reached the filter with no reply, she put out her cigarette on the sole of her boot, dropped it into the garbage—smoking was bad, but to litter would have been out of the question—and went into the brightly lit, chlorine-scented building.

Alice had been hard to pin down for weeks. Pen knew that these unexplained absences had more to do with Julian than with rehearsals, but she was careful not to let on. Jo had suggested to Pen, after a particularly awkward tutorial in which Julian and Alice had seemed to be undressing one another before the whole class, that they might at least raise the subject with Alice, but Pen had warned against it. Alice, she'd explained, hated to feel judged. And she could read Pen's face, so it would have been of little use to act as if she thought sleeping with a married tutor was normal or fine.

Soon after that conversation, Jo, too, had become elusive, not answering Pen's messages until the next morning, and letting her phone ring through to voicemail. She claimed to be spending nights in the twenty-four-hour computer lab known as "the bunker," working on last-minute essays, but Pen wondered if Jo had decided to tell Alice that she knew about Julian. If so, it would have been easy for her to show, in that relaxed, neutral way Jo had, that she wasn't condemning Alice for it. If this was the case, Pen thought, the shared secret would have brought them closer and made them want to spend more time just the two of them. She couldn't blame them. She knew she had been acting like a wet blanket since her disappointing second visit to Stonehaven, and she had not told either of them why. She had only told them that Alice had been right, Sasha was not going to set her world on fire. Their compassion would have been far worse than their current silence.

On returning to her room after the dinner with her dad, Pen had opened her laptop and dragged the instant messenger program into the trash. Her whirring mind, ever prepared with a well-chosen unkindness, told her that even Christina's warmth toward her had likely been an enactment of duty, not the result of real affection. This hurt as much as Sasha's indifference. She remembered how Christina had feigned ignorance of her fame in town, and how all of them had tried to maintain the fiction that Freddie was not in the house. The whole family was too good at pretending, she decided; she would never get the truth out of any of them.

Meanwhile, Fergus's attentions to Pen had become more obvious. He had amassed a collection of words beginning with "Pen" that he produced as pet names in the same tone one might use to address a dog or horse. Pen generally liked nicknames. She was oddly touched by Jo's unexplained use of "Stinky" from almost their first meeting and had never wanted to ruin it by asking Jo of what, exactly, she smelled. (Of nothing, Jo would have answered, for in Jo's mind, Pen's odorless, New World purity was a source of genuine and affectionate awe.) Fergus's belabored terms of endearment did not quite do it for her, but still Pen had begun to play along, in hopes that it might distract her from thoughts of Sasha.

Pen was mostly successful at banishing him by day, but by night he haunted the edges of her consciousness. No matter how much she tried to think of other things while falling asleep, there he was as she lay on her back in her single bed, standing in the doorway, noticing the gap between her buttons. The more she tried to suppress the memory of him, the harder he was to dislodge from her brain. Her desire to be looked at by him, to be touched by him, only grew. When she thought about Sasha, however inadvertently, she could feel a loosening in her joints. She knew Fergus could sense a change in her, and she wasn't sure she minded.

"No Alice then?" Charlie asked when Pen arrived at the student union pub on her own and took her seat at the high, wobbly table.

"She's not answering," said Pen.

Fergus approached with several glasses pressed together. He placed one in front of Pen and pulled his barstool close to hers.

"She's spending more and more time with her fellow ac-*tors*," said Jo, mocking Alice's insistence upon the gender-neutral noun. "Especially that man-angel Neville. God is he gorgeous. He looks like he just fluttered out of a frame at the Uffizi, doesn't he?"

"He seems nice," said Charlie, in a voice that convinced no one.

"Chin up, Charles," said Jo, putting an arm around Charlie's shoulders. "Neville's more likely to fancy you than Alice."

Charlie sat up straighter.

"Oy! So you recognize one another, do you?" asked Hugo with evident delight. "Have secret meetings or some fink?" Hugo's phony habit of sometimes pronouncing "th" as "f" annoyed Pen more than usual that afternoon.

"Yes," answered Jo dryly. "We get together once a month to howl at the fucking moon."

The other members of the planning committee joined them around the table and the meeting began. Pen had trouble keeping her thoughts on the menu.

Her mind alighted instead, for no reason she could fathom, on George and Danny. Danny was, it occurred to her, the first baby she had held as an adult. She wanted to feel his sturdy mass in her arms again and to let him pull on her necklace with his chubby fingers. This led her to think of the gossiping women outside of the tearoom. She tried to return to the meeting. When she looked down at her notebook, someone had scribbled:

Pen is daydreaming.

Pen is thinking impure thoughts about Fergus.

Pen is wondering whether his sword is mightier, after all.

She looked at him and laughed. He was careful to ignore her.

Committee members were busy moving chairs and tables aside to make space to practice. Pen's second gin and tonic had gone down too easily. Fergus waved his hand in the air.

"Monsieur!" he said to no one. The student pub, as he knew very well, did not offer table service. "What can one expect from a union establishment," he muttered, and went to the bar. He returned with two glasses, plunking one before Pen. "Down it, fresher."

The music started up. Charlie stood to remove their table, which was now in the middle of the dance floor.

The dancers had formed two parallel lines, one made up mostly of men, and the other of women. "I know it's against your religion, but try to stop thinking and just follow me," Fergus said in Pen's ear, positioning her across from him. They set to one another, a kind of curtsy with one foot and then the other. She raised her right hand, I'm-a-little-teapot style, to meet his, before walking in a circle.

Pen then raised her left hand to meet Charlie's and circled once with him, back to her own line. The next sequence was similarly straightforward. Pen felt warm and light. Fergus was watching, ready to show her what to do next with a subtle gesture, or to reposition her if she started in the wrong direction. By the end of the second reel, she felt she was achieving a satisfying level of proficiency. Fergus had been right: not thinking was doing her good. The gin had settled over her mind like a thick layer of mist. Each time she spun around she felt less moored. It was like a fancy hokey pokey, she thought.

"What was that one called?" she asked Fergus while catching her breath.

"The Dashing White Sergeant, of course," he said, wiggling his fair eyebrows mock-suggestively. "I'm impressed with your progress, Pentecostal," he added, his face close. The music started again.

"Strip the Willow," Fergus announced with something resembling glee. He positioned them as the first couple. Pen and Fergus began a dance that involved clutching each other's crossed forearms and spinning round and around, and then whirling into another partner with whom to link arms and twirl. Pen worked her way down the parallel lines of dancers in this way, always returning to the merry-go-round with Fergus.

By the time they reached the final armlock, Pen was so proud to have made it through without crashing to the floor that she let Fergus spin her around triumphantly, at full speed. It reminded her of being four and sticking her arms out to spin as fast as she could, marveling afterward at how long it took for her to regain stillness, and for the world to return to its right-side-up position. She was in exactly this exultant, dizzy state when he placed his hands on her shoulders and kissed her full on the mouth. She drew her head back, startled. Seeing sincerity and longing in his pale-lashed eyes, and feeling reckless, she kissed him back. She could hear clapping and whooping as she put her tongue in his mouth and felt him respond.

What Fergus saw in her, Pen had no idea. Maybe it was just her foreignness. But she liked the parts of him he was careful not to show. She was also flattered by his attention. And so she kept kissing him, tasting the spearmint of his toothpaste. When he led her by the hand, each of them three gins deep with no dinner, into a taxi that sped to his room in Holland House, she followed. She had spent the evening learning to follow his lead and found it remarkably easy to continue.

Fergus's room was bigger than hers. It had a window that opened out onto the quad. It was tidy: the bed made, clothes folded on the desk chair. She moved the clothes onto the desk and sat down. Fergus leaned over her to reach his laptop. His sleeves were rolled up and she could see the pale hair on his forearms, the muscles taut beneath translucent skin. Music came up through the laptop's speakers. It was like the reeling music but slower, more mournful. A bass thrummed under the melody of a lone violin. She pictured the velvet interior of her violin case in elementary school. She remembered how she had loved the instrument's reddish sheen, the careful steps of rubbing resin onto the bow, of affixing the foam chin piece, of unfolding and tightening the metal stand. All delicious distractions from the act of playing, which she had hated.

Pen opened her eyes to find Fergus standing in the middle of the room. She saw hunger on his face, in the set of his mouth, but she saw vulnerability, too. He held out his hands, waiting. She stood up and took them.

"I'm not going to have sex with you," she told him honestly, examining the long fingers with no calluses, the maintained cuticles and ridged nails, the blue-veined undersides of his wrists.

"I wasn't offering," said Fergus.

He took back his right hand, placed it between her shoulder blades, and led her in a slow waltz around the room. With her elbow resting in the crook of his, she lowered her left hand onto the base of his neck. She let her body follow his as he twirled her, lifted her off the ground.

He brought his face to hers and kissed her, slowly. It wasn't unpleasant. This time it was his warm, wet tongue that caressed hers. She breathed through the kiss, inhaling the gin fumes on his breath. He brought her closer still, pressing her body up against his, half dancing her toward the bed. *You might enjoy it*, Pen reasoned with herself. Part of her was fixated on it all day every day. On finding out what it would feel like. On getting it over with. But it wasn't Fergus she pictured. She had never once thought about Fergus standing in her doorway.

They were still dancing. She took over the lead and spun herself toward the door.

"Bye, Fergus," she called, turning the knob and running silently down the hall, the sad music following her out.

24

Alice could not move. Julian had pinned her down with his body. She could feel the weight of his femur bones, the musculature of his thighs crushing hers. They were in the small, spartan bedroom in his flat. He did this often after they had sex. He settled, spent, on top of her. They were very nearly the same height, meaning that their wingspan was also the same. He covered her perfectly. He was heavier, though. She was trapped under him, her lungs compressed beneath his ribs, while he pretended to fall into a deep postcoital sleep.

At first, she had found this funny. It had been one of their games. The idea of a power struggle, mutually conceived, had excited them both. Now she tensed her muscles to shake him off and he twisted his ankles to hold her feet in place. But her resistance, she knew, was what kept him on top of her. She gave in, lying still beneath him like a corpse. When he got tired of pretending to sleep on top of a dead body, he rolled off. This was now her only way to win. Afterward, anyway.

Before and during sex Alice still had many ways to win. She used all of them. She tormented him with the way she dressed, he told her. No matter what she wore he accused her, while taking the jeans or the dress or the plain white T-shirt off of her later, that she had chosen it explicitly to drive him out of his mind, to make him lose his job. The way she looked at him in their tutorials turned him into a wretch. She had too much power over him. At least, that was what he told her. She didn't entirely believe him, but she liked hearing it all the same.

On an unseasonably warm day in October, she had intercepted him before class in the lobby of the David Hume Tower wearing a short skirt and no tights. She'd been early on purpose, hoping to catch him when he came in from lunch. Up to this point they had only kissed. And touched. That was as far as it would go, he claimed. She had known this not to be true.

She'd taken the stairs, climbing the twelve flights slowly. Julian had followed, watching her, his breath shortening. During the tutorial, she had noticed him staring at her with something close to violence in his eyes. She had evaded his gaze, fearing that the other students might notice.

After class she'd sat still, waiting, her legs clenched together, heat building between them. As she bid her friends goodbye, she mentioned as calmly as she could that she was staying behind to ask Julian a question. Jo rolled her eyes, Pen gave her a "be careful" kind of smile, and they left. Checking that the students had all disappeared down the stairs and into the elevator, Julian hadn't even taken her into his office, which was just down the hall. He had closed the classroom door, pulled aside her underwear, and sunk into her with a moan, propping her up with his body. They had both come quickly, laughing, embarrassed, her skirt hitched around her waist.

Every subsequent Tuesday they'd met on the tower's fifth-floor landing, which was more discreet than the lobby, at the start of the lunch hour. He'd follow her up the rest of the stairs. She'd wait for him at his office door, slightly out of breath. He'd turn the key in the lock, hold the door open for her, as if she were any other student who had come to ask him about moral philosophy, and close it behind her. They'd have nearly an hour to play their games. He liked to bring her to the brink slowly and then stop, leaving her to tremble, furious, before holding his palm over her mouth to keep her from screaming out as he took her over the edge. This was intended to prevent them from spending the whole of the tutorial making eyes at each other. But it wasn't enough.

Her strategy now was to shake Pen and Jo by leaving before they did and ducking into the ladies' room on the eleventh floor. There she counted to two hundred, staring at her inflamed cheeks in the mirror. When she was sure the other students would be gone, she took the single flight of stairs in three bounds, rounded the dark corner, and found his office door unlocked. Julian sat in his swivel chair behind his desk, waiting for her.

He waited for her after her rehearsals, too. He leaned against the statue of Greyfriars Bobby until she saw him, then disappeared into the shadow of a doorway while she lied to her castmates to get free. Neville and a few of the others liked to debrief over a pint at the Greyfriars pub. She told them she had readings to do, an essay to write. The first few times she had done this, it had been with her heartbeat in her ears and warmth creeping up her neck. Alice loved listening to Neville talk—he was an expert in the style of conversational jousting that one seemed able to learn only in Great Britain—but the pull toward Julian felt like gravity, or some other physical law that she had no choice but to obey. One flash in her mind of how he looked at her under the brightly lit bare bulb above his bed, and her feet stopped walking, a lie dropped from her tongue.

Now that it had become a regular occurrence, she had primed her cast-mates that with exams coming up, she'd have to go straight home and study most nights. If it was late and Neville insisted on driving her back to halls, she'd wave him off by getting into a taxi. Then she'd ask the driver to circle the block, she'd pick up Julian, and they'd ride in electrified silence to the flat he kept in Marchmont.

Alice knew that Julian had owned this apartment since his student days, and that he usually rented it out to postgrads, but had decided to keep it that year as a place to write. She knew his father had bought it for him. His father, who had deposited Julian and his younger brother Paul in boarding school when they had turned eight, and who had then divested himself of his filial load when his sons had "come of age," purchasing a one-bedroom apartment for each near the university of his choice. The apartments were, Julian had explained, their inheritance, on one level. But really, they had been a signal that from age eighteen onward, Julian and Paul were no longer expected to "visit" for the holidays.

Alice knew that Julian had written his PhD thesis on "Virtue Ethics in the Digital Age," and that part of it had been published in a reputable journal, which had resulted in a book deal. Four years later, the book was as-yet unfinished.

Alice also knew, because he had told her matter-of-factly one afternoon while she'd lain in his arms, when and how his mother had died. It had been three days after giving birth to Paul, when Julian was four, from a postnatal hemorrhage that had gone undiagnosed and led to septic shock. Their father, an oil engineer, had remarried quickly. He and Julian's stepmother, Julian had told her without apparent feeling, had together embraced an untethered expat life, moving to a different oil-rich country every four or five years, drinking the first of many strong cocktails each day at 5:00 p.m., and seldom letting anything pass beneath the surface of their evenly broiled skin.

She knew that Julian had met Emily, his wife, while they were both students, and that they had married in their late twenties. Alice desired no more knowledge about Emily than that which she already possessed: she was an elementary school teacher who went to bed early and did not enjoy sex, and she thought Julian spent several evenings a week either writing his book or watching football at the pub.

Knowing these things about his life did not make Alice feel guilty, or so she told herself; they made her feel powerful. One way of showing respect for her fellow humans was to accord them the dignity of choice without judgment. She didn't judge Julian for wanting to have sex with her. She didn't judge Julian's wife for having married a man who slept with his students, for she assumed she was not the first. Nor did she judge herself for the intensity of her attraction to this man. From that first day in his office—from the time he had stopped her in front of the library—she had imagined sleeping with him. She had pictured what it would be like to make his breathing ragged, to be the one to bring about the jerking release of his orgasm. She knew the affair would not last; she had no intention of taking the place of Julian's wife. The only thing she asked of him was to wear a condom. And except for that first time, after which she'd gone to the student health center for the morning-after pill and an STD exam, he always had.

Recently, however, it had become clear to Alice that Julian wanted more control over her than she was willing to give. This should not have been a surprise: in her experience, so did most men. He had begun to ask whether she had ever let another guy do this to her, or that. He asked whether she was fucking Neville or Charlie. He asked these things roughly, with something hard in his voice, even as he touched her gently. For as long as she wanted him to keep going, she didn't mind—"No," she told him, "just you"—but later, sated, bound under his leaden limbs, she wondered if the hard thing wasn't hatred. Who was this person who had given her a mediocre grade to get her alone in his office, when she would have gone willingly? she wondered. Men who made women feel weak in hopes of shifting the balance of power in their favor were not rare; she had first encountered the strategy at age fourteen, in her acting coach. Back then it had almost worked. Now, she knew how to play. If he gripped her thigh and whispered in her ear that she was gaining weight, she reached for his groin and told him he must have a thing for fat girls, in that case. If he called her outfit slutty, the next day she wore no bra. Once he'd announced in front of the class that her argument was fallacious, and she'd pretended not to understand. "What does fellatio have to do with it?" she'd asked in a loud, slow voice, causing Jo to fake a coughing fit.

Thinking about all this too soon after climaxing was like walking down the meat aisle of a grocery store after a heavy meal. It was hard to imagine, in the absence of hunger, that the rows of Styrofoam-backed, slack-skinned chicken thighs straining under their plastic wrap could ever become food. Her drives to survive and propagate must have been strong, Alice told herself, for her appetites always returned sooner than she expected. Within a few hours, her imagination and body once again conspired to make Julian's flesh appear not only appealing but essential.

Alice had still not told her friends that she was sleeping with their philosophy tutor three and sometimes four times a week, although she assumed that Pen knew. She used the play as her main excuse, pretending to have lunch-hour rehearsals that she had to rush to, saying that the evening ones ran later than they did. She had never needed to lie to Pen, historically, nor had they ever gone so many days at a stretch without talking. But Pen would sermonize, even if she tried not to. Alice didn't want Pen to remind her why they both hated the unoriginality of aging men who needed to reassure themselves of their virility by seducing any younger woman naïve enough to fall for it. They had spent many a high school free period railing against this cliché while sharing an illegally purchased cigarette in the back alley behind the coffee shop. Alice's father had done it throughout her childhood and adolescence, and while Alice didn't see it as a moral failing the way Pen did, she didn't like it either. Alice's mother had chosen not to see it, making him pay in other ways.

Pen being Pen, she might also point out that Alice could have been trying to understand this dynamic from the young woman's point of view. Maybe she was attempting to find out how much power this so-called naïve woman could amass over the aging man in question. Or maybe she was investigating whether an adult capable of making a choice that might destroy his marriage with the brain inside his boxer briefs might be deserving of pity. Alice pushed these thoughts from her mind. She did not want to think about her parents. She was her own person. She did not want to see her behavior from any point of view but hers. She was experimenting, she told herself, which was exactly what university was for. When Julian's physical power over her weakened, as it had already begun to do, she would find a way to extract herself from underneath his sluggish mass.

25

It was the week before Christmas exams, and night was falling in the middle of the afternoon. Pen was alone at their usual table in the JMC attempting to eat a balanced dinner when Flossie appeared at her elbow and asked if she could join her.

"I'm so glad you're here," Flossie said in her doll's voice. "I could never face sitting *alone*."

"Of course," Pen said, closing her book.

Flossie put down her tray, which held nothing but a shallow bowl of canned tuna from the salad bar and two syrupy Diet Cokes from the soda dispensers. She pulled a stack of magazines from her shoulder bag and began to flip through them while taking tiny, hamster-like bites of her tuna.

"Oh look, Sasha Lennox. Ferg said he's a friend of yours?" she asked after a while, pushing the fattest and glossiest of the magazines toward Pen. She was pointing a bubble-gum-pink fingernail at a small photo on the back page dedicated to Lady something-or-other's twenty-first birthday party in Sussex. Sasha was wearing a pirate costume and squinting into the flash beside a girl dressed as a mermaid. The girl had symmetrical, well-brushed eyebrows under a cascading wig, and the purple sequined bikini top she was wearing revealed tasteful décolleté and a long, slim torso. One of her sinewy arms was wrapped possessively around Sasha's waist—more Ursula than Ariel, Pen thought, annoyed to be seeing this.

Pen slid the magazine back to Flossie. "Not really," she said.

"Here he is again," said Flossie, turning the spread back around so Pen could see it.

Pen could not help but look. She was drawn to evidence, even if it was gruesome. The second photo was a candid. Sasha was seen in profile in a red velvet booth, tilting toward the same girl. She had a platinum pixie cut and those perfectly arching eyebrows. Now her bow lips were painted burgundy. Her eyelashes looked like the fat, hairy legs of a spider, but there was no denying that she was beautiful. The distance between Sasha's mouth and her dainty, well-formed earlobe, and the way his torso was pitched toward her as if he couldn't quite be trusted to remain upright, made Pen feel queasy. Or maybe it was just the smell of tuna. *At the opening of Harriet's Bar in Mayfair*, read the caption, *royal ex Lady Charlotte Rutherford cosied up to old friend the Hon. Sasha Lennox.*

"Apparently, they've been seen together quite a lot since the prince dumped her and left for Sandhurst," said Flossie helpfully, peering over Pen's shoulder. "My older sister knows Lottie from school. She's *so* pretty. Sasha has a brother who's our age, you know, and a good laugh," she added helpfully. "Have you met him?"

"No," said Pen. She returned the magazine with a smile that she was fairly certain was convincing and excused herself.

On the way out, she pulled her phone from her bag. She dialed Alice first, and then Jo. Predictably, neither answered.

Outside, it looked like midnight even though it was not yet 8:00 p.m. Her limbs felt heavy as she climbed the dank stairs to her room and flopped onto her bed. She thought about calling her mom, but she knew she would break down if she did, and she didn't want to scare Anna. Instead she looked at the picture of their dog, Olive, on her bulletin board and let the fat tears roll down her face. Taken when Olive was a puppy, the photo showed her discovering snow for the first time. She was rolling on her back, legs in the air, and what looked like a grin on her face. Pen ached to sit on the floor of her mother's kitchen with Olive's warm, silky weight in her lap. *Go on, revel in your self-pity*, she thought. *This is all your own doing.*

In the aftermath of her run-in with Flossie, Pen stopped going to the JMC for meals. She spent most of her time studying alone at the library or in her room. There was a communal pantry at the end of her corridor. Its counters were thick with crumbs and slime, and no one ever wrung out the rag in the sink, but the plug-in kettle was serviceable, and so was the mini fridge, where she kept a pint of milk among the forgotten sandwiches and half-eaten boxes of microwavable pasta. She lived on cups of milky tea, chocolate digestives, and wine gums. She was aware of her mounting isolation but made no effort to escape it until one evening, after watching a French New Wave film for her European Cinema class that doubled the load of amorphous dread weighing on her chest, when she gave in and re-downloaded the instant messenger application on her laptop.

Chet messaged her first, his innuendo a welcome distraction from the loneliness that had encased her. But it was Sasha she was waiting for. When he came online, she nearly slammed her computer shut. He went right back offline. Great, she told herself. There's the proof you were looking for.

She was feeling faint and had been on the verge of saying something borderline flirtatious back to Chet just to keep him talking to her when Sasha's blue dot appeared again. A split second later he sent her a message.

SASHA: Hey! My pigeon's been looking everywhere for you.

Pen looked back through their message history, which she already knew by heart. She was trying to seem too busy, or maybe too deep in another conversation, to reply right away.

PEN: Maybe you should have tried an eagle.

SASHA: You're not going to make another insensitive bald joke, are you?

PEN: Or a lark. You seem to be someone who enjoys a good lark.

SASHA: Fair enough. Just don't pluck it and sing to children about it, like in that scary French song.

PEN: No promises.

She was being too intense. She needed to calm down. She opened her window and lit a cigarette. Smoking in her room was a first, which made the rush of nicotine that much more powerful. Or maybe she was just hungry. Dizziness nearly tipped her out of her chair. Why wasn't he replying?

SASHA: We've missed you. Dad keeps asking about you. Danny too, or at least I think that's what he's ranting about. You seem to have cast a spell on the men of the house.

Pen wanted to ask, *Does that include you? Or your outlaw brother who you pretend doesn't exist?* She held her fingers over the keyboard, fuming. But he was typing again.

> SASHA: Not that the women are insensible to your charms. Mum is choosing to believe that your studies are as all-consuming as you claim, and George says you've probably just met a boy.

Here we go, she thought. She pressed hard on the keys.

> PEN: George is right.

He typed for a while. She wondered if he knew that she could see him typing. It was possible that he hadn't downloaded the latest version of the program.

> SASHA: Nice guy?

She wasn't falling for it. There was no greater insult among men than "nice." Besides, nice wasn't the first word she thought of in connection with Fergus.

> PEN: Not especially.

> SASHA: Didn't know that was your style.

Oh, you didn't? Having made me develop a pathetic crush on you and then lured me to your parents' house only to ignore me from close-up—are you not exactly the kind of not-so-nice guy who is my style? She lit another cigarette with a shaking hand even though she had no desire for it. She needed to eat some real food. Maybe Alice was home for once. Maybe she had peanut butter.

PEN: I guess it is. Got to go.

She closed her computer before he could say bye. Her heart was beating like a squirrel's. She called Alice. It went straight to voicemail. She tried the landline in her room. It rang and rang. She tried Jo, who didn't answer either. This time she felt certain that they were together, and that both had looked at her name flashing on their phones and decided not to answer. This made her want to throw up.

She got into bed with her clothes on—something she had only ever done on two other occasions that she could think of—and lay on top of the base sheet, rolling herself into the blanket. None of the comforting places in her head were available. She picked up a book. Sartre. Perfect. She hadn't even brushed her teeth. Her mouth tasted like tar. She felt disgusting. She lay there for a long time, staring at French words, until she fell into a fitful sleep.

She dreamed that she was sitting beside her dad on a public bench near a busy intersection in Toronto. It was evening. She was waiting for Fergus, who in the dream was her boyfriend. "You haven't taken up smoking, have you?" her dad asked. She tried to evade the question, not wanting to lie. Fergus was late, and finally she told her dad she was leaving. She jaywalked through four lanes of traffic, and there he was with a group of boys, including Sasha. Her dad followed her across the road. He was wearing a three-piece suit with shiny shoes and a tiny oval backpack. She had never seen her dad wear a backpack before, let alone a dinky one like this. She wondered what was in it. He shook the boys' hands. Fergus hugged her awkwardly, bending at the waist like a marionette. Sasha just waved. She said "See you later" to her dad, hoping he'd take the hint. He loped off, backpack bobbing.

The next morning, Pen opened her phone to find two texts, one sent at eleven thirty and the other after twelve.

> ALICE: Just leaving rehearsal. Our director Maxwell is such a pompous arse. He probably masturbates to pictures of Queen Victoria. I'm going to crash but if you're still awake call me.

> JO S-M: You all right Stinky? Sorry I missed your call. Back in the bunker atoning for my sins. Mill or Kant? Which horse would you bet on? See you in the morn. X x x

Pen brushed her teeth twice and cursed herself for having such transparent dreams. Her dad's baggage—really. Did her unconscious mind think she was stupid?

26

Just after seven on the last Friday night of the first term, Pen climbed the stairs to the New Club's second-floor ballroom with Jo and Alice beside her. Exams were over, and those who had sat them were ready to let the information they had absorbed seep quietly out of their brains. For ten tense days of feverish scribbling in intimidatingly large halls, the three of them had, without acknowledging their weeks of distance, returned to something like their previous routine.

On the morning of Pen's first exam, they had waited for her in front of the JMC with a takeaway coffee and a muffin. Pen had been overwhelmed with gratitude at the sight of them. Even if the intimacy between Alice and Pen had not been fully restored—and some trust had been lost during Pen's weeks of isolation—she was deeply relieved that the lull in their friendship had been just that, a lull. Not a permanent break.

And although she would not have said it aloud, Pen loved exams. She found pleasure in the kinetic and mental challenge of churning out three essays in three hours, some in English and some in French, inside the regulation blue-lined booklets. Studying hard forced her out of the claustrophobic recesses of her mind. She had sunk with relief into worlds in which she did not exist and emerged feeling peaceful and strong. Her suitcase was packed for the morning, and she planned to leave on a high note.

She had spent much of that day in the ballroom, with its ornate, fifteen-foot ceiling, smoothing out table linens, lining up champagne flutes, and placing candles. In daylight, it had looked the way a dressed stage does when the house lights are up. Now, the sky was dark outside the vast windows, the lit candles were sparkling, and the room was filling up with young men in tails or kilts, and women in gowns that fell to the floor.

Jo's faded turquoise sheath fell only to Alice's mid-calf, but it made her look like Titania the fairy queen, so Pen knew that even Fergus, the self-appointed enforcer of the dress code, would not dare to comment. Jo was wearing the simple emerald gown that Pen had worn to her senior formal the previous spring, and Pen was in a pale gold, diaphanous number that was calf-length on Alice but fell to the floor on her. They had spent longer than usual on makeup, with Alice teaching them how to highlight their brow bones and the bridges of their noses. Pen felt eyes on the three of them as they reached the top of the staircase and made their way into the room. The feeling of being on display made Pen trip over the long dress. Jo and Alice kept her upright.

Fergus, who had been watching the stairs, extricated himself from a ring of boys in white tie and cut a path across what would soon be the dance floor toward them.

"Ladies, you are resplendent," he said, kissing each in turn. "Especially you, Pennsylvania," he said in Pen's ear, clasping his fingers through hers, which were cold to the touch.

Fergus had been conspicuously absent during the pre-exam period. He had gone home to Buttons to study, Jo had explained. Pen had found herself missing him, and not only because he was meant to be chairing the planning committee with her.

Pen had overseen the seating chart. She had put herself between Archie Bloomfield, a fellow planning committee member from Bath with a good sense of humor, and, daringly, a second year studying Arabic whom everyone called Fit Jasper. Fergus used the golf pencil on the end of his dance card to doctor the seating plan, banishing Jasper to another table. He did this with one hand: the other was still clutching Pen's. The reeling had not yet begun. Fergus requisitioned Pen's dance card and wrote his name in every slot. She crossed it out from all but three dances, wishing they had sprung for the golf pencils with erasers attached. Then she wriggled free to find some other partners. It didn't take long. She was surprised to learn that she was somewhat in demand. Even Fit Jasper sought her out.

A few minutes later she was standing against the wall, surveying the room, when Fergus took up the spot beside her and brought her a fresh glass of prosecco.

"You do look beautiful tonight, Penhaligon's," he said, his tone serious. "And you've done astonishingly well. I'm sorry for having been a useless co-chair."

"First you make yourself missed, and then you flatter—is that what they teach you in rake school?" she asked.

"So, you did miss me," he said triumphantly. "I knew the French method would work on you, Napoleonic traitor that you are."

"What do you know about the French method," she said, turning to face him. "I've never seen a more English boy in my life."

"How cold of you, Snow Nymph," he said. "I'm Scottish."

"You're about as Scottish as the Queen."

"The Queen *is* Scottish. Her mother was brought up at Glamis Castle. What do they teach you in Canadiashire? Surely you've at least read Macbeth."

The music changed from Ambiguous Classical to Distinctly Celtic. The reeling was about to begin. The dancers organized themselves into lines facing one another. Pen had a sudden memory of line dancing to "Cotton Eye Joe" at bar and bat mitzvahs. She tried to catch Alice's eye. Here they were again, playing dress-up and trying to look socially adept.

Fergus took Pen's hands back in his. "May I have this dance?"

"You may," she said with a curtsy.

"And later, if you're good, I'll show you the other French method," he said.

"Is that supposed to sound enticing?" she asked, pulling her head back.

"Vive le Québec libre," he said gravely. His accent was terrible. She didn't need to think up an answer to this non sequitur, because the dancing began in earnest. They took their place in the formation. She made the requisite loops and twirls, following his competent, firm-gripped lead, and enjoying it as much as she had during their practices.

Nearby, Alice and Jo had partnered up. Jo was leading, and Alice, who had missed more than one rehearsal, looked like a baby horse trying to walk for the first time. Pen had to turn away to keep from laughing and losing her place in the footwork.

The next partner on Pen's dance card was a small, sure-footed boy called Tim from her Medieval Poetry class. She didn't dance as well with him as she had with Fergus, but aside from a stacked heel to the metatarsals, he got off lightly. When they parted, she drifted over to Alice and Jo, who were on their way to the balcony with Hugo and Charlie.

"I can't reel for shit," said Alice.

"You really can't," said Charlie, who had just been her partner. "You act like you know where to put your feet, but you don't have the first idea, do you." He said this in an admiring tone. Judging by his unwillingness to let go of her hand, Charlie had not found reeling with Alice to be a hardship.

"No," said Alice simply, looking straight at him. They shared a smile.

"It only makes us love you more," said Jo, pulling Alice into a clumsy twirl. "Let's take some air and try to forget our shortcomings." On the balcony she turned to Pen. "You and Ferg are thick as thieves, Stinky. Are his charms finally working on you, or are you just tired of fending him off?"

"I can't tell," Pen said truthfully. "He's being nice. It's disorienting."

Jo looked as if she was tempted to say something, but she held back. Fergus was crossing the room, about to join them.

Pen checked her dance card. The next reel was her least favorite, the Eightsome, which involved dancing around in a circle in a very confusing way. She had promised it to Fergus knowing that only he would have any chance of guiding her through the steps. Dinner wasn't for another two dances.

"Let's skip this one," Fergus said, taking Pen's hand. "I'm all for a threesome or a foursome, but eight is too many bodies to keep track of."

He led her back inside and then out through a door that was semi-hidden by the wallpaper and wood paneling. It led to stairs that they followed up to another door two floors above. Now they were in a small library. The walls were lined to the ceiling with shelves of leather-bound volumes. A ladder stood in one corner, affixed to a track.

Pen went over to the ladder and started climbing. He followed her up until they were balanced on the same rung. She leaned against the books to steady herself. He turned her around slowly until she was facing him.

"I wouldn't let you fall," he said. He brushed a lock of her hair behind her ear. Then he tilted her chin up and kissed her. They were less tipsy than they had been at the student union pub. His kiss reflected this. There was something starched and formal in it. Like a neatly wrapped bar of guest soap. But Pen's mind was in the library scene from *Atonement*, and she wasn't in the mood for guest soap. She moved her head back and looked at him.

"You call that the French method?" she asked.

She kissed him then, hard, and he returned her kiss. She swayed a bit, and he guided her down the ladder. He sank into a leather club chair in the corner of the room and pulled her into it with him. They made out like teenagers. When they came up for air his blond hair was tousled, and his lips were red and bitten-looking.

"Everyone will know," she said. "Look at you."

"Look at you," he said, and he did. "Who cares what they know." He kissed her again, with greater sincerity than she would ever have guessed.

Her dress was fastened with dozens of silk buttons with flimsy loop closures. It would have been impossible to remove without a hurricane lamp and enormous patience. To her surprise, Fergus didn't even try. He seemed content with exploring her mouth, her face, her throat. And he was the one to whisper, "Let's go back. We mustn't miss the dinner you've planned."

They slipped down the two flights of stairs, back through the hidden door, and into the ballroom, where the dancers were starting to find their seats at the long banquet tables. He rested his hand on her knee. She drank a gulp of ice water and tore into a bread roll, trying to look normal.

"Hello, you two," said Archie from beside her. "We missed you during the eightsome."

"Sorry, Archie," said Pen. "How was it?"

"Predictably shambolic," he said. "We could have used your steadying hand, Ferg."

The starter came. Pen was pleased with how it looked. Fergus acted like she had cooked and plated every morsel herself. "This is divine," he said, gathering a bite of lettuce and cheese onto his fork with a push of his knife. "Rocket was an inspired choice."

Alice gave Pen a look from across the table that said, "Really? Are you sure this is what you want?" Pen laughed and took another sip of red wine. Her spirits were higher than they had been in a long time.

"What is this stuffing?" Alice asked when the main course arrived. "It's amazing." Pen glanced at Fergus. She knew very well what the chicken was stuffed with; the choice had not been hers. She'd tried to block it, in fact, on the grounds that their ticket-buying demographic contained more than one person who, like Alice, preferred grilled cheese with ketchup to most things and would be neither intrigued nor awed by the presence of offal on the menu. But the planning committee, and Fergus in particular, who had made a point of phoning into that meeting, had wholeheartedly disagreed. No one who was unwilling to try haggis had any business living in Edinburgh or engaging in traditional Scottish dancing, they argued. Even the vegetarian main, in the end, was to consist of roasted red peppers stuffed with vegetarian haggis.

Fergus squeezed Pen's knee under the table. For once, he could not summon a haughty poker face: mirth had conquered his features, and Pen was smiling, too.

"Penelope," said Alice, knowing that she had become the butt of their joke but not minding very much. "Control your man-friend."

"Alice, dear Alice," said Fergus, pulling her to her feet, causing her fork to clatter to the floor. "How happy you have made me. For a Godless colonial such as yourself to pledge her palate's allegiance to Queen and country." He gave her a smacking kiss on each cheek.

"What's in the damned chicken?" Alice asked Jo while Fergus spun her in a mini jig.

"Haggis," said Jo.

"Really," said Alice. She reached across the table, took Fergus's fork, and returned to her plate. "I like it."

More wine and a wee dram of whisky later, the opening bars of "Auld Lang Syne" filled the ballroom. Fergus stood, and when the vocals came in, he sang along.

Should old acquaintance be forgot and never brought to mind?

His singing voice—warm, soulful, perfectly in tune—was a revelation, and it hit Pen right in between the ribs. All the more because it hinted at the depths of emotion that she knew existed in Fergus, and that she felt certain he carefully hid from most of the world. Jo, a smile taking over her whole face, stood to join her brother with her own husky and equally tuneful voice:

Should old acquaintance be forgot in the days of auld lang syne.

Charlie, Archie, and at least three quarters of the table were soon on their feet, too, and singing their hearts out:

For auld lang syne my dear
For auld lang syne
We'll drink a cup of kindness yet,
For the sake of auld lang syne.

When the song ended, Pen's body was tingling. She glanced at Alice, who looked back at her, equally moved. "I get it now," she mouthed, tilting her head toward Fergus.

Fergus, his cheeks flushed, sat down as if nothing out of the ordinary had happened. Pen squeezed his hand. "You're good at that," she said.

Not long afterward, when Pen and Fergus had found their way back to the secret library, Pen stopped kissing him abruptly.

"Do you want to have sex?" she asked. She was tipsy and out of breath, but the question was sincere.

"With you, or in general?"

"Both."

"Yes."

"Yes to which," she said, studying him.

"Both?"

"Both," she repeated.

"Yes," he said.

They exited the ball as quickly as humanly possible, creating a stir that they failed to notice, and climbed into a waiting taxi on Princes Street. At Holland House, Fergus followed Pen up the stairs. She got lost trying to find his room and he tugged her by the hand to the right door, and then fumbled with his key.

They kissed standing up for a while, and Pen tried to lose herself in the moment. But nerves, and the fear that she'd lose hers, caused her mind to wander. She thought it would be best to expedite matters.

She turned on his bedside lamp and sat on the edge of his bed with her back to him, shivering.

"This is Alice's dress. Please don't hurt it."

Fergus had already begun to undo the buttons with adroit fingers.

"Raise your arms," he commanded when he reached her lower back. She obeyed, and he lifted the dress over her head, shook it right-side-in, and laid it neatly over the desk chair. She was in her underwear now, and he was still fully clothed. She felt the imbalance keenly and had just begun to untuck his dress shirt from his suit pants when the door to his room was flung open.

"FERGUS ST. JOHN SCARLETT MOORE, ARE YOU IN?" came Hugo's booming voice. He was holding a bottle of vodka in one hand and was flanked by two boys Pen recognized but did not know. Hugo looked high, his pupils as big as pennies, but embarrassed. He did not move. The other two openly leered at Pen's exposed body. She let go of Fergus's shirt and dove under the sheets of his single bed. Fergus crossed the room in three steps and forced his friends out, turning the lock.

From under the covers, Pen felt childish, idiotic, and distinctly un-aroused.

Fergus, failing to notice that a change had come over her, returned from closing the door to find her in his bed wearing nothing but matching lace underwear. He climbed onto the bed and tried to pick up where they had left off.

Pen felt nothing, now, but the wetness and enthusiasm of his mouth. She tried to figure out what to do next. *She* had initiated this. When his body had sought hers, and with increasing urgency, hers had responded in kind. Or at least, she'd thought it had. Why was she cold now? And how in hell could she tell him that the sex idea was no longer a good one?

While she worried, he got down to his boxer shorts. She was not surprised, but was nonetheless a bit dismayed, to find that they were printed with an enormous Union Jack.

"Fergus," she said, gently de-suctioning his lips from her neck.

He looked up.

"Fergus," she repeated. "I know I was really gung-ho about the whole sex thing before, but do you think we can just . . ." *Gung ho?* Where had that come from? If she ever wrote a glossary of words to de-escalate a sexually charged situation, "gung ho" would need to be at the top of the list.

He glanced at the door and back at her. "They won't bother us again, don't worry," he said, and went back to kissing her.

She tried returning his kiss. *It's not that bad,* she told herself. *You do like him, freaky as his underpants might be. He's Jo's brother. He's a good person, probably, persona aside. Certainly, he's been good to you. He likes you. He's attracted to you, which you can't say of everyone. You can't say it of Sasha. So, if you are going to have sex with someone at some point, which you probably should because this is the end of your first semester at university and soon it will be very weird for you to still be a virgin (if it isn't already), you might as well have it right now, with Fergus Sinjun Scarlett Moore.*

"Fergus, how do you spell your middle name?" Pen asked, pulling her face away again. She needed to buy some time.

"Hmm?" Understandably enough, he did not seem enthused about this turn of the conversation.

"Is it S-I-N-J—"

"Oh," he said. "No, it's spelled like St. John."

"Hold on," Pen said, excited to have found something so clearly non-sexual to grab on to. "'St. John' as a first name is pronounced Sinjun? So, the hardcore missionary cousin in *Jane Eyre* is called Sinjun? You're blowing my mind."

"Am I? I'm glad," he said, and went back to doing things to her neck.

Pen was discouraged. Why had she just used the words "hardcore," "missionary," and "blowing" in one breath? These words were most definitely not in the glossary. What was wrong with her?

Sinjun, Sinjun, she repeated in her head, committing the pronunciation to memory like she did with French vocabulary. This one was easy: "sin" and "gin." Tonight, it had been sin and prosecco, but it would surely be gin again soon. Sin gin. She tried to return her brain to her body.

Fergus plowed onward as though sex were still the natural endpoint of this exchange. Which in most ways, it probably was. Except that Pen had made a terrible mistake and could not have sex with a boy she wasn't even all that attracted to, if she told herself the truth.

She searched her mind for ways to derail his efforts without hurting him. Should she tell him she had chlamydia? No, then no one would sleep with her. Say she'd gotten her period? She could not imagine discussing any bodily function with Fergus. That was part of the problem. Admit she was a virgin? She had been so forward that she doubted he would believe her. She wasn't sure she would have believed it, in his place. Second thoughts, then. Clean and simple. Also, true. It was the only way. She had the words all lined up in her head when she realized that he was no longer kissing her neck. In fact, all progress had ceased. She met his eyes. He was looking at her with an expression she couldn't place. Had he guessed? For a moment, Pen was so touched that she thought she might be attracted to him after all.

Then she figured it out, courtesy of the Union Jack, and what she felt was relief. Pure, glorious relief. A get-out-of-jail-free card. A mulligan. Another word for the glossary.

Fergus sat up on the bed, unable to meet her eye. "This has never happened before," he said in a voice more naked than he was. He cleared his throat. "Must have been all the drink."

"I think it was your partner," she said, trying to assume responsibility without making her relief obvious.

"Hmm, perhaps," he said, covering himself with the sheet and searching for his normal voice. "Wouldn't do to mix with a colonial, would it?"

"Probably not, Sinjun," Pen said, grateful for his joke. Assuming it had been a joke.

She covered herself, too. She tried talking, but their usual rapport was gone. He turned to face the wall. Soon, he was asleep, or pretending to be. He was thin but long, and his body took up most of the single bed and almost all the covers. The hair on her arms stood on end. After what she deemed an acceptable interval, she got up, tucked him in, and slipped Alice's dress over her head. It would have been impossible to fasten the buttons on her own, so she held it closed around herself, stepped into the heels she'd left by the door, and escaped down the stairs and across the empty quad. The stars were out. Silently, Pen thanked them.

27

The airport shuttle bumped and rattled along the cobblestones. Alice, who had taken the window seat, watched the sun struggle to lighten the heavy sky. Pen was beside her. She looked small, even for Pen. Bundled in her winter coat and hat, she could have been a third grader again. Alice remembered the lunches—peanut butter sandwiches, mostly—that third-grade Pen used to bring in her Winnie the Pooh lunch bag. She remembered how one afternoon Pen had forgotten it under the bench by the big kid playground. The next morning, they'd looked everywhere for it. It had been Alice who had found the remains, Tigger's face mauled by raccoons. Alice had presented the torn-up fabric to her friend and then held her while she cried bitterly, as if mourning the loss of a family pet.

They did not talk. Each was wearing her own headphones, listening to her own music. Antisocial behavior was normally one of the perks of their long friendship, but today it felt oppressive. Alice wished that Pen hadn't finally bought an iPod that summer so they could share hers, each wearing an earphone, splitting a song the way they had on so many past bus rides, one getting the bass and the other the vocals. She didn't even know what Pen was listening to.

While they'd waited for the bus, Pen had told Alice that she'd spent part of the night in Fergus's room, that Hugo and some of their school friends had walked in on them, and that nothing major had happened. This was all she'd told her.

Just a few hours before, after Pen and Fergus had reeled out of the ballroom in the middle of the last dance, the rest of them had piled into taxis and gone to Hugo's room for an afterparty. There had been more drinking. Hugo, who was always working on a new business idea that would make him rich enough to leave uni and spend the rest of his life between a yacht and a private island in the BVIs, was experimenting with a product that he called "Sweeties Vodka." He had several bottles of off-brand vodka lined up on his bookshelf, competing for space with alarmingly few books, and was pouring out "free samples." The liquid in each bottle was tinged with a different color, from the reddish one Alice tried to a creepy grayish-blue, and all contained what looked like pebbles at the bottom. Hugo wanted them to guess the flavor. A few of the boys, Hugo included, had taken pills, and were becoming all dopey and lovey-dovey, like drugged puppies.

"Cinnamon nail polish remover?" Alice ventured, wincing. Hugo chortled and slung a sweaty arm around her in a half hug, his enormous pupils crowding out the watery blue of his eyes.

Charlie, arriving at her other side, told her that the pebbles had once been cinnamon hearts, but the vodka had stripped away the red food coloring. To Alice's surprise (given that he went out nearly every night, and his sneakers were ten times dirtier now than they had been in September to prove it), Charlie had refused the small white pill Hugo had held out. So had she. They were sticking to the vodka. "Delicious, isn't it?" Charlie said, lifting his cup, deadpan. "Hugo's going to be a billionaire."

"The thing is, he will," Alice agreed, gently removing Hugo's arm from her shoulders and returning it to his side, where Hugo watched it flop down as if it weren't attached to his body. "Not from Sweeties Vodka. But he will. To Hugo's immense riches!" she said, taking another throat-scalding shot.

Then a pair of boys, school friends of Hugo's and Fergus's whose faces Alice recognized but whose names she did not know, grabbed Hugo in a tackle and pushed him toward the door. "Where are we going?" Hugo asked dreamily. "To Scarlett Moore's room," the handsomer of the two boys, whose name Alice thought might be Jack, replied. "Apparently he's got Snow White in there."

Alice had a pretty good idea of who Snow White was. So, it appeared, did Charlie. They both sprang across Hugo's room and tried to block the boys' path to the door. But it was too late. The boys were quick, and when they returned five minutes later, it was to report, in excited voices, that "Snow White" had been discovered in Fergus's bed.

Initially, Hugo reported that she'd been semi-clothed, and they'd only been kissing. Later, the boys who had been with Hugo had managed to convince him and everyone else at the afterparty that Pen had in fact been fully naked, straddling Fergus on the bed. This had become the official version of events, despite Alice's and Charlie's protests. Jo, whose voice might have carried more weight with this set, had slipped away from the reeling ball without saying goodbye, as had become her standard practice. The more Pen's friends had argued that the story was impossible, or at least exceptionally unlikely, the more those who hardly knew her had wanted to believe it had happened, and the more embellishments they'd added. Alice had tried confronting Hugo, furious that he had not shown more loyalty to Pen after all the time they had spent together, but Hugo, two-thirds of a bottle of cinnamon heart vodka and at least one pill into his Christmas vacation, had only laughed his easy laugh and said, "Kissing or shagging, what's the difference? They're just winding her up."

Alice did not tell Pen about the rumor, which at that very moment was flying between breakfast tables at the John McIntyre Centre like an airborne virus. New gossip, Alice was certain, would cover it within days, like a fresh snowfall.

At the end of the night, Charlie had walked with Alice back to Baird House. She'd loved the sensation of the cold stone on the soles of her feet, and of Charlie's reassuring body nearly touching hers. Standing beside him in the elevator, she'd wanted to put her head on his shoulder. She'd wanted to tell him about Julian, that it had been a mistake, that she was ending it. She'd stopped herself, however, and she was glad of it now. She liked Charlie too much. She did not want his opinion of her, whatever it was, to change.

Now Alice looked at her friend's face in profile and wondered what had really happened with Fergus. Not feeling comfortable asking Pen outright was profoundly weird. How could they have created so many new roped-off areas in only a few short weeks? It was to be expected, Alice told herself. She knew her own behavior was largely to blame. She had not been as open with Pen as she usually was, which had made their old custom of debriefing and analyzing impossible. This had been fine, at first. Healthy, even. Alice hadn't had the energy for such conversations, between *Arcadia* rehearsals and Julian, and Pen had been busy with her Lennoxes. But as Julian had become increasingly possessive, and as Alice had watched Pen close in on herself like a turtle going into its shell, she had begun to miss the openness they had lost. Most of all, she had begun to miss her best friend.

It occurred to her, in a wave of hungover clarity, that she had been deliberately avoiding Pen in an attempt to prove something to herself. Alice, for the past few months, had not wanted to be constrained by Pen's restrictive code of conduct. She had wanted to feel her independence with every part of her body. She'd needed to know if she could manage alone. Now she knew that she could, and that she didn't want to.

She hated that, as they sat side by side on the bus, she could not tell Pen how hard it had been to breathe during the last few weeks of term, or how she'd itched to be rid of him. It was too late for such confidences. She didn't know where to start. She was glad to be going far away. She was bypassing the Toronto winter and meeting her family in Mexico, where she would lie on a beach chair between her mother and Eli at a resort on the Mayan Riviera, turning the color of gingerbread cookies while her dad stayed behind to "work." She was ready to plunge into the salt water and wash every trace of Julian off her skin and out of her hair.

The bus stopped. Alice and Pen together hauled Alice's overstuffed hockey bag from the luggage rack, and they clambered down into the diesel stench of the airport's drop-off area. Pen was traveling with nothing but a neat black suitcase that looked exactly like everyone else's neat black suitcase except for the yellow smiley face luggage tag affixed to one of the zippers. Alice had the same tag on her duffel; they'd bought them together on a class trip to Niagara Falls in grade seven. They stepped through the automatic doors of the departures terminal and looked for their separate airline counters. They hugged as if they might never see one another again.

28

Pen saw her dad right away and was slammed with a feeling of relief so powerful that she thought she might have to sit down in the middle of the arrivals ramp. He was reading a newspaper that was carefully folded so as not to get in anyone's line of sight. He gave her a warm hug. They didn't say much as he whisked her through the short-stay parking lot to his car, and they sped along the stretch of highway into Toronto.

There were many things she wanted to tell him, but none of them seemed right, somehow. By day, without the loosening effects of darkness, dinner, and a glass of wine, Ted mostly stuck to a narrow script with her, the way he did when he was talking to shareholders. The news was always a safe subject. She brought up Iraq—the US was considering sending more troops, but public opinion was against it—and helped herself to a butterscotch from the glove compartment.

"Your mother will be glad to see you," he finally said, pulling into the driveway.

When ferrying Pen to friends' houses, Ted had always waited for someone to come to the door before driving away. She'd always turned and waved before crossing any threshold. But from the day Pen and her mom had moved with the family dog into this other house, he'd stopped waiting. Maybe it was because she was older. More likely, she thought, he didn't want to see what he had left behind.

As soon as she got out of the car, he backed onto the narrow, one-way street. It was cold, but the pavement was dry; no snowbanks had yet collected along the curb.

The doorbell hardly had a chance to clang before her mother appeared. She looked healthy. Thin but not scrawny. Her dark hair was up in a chignon. She took Pen in her arms and held her close. They were the same height. They embraced for a long time.

Olive poked her silken head out from between Anna's knees, nearly toppling them both over, and began panting heavily. She was in between them, sandwiched in their hug, her fur smell mixing with Pen's mom's lavender soap. Pen felt as if she had been born prematurely and had somehow managed to return to the safety of the womb, where she wouldn't have to breathe for herself any longer. The dog was circling them, wagging her tail.

"Come inside, come inside," said Anna. "Oh my love, I'm so happy you're here."

❦

Anna pulled back to take a good look at her daughter, whom she had missed like a part of herself. Pen's haircut suited her. Her face was narrower and her green eyes brighter and more penetrating. The shadows under them looked deeper, too, but Anna tried not to let that worry her. It was normal not to sleep much as a student, she knew.

Anna Sinclair had once been a student herself, and her life was full of them. She taught French and comparative literature at the same university she had once attended. She had arrived on a scholarship at seventeen from Longlac, a former mining town a twenty-hour bus ride northwest of Toronto. When she had first emerged from the bus into the downtown throng of this strange city, the shock had felt interplanetary. Her foster mother, Marie-Helene, had warned her that Toronto held nothing but peril, greed, and hellfire; to Anna it was a Technicolor paradise. It was far from the small-windowed bungalow, from the Église de Saint-Jean-Baptiste, and she'd absorbed it thirstily, a desert plant under torrents of rain, great fat drops of newness to be taken in, made a part of herself. And so Anna understood, looking at her daughter on the doorstep, how strange it can be to come home.

The house Anna had moved into after leaving Ted was a slim, semi-detached Victorian only blocks from where she had first lived as an undergraduate. It was the neighborhood in which she felt most herself. She liked hearing student voices in the dark as they made their way home from the bars and restaurants on Bloor Street, and watching them glide around on their bicycles, still young enough to believe in their invincibility. They reminded her of a version of herself that she had lost for a while and then, slowly, beginning when Pen was small, built back up into existence.

Stepping out of her boots and into her mom's house, not her childhood home but an in-between place where they had started over, Pen thought that it had never before felt as much like her home as it did now, when it wasn't anymore, not technically. Anna had readied it for Christmas. The tree was up in the front room, and roasting smells came from the kitchen.

Just inside the front door, Pen sat down on the floor. She patted her lap for Olive, who plonked onto her knee. Pen had forgotten how clean her mom kept things. After Lee House, with its spongy wall-to-wall carpeting full of fermenting secrets, her mother's cozy, well-cared-for space felt like a luxury hotel. But while part of what people pay for in a hotel is its neutrality, every chair and plate in this house was freighted with memories. Anna was not a wasteful person and had not seen the point in getting new things. The present was like a dust sheet covering the heavy shapes of the past.

"I'm making that cauliflower dish you like," she said. "I'm sure your clock is all messed up, but I figured you'd be hungry at some point. You're dying for a bath, aren't you. Go up and run one and come down whenever you're ready."

Pen's room was still her room, and she half expected to encounter herself and Alice, aged sixteen, sprawled on the floor eating Cool Ranch Doritos while running lines for the school theater production of *The Crucible*.

There was a vase of chrysanthemums and a stack of novels on the bedside table. The flowers were a private joke, a reference to a remark Tilda had once made, on entering the old house and seeing a modest bouquet of corner store flowers in a vase. "*Chrysanthemums*, Anna?" Ten-year-old Pen, who had proudly bought them with her allowance (mums for her mum), had nearly crumpled under her grandmother's disdain, until she had seen the frozen laugh on Anna's face. Since Tilda's death they bought each other the flowers as a sort of tribute.

Pen chose one of her old CDs from the stack on the dresser: a Destiny's Child mix that Alice had burned for her in middle school. She turned it up and went into the bathroom. The soaps and lotions in the cupboard were several years old. She opened one of the tubs—WHIPPED VANILLA said the label—and inhaled its cloying, melted ice cream smell. She and Alice used to roll down their knee socks and rub it into their bare shins by the handful while watching after-school sitcoms. Sometimes at night Pen would feel an itch in her skin that no amount of lotion could soothe, and would scratch at herself until she bled, digging little pits into her legs, and wearing tights to school in June.

After her bath she wrapped herself in a large towel and flopped onto the bed. The pillows were puffy under her head, and for a moment she was tugged under by sleep. It was past midnight in Scotland, and she'd hardly slept the previous night. But she was home. She roused herself and dressed in a pair of oversized flannel pajamas from the bottom drawer of her dresser. She found her old slippers in the closet and padded down to the kitchen.

Anna was at the island, struggling with the chronically unreliable corkscrew. Pen, who looked about eight in her old pajamas and elephant slippers, took the bottle of white wine from her, and uncorked it.

"I'm not going to ask how you got so good at that," Anna said, taking the bottle back and pouring two glasses. She picked up a tray of crackers and cheese and brought it to the couch, where she placed it atop a stack of books on the coffee table. She settled into a corner of the sofa and looked at her daughter.

Sitting on the living room couch, surrounded by familiar comforts, with roasting smells in the air and her mother's sensitive eyes on her, Pen began to talk. She was not in the habit of confiding in her mom about boys, but that was mostly because there had never been anything much to say. In high school she had had boyfriends, sure, in the sense of someone to kiss at the movies on a Friday night, but she had never felt anything for them that resembled what she felt for Sasha, or even for Fergus. And so, loosened by her mother's love and the warm fire and the jet lag, she began to speak the thoughts she'd been keeping to herself. She started with how she had made her way to a beautiful place called Stonehaven to stay with the family of an old friend of her dad's, Elliot Lennox.

As Anna listened, she tried to keep her feelings from showing on her face. After a while it became too difficult. She stood and gestured for Pen to join her at the dinner table.

Once they moved to the table, Pen could quickly tell from her mother's eyes, which seemed to be scanning the room for an emergency exit, that she should not continue her story. Whether it was the Lennoxes themselves Anna found distasteful—she had little patience for grandeur, and the double whammy of aristocracy and fame would make them suspect—or their connection to her dad, Pen did not know. She cut her story short and, swallowing her disappointment, steered the conversation toward Proust. They remained in the safer waters of fiction, in the narrator's memories of his childhood in Combray, through herbal tea and raspberry tart.

"I put some books I think you'll enjoy by the bed," Anna said when she came up to kiss Pen good night. "Sleep for as long as you can."

Pen woke up feeling refreshed. Her clock radio said 6:30 a.m. She propped herself up on pillows and shifted the stack of books into her lap. She looked at the covers and selected a Gallimard edition with a strange title.

Two hours later, Pen was roused from the story by the smell of French toast. She closed the page on her finger and listened for the hiss of battered bread in the pan. Still in pajamas, she went down, bringing the book with her. It was a Sunday. She had nowhere to be until dinnertime, when her dad was expecting her. It was her intention to read all morning, and possibly all day.

"Sleep well?" Her mother turned from the stove, spatula in hand, to kiss her. The coffee pot was full. Pen found her bowl-sized mug in its usual cupboard. Olive was splayed on her back in her bed by the kitchen table, her paws in the air, snoring.

"Like a corpse. Thanks for the flowers," Pen said. "And the books. I started reading the elegant porcupine one."

"The what?" Her mom noticed the book on the counter. "Oh— hedgehog, love."

"Right, hedgehog." Pen drank her coffee and set the table.

They took their usual spots. Pen could feel tension building in her mother's body. She thought it must be because Pen was having dinner at her dad's that evening. Her parents tried to conceal their still-open wounds from her, but she could sense the effort it took. She was fairly certain it was worse when she was around to remind them of each other. She concentrated on her breakfast, closing off part of her mind to blunt the impact of whatever her mother was feeling. She drowned her plate in dark, treacly maple syrup. It was the same jug that had been in the fridge when she'd left. Of course it was. Her mom didn't go through half a liter of maple syrup in four months. This conjured a ridiculous image of Anna drinking maple syrup from the bottle. Pen smiled. That was probably how Fergus thought she was spending her holiday. She should text him when she went back upstairs. She hoped he wasn't embarrassed by what had happened, or not happened, between them. She knew he would do anything to avoid seeming fazed, but she also knew that he was more sensitive than he would ever let on. Had she tried to make herself feel something for him in part to lessen the blow of Sasha's rejection? It was an unsettling question because she knew she had.

"I'm sorry I was evasive on the subject of the Lennoxes last night," said Anna. Pen looked up. She often had the sense that her thoughts could be penetrated by an acute enough intelligence, and her mom's certainly counted.

"Hearing that name again brought me back to a difficult time. I wasn't quite ready to go back there," Anna continued.

"Don't feel like you have to go there now," said Pen. Based on the look on her mom's face, she was not at all sure she wanted to hear whatever was coming. She yearned to return to the safe fictional world of her book.

Anna considered her daughter again. Yes, Pen's face had lost some of the softness of girlhood. She was sharper-looking now, even in those ridiculous pajamas. The inflection of her speech had also changed, ever so slightly. There was no trace of an accent, but she emphasized different words than she had just a few months ago. It galled Anna to remember how Ted had clung to those acquired speech patterns, to the vocabulary he had picked up, even once he had been back for years. As if he were afraid that if his voice became fully Canadian again, whatever had happened there would no longer count for anything. It would be as if he had never gone at all. Pen was like him, Anna thought. She had the same ability to compartmentalize, to smile in that polite way, even when something painful was roiling beneath the surface. Anna tried to observe this without bitterness. It was she, after all, who had married him.

Pen could feel her mom watching her, and wondering how much of an adult she really was. Probably, she knew exactly.

"I believe you already know that your father asked me to marry him the summer before he went to London for graduate school," Anna began.

Pen waited for more, trying to stop her mind from drawing hasty conclusions.

"We had been seeing one another for just over a year by then. I was still a student, and he was working at Winter Corp. His program in London took one year. We didn't plan to 'settle down,' as people called it then, until the following summer, when he was due to return. I was working on my master's at that time, and had plenty to keep me occupied. Phone calls were too expensive, but we wrote. I sent him long letters about my friends, my research, my job at the library, and he sent me ironic postcards. I wasn't entirely sure he would come back. But he did, exactly when he'd said he would. We were married that summer. It sounds strange, now. But it was not unusual, in those days, to marry while you were still in university."

Anna brought her mug to her lips. It was empty. She picked up her water glass. Pen poured more coffee from the pot into both of their mugs. She wondered if her mother's foster parents had been at the wedding. Pen had met Marie-Helene only once, as a child, when Anna had bundled her into the car and made the long drive to Longlac for Easter. She couldn't remember much from that visit except for the waxy smell of the church, the fact that there had still been a foot of snow on the ground, and a look of scalding rage that had flashed across Anna's face in response to something Marie-Helene had said or done. She'd always known, although Anna had never said so explicitly, that Gregory had been nicer. Gregory had died before Pen was born, but his name made her mom smile.

"The first time it happened—the first time I had a miscarriage, I mean," Anna clarified, rushing past the word, "we blamed ourselves. We had been on our honeymoon. Riding bicycles in the South of France, up and down hills, and I was sure I had caused it. After that, I vowed to be more careful. We stopped trying for a year. I finished my master's and was accepted into a doctorate program, and your father took on more responsibility at Winter Corp, as his family had always intended. He expanded all across Europe, which Edward Senior, from whose mind the war never receded for as long as I knew him, found difficult. Your father carried on, though, traveling constantly, meeting prospective customers, and buying new equipment. He and your grandfather had something of a silent falling-out, but the company was booming. Your grandmother was in raptures, and your father seemed in his element."

She drew a breath. Pen did not interrupt.

"It was while I was pregnant for the second time that Gregory died. Complications from a surgery I hadn't known he was having. Not saying goodbye was hard."

Anna was holding her voice steady. Pen brought her the box of tissues from the desk. She smiled and twisted one between her fingers.

"I went to Longlac for the funeral. It was easy enough to assume that the second miscarriage had to do with the shock of Gregory's death. After that my doctor advised me to remove all stress from my life, good and bad. I decided to put my doctorate on hold for a while. I gave up my job at the library, which I had loved. I stopped seeing friends. My closest friend, Renée, fell in love with an Australian man and moved to Sydney, and the others sort of faded into their own lives. It was a lonely time. The third was the worst. I carried for twenty weeks, long enough to find out it was a boy. We had chosen a name: Elliot. After that, we stopped trying for a while."

Anna paused, collecting herself. Pen felt tears sting her eyes. She had known none of this.

"Your grandmother did not mean to add to my guilt. But in those days, there was an unspoken understanding that if a woman couldn't get pregnant, or, worse, if she couldn't stay that way, it was because somewhere deep inside of her she didn't want to be a mother. I knew Tilda believed that about me. She was aware that my childhood had been less than idyllic, that my birth mother had been 'unfit,' as they say, and that my relationship with Marie-Helene was strained. She assumed, I think, that it made me ambivalent about wanting children of my own. But it was the opposite. I wanted a family more than anything else in the world. I yearned for you with my whole heart.

"Between your father's success, which allowed him to dress up and go out into the world as if nothing were wrong, and my misery, from which

I allowed myself no distraction, the connection we'd had was hard to find, some days. I reached a low point."

Pen, who had been staring at the sticky pool of maple syrup on her plate, stood up and draped her arms around her mother's shoulders from behind her chair.

"But we hadn't given up," said Anna, speaking faster now, "not entirely. Eventually I sought help from a specialist, which your father had initially opposed but finally, thank heavens, decided to embrace. A few years later, along came the greatest joy I've ever known. You were—and are—the love of our lives."

Pen rested her chin in her mother's warm neck. "I'm sorry," she said.

Anna closed her eyes and held on to her daughter's cold hands, accepting the embrace. And then she realized that she hadn't explained how the Lennoxes factored into any of this. She had planned to tell Pen more, but now it seemed like too much all at once.

"Thank you, my love, and I'm sorry to drop all this on you. Both your father and I have come a long way since then. It was in part to remember how far we'd come that we gave you that name. And in part because it sounds pretty, Penelope Elliot. Don't you think?"

"Very pretty." Pen hugged her mother tightly. Then she picked up their plates and brought them into the kitchen. Pen had little concept of what a miscarriage entailed. She couldn't have pictured the volume of blood, the clots of tissue, the pain, or the grief, but she had seen enough in her mom's eyes to understand that the low point her mother had glossed over was when the string between her parents had snapped. What had happened later would only have been a delayed effect of that crisis, an effect delayed by Pen herself, by her childhood, which she had long suspected had been a show. Now she knew it had been a show they had put on not only for her, but for themselves.

Pen felt chastened. Her desire to draw a fat black arrow between her dad's onetime best friend and her parents' divorce now looked hopelessly childish. Any number of things could have made the Lennoxes a sore subject. Maybe Ted had tried harder than he'd let on to stay in touch, and Elliot had dropped the ball—maybe his kindness to Pen was an apology of sorts, and Christina had merely emailed Ted to say, "Hi old friend, you'll never guess who turned up." Maybe the continued animosity between her parents was a natural result of layer upon layer of hurt, and of their sadness that they had not been able to find a better kind of love for one another.

They finished washing up. Pen's mother reached for Olive's leash.

"Up and at 'em, you sweet girl," said Anna, trying for a new tone. She tickled the dog's belly with her big toe. Olive grinned in her sleep, and then harrumphed and opened one eye. "Yes you, I'm talking to you." Anna was kneeling now, affixing the leash to her collar. "It's time to wake up and smell some pee. Come on!"

When they got home, rosy from the bright cold and in a very different mood, Pen ran upstairs to shower and unpack. Her phone was dead. She found an adapter in the random electronics drawer at the bottom of her nightstand and set it to charge. When she came out of the shower, it was lit up with messages. The first three were from Vodafone, welcoming her to Canada and warning her about roaming fees. She scrolled down.

ALICE: HOLA!! HOW'S THE T DOT??

JO S-M (1/2): Thank you for your sweet text. Excessively stinky of you not to have said goodbye in person but you're absolved.

(2/2): All fine and ultra-boring here. Shall we switch to email to conserve funds? Much love x x x x

FERRGUS S-M: Hello Penguin, have a lovely time in
Snowyankshire. Try not to revert to all your pagan habits. X

Pen checked to see if she had missed any. She hadn't. She answered
each of her friends, smiling to herself, and then turned the phone off and
went downstairs to read.

29

The next time Pen turned on her phone it was Christmas Eve. It was late afternoon, and already dark out. She was sitting on her bedroom floor surrounded by spools of ribbon and stacks of recycled tissue paper, half watching an old Christmas movie while she wrapped. There was a plate of her mom's shortbread beside her, and her mug was full of milky Earl Grey. She would have to get dressed soon to go to the same party they went to every year, one she always looked forward to, with the same group of her mother's friends she had known since infancy. But for the moment, she was alone.

The past week had been a marathon of festive errands and visits. Pen had spent two evenings at her dad's new condo on the fortieth floor of a downtown building, staring through the wall of windows at thousands of scurrying pedestrians and rows of traffic-clogged cars glowing red and white down below.

It was his first real home since the divorce. When her parents had first separated, Ted had temporarily moved into his mother's house. She had asked him to, and he had never, as far as Pen knew, let Tilda down. When Pen was fifteen, Tilda had been transferred into a luxurious retirement home. Ted had taken a temporary apartment nearby. It was practical, he said. Ted traveled too much to live anywhere with a driveway that needed shoveling.

The sleek condo building into which he had just moved bore no resemblance to the home they had once shared. Unlike her mother, her dad had taken almost nothing from their family house, only books; none of his art or furnishings were familiar to her. Had this been his taste all along? she wondered.

The man across the table, handling boxes of Thai takeout, was as impossible to reach as the miniature people on the sidewalk below doing last-minute Christmas shopping. She had tried. She had asked him pointed questions. Questions about the miscarriages, which he had expertly deflected, with only a twitch of the jaw giving him away. "Yes, that was a difficult time for your mother." Questions about Christina—"A friend," he insisted, looking amused. "Never more"—and about whether they had been in touch this whole time—"Of course not!"

Her last questions of the night were about Lennox and her middle name, and he had answered them with a bit more candor, or so Pen thought. "I still miss him," he said, looking tired. "He was a close friend for many years. The closest I've had." This strengthened her most recent line of thinking and cast the tribute of her name into a different light. "Your mother and I had agreed on the name years before, when it looked like we were going to have a boy. And then when you came, I don't know. It sounded right. It still does."

It was not until Pen used the bathroom, and noticed the stack of embroidered hand towels beside a decorative jar containing fragrance sticks that made the room smell like a department store, that she realized that Ted probably did not live alone in his island in the sky. She opened the cupboard above the sink. Inside, she found three tubes of lipstick, all of them variations on a bright orangey-pink. Pen did not ask Ted any more pointed questions after that. She was happy he wasn't alone. For once, she did not want to know more, or not right away.

Now that she had a moment of solitude, her mind went straight back to the Lennox house. Being so far away, and releasing them from her parents' narrative, had unlocked the part of her that remained fixated on Sasha. During the whirl of holiday socializing, while Pen had smiled until her cheeks hurt and talked of how lovely the architecture was in Edinburgh—yes, even under a perpetually gray sky—part of her mind had been imagining what Sasha was doing. It would be nine there, she thought now. They would be at the dinner table. George would be there with Danny, if he was still awake, and Freddie, and Danny's dad Rosh, and probably the elusive Margot, too. Christina would be cooking an elaborate feast, a goose, maybe, or venison shot by the bloodthirsty neighbors.

The truth was that she missed them. And they had done nothing unfair by her. They had shown her immense kindness. From her current vantage point, nested among home comforts, it seemed wrongheaded to write them off merely on the charge that they were too good at ignoring inclement weather and unsavory subjects. They were British, after all. A stranger had appeared in the middle of a family crisis and begun "ferreting around," as Freddie had correctly diagnosed; how was it possible that she had viewed herself as the wronged party? Pen was beginning to understand how little she knew. Her parents and Christina and Lennox had decades on her; they had each withstood losses that she could not even imagine. What was she doing inventing reasons to feel slighted by them?

As for Sasha, did she really expect him to sit at home every night of his final year of university, pining for some first year? How silly she had been. It didn't matter whether what he felt for her was equal to what she felt for him. What mattered was that he, and he alone, had awakened in her a powerful and unfamiliar sensation that she did not want to ignore any longer. Wasn't it worth continuing to talk to him, even if it did lead to further disappointment? Wasn't that the point of this time in her life, to make these kinds of mistakes and learn from them, to educate herself? She held down the power button on her phone until the screen lit up.

The first message was from Alice, sent the day before: **Hola guapa, estoy borracha en la playa. Como estas? I missyou.**

The next name she saw sped up her heart.

> **GEORGE LENNOX (1/2): Merry Christmas! Hope you're well. Danny sends kisses. Come and see us soon. Xx**

It was accompanied by a grainy picture of Danny in a tuxedo. He was smiling on someone's knee, and Pen could just make out a puddle of drool on his chin. She was putting off closing the picture. She had only been through three messages; there were four left.

> **FERGUS S-M: Happy Chrimbo S. Y. Hope the ice fishing was good today. X**

Smiling, she scrolled on. The following message made her heart soar.

> **+447895733485 (1/2): You're never online, so I asked for your number from George. I can only guess that you have either a) lost your computer, b) been pecked to death by**
>
> **(2/2): a vengeful French lark, or c) fallen so deeply in love with the not-nice boyfriend that you've forgotten about us. As a Christmas present, please tell me which?**

She read his messages several times and saved him as a contact, typing in his full name. Then she remembered there was one more.

CHET (EXCELLENT SHAG): Merry Christmas!! Already the 25th in Delhi. It turns out well don't worry. Xx

This made her laugh. She had forgotten that Chet had keyed his number into her phone late on her first night at Talmòrach. She answered Alice, then George, then Fergus, then Chet. She got dressed for the party. Now it was a quarter to ten for them. They might be in the living room in front of the fireplace, unwrapping presents, a special bottle sitting open on one of the book-strewn end tables. Lennox would be sipping his whisky.

Pen read Sasha's text one last time and pressed reply. d) none of the above, she wrote. I hope Santa has put you on his 'nice guy' list by mistake.

She straightened the wrapping things and left them in the corner to finish after the party. She went to the closet to find a handbag and some shoes. When she came out, her phone was lit up.

SASHA LENNOX: It seems he has, as I've just opened the only thing I wanted. Merry Christmas Pen. I miss your twisted mind. X

She sat down on the bed, letting wave after wave of happiness wash over her. She drifted downstairs in an intoxicating cloud of hope.

Anna ignored Pen's protests and zipped a bar of dark chocolate into the outside pocket of her carry-on. "I know you say you like plane food, which is taking agreeableness to a new level—but something good to find in the middle of the night won't kill you."

She surveyed the trim black suitcase with its dangling smiley face, looking for somewhere to put her final offering. Her daughter's asceticism never ceased to amaze her. Pen's mood had changed on Christmas Eve. Whatever lugubrious thought she'd been torturing herself with for her first few days home had evaporated just before the party. Anna could see that her daughter was in love, but she had the delicacy not to ask with whom. Evidently, it was someone back in Edinburgh; she couldn't get on the plane soon enough. Anna was glad. That was as it should be.

"Is this really all you're bringing? You're such a Franciscan. Do you have room for one more small item?"

"Mom, your shortbread is the best, but I don't think I can handle another—"

"Not that." Anna handed her a hardback journal with an elastic closure. "I realize my account from the other morning was a bit limp. It's been so long since I've thought about those days, mostly because I don't especially want to. This is my journal from that time. I don't think I can reach the person I was at your age very well anymore. If some part of her is preserved anywhere, it's in there. Probably the most self-indulgent part. I haven't reread it, I warn you."

Pen tucked the journal into her bag, grateful to have it and knowing that she was not going to read it any time soon. She understood enough, now, of what had gone wrong between her parents that she could stop picking at it. She could respect what remained of their privacy. Some things, she was learning, are none of a daughter's business.

Her middle name was no longer a puzzle that needed solving. She was named for the ghost of a brother who had never been, and he had been named for the ghost of a friendship. Many of us are saddled with death at birth in this way; it is not a good excuse to get stuck in the past. Now that she was talking to Sasha again, Pen was becoming increasingly interested in the present, and in the future.

Excited as she was to get back to Edinburgh—to be in the same country as him again—Pen hated saying goodbye to her mom. "Are you going to be okay?" she asked for the umpteenth time. It felt insincere to keep asking when there wasn't much she could do if the answer was no—forfeit the term?—but the question kept leaving her mouth.

"I'm the one who is supposed to be asking you that," Anna said, laughing. "Of course I am. And it's just a few months. It'll fly. Speaking of which." She tapped her watch. "I think I can hear your father's car."

Pen hugged and kissed her mom one more time.

"Be good," Anna said. "Actually—don't. You're too good already. Maybe see if you can be bad for a change."

Pen laughed to hide her tears and turned to go. She opened the door a crack and jumped. Her dad was standing on the doorstep. She looked back at her mom to give her a signal, but Anna had approached the doorway.

"Hello, Ted," she said with a strange smile on her face.

"Hello, Anna," said her dad with a formal type of casualness, like ironed jeans. Pen was impressed by the effort. And it certainly made parting easier: she couldn't wait to make it stop.

"OKAY, BYE!" she said too loudly, letting herself into the car's already-warm passenger seat.

"What was that?" she asked her dad when he'd taken his place at the wheel.

"What?" he asked, as if nothing awkward or out of the ordinary had taken place. "Your mother and I live in the same city, you know. We run into each other. It's all very congenial."

"Very congenial," repeated Pen.

30

Alice got back to Edinburgh on a Sunday morning of dazzling light. She stood under the sputtering, tepid shower and dressed all in white to show off her sun-darkened skin. Jo met her in front of Baird House just before lunchtime. They walked through Holyrood Park until they got to a stone archway marking the entrance to the medieval village of Duddingston.

On the other side stood a fourteenth-century inn, rumored to be the oldest pub in Scotland. Alice had been wanting to go since Charlie had told her about it, but somehow in the first term she hadn't found the time. Now she was determined to do these kinds of wholesome, first-year things. She would climb Arthur's Seat, visit the Dean Gallery, take detailed notes in lectures, and write sound essays. She would leave evening rehearsals with Neville glued to her side. When March came, she would be so mind-blowingly good as Thomasina that scouts from the Fringe Festival would beg her to be in their shows. And most of all she would not ever, not even once, let Julian find her alone.

A few mornings before the end of their vacation, Alice had been lolling in bed in the hotel room she shared with her brother while he took the world's longest shower. She had her laptop open and was scrolling through photos Julian was tagged in on Facebook when she came across one that made her slam the computer shut.

Alice had never seen a picture of Emily Sachs before, nor had she allowed herself much curiosity about what she might look like. It turned out she was petite and smiley, with round cheeks—and a round belly. In the picture, Julian was beside her, his arm protectively circling her shoulders, the two of them standing under a cheesy banner that said "It's a girl!"

Alice felt violent disgust. She had known he was married, but not that he was expecting a child. The idea made her retch. She banged on the bathroom door until Eli unlocked it in his towel and she rushed to the toilet bowl. "Are you hungover or pregnant," her brother asked as he left the bathroom, holding his nose. "Or both?"

An hour or so later, unable to wait, unwilling to call in case he was with his *pregnant wife*, Alice composed a text. It was short but clear. **We're finished. I think you know why.** She sent it.

His replies had come thick and fast, filling up her mailbox and voicemail, first pleading for an explanation and then, when she did not reply, a nasty blizzard of vitriol. She'd listened to a few and then started deleting them on arrival before finally switching off her phone.

The pub was made up of large adjoining rooms, each one glowing in the warmth of a well-fed fireplace. There were shelves full of books and games, and beside the U-shaped bar hung the Sunday newspapers on a row of wooden rods. Alice and Jo each ordered a pint of cider. They sipped them at the bar while waiting for a table in the dining room upstairs.

Alice had only slept for an hour or two on the plane, but she did not feel tired. On the walk over, Jo, who looked radiant and was clearly harboring a secret of some kind, had described how their father had made it his project over the break to try to teach Fergus to play rugby. "Poor Ferg, he really is more of a bleeder than a fighter," she'd concluded, unable to keep the joy from her voice.

"Too bad Pen's missing our homecoming luncheon," Jo now observed.

"She likes to book flights on airline rewards points with as many connections as possible, to remind herself she's a woman of the people," said Alice. "But she should be in by five-ish. We can bring her an early dinner to make up for it."

"What is it you have to tell me?" Jo asked. "It was naughty of you to tease me, and now I'm doubly annoyed to see how bronzed you are. You're eloping to Guadalajara, aren't you. Can I come? I'm very handy around the casa."

"I'm sorry. But I didn't want to explain over email. No, I'm not eloping. The opposite," said Alice.

"You're getting divorced?"

"No, stupid. But I do need to get rid of somebody."

"*Rid* rid? That sounds dark."

"Just one rid. Please stop looking like that. I'm trying to tell you something serious."

Jo dropped the act. "Julian?"

Alice was surprised. "How did you know?"

"It's not exactly a case for Miss Marple. The whole tutorial knows he's bloody obsessed with you. And it's been clear for some time that you have . . . reciprocal feelings. It felt like we were all extras in a blue movie for a while there. Some of us had a contest going to come up with the best name for it. I suggested Lick My Kant, which I still think is quite good."

"Gross," said Alice. "Does Pen know?"

"Of course Pen knows. She told me not to get involved. She said you wouldn't be keeping it a secret if you wanted our opinion, and that you certainly wouldn't want hers, which I can appreciate because she does have a puritanical streak, or she did, I should say . . . Anyway, she said you can be trusted to know what's best for you. I wanted to at least ask you about it. He seems like such a grasping Gollum type. But she told me not to. Said you'd made some kind of pact not to meddle in each other's affairs. Quite sweet."

Alice had forgotten about the promise they'd made almost a year ago. She was touched by Pen's faith in her.

"What do you mean she *did* have a puritanical streak?" she asked. "What did Fergus tell you?"

"He refuses to confirm or deny what the others are saying. But he was sulking all break when he wasn't being bludgeoned by a rugby ball. I know he acts like a callous twat, but Fergus is surprisingly human."

"What are the others saying?"

"Oh, nothing important. Or nothing as important as your metatextual quagmire, anyhow. How are you going to shake your Septimus?"

"Jo. What are they saying about Pen?"

"I'll spare you the details, but the take-home message is that beneath her modest veil, our very own Prudent Penelope is a minxy sex bomb. There are the stories from the night of the reeling ball, obviously, with even Hugo claiming that he walked in on some pretty out-there fetish behavior. Charlie has tried to shut them up, but Hugo keeps tittering and saying sex is beautiful, it's nothing to be ashamed of. A few from that group are saying Pen's been trying to have it on with them for months, undressing them with her come-hither eyes from across the library and so on. And apparently Sasha Lennox is back in the mix. We ran into his flatmate Chet at a house party on New Year's. He told Ferg that Pen and Sasha are messaging day and night. Ferg won't talk about it, but I can see he's gutted."

Alice was furious. Not at Jo, who was too loyal to her brother to see any of this clearly, but at the jerks who were spreading lies about Pen.

"*Come-hither* eyes?! Fetish behavior? Who do these fuckers think they are? They probably just got in the way of her eyeline while she was thinking about Zola. Why does everyone have to assume it's always about sex?" Alice's voice was becoming loud.

"Isn't it, usually?"

"Not for Pen."

Jo considered this.

"But I know the look they're talking about. She does kind of eye-laser people, doesn't she?"

"That's just what her eyes look like when she's paying attention!" Alice was yelling, and people were turning around. She lowered her voice. "She gives me that look all the time, and she's sure as hell not trying to seduce me. Jo, Pen is not a *minxy sex bomb*. She did not have sex with Fergus or with anyone else. I can tell you that with absolute certainty."

"What?"

"Yes."

"She's——"

"Yes."

"Why?"

"I don't fucking know, but she is, so can you please tell all these Eton messes with their pink pants to just fuck off and stop spreading lies about her?" Alice was shouting again. She took a deep breath.

"Trousers."

"Fine."

"Because pants are—"

"OKAY. Underpants. I know. JESUS." Jo found Alice's hand and placed hers on top of it.

"Would you get this riled up to defend my honor, too?"

"Yes, I would." Alice was calming down.

The waiter came to tell them their table was ready. They followed him upstairs and ordered right away. When their shared starter arrived, Alice tried changing the subject.

"What about you? Did you meet anyone over the break?"

Jo let out an unnatural laugh.

"Me? My only fetish behavior was sitting by the fire playing Patience and eating Rich Teas." Jo forked smoked salmon onto her side plate, avoiding eye contact. "Can we talk about your torrid affair with our philosophy tutor now?" She took a bite.

Alice found Jo's eyes. "Josephine Scarlett Moore. I don't actually know your middle name, which is kind of messed up. But I just told you my secret, and then I told you Pen's. Legally speaking, it's your turn."

"Henrietta."

"That's a terrible middle name."

"I know."

"But it's not what I'm asking for."

"I know."

Alice ordered another round of drinks and waited.

"Remember how I told you Sylvia Clarke is here?" Jo began, her mouth twitching at the corners when she said the name.

Alice nodded.

"And remember when I had an essay due and had to spend the night in the bunker instead of going to your Canadian Thanksgiving do-lally?" Jo continued. Alice remembered. She and Pen had tried to arrange a small

Thanksgiving dinner, but no one had been available, so they had eaten turkey sandwiches in Alice's room and shared a bottle of Ocean Spray cranberry cocktail.

"Well thank God for my procrastinating," Jo continued.

It turned out Sylvia had also been in the bunker on a deadline. They happened to take a break at the same time and, smoking in front of the building, had made small talk. There had been what Jo described as a charge between them, and Jo had not been able to tell whether it was the memory of what had happened all those years ago, or something else.

During a second break two hours later, this one planned, Sylvia had found a quiet place for them to sit. It had been just the two of them, then, and getting close to midnight. As they'd sat side by side with their backs against the cold concrete, Jo had felt Sylvia move her hand toward Jo's. They'd sat there, just the tips of their fingers touching for a while.

On the third break, they'd gone to the same place, and Sylvia had lain her head on Jo's shoulder. It had felt like an admission, Jo said, of what they had been through. After they had both printed their essays, at around three in the morning, they had walked back to Pollock Halls together.

At Chapel Street, protected by the darkness, Jo had taken Sylvia's hand. They'd held hands for a few blocks, and then Sylvia had pulled her under a stone archway on Buccleuch Street and kissed her. Jo had been surprised and a bit afraid of what might happen, but euphoric, too. They had made out for a long time. When they had finally reached Chancellors Court, Sylvia's residence building, an hour later, they had kissed chastely on the cheek. Jo had not been able to sleep that night. Since then, they'd been "seeing one another discreetly," Jo said. Sylvia was not yet ready to tell anyone, and Jo respected her wish to keep whatever was happening between them to themselves.

"We both told our parents we had to come back early to study," Jo said, looking happy. Alice could find no words. She put her arms around Jo and hugged her. "Right," said Jo finally. "Time to pretend this conversation never happened."

Downstairs, they found Fergus and Hugo drinking pints at a big table by the main fireplace. Hugo stood up. He pulled out the chair beside him and gestured for Fergus, who was in it, to move so Alice could sit beside him. She remained standing.

"You're looking well, Alice. Where's your smaller, saucier half?" Hugo asked, moving in to kiss Alice on the cheek. Alice stepped back so that he stumbled forward a bit.

"Not here yet, in case you want to talk a bit more shit," she said, her voice cold. "I've heard the most creative stories about the night of the reeling ball. Fergus, maybe you can tell me what *really* went down?"

Alice, to whom Pen had not told the whole story, had no idea what effect this choice of words would have on Fergus. Mottled patches crept up his throat.

"I'll tell you when you're older," he said.

"I look forward to it," said Alice, and she turned to go. Jo followed.

Dusk had fallen by the time Alice and Jo crossed the courtyard and let themselves in the revolving door of Lee House. Alice, ebullient from Jo's revelation, the desire to see her best friend, and her missed night's sleep, leaped up the stairs, clutching the paper bag containing Pen's dinner and a bottle of the JMC store's finest five-pound wine.

The news of Pen's supposed exploits had evidently reached her neighbors: her name tag had been revised in thick black marker. It now read: "Penis Winters," with a small illustration.

"Penis? Oh Penis!! Are you in there?" they called, banging on the door.

Pen opened the door and, in an uncharacteristically spontaneous gesture, threw her arms around them. "I'm so happy to see you," she said into Alice's hair. She pulled them into her room. "Apparently, I'm Lady Chatterley."

When she'd first come back and seen her defaced name tag, Pen had felt a kind of prickly effervescence in the pit of her stomach. She had understood, all at once, how little control she had over what people thought of her. The revelation was liberating. Why, if it wasn't up to her anyway, had she spent the last eighteen years playing by such a confining set of rules?

"Pleased to meet you, Lady Chatterley. I'm Orlando," said Jo, curtsying.

"Fun! Who am I?" asked Alice.

"Lydia Bennett," said Jo.

Alice snatched Pen's pillow from the bed and threw it at her.

"Yum. Thank you for this!" said Pen, opening up the fish and chips they had brought her and eating a fry.

"I hope you had a splendid holiday and a smooth crossing and whatnot, but can you please tell me immediately what happened between you and Ferg?" Jo asked Pen as she opened the wine. "Because he refuses."

"I think he discovered I'm better in theory than in practice," Pen replied carefully.

"I very much doubt that," said Jo. "And is it true about Sasha?"

Pen looked at Jo. "What about Sasha?"

"Only that you've been talking online nonstop and probably having lots of internet sex," Jo replied, taking a swig of wine.

Pen felt a clasp of guilt. She looked down, ashamed. She could tell that Jo was trying to make light of the situation, and to view it as Pen's friend, not only as Fergus's twin. Fergus had shown more of himself to her than he showed to most people. Pen had known this, had encouraged it, and then had repaid his trust by resuming her crush on Sasha without a second thought. If he retreated back into character, if he'd joined in on spreading gleeful rumors about her, she could not entirely blame him.

Pen was blushing. "We *have* been talking. But only talking," she said. She almost added "for now," but held back.

Alice noticed with a sting that Pen did not even glance her way once during this exchange. She sat on Pen's desk, opened her window, and lit a cigarette. She stared at her friend, willing her to say more. But Jo spoke first.

"The suitors are piling up, Penelope," she said. "You'd better start weaving and unweaving a shroud, or they'll eat your meat and drink your wine."

"Okay, Orlando, no more wine for you," said Alice, taking the bottle.

"Something is rotten in the state of Ithaca!" murmured Jo, flopping onto Pen's bed.

"We've been drinking since lunch," explained Alice apologetically, looking closely at Pen. She was still flushed from the mention of Sasha, and her eyes were bright with something. Excitement, maybe, or hope. Alice saw that her suitcase was still standing in the corner. "You haven't unpacked," she observed, half teasing.

"Have you?" Pen was smiling. They both knew that Pen liked to unpack within minutes of walking through the door, setting everything in its correct place as if reestablishing the conditions of reality, and that Alice sometimes put the chore off for weeks, until she couldn't find something important and had to dump all her duffel bag's balled-up contents onto the floor.

They had a lot to talk about, but this wasn't the time. They all needed sleep.

When Alice cut across to her own building the air was damp and cold, but the sky was still unusually clear, and the buildings of Pollock Halls were lit by a full moon.

She fell into her unmade bed and then into a dream. She and Pen were in Mexico together. They'd signed up for one of those day trips where you get your picture taken swimming with dolphins. It wasn't until they were already underwater that Alice realized the dolphins were not dolphins at all, but sharks. Pen swam away at speed; she'd always been a fast swimmer. Alice's legs felt heavy and crumbly, like they were made of wet sand, and her arms rotated in the water without moving her forward. She saw Pen turn around to look over her shoulder. Salt burned her sinuses, and she woke up gasping for air.

31

The next morning, Fergus sat at Flossie's table with his back to the cafeteria's entrance, his long legs outstretched in a contrived show of ease. Jo swatted him upside the head on her way past. He smiled in the direction of Alice, Pen, and Jo as if he couldn't quite place them. Hugo arrived, looked confused for a moment, and then pulled up a chair next to Flossie.

A few minutes later, Charlie entered looking like he had just stepped out of a commercial for laundry detergent. Even his sneakers were bright white. He put his tray beside Pen's without a moment's hesitation.

"Charlie, what happened to your shoes?" she asked.

"Mum binned the good ones," he said sheepishly. "I tried to rescue them, but she'd buried them under coffee grinds and something cabbagey. Cunning lady, she is. Gave me these new ones for Christmas to make up for it. I'll need to do a few laps up and down Arthur's Seat to break them in," he said.

Alice had forgotten what his r's sounded like. "Can I come?" she asked. His dark eyes met hers. His expression changed almost imperceptibly, and only for a moment. It made her stomach drop. "I haven't been up there yet," she added as casually as she could manage. What was happening to her? This was Charlie.

"Of course," he said.

Pen and Jo ate their porridge, politely ignoring them.

Later, during a break between lectures, a glacial wind pressed against Alice as she crossed the raised platform from the George Square Theatre to the David Hume Tower. She went down the stairs to the close, neon-lit basement, where neither air nor natural light circulated, and which she knew Julian avoided. Around the corner from the ladies' room was the film lab. It was a poky, pitch-black room and, she thought, a good place to hide during the seventy-minute gap before her next class. There was an anteroom where a clerk would find you the film you were looking for, and on the other side of a soundproofed door was a square-shaped lab with desks lining the perimeter, each bearing a small television and pair of headphones, with chairs facing the walls. Alice planned to position herself in front of a screen and sink into an Almodóvar film for an hour or so.

Only, when she got to the clerk's desk, a folded piece of paper stood, tentlike, on top of the sign-in sheet. On it was scrawled in pencil: *Be right back* ☺. She felt conspicuous standing there, so she went into the dark inner lab to wait. When her eyes adjusted, she saw that she was alone. The screens were all black. It was only the second day of the second semester, she realized, a bit early to be slacking off with a movie.

She chose a TV in the back corner and turned it on, thinking there was a slim chance it might have cable, when she heard someone enter the anteroom, no doubt the attendant back from a tea break. She rose and crossed toward the door. Julian came through it and closed it, sealing out both light and sound. He backed her against the wall.

"Hello, little mouse," he said, kissing her urgently on the mouth. He tasted like stale coffee. "Why are you making me chase you?"

She pushed him off.

"This is a silly game," he said. She felt one of his hot hands lock around both of her wrists. "But it's working." He lifted her crossed forearms above her head and shoved them against the wall like he had her in handcuffs. He pressed himself against her.

"Get off me," she croaked. She struggled to free her arms from his grip. He used his other hand to feel under her sweater, undo his fly, pull her jeans down over her hips. He started touching her, brusquely, his fingernails sharp. She felt herself contract with loathing and fury. He kissed her again, harder than before, and she bit down on his lip. She tasted blood. Off guard, he let go of her hands and she kicked him in the shins.

"Get the FUCK off me." She pulled up her jeans and tried to get out. He caught ahold of her arm and dragged her back. He licked the blood from his lip.

"What are you playing at, you little whore?" There was savagery in his voice. "You send me a cunty text message and then you attack me? Is this your version of hard to get?"

"I mean it. This is not a game." Alice was shaking her arm, trying to get free.

He yanked her toward him. She felt her shoulder scream in its socket.

"Found another cock to suck, did you?" He released her. "Fine, go then. I know you. You won't last long."

She escaped the dark hole of a room and stumbled, blinking, through the anteroom into the main basement corridor. It was the middle of the hour, and no one was around. The campus convenience store was straight ahead, and Alice could see a handful of students inside. She entered through the sliding glass door and stood beside the air curtain fridge, forcing breath in and out of her lungs. She watched the door, pretending to look at the sports drinks and premade sandwiches in triangular containers, until she saw him leave the film lab and head for the stairs. She stayed in the store for an indeterminate amount of time, clutching a bottle of Lucozade, thankful for the concreteness of its cold plastic surface, and then put it down and sprinted as fast as her legs could carry her toward the French building.

32

Twelve minutes into the afternoon tutorial, Julian felt his disappointment turn to rage. He had warned himself that she might not come, after their argument that morning, and yet he'd believed she would. He'd believed she would always come when he wanted her. But she'd not been herself that morning. She'd acted like he was trying to force himself on her, for God's sake. She, who had consented so often and with such liquid enthusiasm, who had begged for him in a voice hoarse with desire.

It was only frustration and hurt pride that made his fists clench and blood run to his face, he told himself. It was only that Alice was a rousing partner, and that Emily's maternal transformation, the inflation of her stomach and thickening of her ankles, the strange darkening of her nipples and the stripe of hair that ran down her belly, had made it impossible for him to view her sexually for months.

When he and Emily had married, they had agreed that they did not want children. He had shared his reasons and added a few supporting arguments about melting glaciers and rising sea levels, about the Earth's carrying capacity, about the pull of individualism versus the requirements of the collective, and she had said she was of the same mind: they had each other, and their work. That was all they needed.

But when Emily had turned thirty-eight, she had gone without his knowing to a fertility clinic, where she had been told (they are paid to say this, are they not, like a gym that tells you that their special membership offer is valid for today only, *the future starts now!*) that her eggs were rotting on the vine. For three nights she had come home from work despondent, cried herself to sleep without saying why. He had held her in bed as she'd choked on her tears, convulsing with misery. On the fourth morning, she had blindsided him with the calm assertion that it was a baby she wanted. That a baby was, in fact, something she could not live without.

Julian had felt such relief that an end to her anguish was within his control that he had, with the purest of intentions, put his own interests aside. Thinking only of her happiness, of the life she deserved, he had said, running his thumbs along the sensitive places under her eyes, "Okay, then we'll have a baby. Let's have a baby." Because she was his only real family, and he wanted to do right by her. And he had been right: her eggs were fine.

He tried to tell himself he was not hurt, could not be truly hurt, by Alice's unfaithfulness, because he could only love one person, and that person was Emily. The rest was merely mechanical, a release of tension, both infinitely replaceable and morally neutral. Emily, he was almost certain, knew that he needed other outlets, in the same way that some needed massage therapy, or a personal trainer.

But there was something else contributing to his unease, he now recognized, as he surveyed the semicircle of students. He had told Alice things in confidence, things he'd never told any of the other girls. Things about his father and brother. Things about his mother. He'd trusted her, in his spent haze, because he could see that she did not look up to him, the way they usually did. The way Emily once had, and perhaps still wanted to. Alice had never held any illusions about him. From the first she'd seen past the wallpaper to the moldering structure beneath, and she'd still wanted him. But she didn't, anymore. And she had been wrong, in her brutal text message; he did not know why.

Alice had sworn that she'd told her friends nothing, that she'd taken pains to disguise their time together. He'd believed her because the other option had been to stop seeing her. In the end, she'd held all the power, he thought, smiling. And she'd known it, the bitch.

Penelope and Josephine—wives' names, both of them—had abruptly stopped talking to each other when he'd entered the tutorial room. Now, as he opened his briefcase to take out folded photocopies on cheap printer paper, it occurred to Julian that these child-women with their androgynous nicknames might have shared in intimate gossip about him. Might know better than he did why Alice had sent that message. He felt exposed, like an old mattress left on the curb, its private stains visible to passersby. As he considered how best to engage with the closest companions of the girl who had humiliated him, it struck Julian as appropriate that the day's readings should be about friendship.

"Who can tell me what Aristotelians say of friendship?" He interrupted their chatter and pretended to survey the oily faces. He met a pair of eyes that glowed green like a cat's. "Penelope?"

"That it's a virtuous relation between people," said Penelope, who always did the readings. "Underpinned by the mutual recognition of virtue."

"Do you agree?" Julian asked. She did not blink.

"To a point. I believe true friendship, as opposed to acquaintanceship or situational friendship, is formed upon seeing and appreciating one another's finer qualities." She paused, glanced down, and then fixed him again, color creeping across her straight nose. "But I don't think true friendship dissolves when virtue fails."

The way she stared at him while she said this caused Julian to remember the first tutorials, before Alice had appeared, which he had spent imagining what Pen might look like under her clothes. He had mentally slipped the skirt down her narrow hips and pulled the tights from her legs; he'd unbuttoned the men's white shirt, which she kept primly closed at the throat, and imagined finding underneath a black lace number, an expensive one. Her face was delicate and alert, and there was something undeniably appealing about the intelligence that radiated from her eyes. He remembered being surprised by her that day in the café and wondering if perhaps she would be exciting as a conquest after all. But he'd forgotten her the moment he'd tasted Alice. Alice, whose body he could almost hear humming for his from across the room, turning the rest of the class into a homogenous sludge of undergraduate affectation. But today, something was different about Penelope. In the absence of her friend, she appeared to be inviting him to reconsider.

"Please elaborate," he said.

"I mean that once a friendship has become its own entity, it should not disintegrate just because one or the other has a lapse in virtue," she said. "It has to be durable enough to withstand the weaknesses of its participants. Or else friendship would be too rare, and too short-lived, to be of much use."

Julian broke the spell of Penelope's eye contact and glanced around at the other faces. Josephine's wore an expression that he could only describe as "What the fuck," which made him smile. He read it as a confirmation of the suggestion he thought he'd heard in Penelope's voice, and certainly saw in her eyes.

"So is the old joke accurate—that a friend will help you move house, and a true friend will help you move a body?" Julian asked lightly. "What do you think, Josephine?"

"I'm sorry, what?" rasped Jo. She had been staring at Penelope with open dismay.

Julian tilted the conversation toward Orwell so he could take a few minutes to savor the new possibilities that presented themselves. Beyond the meeting of his immediate needs, however pressing, he saw a way to regain Alice's attention. At this age, girls took friendship so very seriously.

When the bell released them from their seats, Penelope stayed in hers. Julian, too, took his time packing up. Jo, witnessing their mutual dawdling, shot Pen a look of disbelief on her way out.

When Julian was alone with Penelope, she turned her eyes on him once again and erased any lingering doubt. He felt a stirring of anticipation. There was no way she would have Alice's expertise—her lack of experience was obvious in the way she held herself—but that made it even more of a novelty. He would enjoy describing to Alice, in minute detail, how he had deflowered her lily-white sidekick.

Pen didn't speak. He watched as she flipped to the back of her immaculate notebook and wrote out a phone number. With an almost imperceptible tremor in her hand, she tore out the page, folded it twice, and tucked it into the inside pocket of his jacket. Then she left, not turning as she closed the door behind her.

Back in his office, Julian bit into an apple and sent her a message. When can I see you again?

PENELOPE: Are you questioning my virtue?

JULIAN: It's your virtue I'm after. Tonight?

PENELOPE: No, tonight I'm busy.

He took another sour, crunchy bite. She was making him wait. That was fine. He had another idea in mind for tonight.

Tomorrow evening then, he replied. **Half nine. Don't be late.**

A message came through from Emily asking if he could stop at the pharmacy on his way home to get her some tablets for acid reflux. **Of course, my love,** he wrote back. He was a good husband, a helpful husband. She was helpful, too, in her way. These days she fell asleep at eight, beached on her side with a pillow between her knees, eyes hidden behind a polyester mask that read SHHH. This gave him his evenings free, no questions asked, while she slept the sleep of the whales.

That night Julian set out, his coat buttoned against the chill, past the National Gallery and the Mound and up the Playfair Steps two at a time until he reached the George IV Bridge. He took his place behind the statue of Greyfriars Bobby and waited for the rehearsal to end. He needed to see her, at least.

Partially obscured by the structure, he felt her approach, smelled her familiar perfume. It smelled different on her tonight. He clenched with rage thinking of the other man, whoever he was, but got ahold of himself.

"Guess who," said a voice on his neck. He whipped around to find Penelope's face close.

"Did I scare you?" She was smiling. "Sorry to sneak up on you. My plans for tonight fell through, and I couldn't wait. Take me for a drink?"

That she had known he would be waiting here sent another jolt of anger through his body.

Pen stood up on tiptoes to whisper in his ear.

"Alice didn't tell me. I'm just not stupid. And maybe I've been the tiniest bit jealous."

Her breath tickled his ear. She put her cold hand into his coat pocket, as if to warm it. The certainty of success, after over a month without sex, made Julian want to skip the drink and take her straight to the flat. But if he was going to stretch this to last beyond a single night, it would be better if he flattered her a bit.

Julian brought Penelope to a nearby cocktail bar that was too expensive to attract many students. Some of them were loaded but it wasn't cool to let on; they preferred to drink on the cheap. It hadn't been that long ago that he'd been one of them, so he knew how to disappear from their small, warped map of the city.

She perched on a barstool, giving him a view of her slim legs, crossed at the knee. She wore a short suede skirt that rode up at the thigh. When she picked up her glass, a single gold bracelet slid up her white wrist to her elbow. "You're beautiful," he told her matter-of-factly. "I hadn't noticed."

"Thank you," she said. "You're not bad-looking either. Though I had noticed."

He gave her his slanted smile. "I thought you were a clever girl, Penelope. But that isn't true, is it."

She uncrossed and recrossed her legs.

"Don't lie. You didn't think of me at all. You only saw Alice. Don't feel badly; everyone does."

"She is rather visible," he said.

"Yes. Changeable, too."

"Is that a fact?"

"It's a justifiable true belief."

He raised his eyebrows. She really did do all the readings. "I wouldn't know."

"Wouldn't you?"

She slid off her barstool. She was just below his eye level. Her breath was sweet. "Thanks for the cocktail," she said, and left the bar. He started to go after her, considered overtaking her and pressing his mouth to hers, her small body against his, but he held himself back. He was a grown man. He could wait one more night.

33

Pen called Alice from Neville's car, her whole body shaking, whether with fear or relief she did not know.

"Are you out of your mind?" said Alice when Pen came to the door of Jo's room. She pulled Pen inside and flung her arms around her. "Please tell me you'll never do anything that stupid ever again."

Jo was sitting cross-legged on her grandmotherly bedspread. Her room in Mason House, the smallest and most sought-after of the residence buildings, had a double bed with a window overlooking the back of the desolate quad.

"Stinky, you look like a burlesque dancer. What in the blooming flowers of hell have you been doing?" she said.

Alice released Pen. They climbed onto the bed with Jo, who moved frilled pillows aside to make room.

"Pen just risked getting herself hacked to pieces and tossed into the North Sea for me," said Alice.

"Not true," said Pen. "I had backup. Neville was right behind us the whole time, in his wig from the play. He's the one who drove me here."

"Does this have to do with the eye sex you were having with Julian this afternoon?" Jo looked between them. "Holy Hades. I *knew* you were up to something. How was I not a part of this plan?"

"You were," said Pen. "You had to look disgusted with me, otherwise he might not have bought it. You were perfect."

Jo opened her bedside drawer and pulled out a large bag of Haribo gummies. "For emergencies," she said. "This qualifies." She ripped open the bag and placed it in the middle of the bed. "Alice, please can you catch me up on how getting rid of Julian turned into lobbing a trussed-up Pen into the night like Odysseus inside the Trojan bloody Horse?"

It was ten thirty, and Jo was in white pajamas with roses on them. Her blonde hair was neatly brushed and braided. Beside Pen, with her smudged red lipstick, kohl-rimmed eyes, and short skirt, the virgin-whore contrast was stark. Alice, who had too often played the Mary Magdalene to Pen's blessed virgin, felt like she was hallucinating.

"There was no lobbing," said Pen. She took Jo's hand in hers. "It was my idea." She turned to Alice, who continued.

"After my morning lectures I went to the film lab, thinking he would never look for me there. But he must have seen me from his office. It turned out to be the worst hiding place I could have chosen—a dark, soundproof room in a deserted basement. He caught up with me, held on to my wrists, pulled down my jeans, and started trying to—" She took a breath, composing herself. "I knew he could be an asshole, but this was the first time he . . ." She did not want to finish the sentence.

"We have to tell Peter McAvoy immediately," said Jo, who had gone pale. "The department head. He's my director of studies. I'll call him right now if you want."

"It won't work," Alice said quietly.

"Why the fuck not?"

"First of all, I got away, so nothing happened—"

"NOTHING happened?" Jo was rattled. "He stalked you. He *hurt* you."

"Second, there's no proof. No one ever believes a former sexual partner and you know it. And third, even if McAvoy gives him a warning and moves me into another tutorial—and that is the *most* that will happen on my word alone, I guarantee you—he's just going to find someone else later in the term, and again next year, and the year after that. He has no shortage of candidates."

They were all silent. Eventually Pen turned to Alice and spoke.

"Jo wanted to talk to you about him before Christmas and I told her not to interfere. I'm sorry. I was wrong."

Alice squeezed Pen's icy fingers. Pen was the person she knew best in the world, and she had changed in the past few months. Whereas Alice had always been able to perceive two Pens—the one on the ground, telling funny stories or listening to the others in interested silence, and the one above, criticizing the first and ready to make her pay later—she now saw only one. Pen's movements seemed more spontaneous, and the pauses before she spoke were shorter. Was this what people meant when they talked of someone *coming into herself*? Alice wondered.

She reached for Jo's floral throw blanket at the foot of the bed and pulled it over all of them. "Please don't apologize—I'm the one who's sorry. For lying to you, and for disappearing into my own idiotic psychodrama. I made a monumentally stupid decision. All you were trying to do was keep our promise."

Jo patted their knees through the blanket. "You're both terrible friends. It's a tie. But I still don't understand why you're dressed like that, Stinky. What are you trying to do?"

Pen pulled the blanket more tightly around herself. "I think Alice is right. There is a chance McAvoy won't take our word for it. We have to tell him what Julian did, but what we really need is evidence."

Alice interjected. "Pen reads too many detective novels and is actively insane, so I was tempted not to listen to her. But she does make a good point about needing proof. So . . ."

"Julian has a bruised ego," said Pen. "I figured if I could convince him that I was dying to sleep with him, he'd go for it, if only as leverage to get back at Alice. I wasn't wrong. But we're not done."

Jo reached for the bag of gummies. "We're not?"

"Like Alice said, it's unlikely our word would be enough to stop him. It's not technically against the rules for a tutor to have an affair with a student, although they're meant to disclose it, which he definitely has not done. There are no cameras in the film lab; it would be Alice's word against his that he tried to— If we really want to stop him from hurting Alice, or someone else, we need something concrete to show McAvoy. Something that makes it clear he's a repeat offender."

Pen got out her phone.

"Are all Canadians this mad?" Jo put a handful of sour gummies in her mouth and took a sip of cold tea from a mug beside the bed.

Pen slid the phone open and started typing a message. Alice and Jo leaned over the tiny screen.

It was nice running into you earlier, she wrote.

He didn't answer right away.

"What if he's in bed with his wife?" Jo asked.

"He usually sleeps on the couch," Alice said. She added in a croaky voice, "His wife is pregnant."

"WHAT?" Jo exclaimed. "You didn't—"

"Don't worry, I hate myself enough for all of us," said Alice.

Pen's phone lit up.

> JULIAN: A pleasure. Are you in bed?

Alice felt a dull thrum in the middle of her forehead. Even though she had been very much in on the plan, the idea of Julian sending racy messages to Pen was disturbing. She watched her friend bite her lip as if thinking through the answer to some math problem.

> PENELOPE: What a thing to ask. What do you have up your sleeve?

> JULIAN: Nothing. I'm attracted to your fine qualities and hoping to form a virtuous relation between people.

> PENELOPE: That's touching. But are you sure? Maybe you should check your jacket, just in case.

> JULIAN: You're touching. Or at least I hope you are . . .

"Pen, what are you doing?" Alice asked. She was overcome by a panicked, sick feeling. "I thought we just wanted him to send you an incriminating message."

Jo stuffed a towel under her door, opened the window, and lit a cigarette. Alice stole it and took a drag, but it made her feel even more nauseous and headachy. She handed it back.

"I want to make sure our evidence is strong enough," said Pen. "A photo would be ideal."

> JULIAN: Found something in my pocket. Are they yours? They're very nice.

"What the hell did you plant on him, Stinky?" Jo demanded. Pen was focused on typing.

PENELOPE: A present to remember me by.

JULIAN: Would you like me to send you something in return? Something you might find . . . touching?

PENELOPE: How thoughtful. Yes please.

Pen put the phone down on the bedspread.

"What was it?" Jo asked again. She took another slug of tea. "This might actually kill me."

"Let's just see what he comes up with," said Pen.

Alice was squeezing the bridge of her nose with her eyes closed.

"Have you done this before?!" Jo asked.

"Of course not. But part of me has always wanted to. Haven't you?" She looked at Jo and Alice.

"You're asking the wrong woman," said Jo.

Alice just lay her throbbing head back on Jo's pillows. Pen's phone lit up.

"I can't look," Pen said, covering her face.

"What, now you're a prude?" Jo slid the phone open, shouted, and dropped it on the bedspread. "HOLY MOTHER OF GOD."

The phone lay open. The three of them peered over it. There on the tiny screen was a fuzzy picture of something bulging beside a small strip of black lace.

"Hold on, THAT was your present?" Alice was stricken, but also impressed, even through the fog of her headache.

"They're not really mine, I bought them this afternoon. I can't believe it worked," said Pen, whose face had turned a deep red. "I wasn't sure he'd fall for it."

Another photo came through. Now there was no mistaking the subject. Pen used Jo's phone to take a picture of her screen displaying both the photo and Julian's number, sent a copy to herself, turned her phone off, and placed it down on Jo's bedside table.

None of them said anything. Alice did not feel at all well. Jo patted her hand, fetched her laptop from the desk, opened the movie folder, and passed it to Alice to choose. Alice handed it to Pen, who chose *War and Peace*.

They watched in silence.

"Looks like old Julian's stiff out of luck," remarked Jo finally.

"We've got our hard evidence," said Pen.

Alice couldn't bring herself to join in. She just wanted to take an extra-strength Tylenol and get into bed. But her own bed felt miles away. Eyes half-closed, she tried to focus on the movie. "They made Pierre too handsome," she remarked after a while. She let herself grow sleepy watching the birdlike Audrey Hepburn flit through a gilded drawing room in a dress of buttercup yellow, the picture of feminine purity.

"If you were a man, what would you decide to do?" asked Pierre.

"I would become enormously powerful," Audrey-as-Natasha answered in her Holly Golightly voice, leaning dreamily against the mantel.

From somewhere off-screen, the men all laughed. Audrey's perfect face filled the frame, smiling proudly, as if she were in on the joke.

Spring

34

The official story, sent by email to every student in the School of Philosophy, Psychology, and Language Sciences by Department Head Peter McAvoy on a cold morning in February, once the board of faculty members and administrators called upon to decide the matter had reached its conclusion, was that Julian Sachs would take six months' parental leave to support his growing family, effective immediately. This would flow directly into a lengthy, unpaid sabbatical during which he would complete work on a book.

In reality, Peter McAvoy explained to Penelope in his office, speaking quietly because the door was propped wide open (under no circumstance would any member of his faculty ever again hold a meeting with a student behind closed doors if he could help it), Julian Sachs had effectively been let go. That Sachs had a reputation for inappropriate involvement with students was widely known. He had never, however, disclosed such a relationship to his superiors, as school policy dictated he must. Peter himself had issued several warnings—the most he could do in the absence of evidence. Sachs's graphic text messages, combined with the shocking accusation that he had cornered one of his students in the film lab, was more than sufficient grounds for dismissal.

The board had decided that Julian Sachs would not be permitted within five hundred meters of any university-affiliated building for the duration of both leaves, on pain of permanent and public dismissal. He had been made aware that his teaching contract would, at the end of the sabbatical, not be renewed. The softer narrative, Peter explained, had been devised in order to protect Penelope's privacy, as the matter was, naturally, a delicate one. The book in question, he thought it pertinent to add as he stood to signal the end of this uncomfortable conversation, was to contain a chapter on sexual ethics in the "digital age."

But of course, this being the digital age, by the time Pen left his office, most of the School of Philosophy, Psychology, and Language Sciences and at least half of the School of Literatures, Languages, and Cultures had already heard some version of the story. It did not take long for it to become common knowledge across George Square that Sachs had been sacked, and, more compellingly still, that it had been Penelope Winters—the smallish, innocent-looking Canadian—who had unfastened the handsome and popular young faculty member from his job.

In the spring term, a rudimentary message board website had begun spreading from screen to screen throughout the university's computer labs and residence halls. The banner across the top of the page read "Lonely Hearts of George Square," and in the threads below, students hiding behind anonymous usernames wrote notes to and about one another. Mostly, it was used for low-risk flirting. A typical post read:

> Friday 3:13 p.m.: George Sq. Library, 5th floor, Braided blonde in Famous Blue Raincoat: I'd unmake my bed for you.

In that case, even though Jo herself had not yet been following the website, within five minutes, a good Samaritan had tapped her on the shoulder and shown her the post, giving her a chance to glance around, pleased and jumpy, for her secret admirer.

A thread called "Snow White and the Randy Prof" had soon cropped up, where epic retellings of Pen's alleged exploits were rendered in competitively vivid detail, and sometimes in verse. For a day or two, Pen had felt ill, unnerved by the exposure. But she couldn't very well complain when the whole thing had been her idea. She had not so much lost her reputation, she reasoned with herself when she felt eyes on her back on Teviot Place or in the café attached to the library, as donated it to a good cause.

It hadn't been an entirely selfless cause either. The molten rage that had filled her veins when Alice had banged on the door of her French tutorial with a pale face and blood on her lip had cooled and hardened into a plan. By dragging her own name, quite deliberately, through the mud, Pen intended to free herself from the useless burden of other people's expectations.

Pen hoped that her childish notion of selective omniscience for the dead was wrong, and that her grandmother was not watching. Because Tilda Winters had often told Pen that her reputation was her most valuable asset. The Winters name, and the business that had borne it since before the First World War, must never be besmirched. Until the end of her life she had behaved, and taught her children and grandchildren to behave, as if what people thought of them was more important than the truth. Tilda, Pen knew, would be appalled by what her granddaughter had done, and more appalled still by what was being said about her.

Dante would likely place her among the whip-wielding demons of hell's eighth circle, and Kant, if he were watching, would be as categorically disturbed as Tilda Winters. But the consequentialists, at least, might approve of what she had done. Because it had worked. Alice was out of danger. So, for now, were Julian's future conquests.

As a side benefit, Alice's name had stayed out of it. In the weeks leading up to her play's opening night, she could focus on her performance without worrying that whispers from the audience would poison the reviews. With the exception of a few baffled classmates, no one was talking about Alice and Julian. The idea that it had been Snow White who had seduced and then toppled the tutor was just too unlikely a story not to spread.

Even in mid-March, the thread remained active, with new accounts of her supposed deeds dropping from the ether. The most recent post had gone up just a few minutes before. It read:

> Thursday 8:32 p.m.: There was a young lady named Pen,
> Who liked a good romp now and then.
> She hailed from the snow,
> And well did she blow.
> Said suitors to tutor: amen.

Pen, sitting at her desk, laughed out loud at her screen. *A limerick?* She knew immediately who had written it. It made a strange sort of sense to her that for Fergus, revenge might be a dish best served in an AABBA rhyme scheme.

She also knew him well enough by now to see that there was no real malice in it. This was his schoolboyish way of trying to make it abundantly clear, to Pen herself and to whoever else might like to know, that his feelings had not been engaged.

While Pen knew that this was not strictly true, she no longer felt as guilty about how she had handled things. Fergus had moved on. He and Flossie had recently begun sitting so close together at breakfast that they might have been sharing a chair.

A message popped up on her computer screen.

SASHA: Gorgeous poem. Mind if I send to Mum? She does love hearing your news.

She smiled. Since Christmas Eve, Pen and Sasha had been carrying on one long conversation via messenger and text that rushed around obstacles like classes and meals like a river around rocks. The dopamine that flooded Pen's brain every time his name appeared was anesthetizing her against the humiliation that still sometimes threatened to encroach when, for example, she came back from George Square to find stacks of *Penthouse* and *Razzle* magazines at her door, some of them worryingly well thumbed.

Sasha understood that it was not Pen herself, but a character she had invented, who had become infamous. Others encouraged her to ignore the attention; Sasha confided that he knew what it felt like, having created characters of his own to throw people off the scent of real blood. It was impossible to have Elliot and Margot as his father and aunt, he told her, and to avoid being grist for the mill now and then, "on the days when they really had nothing else to write about."

It did not take long for her to see exactly what he meant.

Barely a week later, Pen was sitting cross-legged in her desk chair having a late snack of dark chocolate and Earl Grey, trying to focus on semiotics in Proust, when her phone rang. It was Jo.

"Go to a news website," she said.

"Which one?"

"Doesn't matter."

On the homepage of *The Times* was a picture of Lady Charlotte Rutherford on a mountain, beaming in a slim-fitting red ski suit, goggles holding back her well-highlighted bob, with the arm of the future monarch slung possessively around her waist. 'LADY LOTTIE' BACK ON PISTE, read the headline.

There were rumors, as yet unconfirmed, that Sasha's old friend had not only reconciled with her on-and-off boyfriend the prince, but had, on a ski holiday in the Alps, accepted from him an enormous and very ancient jewel. The press was, as Jo put it, in a lather.

Among the angles taken by the tabloids in their swift torpedoing of whatever privacy "Lady Lottie" had once enjoyed were a few involving her alleged involvement with Sasha. Photos of the two of them together could now be found all over the internet with headlines like CUCKOLDER-IN-WAITING and LOTTIE'S LENN-EX. As Pen clicked her way toward the most disreputable papers, she found a headline that made the hungry, unknowing part of her stir in its sleep: CRIME FICTION? SOURCE CALLS YOUNGER LENNOX BROTHER "DERANGED AND DANGEROUS." She began reading.

> A government intelligence insider with intimate knowledge of the Lennox family has accused Frederick "Freddie" Lennox, younger brother to Lady Charlotte Rutherford's ex Sasha Lennox, and son of well-known crime writer Lord Elliot Lennox, of "deranged and dangerous" behavior during his gap year and called the Lennox family "a national embarrassment." This source, who shall remain anonymous, cautions the Royal Family not to invite anyone with the surname Lennox to the royal wedding, to avoid a possible high-level risk to national security.

She stopped reading and sent a message to Sasha.

PEN: You okay?

He wrote back right away.

SASHA: Yes, fine. Thanks. Which one made you ask?

Pen sent him the link.
Sasha took a moment to reply, presumably to read the piece.

SASHA: Right. Well, thank God for the timing. We might
be in much worse trouble had this happened sooner. Back
in a bit.

Pen had no idea what he was talking about. She began typing, but
Sasha was offline.

It took what felt like hours for him to reappear. Pen couldn't help herself. She looked at every image she could find of Charlotte, who really
was absurdly beautiful, and read every detail she could find about her
supposed fling with Sasha, until the pinging noise roused her.

SASHA: You there?

PEN: I'm here. Just reading about you on the internet.

SASHA: Anything good?

PEN: Some quality journalism, yes. Especially regarding you
making out with the future princess. Is it true then?

SASHA: That Charlotte and I have kissed? Yes, it's true.

Jealousy tore through her. Even though she'd known it already, and her question had in fact been about Freddie, this was the first time he'd mentioned Charlotte's name to her. She wasn't about to let the opportunity drop. She needed more information.

PEN: What do you mean by that exactly? Because I've heard Chet use "kissed" to describe any number of activities. In North America we use a baseball metaphor, for clarity's sake.

SASHA: I'm aware. I've seen the movies.

PEN: First base is what we think of as kissing.

SASHA: Mouth to mouth contact unrelated to resuscitation.

PEN: That's right. Second base involves what young adult books of the '90s referred to as "heavy petting."

SASHA: I'm following. And third, in your estimation?

PEN: All acts after heavy petting up to and including "everything but."

SASHA: Third Base: Heavy Petting $\leq$ Everything But

Pen was glad that he had gone to the trouble of finding the "less than or equal to" symbol on his keyboard. It suggested that he was taking the subject as seriously as she was, which, on a night like this when there must have been a lot competing for his attention, was frankly very flattering.

PEN: Exactly. So when you say you and Charlotte have "kissed" . . . or when Chet told me you've "kissed" half of the history department, does that mean first base or . . . ?

SASHA: Chet is more of a cricket player.

PEN: Be that as it may

SASHA: Chet fancies you.

PEN: Don't change the subject!

SASHA: I'm not. It's in Chet's interest for you to think I'm really good at baseball.

PEN: Why?

SASHA: So you think I'm a roué.

PEN: Why would that be in his interest

SASHA: Hi Pen, it's Chet. Sasha's having a tough night, what with all the news and everything, and he's just dropped quite a lot of acid, so I'm taking over his keyboard for everyone's safety.

Pen smiled, her hands hovering above the keys.

SASHA: And just so you know, he is really very good at baseball. But he's hopeless at cricket.

PEN: Thank you for the warning, Chet. So nice we're all talking like this.

On the bedside table, Pen's phone began to vibrate. Sasha had never called her before; until now their exchange had been safely confined to words on a screen. She picked it up, her heart pounding.

"Hi Pen," said the slightly breathless voice coming down the line. It was a nice voice, clear and soft.

"Hi."

"Sorry. I didn't hear Chet sidle up. He's quiet on his feet. I should make him carry Tic Tacs."

This was the first *Seinfeld* reference Pen had ever heard from a British person. God, she liked him.

"Sasha?"

"Yes?"

"What did Freddie do?"

He paused, as if hesitating. She could hear him walking, Chet's voice fading, and a door closing.

"Can I ask you a favor?" His voice was lower now. It sent a jolt of excitement through her. "It's Danny's first birthday this weekend. George decided last-minute to throw him a party. My aunt Margot is coming, and possibly Freddie, too. It's a bit of a story, the Freddie thing. It'll be easier to explain in person. George has been asking after you for months. I think everyone would love it if you came."

Pen did not answer for some time.

"So you're inviting me for George?"

"No," he answered quickly. She let her breath out slowly, away from the receiver. "But I'm afraid you'll refuse, so I'm using your affection for my cousin and her child as a lure." His voice sounded a bit shaky, as if he, too, was nervous. "I'm coming to collect you tomorrow. Is ten too early?"

"In the morning? Tomorrow?"

The next day was a Friday. She never cut class, but she only had two lectures. One day wouldn't hurt.

"I know you don't entirely trust me. I'm not sure I would either in your position. But please say yes."

"Yes."

She could feel him smiling.

"I'll see you in the morning."

She hung up.

Pen stared at the yellowish wall for a minute and then began making a list in her head.

First, she texted Alice. **Stonehaven ho!!!**

Alice wrote back immediately. **Ho ho hold the phone** And then followed up with: **For real?! Ho shit! GODSPEED!**

Then she got to work. She scrubbed her body down and shaved her legs under the chilling trickle of the shared shower. She covered herself in lotion, tweezed her eyebrows, rubbed useless cream into the shadows under her eyes, trimmed her nails, painted her toenails a neutral color that no one would ever notice, packed her bag carefully, brushed her teeth twice, and fell into bed to confront the tangle of hope and realism in her chest.

What was she expecting—for Sasha to take one look at her freshly polished toenails and decide that she was not just a too-available blue dot on his contact list, a few steps up from an online Scrabble buddy, but his girlfriend? And even if he did try to "kiss" her, whatever that meant, was she willing to take her place among the hordes of women who no doubt followed him around St Andrews and London? Was she really pushing down her cuticles and worrying about the fine bumps on the backs of her arms in hopes of throwing her heart at his feet like one of those women at concerts who hurl their bras at the stage?

As she lay under the covers, she felt the way she imagined people did when they took MDMA. Her pulse was rushed, her jaw was restless, and thoughts bounced across the surface of her mind like hollow balls along a Ping-Pong table. She felt cramped in her body, and yet was filled with a fireworks display of energy that was sort of wonderful. *Whatever this is, at least it's the opposite of numb,* she thought.

35

P en awoke before her alarm. She splashed her face with cold water at the sink in her room, dressed in the outfit she'd laid out, and examined herself in the full-length mirror on the wall. As always after a frenzy of ablutions, she was dismayed to see that she looked the same as ever: slightly unfinished. If anything, the restless night had only accentuated her library pallor and the purple stains under her eyes. She laced up her ankle boots, sipped her tea, sat down in the armchair beside her desk, and waited. Just before ten o'clock, she had her coat on and was about to go down to the courtyard when there was a knock at her door. She glanced around her room like an animal in a trap. The narrow bed against the wall was made. The sink was clean, the desk tidy, and—what did he care? She opened the door.

"Penis Winters, hello," said Sasha. He was tall in her door frame. He wore the green sweater she had first seen him in, which looked incredibly soft. It had a small moth hole at the left wrist, and he had poked his thumb through it.

"May I—?" He was waiting for her to invite him in. She saw the first-year residence corridor through his eyes, with its odor-infused carpeting and scribbled-over name tags. She wondered how long it had taken him to find her door, and what horrors he had come across in the process.

She backed up and let him cross the threshold. She didn't know what it was he smelled like, only that she had to fight an urge to press her face into his sweater and inhale. He took in the eight square meters she inhabited, resting his gaze on the bookshelves above the desk, the spines of the novels she had collected from secondhand shops since arriving, the heavy dictionaries and anthologies. She followed his eyes to her bedside table, where the room's landline stood beside a pile of books. He glanced discreetly over the bed, with its blankets pulled taut, and above it, the bulletin board where she had pegged photos of Olive as a puppy, the flyer for Alice's play, and postcards of paintings she liked by Whistler, Degas, and Toulouse-Lautrec. Seeing all this from his perspective was excruciating. He stepped toward the bed, and she saw that he was admiring her photo of Olive rolling in the snow.

"She looks just like you," he said. "Although her eyes are brown. Those must be from her dad."

Only then did Pen realize that she had not offered him any kind of greeting. She touched each of her scalding cheeks to his. They were freshly shaven. He smelled like woods, she realized. How was that even possible? "I was about to go down," she said.

"I know. I was early on purpose. I wanted to see where you live."

"Can I offer you a cup of tea, or . . ."

He smiled. "It's just how I pictured it. Except for the curtains. Those are nicer."

He crossed to the awning window and fingered the flameproof fabric, a riot of vertical stripes in tones of sunburn and marigold.

"Thank you. I made them."

"I thought you must have done." He found her overnight bag on the armchair and slung it over his shoulder. She followed him out the door and locked it behind them.

It was freezing out. His small green car was parked just outside the building's heavy front doors. He let her in and gave her a sideways look before turning the key in the ignition. He shook his head.

"What?" she asked.

"Jesus," he said, smiling to himself, and drove through the still-sleeping residence compound toward the road.

In the car, Sasha began to tell Pen, seemingly apropos of nothing, about a cousin of his on his mom's side, Hugh Campbell, the eldest son of Christina's brother James. Hugh had gone to the same boarding school as the Lennox brothers, in Sasha's year. He was tall, clever, and mean. While not popular, he had a following: a group that took its chief pleasure in the persecution of younger boys. A prefect and a top student, Hugh was never suspected of any wrongdoing. Freddie, three years younger, small for his age, and gratifyingly easy to wind up, had been an obvious target. Aside from the usual shows of power—making Freddie toast his bread and bring him his tea—Hugh had come up with some creative means of tormenting his cousin.

His favorite of these, he called "hooking." Thirteen-year-old Freddie would, in one moment, be walking along minding his own business, and in the next would be borne aloft by a cluster of older boys and hung by the back of his coat on a hook in the cloakroom. There, legs flailing, he would be jeered at by all who passed until word reached Sasha, who would come and unhook him. In the warmer months, finding Freddie's clothes insufficiently sturdy for hooking, Hugh and his goons taped him to the wall instead, using full rolls of heavy-duty cloth tape. That it was a family member—one who should by rights have been an ally—leading the charge made the humiliation cut deeper, and Freddie developed a seething hatred for their cousin.

Last summer, Sasha continued, Cousin Hugh graduated from Oxford and began working in the secret Palmer Street office of the GCHQ, the same government department where their grandfather had begun his career. And very recently, Hugh had revealed himself to be even more vindictive than they had imagined.

Pen looked at Sasha's face in profile while he focused on the road. She was completely at a loss.

"He's the government intelligence official," Sasha said, glancing sideways at her. "From the story you sent me. That was why I had to go—I had to tell Mum. She's already sorted it out. There won't be any more stories of that nature. Cousin Hugh obviously didn't realize who he was dealing with."

Pen was still a bit flummoxed. She waited for Sasha to go on. And so he told her about his mother's family. He told her about how his grandfather, William Campbell, was a knee-jerk conservative who insisted on calling Christina "Teensy" to this day, and had never taken her seriously, even when she'd proven the only one of his children with any aptitude for languages or diplomacy. Here Sasha put on his best Old Boy accent. "Impossible to be an ambassador without an ambassador's wife, Teensy. So unless you plan to become a homosect-*sual* . . ." When Christina had been recruited out of Edinburgh for a role at the GCHQ, her father had chuckled that "perhaps intelligence is no longer a prerequisite for intelligence work," and that they must really be "scraping the bottom of the jam jar."

When Cousin Hugh appointed himself his grandfather's successor twenty years later, however, William rolled out the red carpet. He made sure every dinosaur still in action and all their well-placed progeny were aware that Hugh was a third-generation signals and cybersecurity wunderkind, poised to make his mark on the world. The Lennoxes had found this to be a bit much. Unbeknownst to any of them, however, Freddie had come up with a retaliatory plan.

"I should let Fred tell you the rest," said Sasha. "You'll meet him shortly. He can do a better job of explaining the inner workings of his mind, which remain opaque to me. But related to all this—" He made eye contact with her briefly, which had its usual effect. "I owe you an apology. The last weekend you came home, when I was late and hungover, I was truly awful to you. I behaved dreadfully, and there is no excuse. I'm sorry. Please forgive me?"

She considered this. "I met Freddie that weekend," she said.

"What?" His eyes darted to her face and returned to the road. "How?"

"I went into his room by mistake," she said. "He was smoking a joint in the middle of the day. I assumed he'd done something involving drugs and an airport."

Sasha shook his head. "No. He's not daft, Fred. Nor does he have any evil intentions that we know of. He's just a bit . . . thoughtless. I can't believe you knew all along that he was home. Is that why you put Dad in his place after the polo jab?"

Pen reddened, remembering.

She did not have a sibling, but she could recall the metallic panic in her throat when Alice had been in trouble. How incapable she had been, in the following hours, of caring about anyone or anything else. She knew Freddie wasn't the only explanation for Sasha's coldness toward her that weekend, but she had already forgiven him.

When the car crunched slowly over the gravel of Talmòrach and Pen watched Sasha pull the stick shift into park, she still couldn't be sure which parts of him were real and which parts she'd invented. That was the problem with epistolary crushes, she thought. Well, one of the problems. It was a relief when he opened his door and cold air rushed in.

Carrying both of their bags, he led her around the side of the house and up through the boot room. The kitchen smelled like vanilla and hot sugar. Christina, in a navy wrap dress and an apron, was washing dishes. She started when she saw Pen but recovered herself quickly.

"Kids!" she said, pulling first Sasha and then Pen into hugs, as if they were both her children, and as if no time had passed. Pen hugged her back. Sasha kissed her on the cheek.

"Pen, what a delightful surprise. George will be overjoyed. Are you famished? I haven't got much of a lunch planned, I'm afraid, but dinner won't be too far off. George wants to get an early night before the party."

"Don't worry about us, Mum. When's Bolter due?" At the name Bolter, Christina blanched. Sasha did not notice. He took three mugs from the cupboard and put four crumpets from the bread box into the toaster.

"*Margot* is due before supper. Kettle's boiled if you're after some tea."

"Unless you'd prefer coffee, Pen?" offered Sasha. She nodded gratefully and he set about brewing some.

"Are you making a cake? It smells amazing," Pen said to Christina.

"The cakes!" Christina reached into the oven with a tea towel. The cakes were a perfect caramel color. "That was close. I'd forgotten what a brilliant help you are, Pen. We *have* missed you."

They drank their hot drinks and ate crumpets with butter and honey. Sasha also put out a thoughtful array of snack items including carrot sticks, hummus, miniature pitas, and a plate of biscuits. Christina explained how she planned to layer two of the cakes and cut the third into ears to make Danny's favorite cartoon pig. "I found a baby-friendly recipe online, and I even ordered some natural food dye by post. It's made from beetroot, apparently. Is that not the cleverest thing?"

"How can we help?" Sasha offered, rinsing the dishes.

"Thank you, my darling. Could you give the horses some attention? Hector is off today, and I've been neglecting them terribly."

The stables were surprisingly warm. Nellie, who had been dozing in the hay, did her Sasha dance. He carried her under his arm while he went to get two buckets of brushes.

"Do you want to take Cindy?" he asked, stroking Kevin's nose. The horse's lips twitched with pleasure.

Pen went over to Cindy's box stall and let herself in cautiously. She began making circles across Cindy's body with the rubber curry comb and watched the dust and dander fly. She went over her coat until it shone, and then lifted her hooves as she had learned to do as a child, running the pick gently along the V-shaped grooves to remove dirt and stones. When she put down the last hoof, she saw that Sasha was watching her.

"Do you want to take them out?" he asked. "Shooting season is over."

Pen followed him into a small tack room made cozy by a space heater. It was well organized and had a strong smell of leather and wax. There was a large sink and a dusty old sofa with boot winches around it. Sasha chose two bridles and took up an armload of saddles. They carried everything back to the stalls and tacked up the horses.

They made their way through the back fields at a trot in companionable silence. Pen felt a drop on the back of her neck. After several more, Sasha, who was up ahead, slowed.

"Time to turn back?" he asked.

She shook her head. After having been trapped beside Sasha in the car, unsure of where to look and convinced that she was swallowing more loudly than was normal, the freedom of being beside him in the open air was exhilarating. She took a chance and pressed into canter.

Cindy's gait was confident and smooth; Pen gave her a loose rein and let herself be carried.

It began raining harder. Soon her jeans were soaked through, and she could feel the damp seeping through her jacket. Sasha brought Kevin to a walk. Cindy slowed, too, without waiting for a cue from Pen, and walked up beside Kevin, so close that Pen's shin grazed Sasha's.

"Sorry," she said.

"She's all right there," Sasha said. "Kev's in love with her; he won't try anything."

Obligingly, Kevin half nipped at Cindy's neck in what looked like a playful nuzzle.

Pen could feel rain dripping down her face and into her mouth. "Your lips are turning blue," Sasha observed. "We should go in." But they stayed there, looking at each other, until Cindy grew bored and began walking forward, separating them.

"Bye then," Sasha said, laughing. He pressed Kevin seamlessly into a canter and made a figure eight, changing leads halfway through.

"Show-off," Pen called, as Cindy followed after Kevin.

Back in the stables, they untacked and dried off the horses, and Sasha gave them each a drink of water and an armful of hay. In the warm tack room, Pen realized her teeth were chattering.

"I've turned you to ice," Sasha said. They were facing each other. He took her hands in his. She had thought they were nearly numb with cold, but evidently not. Her fingers burned where he held them, and the heat spread rapidly through her body.

"Here," he said, and placed her hands under his shirt, laying her icy palms flat against the warmth of his bare sides. She could feel the muscles in his stomach tense under her touch. *So this is what it feels like to lose one's mind*, she thought. She wanted to run her hands across his back and up to his shoulder blades. Instead she just stood there, mouth slightly open, looking at him. He was looking at her, too, in a way that she couldn't read.

"We should get you out of those wet clothes," he said.

Pen nodded.

"I just heard how that sounded," Sasha said. There was color rising from his neck to his cheeks. "What I mean is, you should get out of those wet clothes and into a hot bath. Alone." The blush spread to his ears. She wanted to cup them in her hands.

"A bath," she repeated senselessly. "Yes. Good." He followed her as she ran across the short distance to the house.

36

While they sat on the bench by the side door, peeling off their saturated jackets and boots, an unfamiliar voice came from the kitchen. It was low and prowling, with an authoritative languor.

"Margot's arrived," Sasha said. Pen got her second boot off and found him looking at her in that same way again. She wondered if he knew what he was doing to her.

They went up into the kitchen. An elegant woman dressed in a black suit, her hair tied at the base of her neck, was standing with her back to them. She turned and looked Pen up and down coldly.

Under Margot's appraising stare, Pen realized what a sight she must be. Drenched sweater clinging to her skin, wet hair plastered to her head, and reeking of the barn.

"Darling, you're a drowned rat," Margot said to Sasha, kissing him on both cheeks. "And who is this?" she asked, as if Pen would not be able to hear.

"Pen is our guest," said Christina. She sounded uncharacteristically off-balance, like she had not yet had a chance to explain Pen's presence. Why her presence should need to be explained in a household so accustomed to absorbing people that errant younger sons were sometimes stashed away in their bedrooms was something to wonder about later. For now, Pen tried not to think of what those accusatory eyes were seeing and focused instead on observing Margot Lennox in return.

She was of medium build like George, and shared her wide-set eyes, but her irises were a striking amber. Her brown hair was going gray in a way that struck Pen as both intentional and chic. Margot's face, which Pen had seen in countless photographs, seemed bare of makeup save for red lipstick.

But Margot was no longer looking at her, and now Pen was the one staring.

"It's lovely to meet you," she said quickly.

"You're looking well, Aunt Margot," added Sasha. "Did you bring Freddie with you?"

"No," Margot said, shooting Christina a rapid but unmistakably defiant look. "Our arrangement was that if I took him on, he would work. And so he's working tonight. He'll arrive in time for the party tomorrow."

"Up you go to thaw out," said Christina to Pen and Sasha, ignoring Margot. "I won't have any funerals this weekend, there simply isn't the time."

Sasha picked up their overnight bags and Pen followed him up the back staircase. They ended up in a different part of the second floor. It was narrower and less grand than the hall she was used to, with family photographs instead of paintings on the walls.

Sasha didn't play tour guide the way Lennox would have; he just continued with her down the corridor, leading her past what she now knew was Freddie's bedroom to the green guest room. He held the door for her, placed her bag on the bench at the foot of the bed, and then turned quickly and left the room, closing the door gently behind him.

Pen stepped out of her wet clothes, hung them up, and wrapped herself in a towel while waiting for the water to fill the tub. She replayed the day in her mind. She was still incapable of understanding how Sasha saw her (objectively she was a bedraggled mess, as the mirror confirmed), and to what extent she was conjuring the desire she thought she could see in his eyes and hear in his voice. How much of what she perceived was the real him, and how much was her illusion of Sasha, the Sasha she wanted to see? Maybe one never knew for sure. The idea came with a clamp of fear. But it would, she thought, explain a lot.

She floated in the hot bath for an unreasonably long time, letting her hair fan around her face, imagining herself in a river surrounded by flowers, like that painting of Ophelia that hung in the Tate, which she found at once eerily beautiful and intensely depressing.

She was unpacking the two dresses she had brought when there was a knock at the door. *George*, she thought, and opened it in her towel. Sasha wore black jeans and a different soft sweater, this one navy blue. His hair was still wet and brushed back from his face. He held out a tall glass.

"I'm sorry—" he said, turning to leave. She didn't want him to go. She wanted to settle this, to know one way or the other whether he wanted what she wanted.

"Where's yours?" she asked, holding the door open for him.

Sasha retrieved his drink from a table in the hall and entered the room, keeping his eyes politely averted from her naked arms.

"I'm still deciding what to wear. Your aunt is a bit intimidating," said

Pen, trying to sound relaxed. Pretending she wasn't wearing just a towel and ignoring the goose bumps on her arms, she showed him the dresses. One was made of black jersey and was short with long sleeves. The other was a clinging slip dress made of dark red silk. Alice had persuaded her to buy it at their favorite vintage store in the Grassmarket and had instructed her to wear it for Sasha, but really for Margot. He cleared his throat.

"That one," he said, pointing to the red dress.

Pen smiled. She went into the bathroom and put on the dress. It hugged her figure and fell to just above her ankles. There was space between the fabric and her skin, but not much. She ran through her damp hair with a brush, rimmed her eyes with smudged dark shadow like Alice had taught her, and went out before she could change her mind.

Sasha stood up from his seat by the window when she came back in. He looked directly into her eyes for a moment and then dropped his gaze slowly downward. She could feel his eyes lingering on her body, not in the judgmental way that Margot had looked at her, but in a way that made her heart beat faster.

"I would whistle if I knew how," he said finally in a voice that sounded controlled.

"You don't know how to whistle?" She sat on the upholstered bench at the foot of the bed and crossed her arms over her chest to keep warm, but also because she was self-conscious. "How do you hail taxis? Or pick up women?"

"I'm no good at either," he said. He was still standing, and still looking.

"They all come to you?" Pen was straining to regain the ease they'd had when typing. "Do you have any other character flaws I should know about?"

"Oh, many," he said, sitting down again in the window seat. He was too far away from her. "But don't worry, I'm good at hiding them."

"That's a comfort."

She wanted him to come closer, to sit beside her on the bench. She wanted him to uncross her arms, to lift the dress over her head. She wanted him with an intensity that scared her. To feel his mouth press against hers, to feel his head in her hands as she pulled him closer. What had been a small, dull ache at her center was now an unbearable lack.

"I'm probably not very good at baseball," she said quickly, and then flushed the color of her dress.

He let out a startled laugh. "What do you mean?"

She thought, in rapid succession, about how she didn't even really know the basics of a hand job, about whether Sasha was the kind of person who would carry a condom in his wallet, and about the annoyingly perfect belly button of Charlotte the mermaid in her purple bikini top.

"I haven't played much," she said, hoping she wouldn't have to spell it out further.

He crossed the room and sat beside her on the bench. Her leg began to shake. He placed a steadying hand on it, which made it shake harder.

He took her hand, which meant she had to uncross her arms, and smiled in a way that at once put her at ease and intensified the jangling inside her. His eyes were back on hers.

Just as she began to let herself believe that he was about to lean forward and kiss her, to put her out of her misery, he said, "We should go down."

"Right," Pen said quickly, feeling like a bucket of ice water had just been dumped over her head. "Of course. You go first."

He stood. He went. She finished getting dressed and stood in front of the bathroom mirror. Her heart seemed to be shaking her whole body. She unpacked a black blazer and turned the wrong way out the door. She went a few steps before realizing that she wasn't wearing any shoes. She went back, and then turned the wrong way again.

She paused at George's door. It was half-open and she could hear

George singing. Pen watched her circle the dark room, swaying Danny in her arms. She kissed him on the forehead and laid him down in his crib. She nearly collided with Pen in the hall.

"God! Pen. Sorry."

She took her by the arms and kissed her on both burning cheeks.

"Well. We've finally dragged the cat back in," she said, looking Pen in the eyes. "You look gorgeous. You stayed away a long time. What did we do? Never mind," she said as Pen started to answer. "Join me for a cig?"

Pen nodded. George took her arm, and they went back down the hall and through the library. On the balcony, they could see their breath. George handed Pen a pack of Gauloises and a book of matches.

"Nicked from my mum," George said, seeing Pen looking at the pack. "Did you meet her?"

"Only briefly," said Pen.

"Was she very rude?"

"I don't think I made a good first impression."

"Diplomatic," said George. "Mum's perfectly capable of being polite, but for some reason whenever she comes back to this house she acts like a thwarted teenager. It might have something to do with the nickname."

"Bolter?"

"They shouldn't call her that. She's a bit too comfortable in the role, if you ask me. But people seldom do." George blew a column of smoke up into the sky. "Ask me, I mean. You'll notice when you have a baby—if you have a baby—that people stop asking you things that don't relate to nappies and sleep schedules. I don't mean to sound resentful. I mostly want to talk about Danny anyway. But after twenty-six years as a separate person, it's almost funny how completely the world's perception of you shifts." George blew out another plume of smoke. "It's one of the things I'm guessing she was not okay with."

"Your mom?"

"Mothering was never going to be her main job. There were too many things she needed to do. I'm glad she does them. I respect her for it."

Pen waited, watching the fog their breath made in the goldish light from the library, hoping she'd say more. She didn't.

"What about Christina?" Pen finally asked.

"Thank God for Christina. We lived here on and off when I was little. Later, we moved to Paris, but I always came here for holidays and while Mum traveled. When Sasha was born, I thought he was my little brother. I don't think Christina minds being the responsible one. I can't tell if it's temperament or a choice, or a combination of the two, but some women are just better at being selfless." She blew a perfect smoke ring. "I'm still waiting to see where I fall on the spectrum."

"What about your dad?"

George gave Pen a hard look. Pen felt as if a door had been slammed in her face. George's features softened again, and she patted Pen's hand as if forgiving her for the indiscretion.

"Sorry for making you listen to that. No wonder you didn't come back for months. How are you?"

Pen laughed, relieved.

"Good," she said.

"Good," said George, meeting her eyes. She looked like she meant it. "Now let's go in, it's freezing out here." They stubbed their cigarettes in the tin and went back inside.

At the doors to the living room, Pen could hear Margot's throaty laugh and Lennox's narrator's voice. She buttoned her blazer. George unbuttoned it.

"Stop hiding," she said.

Lennox was standing beside the fire. Margot was close to him, their eyes locked in some shared joke. She was wearing a man's tuxedo jacket, perfectly tailored, over an open shirt of the crispest white. Sasha sat opposite them on the couch, one long leg crossed over the other.

"Ah, Penelope," Lennox said, kissing her. "You've returned at last. I was afraid the suitors—or whatever was detaining you—had swallowed you whole. But now we're mixing our references." He took in her dress. "I'm so glad Danny was inducement enough, as we evidently were not. Have you met my sister Margot?" He guided her toward the mantel. Only then did Pen realize that George was no longer beside her.

"Yes, we met earlier," said Pen, with a self-possession she did not entirely feel.

Margot held out her cheek for Pen to kiss.

"Right. Who needs a drink?" Sasha offered, rising from the sofa to where a bar was set up on a side table.

Margot went with him. "So, pet," she said, "what's doing at St Andrews. How's your old friend the prince?"

"He graduated last year, Margot. Last I heard he was getting engaged," said Sasha, with some irony.

"Oh yes," Margot said, as if remembering. "To that girlfriend of yours. It would be good to get her something of mine to wear. She must need frocks. Do tell her I'd be happy to get her in for a fitting, would you?"

Sasha uncorked a bottle of white wine and poured out glasses. He handed one to his aunt. "Ex-girlfriend," he corrected her.

"You're admirably community-minded, Marg," Lennox interceded in a gently mocking tone. "I'm sure you've been a wonderful influence on our Freddie. How's he getting on?"

"Quite well, surprisingly," said Margot. "I've got him working on the reception desk. He knows every employee and vendor by name. His French is god-awful, he more or less speaks in Spanish with a French accent, but no one minds. Everyone adores him."

"*Tant mieux*," said Lennox.

"Hello Mummy," said George, who had just reappeared.

"Darling!" said Margot, pulling George into an embrace. "Where have you been?"

"Checking on Christina. She says she has it in hand."

"She always does," said Margot, ushering George onto the sofa and curling her feet—shoes on—up under her. Lennox took the armchair facing them.

Pen watched from a straight-backed chair near the wall. George was animated as she answered her mother's questions about the new words Danny was saying and the first steps he was surely going to take soon. There was a quality about Margot that made the people she loved soften, even though she herself was as hard as black ice. She loved the three who were assembled around her, that much was clear. She took her brother's ribbing in stride, seeming to seek out his approval, and responding to it like a cat to sunshine. And Pen had pictured Margot as the sort of mother who seldom hugged or kissed, but Margot held George's hand and caressed her cheek, and George allowed it.

When Christina came in from the kitchen the tableau rearranged itself. Sasha jumped up to offer her a glass of wine. Christina perched on the arm of the sofa beside George, and Margot moved away from her daughter. George and Christina fell into talking about the next day's festivities. Margot shrank back into the remote, appraising version of herself Pen had seen earlier. Pen had become so engrossed in her study of Margot that she did not notice Sasha until he was right at her side.

"I'm not sure anyone has ever actually sat in these chairs," he said.

Pretending to examine the carvings in the wood, he slipped his hand up the back of Pen's blazer. Lightly, he ran his fingers up her spine, sending an electric shock skittering through her. "I'm sorry I left so abruptly," he said in her ear, his voice low and hot against her cheek. "All I wanted was to kiss you. But if I'd started, I'm not sure I would have been able to stop." His fingers traced her bare shoulder blades. She turned and met his eyes, which held hers. They stared at each other in silence until the others began moving toward the dining room.

At the table, Pen sat between Christina and George, whose talk required little intervention, only the odd nod of agreement that yes, it would probably be too wet to have the piñata outside. Lennox and Margot were engaged in a tête-à-tête at the far end. Pen, who by this point could not trust herself to so much as glance at Sasha, did not notice what or whether she was eating, nor did she see or feel Lennox's eyes roving between her, George, and his sister.

As soon as coffee and digestifs had been served, she thanked Christina and excused herself.

"You must be beat after your soaking this afternoon," said Christina, kissing her cheeks. "Thank you for your help with the horses. That color is pretty on you, by the way," she added more quietly.

"Night, kid," said George, squeezing Pen's forearm. "I'm glad you came."

Pen waited in the darkness outside the dining room. She listened in petrified silence until Sasha echoed her excuses.

She could hear his breathing as he came closer to her in the dark. Her rib cage felt tight. He found first her wrist, and then her fingers, which he wove through his. He tried to lead her somewhere, but she could not go. She had waited long enough. She moved toward him in the blackness and stood on her toes, feeling for the sides of his face. She found his mouth and kissed him with all the intensity she had been suppressing. Without a moment's hesitation he pulled her closer and kissed her back, matching her intensity.

After a few minutes of the purest physical thrill Pen had ever known, he abruptly drew back. He continued to hold her, tucking her head under his chin, while they caught their breath. She could feel how fast his heart was beating.

"Can I see your bedroom?" she asked.

"Yes."

"You've seen mine. It's only fair."

"That's true."

Whatever skin she had just shed she would be happy never to see again, she thought, as she followed him up the back staircase.

37

Sasha's room felt cut off from the rest of the house. It was three
flights up, each narrower and more corkscrewed than the last. At
the top he touched an inside wall and low pools of light brought the
room into focus. It was circular, with exposed beams. At one pole there
was an open fireplace, and at the other, a low bed that he rushed to
make, straightening the sheets and fluffing up the pillows. Under one
of the small windows stood a desk scattered with pens, books, pads of
legal paper, and a laptop. Beside it, a bookshelf was crammed with more
books whose titles she would examine later, and beside that on a low
table stood a CD player.

He knelt to light the fire. It flickered to life as the newspaper caught,
and then a log. He chose a disc from a tall stack.

Pen sat on the edge of his bed, watching him. It took her a moment to
place the music.

"*Tommy?*" she said. She liked The Who well enough, but a rock opera
wasn't what she would have chosen for such a moment.

"It's a good album," he said.

She lay back with her feet on the floor as if testing the mattress. It was unreasonably soft, and she told him so. She kicked off her shoes.

"I suppose the others slept on slabs of Canadian Shield?" said Sasha.

Others, she thought.

He lay down beside her and placed his hand on her chest. Her heart was going haywire.

"What's going on in there?"

"Pinball."

She was waiting for him to slide his hand under the loose silk. It would have been easy. He didn't. He left it there over her heart, which continued beating too fast, giving her away completely. They had been on the same page a moment ago, but she could sense something in him pulling back now, reconsidering.

It's because I told him, she thought. Only perverts want to sleep with virgins, and he's not a pervert. She wished he would speak. Once Daltry began singing, "Tommy, can you hear me?" in that pleading voice, it was becoming ridiculous.

Pen sat up. Her hand shook a bit as she found the volume knob on the stereo and silenced the song. She put on her shoes.

"Where are you going?"

"Don't worry," she said. "I get it."

"Get what?"

He followed her to the door.

"It's fine, I understand. There's no need to humor me."

"Humor you?"

"You're being polite, to let me down gently. It's fine."

"Polite?" He took her hand, which was still shaking, and held on to it tightly. "You think I'm being polite?"

"I get it. I appreciate it, even. I don't want my first time to be with a lunatic in an attic either. It's too *Jane Eyre*, and not in a good way." Pen was mortified that these words were coming from her mouth, but she had no power to stop them.

"Hey," he said, closing the space between them. "That's excessive. I may live in an attic, but I'm not a lunatic. I've never set fire to anyone's bed, for example."

He touched her cheek, and she could see he was fighting a smile.

"No, I can see that," she said. The corners of her mouth started to twitch. She was terribly nervous.

"Is that a challenge?" He kissed her twitching mouth. "It's hard to kiss you when you're laughing at me," he said. "Maybe I'd better humor you instead."

He kissed her again, not at all politely. She ran her hands across his back under his soft sweater, feeling the ridges of his spine, the strength in his shoulders. She pulled the sweater over his head, wanting to see all of him, to feel his body against hers, to feel all of him at once. She went for the T-shirt, and he held on to her hands, stopping her.

"Pen. I don't want to rush you. We can just kiss. We don't need to do more," he said, breathlessly.

She shook her head furiously. "You're not rushing me."

"But if you change your mind—" She got his T-shirt off and moved a hand down his chest and stomach, felt him inhale sharply.

"I won't," she said.

"Let's have a word. How about 'golf'?"

"Golf?"

"There's nothing less hot than golf. If you bring up golf, I'll know you want to stop."

"You really are a lunatic."

He led her back to his bed and lay her down as before. This time, though, he did not keep his hand on her heart. He touched her through the silk. He moved the fabric aside, and, watching her face, traced a spiral around the curve of her breast. A sound issued from the back of her throat. He lifted the dress up over her head.

As dawn was casting diamonds of light on the walls, he was asleep with his arms around her. She lay awake, her left forearm and hand slowly going numb, her mind racing. His bedside drawer had contained mangled playing cards, an old wristwatch, and some loose condoms. She'd watched him rip open the foil packaging.

While he'd touched her with his fingers and mouth, she'd stopped thinking entirely, had dissolved into sensation. But then, wanting more, she'd pressed him closer, deeper, and her sharp drawing in of breath had shocked them both. He'd stopped. She'd asked him to continue, had tried to bring the desire back into her voice. Soon it had been better, if not quite the stuff of poetry. But she had remained too aware of the strangeness of the pain, like a third person in the room, to forget herself again. He'd warned her he was close and apologized. She'd told him not to apologize and, after holding him in that moment of intense intimacy, she'd thanked him, not knowing why she was thanking him exactly, or why her face was wet. The spot of blood was tiny, hardly bigger than a quarter.

She liked being there with him, in the warm crook of his body, but she had to get up. To be caught on the stairs in the red dress would be too damning. She needed to change, to text Alice, to think about what had happened.

"Where are you going?" he said, not letting go.

"To play a round of golf."

He released her. "You're cruel," he said. She dressed and made her way slowly back down all the winding stairs, careful not to let them creak.

38

With Alice's incredulous replies and demands for more information buzzing in her pocket, Pen went down to the kitchen. She was hungry. She planned to make herself a vat of tea and the world's largest bowl of cereal, and then to go for a walk. It was barely seven. She thought she'd have at least an hour until Christina appeared. But the kitchen was already occupied. Seated at the round table, Lennox was reading the newspaper. The soggy tags of three PG Tips tea bags were plastered to the side of the white teapot before him.

"Penelope," he said, setting down the centerfold of a lurid tabloid. "Good morning."

Though they were both dressed for the day, Pen, who had never once encountered Lennox before noon, felt as if she had walked in on him in his dressing gown and slippers. She knew from Christina that while he was working, Lennox wrote seven days a week, even on Christmas, and always in the morning. This must have been his pre-writing ritual. She reprimanded herself for not having thought to give her host dominion over his kitchen at this hour.

Her horror was compounded when she noticed how he was looking at her: like he was dusting her for prints. Just as Sherlock Holmes could deduce, from the worn-out knees of a man's trousers, that he was planning to rob a bank vault, she realized that Lennox would probably find evidence on her person of where she had spent the night, and how. The thought was intolerable. She plastered an artificial smile onto her face and forced herself to go through the motions of cheerful human interaction.

Lennox was pouring her a cup of tea. It was still steaming hot, though it had steeped almost to the point of opacity.

"I'm glad to have company," he said when she offered to leave him in peace. "I've been conscripted. No writing today, the General was firm on that point. But I'm free to read salacious newspapers and drink builder's tea until the shops open. Do join me." He gestured toward the chair in front of him. She sat down and took a sip of tea. She could not imagine helping herself to a bowl of cereal under the circumstances, though she wanted one badly.

Lennox handed her the front section. PRINCE'S ENGLISH ROSE TOPS POLL OF "NATURAL BEAUTIES" ran the headline, under a picture of Charlotte looking fresh-faced and demure.

"Now Margot won't rest until she gets one of her frocks over the poor girl's head," he said, as if Charlotte stood to suffer a great deal as a result.

Pen scanned the article and saw that the judgment on "natural beauties" had been commissioned by Fox's biscuits, "to support the launch of its new Naturally Fox's range." These women, for whom the maintenance of "natural beauty" surely precluded the eating of very many chocolate-dipped wafers, were being ranked by strangers at the behest of a cookie company? She looked up, smiling at the absurdity, to find that Lennox was considering her again.

"Had you heard of my sister before coming to see us?" he asked.

Pen was surprised by the question. Lennox usually took pains to seem oblivious to his family's fame. "Of course," she said. "I've known about her for years."

"Have you?" He was visibly intrigued.

"Sure." She paused, doubtful that he would find this interesting. But his look urged her to continue, so she went on. "My friend Alice told me about her. She used to clip out every picture of Margot and her clothes that she could find and tape them to her bedroom wall."

He raised his eyebrows encouragingly, but she could sense he was disappointed by this answer.

"Did your parents ever mention her?" he asked. His tone was light, but Pen knew the question was not.

"My parents?" she said. "No. Why?"

"Oh, nothing in particular," he said, shaking the newspaper back into a stack. He must have seen that this was unsatisfactory, because he added, "I wondered if she might have come up at some juncture. I think your father had a soft spot for her, at one time."

A soft spot for Margot? Pen thought. "When?" she asked.

"Oh, when we were young. Your age. She was something of a beauty, or so I was relentlessly told."

"Were they . . ."

"Heavens no. The age gap was a chasm at that age, and I'd have skinned him alive."

He wasn't telling the truth, or at least not all of it.

"How did you know, then?"

"The signs are easy enough to spot." The detective look had returned to his eyes.

Irritation emboldened her. Pen went over to the cupboard where the bowls were kept and helped herself to cereal. If Lennox had something to tell her, let him say it, she thought. But he didn't, of course. He just went on drinking his tea and reading his newspaper.

After devouring her breakfast, Pen put her bowl, mug, and spoon in the dishwasher, and told Lennox she was going out for a walk. He smiled up at her with a kind of wistful affection, but she didn't see it. She had already made her escape down the boot room stairs.

Pen was still on edge when she came back in from her walk. The damp air had done nothing to dispel her confusion. The kitchen was now full of activity. Danny was in his high chair. His chubby fingers were busy squishing up pieces of buttered toast and tossing them on the floor. He muttered to himself in gibberish as he did this. Beside him, silicone spoon of yogurt suspended in midair, George was watching a situation unfold between her mother and Christina.

"Your snout is too small," drawled Margot. "And the ears are lumpy. You'd better let me fix it."

"It doesn't need fixing." Christina was piqued. "It's not meant to look like I bought it. It's homemade."

"The children won't recognize it, and the whole undertaking will have been pointless. But do as you like."

Christina tossed her spatula into the bowl of pink icing and untied her apron. "Have at it," she said to Margot, and pushed through the door to the dining room.

Margot took the apron and hung it disdainfully on the back of a kitchen chair. She surveyed the cake, chose a sharp knife, and began making incisions.

George's relief at seeing Pen was obvious. "You're just in time to see my mother perform a facelift on a pig," she said. Pen understood the value of a non-family-member in maintaining the peace. As ever she was glad to have a job. Giving Margot and the cake a wide berth, she tapped Danny on the shoulder and ducked down to hide. He looked around, puzzled. Catching sight of her cowering behind her fingers, he shrieked. He tossed a handful of toast down to her. Pen pretended to gobble it up.

"Who's having a party today?" she asked. Danny grinned, revealing a new pair of well-spaced front teeth.

"Is it my party?" Pen pointed to her chest.

He shook his head. "DADDY POTTY!" he squeaked.

"It's Daddy's party?" asked Pen.

The boy shrieked again. "DADDY POTTY!" he repeated, vibrating in his chair.

"He calls himself Daddy," said George. "I try not to read too much into it."

Pen held up her hand for a high five. Danny smacked it with his sticky palm.

"I can't believe he's talking. Who's coming today?" Pen asked George.

"His dad is on his way up as we speak. Freddie should be here soon, too. And Christina has invited all the young kids from the village, plus a few from the countryside around here."

"We're expecting a good turnout," said Christina, reentering from the dining room with renewed alacrity. Pen caught a glimpse of Lennox blowing up balloons through the two-way door.

"Morning darling, how did you sleep?" Christina asked. Pen did not detect any innuendo. Either Lennox had not told her, or Christina had other things on her mind.

"Very well thanks," said Pen. "Please, put me to work."

"We're in fine shape, actually. They're not expected until one, and we're only"—she consulted her watch—"a quarter past nine. The potatoes are peeled, the ham has been soaked. I'll put it in at half ten, and—"

"You're serving *ham*?" Margot interjected.

Christina peered into a roasting pan. "Yes, a beautiful joint from Hector's brother. With a mustard and demerara sugar glaze."

"You're not afraid it will traumatize the children?"

"Why should it?"

Margot swept her arm over the cake, bracelets clattering. She had outlined the face, ears, and snout with icing in a darker shade of pink. She had even added eyes and rosy cheeks. The effect was considerably more porcine.

Christina covered her mouth. "Peppa!" she exclaimed.

Danny's eyes opened wide in expectation. George let out a dark laugh.

"You're both getting batty in your old age. If we agree that no one is to connect the dots for the children"—she looked pointedly at her mother—"I don't think we'll need to hire a social worker. Our guests are mostly under four, remember."

She turned her attention to Danny. "Right, bath time for you, sir." She lifted him up from under the armpits. He threw his head back and yelped in protest. Pen helped to extract his pudgy legs from the high chair. She found a pacifier on the ground, washed it, and handed it to Danny. He stuck it in his mouth and lay his cheek on his mother's shoulder, overcome with drowsiness. George went out, nearly bumping into Sasha as he came in from the dining room.

"You're good with kids," Margot observed. Pen, who was trying hard not to look at Sasha or to reveal the havoc his presence in the room was stirring in her chest, noticed that once again Margot was appraising her. "Do you plan on having them?"

"I don't know." She was able to keep her voice steady by concentrating on her dislike of Margot.

"A bit early to have decided that." Christina laughed, squeezing Sasha's arm by way of greeting.

"Not necessarily. She might already know she'd prefer a career," said Margot. "My brother mentioned that you want to be a journalist?"

"It's not the nineteenth century, for heaven's sake. It's possible to have both," Christina countered.

"Is it?" said Margot. "You don't."

Christina refused to be baited. Her face was set in a gracious smile. "Well, you do, don't you?"

"Margot," interrupted Sasha firmly. "Running this place—and with the minimum of help so she can put every extra penny into the village, where she does the work of a local representative, head of school, church warden, conservationist, therapist, and entire business development council combined—*is* a career, as you, of all people, should know."

"Don't forget defense lawyer," said Freddie, surprising them all. He had silently come up from the boot room laden with two carrier bags, one bright orange and the other light green, and a large wrapped box. He was dressed nattily in a navy wool coat and looked very different from the rumpled boy Pen had stumbled on in his bedroom. "Without you on my side I'd be a cooked goose, Mum. I only wish you had one of those lovely barristers' wigs."

He swept his mother into an enormous hug, and she wrapped her arms around him tenderly. "Hello my darling," she said. "You're very sweet, but don't think yourself exonerated. What's all this? You'll forgive me for not being overly enthusiastic about parcels from *you*."

He laughed, gave the orange bag to his mother, and set aside the other packages for George and Danny.

He then flashed Pen a smile that contained only a hint of wickedness. "Lovely to see you again, Nancy," he said.

"This is *Penelope*, darling," Christina said.

Pen leaned in to accept Freddie's cheek kisses.

When she pulled back, hoping to find Sasha's eye, it was Margot who met her gaze and held it. Her way of looking made Pen feel like a fish at the market, gutless and splayed on ice chips, on the verge of being sliced up and eaten raw.

39

From the moment Danny reappeared, bleary-eyed in elasticized slacks and a blue button-down, and began helping himself to fistfuls of the Twiglets and potato chips Christina had put out, Pen was able to disappear into the flurry of the party. George was radiant at the center of a knot of admirers. Diana-like in her patterned trousers and ruffled blouse, she anticipated the needs of her guests large and small, carrying presents, wet wipes, toys, plates of ham, dishes of cake with ice cream, and the pastel-colored macarons Freddie had brought hither and thither, and switching seamlessly between the crouched complicity of toddler-speak and the different register required by the assembled adults.

Danny's father, Rosh, who had pulled up an hour before the party was due to start and been greeted as a conquering hero by Lennox and Christina, followed George closely with his eyes. Olive-skinned and handsome, with a high forehead and clean-shaven jaw, he wore a smile that invited approach and a blue and white graph paper shirt that looked professionally starched. His hands were kept busy, though mostly he waited for George to put things into them. Margot teased him in a way that suggested he was more one of the family than George had let on.

Lennox was a benign absence from the octagonal sitting room, which heaved all afternoon with balloons, ribbons, and small tumbling bodies. He had instead established himself at the dining room table, where he spoke in confiding tones to the other men of his generation in attendance, most from the farms and village, each with a tumbler of whisky in hand.

Christina, meanwhile, with the silk scarf Freddie had brought for her tied elegantly at her neck, was the cog around which the day turned, providing not only its structure and sustenance, but also the low, nearly imperceptible hum of order and compassion that made the house comfortable, and which, like running water or electricity, would only ever be truly noticed if it stopped.

At one moment, after the excitement of the piñata, Danny, indignant that the candy was being put away, had thrown his head back in protest, striking it against a side table with a sickening thunk. From the other end of the room Margot, who had been sunk in a tête-a-tête with Rosh, cried out as if it were her head that had been bumped. After a shocked pause, Danny burst into loud sobs at both the pain and the injustice. George, who had sprung up to buffer the fall and missed by a split second, held her son to her chest and rocked him back and forth, whispering comforting words in his ear. Margot leaped to her feet and crossed the room.

"You have to watch him ALL the time," she shouted at George, who was busy soothing Danny and paid no attention to her mother. Christina put her arm around George.

"She knows," she said pointedly to Margot. "And she does."

. . .

Midway through the party, Pen stepped out the back door and into the still-dormant flower garden for a short break from the noise. She was hoping for a moment to think—or that Sasha might follow her. She soon heard the terrace door clank, but when she turned toward the house, it was Freddie who came down the steps.

"All right, Nance?" he asked conversationally, tapping a pack of Marlboro Reds against the heel of his palm.

"Hi, Freddie. What did you do in Peru that was so awful?" she asked, cutting right to the chase. "Sasha said it would be better if you explained."

Freddie drew in a breath, as if loath to revisit the subject. "I suppose I can tell you, now that Hugh's had his payout from the *Daily Bugle*, or wherever," he said. He lit a Marlboro and offered her one. She shook her head. "But first, you should know that Hugh is a first-class tosser. He made my life miserable at school. It's normal for younger boys to get teased, but he was sadistic on another level. And we're *cousins*.

"It began as nothing, just a joke between my mate Jake and me," Freddie continued. He stamped his feet against the cold like a horse. "Can we walk? I'm freezing my bollocks off out here." So they walked along the garden's hedge-lined path. "We worked in landscaping for three months to save up, and then we started our gap year in Rome. At a shop in Vatican City, I found this pendant embossed with the pope's face in profile. At first it really creeped me out. Then I had a vision: What if it were to arrive, with no note or explanation, in a velvet box addressed to Hugh at his new job? What would he make of it? All very innocent, as you can see." He checked her face to find out if she was sympathetic so far.

"A couple of weeks later, in Bucharest, we came across a truly massive case of cigarillos—there must have been four dozen of the things, utterly useless because who on God's green golf course smokes bloody cigarillos?—all wrapped in gold foil. It seemed like the kind of thing one might send to grease a palm, had one been born in 1910. So we pooled our funds and purchased the damned thing for Hugh and his prodigious ego, with compliments.

"Things got a few shades darker after Romania," Freddie said, shaking his head ruefully. At a costume shop in Moscow, he told her, they had come across a set of realistic-looking severed fingers, and had been powerless to resist the thought of Hugh's reaction as a thumb tumbled onto the institutional carpet of his prestigious office. But the thumb had not been their undoing. It had been weeks later, while playing chess with Jake on the finely grained sand of Do Son Beach, that Freddie had once again remembered Cousin Hugh and felt moved to send him a souvenir, even though they were quite short on cash by that point.

This time, the arrival in the Palmer Street mail room of a slim envelope addressed to Hugh Cornelius Campbell, Esq., with a Vietnamese postage stamp and no return address, had triggered the evacuation of the entire building and the arrival of a bioterrorism team in hazmat suits. Loose white granules shifting around inside an envelope addressed to a secret government office, as it turned out, were no laughing matter; it had only been a few years since anthrax in the mail had killed several people in Florida.

For weeks Freddie and Jake remained ignorant of the wreckage they had caused. They would never have guessed that the envelope could be traced back to the post office from which they had sent it, in Haiphong. Or that footage from surveillance cameras at an adjacent bank would be used, eventually, to identify their faces. By the time their identities had been confirmed, they were in Peru, trying to board a flight to Buenos Aires. They were alerted that their passports had been flagged and brought to an interrogation room, where they were informed that they were wanted by Interpol.

Christina, after receiving the phone call, had done everything in her power, including getting in touch with several former colleagues who by then were high-ranking officials and—worse—explaining the situation to her family, to ensure that the boys, barely eighteen at the time, would at least be sent back to the UK and charged domestically. Once the substance had been confirmed as sand; once Hugh had acknowledged that he knew the sender; once Christina had made the case that this should be treated as disorderly conduct, not as a hoax threat—and with the understanding that should the story become public, it would be next to impossible not to make an example of them—Freddie and Jake were eventually let off with a fine, including repaying the cost of responding to the perceived threat, and a thousand hours of community service apiece, plus a note on their records, which could be cleared after five years of good behavior. He was currently paying off the fine by working for Margot, who, for all her employment standards with her real staff, was delighted to have a nephew on call around the clock.

"Dad, bless him, buried his head in the—well, sand, throughout the ordeal," said Freddie. "It was Mum who kept us out of prison. And Marg is helping to restore my solvency. So that's the whole sordid tale." He looked appropriately repentant.

They had made it back to the terrace door. Pen shook her head, smiling. "Thank you for telling me," she said.

"You're welcome. Now we'd best go in, or we'll risk missing the ham cake."

After the guests had gone, no one wanted much in the way of supper. George and Rosh, who were headed to London early the next morning, did not reemerge after putting a delirious Danny down at six thirty. He had insisted on bringing the toy train Freddie had given him upstairs to bed with him, and they could hear his fading "choo-choo"s winding their way up the stairs. Margot turned in soon afterward, pleading a headache.

Sasha made tea and took on the kitchen while Freddie took out the bins and Pen and Christina cleared the living and dining rooms and vacuumed up the crumbs that had been ground into the rugs. Lennox, impervious to the sound, snored in his armchair.

"He could sleep through an alien invasion," Christina told Pen, shaking her head in a way that suggested it had long ago ceased to annoy her. Once the last surface had been sponged and the dishwasher was making the satisfying shushing sound that signals order restored, Christina gently roused her husband. He followed her into the kitchen.

"Well done, my love," said Lennox sleepily. "Splendid party."

"It did go well." She said. "You're all poppets. I think there's a miniseries on tonight." She caught a small yawn with the back of her hand. "I can't remember what, but it's supposed to be brilliant."

"What do you say, shall we all watch a miniseries?" Freddie asked after his parents had gone out, stretching his arms over his head in a gesture Pen recalled from their first meeting. He looked at Pen, his eyes twinkling like his dad's. "I think it's *Jane Eyre*. I'll bet that's right up your street, isn't it, Nance? Let me guess—second only to P&P? Or are you more of an S&S woman?"

Pen laughed. "All of the above. But I don't think I'm up for it tonight. Thanks, Freddie." She looked across the table at Sasha. He met her eyes.

Freddie looked between them. "All right then. Night, you two." He whistled to himself as he left the kitchen.

Up in the turret, Pen sat down on Sasha's bed. It was freshly made up, she noticed. He sat beside her, leaving some distance between them.

"Are you all right?" he asked.

"Of course," she said. "Why?"

He took her hand and wove their fingers together. "You've hardly spoken a word to me all day."

"I couldn't have spoken to you in front of them," she said, squeezing his hand. "I'm not a good actor. I'm pretty sure your dad guessed anyway. I ran into him in the kitchen first thing."

"Was it very painful?" he asked.

It took her a moment to realize he didn't mean the conversation with Lennox.

"A bit. But not because of you. You were nice."

He shifted closer to her. "So you haven't been regretting it?"

She touched the place between his shoulder blades, putting pressure there. He seemed to uncoil. "Not at all. Have you?"

"Not at all," he said, sounding relieved. "There's no need to act. They can all know."

She smiled and moved her hands to the slope between his neck and shoulders.

He looked at her, their faces so close their foreheads nearly touched. "Can I ask you something?"

"Marriage," she said. "I was waiting for marriage. You are going to marry me, right?"

He kissed her gently on the mouth, too briefly. "Of course," he said.

"No, you're not." She laughed. "I don't even believe in marriage. I think I just knew it was going to be weird and embarrassing, and I was waiting for someone weird and embarrassing enough to do it with. If that was even your question."

He lifted her hair into a ponytail and kissed the side of her neck. "I'm honored," he said.

"And." She tilted into his touch. "I suppose it also has to do with never having wanted to do it with anyone quite so badly before."

He stopped kissing her neck. "Really," he said.

"Really." They shifted farther onto the bed, and she lay back against the pillows. Her cheeks felt hot.

"Can you tell me how badly that was, exactly?"

"Very, very badly."

"I see," he said. "And was it so weird and embarrassing that you'll never want it that badly ever again?"

"I wouldn't say that." Her voice was growing hoarse. He was moving his hand up her leg. "No, I wouldn't say that."

"I think I can make it better for you," he said. "Would you let me try?"

She couldn't speak. She nodded. He kissed her again.

Afterward, with the windows open and cool air blowing in, lying with her head on his chest, Pen had begun to understand what the fuss was all about.

"Any improvement?" he asked.

"Hmm?" she said. "Oh. No. You're going to need a lot more practice."

His laughter was a bit manic. They had not quite recovered.

"Why don't you believe in marriage?" he asked, running his fingers through her hair.

She was surprised by the question.

"Maybe 'believe' is the wrong way of putting it. I know it can work," she said. "It's just that it usually doesn't."

She was quiet for a while, and then went on. "In a way it's nice that people in our generation are still optimistic enough to try it. It's like how people get tattoos, when on some level they must know they're not going to want those same markings forever." She turned to face him. "You don't have any tattoos, do you?" she asked, recalling Freddie's heraldic rose.

"I can't remember."

She searched the smooth skin over muscle and bone, and through the soft hair on his forearms and legs. There were tiny bumps on the backs of his arms, too. She found a scar just below his left kneecap.

"None," she said.

"What about love?" he asked.

She locked her jaw.

"What about it?"

"Do you believe in it?"

"I'm not sure. Why do you ask?"

"What aren't you sure about?"

She didn't want to tell him about how her parents' love, if that was what it had been, had exploded like a swollen battery, leaking acid into all their lives.

"That it lasts." She was glad he couldn't see her face, but she wished she could see his.

"I see."

She thought, unaccountably, about Margot. That sharp, laughing stare. The feeling of being the subject of an inside joke. And then Lennox's question: "Did your parents ever mention her?" A strange thing to ask.

"Rosh seems kind," she said.

"Mm. He's a good man."

"Are he and George . . ."

"I think so. As much as she'll allow. They do live together when she's in London. But if you're marriage-agnostic, she's probably an atheist."

"Why?"

"Margot. Margot has this idea—I'm surprised she hasn't cornered you to deliver it yet—that all men are jailers. She says women should have children, if that's what they want, but that brides are lambs to the slaughter. Or something to that effect."

"So she chose to raise George entirely alone?"

"I don't think that's how Mum would see it."

"Right. George told me that she had spent holidays here."

"I adore Margot, but she's on her own schedule. She didn't turn up for Christmas half the time, if there was fun to be had on the Matterhorn or wherever. And I think she's made it hard for George to trust anyone. Rosh has been trying to convince her to marry him for years now, and she keeps escaping up here. To be fair, he does work insane hours. He's a banker, but a cool one. He's brilliant, actually. Speaks four languages. He and George met at Cambridge. He and his older brother left Beirut during the Civil War. His brother is a chef at a restaurant near Holborn. Best food in London. I'll take you there." He ran his foot along her leg.

Pen hadn't even known that George had gone to Cambridge. She'd never thought to ask where she had studied, or what.

"How old was Margot when she had George?"

"Twenty-one."

Pen imagined herself pregnant in two years, a mother in three. She pulled the duvet over her body.

"And George's dad was never in the picture?"

"No. It wasn't planned, obviously. He fled to America or something, the coward. She'd been in London, at Slade, but she left and came here."

At the words "America" and "coward," Pen's body went cold. The clarity was painful, a dislocated joint being set back into place. Sasha, unaware, continued. "When George was little, Margot brought her to Paris and set up shop. Everyone was horrified, apparently, but nobody could argue with Margot. You all right?"

Pen nodded.

Sasha shifted onto his side and drew her to his chest. "Thank you for letting me redeem myself," he said into her hair.

His chest was warm, and she could feel the throb of his heartbeat against the side of her face. The pine sap and wood fire smell of him, the weight of his arms around her, and the way their legs were entwined under the covers was intoxicating. But inside her nervous system, all was mayhem. An alarm was blaring, bright lights were flashing, sirens were going off. She knew that she needed to get out. When she could take it no longer, she got up slowly, careful not to wake him. She tore herself away.

Pen folded her things into her bag and straightened the green bedroom. She paced the room, thinking, waiting for the first sign of light. She knew she should leave a note, an apology for leaving in a rush, some lie to keep them from worrying. She riffled through her bag for a pen, but she didn't have one. *Some reporter you'll make*, she told herself. But what did it matter when Lennox and Christina, surely—and possibly all of them—had known all along? Out the window, the sky was turning the purple of a black eye. She crept down the main staircase, watched by a succession of Lennox ancestors. She went through the kitchen and down the boot room steps, feeling for her jacket and boots. The cold handle gave with a click. She exhaled. She closed it gently and hurried up the gravel.

Out on the driveway, she dug for her phone. She had saved the phone number Christina had given her in November, and she prayed someone would pick up at this hour. After ten rings, someone did. She asked for a taxi to meet her at St. Helen's. Twenty minutes, they said. She made her way down the long driveway then followed signs for the village.

When she reached the sleeping church, she waited. Hot pink and DayGlo orange—colors that belonged on an eighties ski suit on the Matterhorn—were rising in the sky beneath a thick strip of mucky cloud. The cab pulled up with its rounded contours and spacious back seat. She named the train station and dug in the silty crevices of the banquette to fasten her seat belt.

She bought a ticket at the machine, and after an interminable wait on the deserted platform, the empty train chugged to a stop. When it began sliding south, she closed her eyes and tried to rest.

She imagined the layers of awareness inside of her, like a diagram of the Earth's crust. The brittle layer at the top told her that she should dismiss the thought that had taken hold of her as an incorrect connection drawn by an overeager mind. Beneath it, in the area of dense rock that becomes molten when a plate slips below the surface, an area that seemed to be linked to her breathing and heartbeat, was the desire to be wrong, and a plea for more evidence. And at her liquid, burning core, there was fury.

She noticed her phone was making noise and turned it off. The refreshment trolley rattled toward her. She held her elbows in and smiled at the attendant in the overfriendly way she had of rejecting wares. As if this man cared whether she bought his Hobnobs. After he had gone, she realized she was thirsty.

She smiled at the ticket man, too, and handed over her ticket and student railcard. She let the train rock her. Her tumbling thoughts morphed as she sunk out of consciousness and into a dream.

Sasha was in the study wearing a black academic gown. George and Freddie were with him, and he was warning George about something, or someone. *Trust me*, he was saying. Pen was watching them from outside on the balcony. She tried to get their attention, but she didn't have the strength to open the doors. She tapped on the glass. They didn't notice her. She smacked on it with her palm but still they did not see or hear her. She looked at the beige pebbles below. *If only I were wearing a gown, too,* she thought, *I would be able to fly down from here.* She looked down at her body and noticed she *was* wearing a gown. She climbed onto the railing and looked. Her stomach dropped.

"Feck!!" said a voice from nearby. Pen blinked. A man across the aisle had spilled coffee onto his lap. She felt crusted saliva on her chin and dabbed at it with her sleeve.

Her room in Lee House felt different now that Sasha had been inside it. She stood still for a moment, letting the hot wave pass through her, and then drew the curtains closed to block out the too-clear day. She opened the drawer of the bedside table, pulled out her mother's journal, and opened it. Then she switched on the bedside lamp and sat cross-legged on the bed. After a while, her landline began to ring. Without thinking, she picked up the receiver.

40

Alice had lice. She had caught one of the fuckers in the tines of a skinny comb she'd bought at the pharmacy as soon as it had opened that morning. She'd matched it to the pictures online and now she was pressing it between her thumb and forefinger. The only thing to do, she had read, was to use a special shampoo and then cover her hair with a whole bottle of thick white conditioner and comb it through. But she had so much hair, and she couldn't reach the back of her own head.

She needed Pen. No one else in the city of Edinburgh, maybe no one else in the world, could be trusted with knowing how vile she was. Alice would sooner have shaved her head and called it a fashion statement than asked Jo or Neville, whom she had known for a mere six months, to comb vermin from her hair. And she could not call her mother. Even if she had not been five thousand kilometers away, Nicola would only have folded Alice's panic into her own larger and more general panic. It had to be Pen. But Pen's phone was off. Alice had listened to her friend's polite-to-strangers voice a dozen times. "You've reached the voicemail of Penelope Winters. I'm not available right now, so please leave a message and I will return your call as soon as I can. Thanks!"

"Pen, I know it's a bad time and you're in a love nest, but I NEED YOU. PLEASE. It's an emergency. Okay, bye."

It was the fifth voicemail she had left Pen that morning. In between, she had sent her texts and alerts on messenger (even though her profile said "offline"), and dialed the landline in her room, which didn't have voicemail but rang and rang in a way that Alice found soothing, because it left open the possibility that Pen could, at any moment, walk through the door and answer it. She had said she would be home on Sunday, but she had not said when on Sunday. It was now half past noon and a gnawing hunger added to the discomfort of her itchy scalp. Alice had bought snacks at the pharmacy, knowing that if she was, indeed, contaminated, she would shut herself up in her room until the massacre was complete, but she wanted to save them to share with Pen.

She twisted open a bottle of Diet Coke. It made a satisfying hiss. She screwed the cap against the erupting fizz and dialed Pen's landline again.

"Hello?" Pen answered on the first ring. Her voice was tentative, as if she didn't know who was calling.

"Oh thank God. Thank fucking God."

"Alice? Are you okay?"

"NO!" It came out as a wail. She hadn't meant to sound so pitiful, but she hadn't slept the night before, and had worked herself into a state of considerable anxiety and self-loathing.

"Stay there, I'm coming."

Alice replaced the receiver and swallowed a mouthful of lukewarm foam. The familiar, chemical taste calmed her. She shoved her clothes into the closet and her shoes under the bed, trying to make her room look less like the kind of slovenly den where one might incubate head lice. She stacked up the magazines and books on the desk and laid out the snacks—bags of gummies and salt and vinegar crisps, a big bar of dark chocolate with almonds, Pen's favorite—in what she hoped was an enticing spread. On the counter beside the sink, she readied the bottles of shampoo and conditioner, the comb, and, in case things went badly, a pair of scissors and a turquoise Venus razor.

Pen let herself in. She was breathless. She crossed directly to Alice, who held her arms out, wrists flexed in warning. "Don't come closer."

"What?" Pen still looked like she planned to hug her. Alice backed into the corner by the sink.

"Pen, don't. I have . . ." The word felt icky in her mouth. "Lice."

"Oh!"

Pen didn't look disgusted. She looked concerned. "How?"

"I don't know." Alice heard her voice rise again into something thin and breakable. "My costumes, probably, or the old couches in the rehearsal room covered in blankets that no one ever washes. Or maybe I'm just gross. But Thomasina isn't, and I can't be her with—" Alice hadn't cried for real since grade ten, when her family's dog had been put down. The tears falling into her mouth felt nothing like the ones she manufactured in auditions; they were scalding and accompanied by deep, throttling sobs. She wanted to go home. She let herself slide down the wall and hugged her knees. She knew she was being childish but now she couldn't stop.

Pen sat down facing Alice, so that their knees were touching. She picked up Alice's hand and held it in both of hers, as if to keep it warm.

"I've had lice, remember?" Pen said.

Alice did not remember. She shook her head, resisting the urge to scratch.

"At camp when we were eleven. See, you don't even remember because it's not a big deal; it's manageable."

Alice's mind jumped to the last summer they had gone to Camp Blue Moon together. She remembered what had happened while they were gone, and what had happened in Pen's life afterward. The memory had the immediate effect of adjusting Alice's perspective on the current crisis.

"I'm sorry," Alice said. She wiped her tears with the back of her hand and changed the subject. "How was sex?"

Pen produced a dry laugh, almost a cough. "How was sex?" she repeated.

Alice gave her a meaningful look that was comically overdone and then started shaking with laughter.

Pen felt a familiar fizziness in her chest. Soon she found herself laughing in the uncontainable way that only ever happened with Alice, the way that made her diaphragm contract in hiccups and her face and stomach muscles sore the next day. The madness of it—of their fallible, animal bodies, of urges that were necessary to the survival of the species and yet obscene in the daylight—was suddenly too much to take.

Alice dabbed at her streaming eyes with the bottom of her T-shirt. She had almost peed her pants, which would not have been unprecedented.

She and Pen had been friends since well before they had discovered the need to construct an outer shell, like that of an invertebrate animal, to protect the soft inner substance of the self. Childhood friendships often lose their hold at that point, when one sees that the person one loved has learned to disguise herself and will no longer be reachable, or at least not often. What made Alice feel certain, as Pen helped herself to the roll of toilet paper on her desk to wipe her nose, that this friendship could take them through every stage of their lives, cushioning them against the bone-crushing loneliness of being human, was that they did not have to pretend with each other. Silently, she vowed to remember this.

Pen held her breath until the hiccups subsided. She found the shampoo and broke off a piece of chocolate while she read the instructions. Alice retrieved her laptop from the bed and put on music. Then she took her place in the chair before the sink.

While Pen massaged the lice shampoo into Alice's scalp, she let her mind return to the Lennoxes. Not to Sasha, not yet, but to Christina and Lennox, to George and Margot, and to what they had all known this whole time. They must have thought that she, too, had known. She was now convinced of this.

"I think I might have a sister," Pen said.

Alice was humming along to *The Miseducation of Lauryn Hill*.

"Hmm?" She looked up at Pen, whose hands had stopped moving.

"I think I have a sister," Pen repeated.

Alice did not speak. Her face, enlarged by the shampoo-coated helmet of her hair, was frozen in a look of anticipation, as if she were waiting for Pen to deliver the punch line.

"George," said Pen. She rinsed her hands in the sink. Her throat felt dry. She still hadn't drunk any water that day, she realized. She reached for the bottle on Alice's desk and took a big swallow.

"What the . . ." Alice was shaking her head. She turned off the music. "What the actual fuck?"

Pen sat down on the bed and took another sip of water. She was parched. She drained half the bottle. Then she told Alice what she had put together.

"Wait." Alice stopped her. "You're saying your dad had an affair not with Christina but with MARGOT Lennox—and that she may have had his child?"

"I think so. Yes."

"You think or you know?"

"I think I know."

"Holy shit, Pen. And you let me go on about lice? Start from the beginning."

Pen took a deep breath in through her nose. Trying to put the streaks of information she had gathered into a coherent narrative would be useful.

"I've been so distracted by my—whatever it is, on Sasha, that I didn't—"

She started again. "This weekend, when Margot arrived, she clearly hated me. She was awful to Christina, too, so I figured she was just not the nicest person, but there was something in the way she looked at me. Like I was a knockoff of one of her handbags and she was noticing all the cheap, fake bits. And then Lennox asked me in this weird way if I knew about Margot when I was a kid. I said of course. I told him about you, and how you've been telling me all about Margot for years, and he said yes but did my *dad* ever talk about her, because he'd had a 'soft spot' for her back in the day."

"A *soft spot*?!" Alice was incredulous.

"Part of me knew there was more, there had to be more, he was being so cagey. But between the party and Freddie and Sasha, it wasn't until last night . . . I started asking Sasha questions, almost without realizing what I was doing. And it fits. They were in London at the same time. She was in art school, and he was doing his master's. He left the same summer she got pregnant with George. He came straight back to Toronto and married my mom that August."

Alice shook her head from side to side. The shampoo was starting to burn her scalp a bit, and she wanted to scratch at it.

"I don't understand. It doesn't really sound like your dad."

"I know. Except that he and my mom were already engaged before he went to London. And he'd been trained from childhood to take over Winter Corp—so he had to go back."

"Who cares?!"

"Tilda would have cared. She would have told him it was his duty to care. He would have had her voice in his head. I still do."

"What about his duty to his child? To Margot??"

"I don't know," Pen said.

Alice gave in and scratched her head, getting foam under her fingernails.

"Wait, the Lennoxes would all know this, wouldn't they?"

"I'm pretty sure. It explains why they've seemed so . . . interested in me," said Pen.

"Right. Because them liking you was the confusing part in all this," said Alice. "But what do you mean you're pretty sure—haven't you talked to George? Or Sasha?"

Pen shook her head.

"Who have you talked to?"

"No one. You. I left as soon as it was light out. I couldn't stay there."

"You *absconded*? And you turned off your phone. They must be . . . Holy SHIT, Pen. Are you okay? I'd hug you if I wasn't . . ."

"I'm fine. It's just . . . yeah."

"Hold on—does this mean you and Sasha are *related*?"

"NO! God," said Pen, who had already been through the family tree in her mind several times.

"Kind of, though," said Alice, still working it out. "Obviously not by blood. Legally you're fine. But his cousin is your half sister—don't look so freaked out! Everyone knows aristos love their cousins."

"What we should do is wash that stuff out of your hair before it burns any more holes in your brain." Pen tipped Alice's head back into the sink and used her tooth glass to rinse her head, careful to keep the shampoo out of her eyes and ears. Then she spread Alice's hair with a thick layer of white conditioner and combed the corpses out one by one.

"When are you going to call your dad?" Alice asked.

Pen shook her head. "I need more time to think."

"Do you hate him?"

"No. I haven't decided yet. But no."

They fell silent.

At length, Pen told Alice that she thought she had gotten them all, and Alice went to shower. Pen opened her cell phone and held down the power button. "Storage full," warned a bar of text on the small screen. She dialed her voicemail. "Your voicemail box is full. You cannot receive any new messages," scolded the officious-sounding recording. The first several were from Alice. She pressed 7 to delete them. The next was brief:

"Pen, it's George. Please call me as soon as you can."

She deleted that, too. While she waited for the next one to play, a new call came through. "Sasha," read the display. She couldn't answer it. Not yet.

The next voicemail was from him. His voice sent ripples down her spine.

"Are you okay? What happened? Trying not to worry. Ring me back."

She shut her phone and turned it off again. She broke off some more of the chocolate bar and ate a handful of chips.

Alice came back into the room wrapped in her bathrobe, her hair in a towel.

"I'd better boil everything I own now," said Alice. "Thanks for saving me."

"Any time."

"Want to stay? Maybe watch something?"

"No, I'm good. Meet you at dinner?"

Alice nodded and squeezed Pen's arm. Pen let herself out.

She crossed the courtyard to her room. Tim from Medieval Poetry made eye contact and waved. She picked up her pace. The sky was an irrational, vibrant blue, as if it were made of bristol board. She had a brief fantasy that she was Jim Carrey in *The Truman Show*, and that everyone else—George, Sasha, her parents, everyone but Alice—was an actor putting on a show for the amusement of some unknown audience. This sensation of unreality grew stronger as she unlocked the door to her room. Something was off. When she opened the door, Elliot Lennox was leaning back in her desk chair, one leg crossed over the other, reading her copy of *Night and Day*.

Lennox looked up at Pen with an expression of welcome, as if she were entering his living room.

"What's the use of writing detective stories if you can't borrow some of the tricks?" he said, standing up to greet her. He replaced the paperback on her bookshelf, first glancing at the page number as if he planned to return to it.

She noticed that he had brought a bottle of whisky with him—the same kind she had given him on her first visit. He cracked the seal, took the two polka dot mugs her mother had bought for her down from the shelf, and poured out large measures of the golden liquid. He passed one to her, but she did not take it. He set it down on the desk.

Nothing in his demeanor suggested that this visit was out of the ordinary. He did not seem to notice that he was half a foot from her bed, where the journal that she had dropped earlier lay, apparently undisturbed. His power was such that she felt like she was the one trespassing. This, she knew, was nuts, and she forced herself to fix him with a neutral stare. She waited for him to speak, to explain his presence.

"Christina sent me," he said. "She wanted me to see that you were all right."

"I'm all right," said Pen, still not sitting down, refusing to drop her guard.

"I've never known Sasha in such a state," he said, trying another tack. "But I know you didn't leave because of something my idiot son has done."

"No."

"Perhaps, rather, it was something his idiot father has done?" he asked, and took a sip of whisky.

"Yes," he went on, as if finding in her eyes some responsiveness that she was trying hard not to offer. "I know you feel we've been keeping you in the dark, Pen. And you're right. But this time, it was not my story to tell."

He took a notepad from his jacket pocket and wrote down a phone number. He held it out to her. When she did not move, he placed it on her desk, centering the paper on top of her closed laptop.

He drained his mug and stood up. "You've become dear to all of us, Pen. Please come back whenever you're ready." He put his hands on her shoulders. There was something in his bearing that made her think of the few priests she had known. He kissed the top of her head. A benediction. And then he was gone.

She sat down in his recently vacated chair—*her* chair!—and smelled the whisky. He had left the bottle. She sat still for several minutes, staring at the wall. Then she picked up the journal from the bed and opened it to the first page, on which was written in black felt tip:

Please return to Anna ~~Sinclair~~ Winters

Her mother's writing had hardly changed. It made Pen think of her own name printed in bleeding Sharpie ink on the tag of every baseball cap, beach towel, and pillowcase that had once gone in her trunk to sleepover camp. Some of these were still in circulation at her mother's house. The image of these objects brought with it a painful flash of the broiling August afternoon when it had been Tilda, not her mother, who had met the returning camp bus in the shopping mall parking lot. To banish the memory, instead she imagined the plastic body of the marker Anna had used to write her name all those years ago, refusing to decompose in a landfill somewhere. *We leave so much garbage behind*, she thought. *If we didn't let ourselves forget about most of it, we'd go insane.*

After learning about the miscarriages and understanding how wrong she had been, Pen had wanted to leave her mother's past closed for a while, the way as a child she had preferred to leave the lid on her green turtle-shaped sandbox, to avoid seeing the potato bugs that hid underneath. But she knew that this wasn't something she could do forever, even if she chose not to read whatever it was her mother had sought to preserve in this notebook.

You can be braver than that, she told herself. *Sapere aude*—dare to know. She opened the journal to the last spread, with a single page of text on the left. Neat words marched to the bottom of the page like black ants, growing smaller and denser as the limit approached. They crowded to the bottom right corner and then veered up the side of the paper and back over to the top margin where they hung suspended, upside-down. Inside the back cover, she knew (because she had some of these journals herself; her mother had given them to her), was a secret pocket. *Relics*, she thought, feeling inside, *are safer than words*. Relics are dead; words are alive.

The first thing she took out was a picture of herself in black and white. Except that it wasn't her; it was her mother. Anna wore a spring dress and a defiant expression. Her dark hair was twisted into a knot at the nape of her neck, with tendrils escaping around her face. She was standing with another woman in front of an ivy-covered building Pen recognized. "Renée and me, Hart House, April '79," her mother had written. Next Pen took out a postcard, a Turner sunset, or was it a sunrise. On the back, fifteen indecipherable words, signed "Yours, Teddy." Next, a wedding invitation, formal, on cream cardstock. *Mr. and Mrs. Edward Winters request the pleasure of your company . . . Saturday, August 22, 1980, three o'clock . . . Dinner and dancing to follow.* Next, an opened faded periwinkle envelope with the original address crossed out, and the forwarding address corrected. The handwriting was loopy but elegant. It was addressed to her dad.

Pen returned to the front of the journal. She imagined herself as a

pelican, hovering above the water's surface, hunting for fish. She began
running her eyes across the rows of words.

*Renée thinks he must have someone over there. Well, so what
if he does. I never asked for celibacy. All I cared to know was,
will he come back? And it appears he will, and our life
together can finally—*

*"You've hardly time to print invitations," Mrs. W said when
we told her. She thinks I'm pregnant. If only. Almost every
night now I have the same dream that used to soothe and
haunt me, except now* mine *is the chest the warm bundle is
resting on, mine the neck she breathes into. I don't care if it's
impossible to retain memories from that age; it* feels *real. He
wants it, too, as badly as I do, I think. So many of our friends
are still refusing to put on shoes, and here he is ready to be a
father. And his love for his mother, his own strong family ties,
are part of what drew me to him. I must remind myself of
that. She hates me, of course. I'm the wrong sort—too poor,
too shabby, too much of a bluestocking with my French books
and my talk of a PhD, but she's accepting me. She knows
accepting me is the price of Ted . . .*

Eventually, Pen would read the rest. But first, she turned to the back
pocket again and fingered the blue envelope. The flap was jagged.

St. Mark's Road

July 19, 1980

Teddy,

Not sending by air because I <u>do not</u> want you to turn around and come back—my decision stands—but I thought (or rather, <u>your friend</u> thinks) you ought to know. Pour yourself a gin. Good, you've guessed. Yes, it happened to us, to me, and yes, I blame you because you said you were taking precautions, although I'm the one who believed you, so there we have it.

I'm keeping it, turns out that's all I'm capable of, joke's on me, and naming it for Father, who would have killed you, so you're lucky he's dead. I have what I need so don't start sending your Canadian dollars, I don't think I could bear it.

With love and less rancor than you might think, only a small amount owing to your ignorance on matters of biology, Yours (in part)—M

41

The London Aquarium was on the other side of the river from the small part of London Pen knew. She took the tube as far as Leicester Square, and then she walked. She was stiff-limbed from sleeping on the train and needed to collect her thoughts.

In Trafalgar Square, low puffs of cloud, dark gray against a pale gray sky, appeared to touch the central dome of the National Gallery. This, too, was gray, as were the portico's impressive columns. A stone carapace protecting the nation's color and feeling. Or keeping them from seeping out.

Pen hurried past the spluttering merpeople of the fountains, and across the Strand and the Embankment toward the river. She had planned this route the previous night, tracing the path she would take across the Golden Jubilee footbridge and along the Queen's Walk, past the London Eye to the Edwardian County Hall building. She arrived at the ten-foot penguins that flanked the riverside entrance with time to spare. There were no crowds; the school groups, she imagined, had yet to disembark from their buses.

Buying a ticket at the information desk, she was briefly alarmed by how much money she had spent in a single day. She let the thought evaporate.

Pen was admiring the round white bellies and long tails of the seahorses, whose silhouettes did not at all correspond to the image she'd had in mind, when she felt a presence beside her.

Margot's coat of ornate silk brocade shone in the strange light of the aquarium and reminded Pen of a suit of armor.

"Good of you to come all this way," Margot said in greeting. Pen nodded. She waited for Margot to say more. She was learning to wield silence.

"Strange, isn't it," Margot continued after a while, as if Pen would naturally be thinking the same thing, "the way the male seahorse is the one to carry the young and give birth, so to speak. His pregnancy only lasts a matter of days, but still. It endears them to me, I must say."

Pen had not come all the way to London to hear about seahorses. She took the periwinkle envelope from her jacket pocket and held it out.

Margot looked down at the envelope and laughed. Her laughter was delicate, like clinking glass.

She reached sideways toward Pen, but instead of taking the envelope, she encircled Pen's forearm and pulled her into an off-kilter embrace. Pen was enveloped in the scent of rosemary.

"Please don't insult me by blaming your father," Margot said at last, releasing Pen. "I had no intention of marrying him, or anyone else for that matter." Margot took the envelope now and turned it over between her fingers.

"My brother hadn't known about your dad and me. He was livid when I told him. He asked what I planned to do. It was possible, if not easy, for a woman in my situation to get out of it." She paused, as if remembering.

Pen had looked it up the night before, and what she'd found was confusing. Even now, procuring an abortion in the UK was technically a criminal offense carrying a life sentence. However, under the Abortion Act of 1967, it was legal under certain conditions, including if two doctors agreed that continuing the pregnancy could endanger the mother's mental health. Pen wanted to pry—how hard would it have been in 1980 to find two willing doctors? How afraid had Margot been? To whom had she turned, and why had she made the choice she had made?—but she resisted. Eventually, Margot continued.

"When it came down to it, Elliot said your father had a right to know, and I didn't argue. Where we disagreed was on what role he might play. Elliot expected him to do 'the right thing' and try to make me his wife. I hoped he knew me too well for that."

Here, Margot paused again. She took out the letter and read it. A self-conscious smile played on her lips, as if the words confirmed a long-held and somewhat embarrassing suspicion. She looked up as if trying to assess whether Pen was flinty enough to hear the truth.

"He had left this address, which clearly did not remain valid for long, and the phone number for his mother's house. He never replied to this letter. I didn't know if he'd received it, and so after a while, I tried calling. When I finally reached him—it took several tries—he offered to come back. He'd get on a plane that very night, he said. He made no mention of anything that would prevent his coming. I told him my decision had not changed. I asked him to please understand."

She glanced at Pen, as if surveying the damage that these words might have caused. Pen kept her face impassive.

"When, a few days later, Elliot and Christina received an invitation to a wedding in Canada that was about to happen, my brother was heartbroken. I was grateful."

He would have left her mother for Margot. He had wanted to. He'd loved Margot more. Part of him had been there, with them, the whole time. This settled on Pen slowly and was unexpectedly reassuring. She had known it. Not the facts, those had been a sunk stone, unreachable, but the ripples they had caused, which she had felt but not understood.

"Why?" Pen asked.

"Because I wasn't made for it," said Margot. "My mother was nineteen when she left her father's house for my father's. She never had a life of her own, never earned a pound, never had her own bank account. It sounds petty to put it in those terms, but she was a dependent her whole life and made to feel it. She had one outlet, one thing that was hers alone, and she never told a soul. She painted. Small seascapes, mostly, in watercolor. Storms. Wide open vistas. She didn't know I knew. But when she became ill, I hung them up. She would look at them and smile in a far-off way. Hers are the only decent pictures in the house."

Margot was still facing the tanks, but there was a film of tears obscuring her eyes. She blinked to clear it.

"I loved your father in my way, but I was not prepared to bind my future to his. I was not prepared to tie myself, at twenty, to his life. Mother may not have had a choice, but I did. I was not prepared to move to *Canada*. Nor was I prepared to ask him to give up all his plans, the promises he had made to his family, to your mother, to live with me here. And for what? My ambitions? He said that he would, that he wanted to, but I knew there would be a cost. And I didn't want to pay it. Do you understand?"

Pen followed her gaze and saw, abstractly, the colors and textures of the thousands of sea creatures trapped in a tank in central London, resplendent behind their wall of glass. Pen did understand, now, or she thought she did, at least partially.

"You know what they call me. Elliot and Christina. They think I'm selfish, of course," Margot continued after a time.

Pen did not contradict her.

"And they're right. It was necessary for me to be selfish in order for both of us, George and me, to survive. But people don't understand that. There is little room for a mother's self-interest in the narrative. There is only the selfish monster and the octopus."

Margot moved on to another tank. Pen noticed that it was empty, or nearly, apart from a structure of rocks that seemed to replicate coral reefs. Red sea urchins that looked like Christmas tree ornaments dotted the bottom.

"What do you know about the life cycle of the common octopus?" Margot asked.

What now, Pen thought. "Nothing," she said.

"After the female lays her clutch of eggs, she devotes herself entirely to cleaning and protecting them for months. She stops looking for food, unable to leave them even for a short time. She begins to waste away— senescence, it's called. It's as if she's used up all her life force hunting, outmaneuvering predators, finding a mate, arranging her den, and then, finally, caring for her eggs. By the time they hatch, she's starved herself to death, or nearly. Her skin, once capable of rapid changes in color and texture, goes pale and develops lesions that never heal. Her eyes go cloudy. She begins to pick at herself. Her decomposing body sometimes becomes a source of food for her young." She smiled a sad, thin-lipped smile. "That's the best she can do for them."

"What about the male?" Pen asked. She thought she knew where this was going. "He keeps mating?"

"No," said Margot. "It's worse for him. He isn't needed to care for the eggs, the way she is. He becomes senescent, too, and usually dies before they hatch. Sometimes the mother of his children eats him."

Pen was silent.

"Don't worry," Margot added in a more lighthearted tone. "I'm well aware that I'm not an octopus. I just find it useful to remember that there's no reason for me to behave like one."

Pen was unconvinced. She thought of Christina and Lennox, who seemed happy and were clearly not wasting away. She thought of her mother, whose eyes had gone cloudy for a time, yes, but who had then begun to build the life she wanted, piece by piece.

"And the only alternative is to be a selfish monster?"

Margot's eyes, still trained on the tank, lost their playful expression. "The mother who insists on keeping that inner self of hers alive *is* monstrous. No one blinks when a father continues devoting himself to whatever it is he most wants to accomplish in this world. But a wife and mother who has priorities of her own and refuses to put them last? Hers becomes a life of conflict, between who she is and what is expected of her. Society deems her selfish and unnatural. If she lets herself believe it, she's doomed, and so are her children."

"I don't think you're right," Pen said quietly. "Maybe that used to be the case, but no one thinks it's selfish or unnatural anymore. Things have changed."

"It would be lovely if that were true," said Margot. She sounded almost sad, as if she had hoped Pen would understand and was disappointed that she did not. "I hope for your sake it is."

"And failing that, the best option is never to fall in love, and never to have children?" Pen asked, a bit defensively.

"God, I hope not." Margot's voice was softer.

"Well, what then?"

Margot turned to her with a look that was nearly tender.

"The only way is to make peace with yourself."

Pen looked back at the tank. Slowly, rhythmically, her supple body twisting and billowing like smoke, the octopus emerged from her hiding place. Her skin, which had taken on the color and pattern of the rocks, now turned a brilliant red. Her eight long, tapered arms with their gleaming rows of suckers looked strong and flexible enough to choke a person to death. Each arm moved with perfect grace, independent of the others. They watched her for a long time, as if hypnotized.

"The octopus is quite intelligent, isn't it?" Pen asked.

Margot turned to meet Pen's eyes. "The octopus is the most intelligent animal on the planet without a backbone."

42

Pen took the Northern line to Angel. At a chain across from the tube stop, she bought two boxed salads, two coffees, and, on impulse, two caramel-smothered Love Bars. She found the blue door of a maisonette on a calm square and pressed the buzzer. Ten seconds passed. Twenty. She shifted the tray with the coffees to her other hand and drank liquid that had started spilling from one and pooling in the crevices of the plastic lid.

"Yes?" came an unwelcoming voice.

"George. It's Pen."

George said nothing. A mechanical sound issued from the intercom and the door's lock clanked open.

Pen edged past a stroller to climb a narrow staircase. George stood on the second landing with Danny wriggling on her hip. She wore pajamas with small pink owls on them. It was past noon.

"Boom! Boom!" yelled Danny excitedly, breaking free. George set him down and took the coffees just in time for him to hurl his compact little body into Pen's arms. She stroked the downy curls on the back of his head.

"Bless you," said George. "How did you know I needed this?"

She ushered Pen through a thicket of outerwear and into a large living space with an open kitchen and dining room. It was a handsome flat in which everything probably had a place, but nothing was in its place. The furniture and rugs were strewn with toys and baby paraphernalia. George put the coffees on the mantel where Danny couldn't reach them. She fluffed the cushions and moved an *Economist* with a soggy, rippled corner aside so Pen could sit.

"We have to read the news fast before Danny eats it," she explained, sitting down on the floor. "Everything in the flat is a teething aid. It's once they start walking that you're really screwed. But you haven't spent five hours on the train to hear about the challenges of sharing a flat with a one-year-old, have you."

Danny drove the fire truck over Pen's foot. "Daddy!" he shouted. "Fire! BOOM!" George brought him to the kitchen and opened a cupboard full of mismatched bowls and kitchen implements. He shrieked with glee and began the process of removing every vessel and utensil from the cupboard, one at a time.

"That should buy us about four minutes," said George, returning to the sofa.

Pen started to apologize. George stopped her. "How is it in any way your fault? You didn't ask for this any more than I did. I assumed you knew and thought it'd be best to let you bring it up. But you never did. Until Friday, when you threw me for a loop asking about my father, I'll admit."

Pen opened her mouth but could not ask the first question that had risen in her chest.

"Please don't feel strange about it," George said, putting her hand on Pen's knee. "I don't think I could handle another parent. Mum's enough of a handful. And Lennox and Christina have filled in the gaps. Giving me a stable home, trying to get me to marry the father of my child, that sort of thing."

George's attempt at humor did nothing to blunt Pen's discomfort. The coffee she had drunk was burning a hole in her stomach. She looked over at Danny, who was muttering to himself while he reached to the back of the cupboard and pulled out a plastic salad spinner.

"So have you ever met my—our—" Pen began, but again, George stopped her.

"Yours, not mine. I want to be clear on that point. I don't want or need one. Yes, I've met him. The first time, I was sixteen. He came over to us in the lobby of a hotel and looked at Mum like she was the ghost of Christmas past. She introduced him as an old friend, which is code for jilted lover. But then we saw him a few more times over the years. He would come to see us whenever he was in London or Paris on business, and he generally brought me a somewhat extravagant gift."

She shook her wrist, showing her slim gold watch on a black leather band.

"She'd always told me my father was an anonymous donor. When I eventually figured it out, I confronted her. All she said was 'What took you so long.'"

Pen remembered those trips, how she had stopped being invited to join him, and how distant Ted had always been on his return. Anger flashed through her, followed by guilt, shame, and then a kind of dissociation.

She had so many questions. *What was he like with you? Did he ever mention us?* But her feelings about Ted were in an ugly jumble that would need to be sorted out when she was alone. For now she wanted to shift her thoughts onto someone for whose actions she felt no responsibility. "Were there many jilted lovers?" Pen asked after a long silence.

"Reams. She doesn't believe in marriage. Thinks it's bondage, and not the fun kind, in her words."

"Do you agree?"

George glanced at Danny, who was now methodically unspooling an entire roll of paper towels. She retrieved her coffee from the mantel.

"I'm not constitutionally opposed. Rosh and I might get married one day if our relationship survives Danny's toddlerhood. But first I've got to figure out what I'm doing with my life."

"What were you doing before?" Pen asked. "I'm sorry I've never asked."

"That's all right," said George. "I worked for a fashion label, in marketing. Not Mum's—a menswear brand, actually. I figured I would go back there, but I've come to realize that they were doing a few things wrong. I've come up with my own small idea for an online business that would be much more efficient. I'm going to try to find some investors once Danny starts nursery in the autumn and see what I can make of it."

They watched Danny as he twisted the lid of a small jar. He sneezed extravagantly. The smell of cumin wafted over to them.

"Hm," George said, walking over to him. "Wonder how that got down there." She took the cumin from his chubby hands and put it up on the counter, then unhurriedly began respooling the paper towels. "Do you know what you want to do?"

Pen picked up the limp, bite-marked *Economist*. "I'm applying for work experience at some newspapers and magazines this summer. But the industry is imploding, so we'll see."

"If you find something in London you can always stay here with us," George said. "And I'm not just saying that for the free childcare. Or because you're sleeping with my cousin."

Pen felt blood rush to her face. "How does everyone know?"

George laughed, not unkindly. "Lennox has been onto the two of you for months. He's like one of those actors who play a doctor on TV and then start thinking they can perform surgery."

The question was cold in Pen's throat. "Has Sasha known this whole time?"

"God no," George exclaimed.

"GODNO!" echoed Danny, who had found a box of crackers and was trying to tear open the plastic sleeve.

"Now I see why you left in such a hurry. Did you think we were all having some kind of deranged laugh at your expense?" George took the crackers away and carried Danny back over to the living room. "I promise you it wasn't like that. Lennox was sure you'd written in the first place because you either knew or suspected. Once he saw that you had no idea, and moreover got to know and like you, he wanted to give your father a chance to tell you himself."

Pen remembered the surprise visit from her dad.

"No one enlightened Sasha in the meantime," George continued. "It wouldn't have been right for him to know before you did, especially given how besotted you clearly were with one another. It was Sasha who invited you for Danny's birthday without warning us. I was thrilled you were there, but I would never have subjected you to Mum. Poor Sasha had no idea what he was doing. I suppose it's for the best, though. And they did tell him after your French exit. He was in quite a state."

A key turned in the lock and Rosh appeared in a suit. He put a paper take-out bag on the table next to Pen's and took in the kitchen with a raised eyebrow.

"DAAADDA," shouted Danny. He army-crawled toward Rosh. Rosh tossed him into the air.

"My one thirty was canceled so I thought I'd drop by with some sushi," he said, greeting Pen with a kiss on each cheek and George with one on the mouth.

"Two surprise visitors bearing lunch before I've even put on a bra. My horoscope did say it would be a day of plenty. Pen, you must be famished—come, let's sit at the table and pretend to be civilized."

Pen made her excuses. George insisted on accompanying her downstairs.

"You know where you're going? It's just one stop to King's Cross."

Pen thanked her and hitched her satchel up on her shoulder. She didn't know what to do with her arms. George hugged her.

"You're a bit of a weird one, you know that?" she said.

"I know," said Pen.

"Good," said George. "Don't be too angry with your dad. She would not have given him a choice, and he did what he could under the circumstances."

Pen hugged George back, feeling the strength of her arms under the layer of thin cotton.

George waved from the threshold in her graying owl pajamas. Pen turned toward the high street. As the blue door closed, Pen approached the crowded sidewalk of umbrella-wielding pedestrians funneling toward the mouth of the tube stop and felt her heart rate slow as she was folded back into anonymity.

That evening, in the fluorescent light of the Lee House hallway, Pen noticed that the sign on her door had been revised once more. Someone had made a mark indicating a space between "Pen" and "is," and it now read "Pen_is sweet." A wrapped box waited on the carpet. There was a note taped to the paper in the shape of a pentagon.

"Far mightier," it read. "I am contrite. Yours, Fergus."

Inside the oblong box she found a fountain pen and a small pot of ink.

43

Opening night arrived like any other Thursday. Alice, Pen, and Jo met in front of the JMC and joined the queue for breakfast. Alice, who had felt cold since her shower that morning, kept her coat on. She spooned jam into her porridge. *You cannot stir things apart*, she recited in her mind.

Charlie sat down. "Alright?" he asked.

The question was addressed to the table but intended for Alice. With the single word he seemed to convey an awareness that she was nervous and an understanding that it would be best not to mention the play directly. To hide her flush of pleasure, she looked down. She noticed that his new sneakers were already dirty. This made her think, with a pang, that their first year was almost over. She wondered whether he would be staying in Edinburgh for the summer.

Fergus interrupted Alice's daydream, in which she and Charlie were sharing a high-ceilinged loft in Leith with a huge window overlooking the Firth of Forth, while he did work experience at a gallery and she was the lead in two different Festival plays (one traditional and one experimental, to show her range), by plonking a bottle of champagne down on her tray, beside her jammy porridge.

"Anesthetic," he said with a bow. "In anticipation of your gammy broken leg."

Jo whistled and examined the label. "Fergus has missed you lot," she told the table by way of explanation. "I told him some atonement would be in order if he wanted to be friends again. We'll need a few more of these before you're back in our good graces, brother of mine," she said, pinching his cheek.

Fergus nodded soberly, like a child accepting his penance. He sat in the chair beside Pen's, picked up one of her discarded raisins, and popped it in his mouth.

"Anyone for a lift?" Charlie asked, taking his last bite of toast. He glanced at Alice.

"We'll catch up," said Jo.

Alice followed Charlie as he wove through the tables, getting hellos from almost all of them.

In the car, Charlie left her to her thoughts. When they pulled up on Buccleuch Place, he opened her door. "You'll be great," he said, kissing her lightly on the cheek. The part of her cheek he'd touched felt hot. She turned to look at him. His dark eyes were steady.

Alice attended lectures in body while running through the play in her mind. When she got to the end she began again.

In the afternoon, Neville found her talking to herself in the sunken area behind the back steps of the Bedlam Theatre. She was at the beginning of her fourth recitation. "If you stir backward, the jam will not come together again. Indeed, the pudding does not notice and continues to turn pink just as before. Do you think this is odd?" she asked in her Thomasina voice.

"No, but you're a bit odd sitting there talking to yourself," he said.

"Well, I do. You cannot stir things apart."

Neville brought her to a café around the corner and ordered her a cheese toastie and a cup of soup.

Later, in the rehearsal room, she sat on the floor well away from the scarf-covered sofa, leaning against the wall with her eyes closed. "There will be people up from London in the audience, people in a position to give you a future doing this, if that's what you want," their director Maxwell had told them after their dress rehearsal, which he'd deemed "passable." He had timed the performance schedule perfectly; Fringe auditions began in earnest that weekend.

He'd given Alice only one note, absently, while fingering his plum-colored ascot: "Remember: you have no sense of yourself as an object of desire. You're a child. You're conscious only of the power of your mind."

The thought had made her want to cry.

Now the green room contained twelve other bodies. Now she was dusted with pale powder and gowned in a long white dress with an empire waist. Now they were all holding hands in a circle. Someone had filled a plastic bin with ice and there were bottles cooling, the one from Fergus among them. She breathed into her diaphragm with the others, feeling the bodice rise and fall, the cap sleeves tight around her arms. "A nightingale knew no night was nicer than a nice night to sing his nocturnals," they recited. "Three fluffy feathers fell from feeble Phoebe's fan."

The lights cracked on behind the curtain. Relief flooded her body as she abandoned Alice, freeing her mind from the grooves of thought it had been following since her first awareness that other people could see her. In this untethered state, she could offer the best part of herself, her soul, maybe, to the eternal, to the collective. This was what she wanted to do every day for the rest of her life.

It was not Alice but thirteen-year-old Thomasina Coverley who stepped lightly over taped-down wires onto what felt like the deck of a ship that was about to set sail and sat down at the large table opposite a tall, handsome man. He took a live tortoise from his pocket and set it atop a stack of papers. She let her eyes adjust. The faces in the audience were invisible to her. If a pale one with deep-set eyes by the aisle was looking for Alice, he was not going to find her here.

"Septimus." Her voice rang out, innocent as strawberry jam, into the packed theater. "What's carnal embrace?"

The French restaurant at which they had reserved a table for the post-play celebration was a tomb. The other patrons sat in their chairs as if trying not to crease their clothes. They squinted nearsightedly at the daubs of food on their plates, pointedly ignoring the noisy mob of young people filing in through the curtain that kept the elements out. In the hubbub of outerwear divestment and Fergus calling for champagne, no one would have noticed a tall figure slip in with them.

A dignified Frenchman emerged from nowhere to pull out Alice's chair and unfurl her napkin. Neville sat down beside her, and Charlie on her other side. For what felt like the first time since the final waltz across the stage, she exhaled. She knew that she had done well because she could not remember acting. She had slowly returned to herself with the pop of the first cork backstage, while the audience was still roaring its approval on the other side of the curtain.

Neville had filled her in on the buoyant walk to the restaurant. He'd promised that, apart from one place where the spray-tanned third year playing Chloë had fumbled a line, the play had been a success.

Alice became conscious that she had not peed in hours. She excused herself. At the edge of the dining room, past the swinging door to the kitchen, she found a sign pointing toward a narrow corridor filled with coats. *Great*, she thought. Narnia. She descended the inevitable stairs and shivered. At the bottom of the staircase, the din of the restaurant was inaudible, as if she had put her head underwater.

At the end of the basement hallway, the ladies' powder room was large, with an upholstered love seat, floral hand soap, and a scented candle. The first stall's door was closed so she went into the second. She hiked up her skirt and waited, crouching above the cold seat. The bathroom was silent. Stage fright, she thought, wishing Pen were there to share in the dumb joke. But then she heard a creaking sound, like the squeak of a rubber sole compressing a toilet seat, and her insides seized. Had Julian been there, in the audience, at the edge of the front row? Had he followed them to the restaurant and slipped in, unnoticed? It was possible. Her breath sped up and she fought, although it felt like willful suffocation, to keep it inaudible. She was now certain it was him in the next stall, waiting for her. The air was hot and waxy, and she couldn't get it into her lungs. There was a dagger of fear in her chest.

Get out, said a voice in her head. *Unlatch the door, cross the room, go.* But the floor grabbed on to her. Her hands and feet felt numb. She tried to call for help, but her voice was lodged deep in her throat. Her ineffective fingers fumbled with her underwear, trying to yank it up, as if it could protect her. She crouched down on the floor, her back to the cold metal of the stall, and choked for breath. She remembered the weight of his body on top of hers, holding her in place. He would pull her underwear aside and jam himself inside her. His breath would be wet on her throat. He would let out an infantile cry. His sticky orgasm would burn the inside of her.

She sat huddled there, shaking, trying to suck oxygen into her lungs, her heartbeat screaming in her ears.

Eventually, she got ahold of her breathing, of her pulse. She opened her eyes and looked up. No fingers clutching the top of the stall. She was alone. She was out of her mind. She stood, straightened her clothes, washed her hands at the sink.

She cupped the glass casing of the scented candle that stood on the ledge beneath the mirror. It was warm in her palms. As a child she had shown her brother how to lick his finger and run it through a flame. He had done it too slowly, touched the blue, and screamed out in pain. "That's what comes of being a daredevil," their mother had scolded.

Nicola had played it safe. Too safe, Alice had always thought. She had never challenged her husband. She had never complained of his infidelities, of the hurt or humiliation they must have caused her. Not openly, anyway. Alice had wanted to rip his head off at times, and her mother had just borne it, ignored it, made soup, driven Eli to hockey practice, smiling.

Alice passed the kitchen, with its thick smells of grilled meats and sauces, and re-entered the dining room.

"Alright?" Charlie asked, pulling out her chair, and looking at her with affection and concern.

"I will be."

She kept her eyes fixed ahead as if she were studying a painting. Something warm touched her forearm and she flinched. It was Charlie's hand, and he pulled it back, a painful look crossing his handsome face. She reached for his receding hand and clasped it. His fingers were strong. He laced them loosely between hers. The faint smell of burning flowers began to fade. From across the table, Hugo had grown glassy with wine and was telling Neville one of his sailing stories. Flossie, in Fergus's thrall, had a piece of parsley stuck to her lip. Alice had a flash of what it would be like when her parents were very old and needed to be fed and bathed, like babies. She wondered if her mother would tend to her father, who was older and would no doubt deteriorate first. Would she spoon-feed him, and wipe applesauce from his grizzled chin? Probably she would, Alice thought. Nicola was generous with her love. She chose to be. She did not punish others for their weakness. Maybe, Alice thought, that was a position of strength, in its way. She tightened her grip on Charlie's hand, and he gave hers a reassuring, unhurried squeeze.

44

The sky was a wispy blue. A warm breeze carried the promise of a fresh round of exams. Pen was sitting on a bench in the middle of the concrete courtyard, trying and failing to lose herself in a novel.

Alice had come to Pen's room early that morning with the student newspaper under her arm. STILTED STOPPARD REDEEMED BY DIAMOND IN THE ROUGH ran the front-page headline. After a livid call from Maxwell accusing her of being an attention-stealing bitch, Alice's phone had not stopped playing the first few bars of 50 Cent's "In Da Club" (her triumphant ringtone). By the time they had sat down for breakfast, Festival People had already summoned her to two auditions and three coffee meetings.

During the three-day interval between her trip to London and Alice's opening night, Pen had woken up early each morning, gone for a run through Holyrood Park, taken careful notes in her classes, done her work, and fallen into bed almost immediately after dinner. She'd told Jo and

Alice she was fine; she just needed some time on her own. They'd brought her chocolate covered almonds and paperbacks, including the one she was holding in her hands.

She had also called her parents.

"Penny. I was beginning to worry," her dad said when he picked up after half a ring.

"Were you ever going to tell me?" she demanded.

"Of course I was." She could hear him cover the mouthpiece with his hand and ask whoever was in his office if they could come back later. *It's my daughter*, he would say by way of apology. This would make him look good. A family man, doing his duty. No one ever spoke of a family woman, Pen thought. The phrase sounded ridiculous.

"Of course I was going to tell you," he said. His voice was heavier now that his witness had left. "I was waiting for the right time."

"Oh, right. Like my first unplanned pregnancy? You'd swoop in with an anecdote about how this happened to you once, but the other way around? And by the way, she kept it?"

Her dad's voice turned serious. "You're not going to be as stupid as I was."

She exploded. "Stupid?! Georgina Lennox, a full person, someone I've become friends with, someone who has a child of her own, exists because of you being *stupid*?"

"Penny—"

"Don't call me that. How am I supposed to avoid being as *stupid* as you when I don't even know who you are? You spent my entire childhood preaching honesty while— And then you came here, and you still didn't have the guts to tell me. You let me feel crazy instead. Is it not obvious that I've been trying *for years* to understand how you and Mom screwed each other up so completely? Don't you think it would've been a lot easier if you'd just told me about her, so I didn't have to pry it out of near strangers who, by the way, must think we're the most repressed people on this planet?"

Her dad was breathing quietly on the line, clearly waiting for her to finish. Her anger was already congealing, like sweat after a run.

She pressed her knuckles to the inside corners of her eyes until shooting stars filled her vision. He didn't try again to speak. What could he say? What would she have done in his place? Not lied to everyone including herself, she hoped. But then, she wasn't him. She didn't know.

"I'm sorry," he said. "I know it doesn't hold water at this point, but I was thinking of your mother. Of course I wanted to tell her the moment I found out, but I couldn't. By the time Margot reached me with the news, we were all but married. We could have called it off, yes, but Margot didn't want anything to do with me; she made that clear. Who would have gained from my telling your mother, besides me and my guilty conscience?"

She could imagine him in his large office with the fogged glass wall. His walnut desk. Small family photographs in silver frames that must get polished by someone. Helga, presumably, or an unseen cleaning woman who came after dark. There was a photograph, in an oval frame, of her grandparents on their wedding day. Pen could picture Tilda's string of pearls and her determined smile. Pen's parents had been married in that same church, although that photo was missing now. There was a triptych, too, of Edward Senior and his two brothers frowning stoically in their uniforms, about to leave for training in England. All three had enlisted as soon as Canada had joined the war. Her grandfather had been "over for the duration." Six years: a master's degree in killing and not being killed. He'd been the only one of the three to come home.

"And then, as we discussed at Christmas, your mother had—*we* had—

some reproductive difficulties," Ted continued. "The first happened during our honeymoon, and several more followed. Each was more devastating than the last. Your mother was not well, Pen. Not for a long time after that."

Had it been for her sake that he'd corrected himself? she wondered. Did part of him really still think that these were women's problems, these matters of procreation, as he had no doubt been raised to believe? No, it could not be that. The miscarriages had been his losses, too, she knew. She did not want to blame him for his inability to express pain. He had never learned it; none of them had, these children of war. Everything paled beside massacre. His generation had been taught to shut up and count their blessings, and that was what they had done.

"She did find out, of course," he said after a while. "Many years later. I ran into them on a trip to London. I began to visit them whenever I was over there. It was after one of those visits that— Well, we don't need to revisit all that right now. She thought I was having an affair."

"Dad," Pen said, her voice firm, severe. It was a tone she had learned from him. "Please don't ever lie to me again."

She could hear him sigh. "I'll do my best," he said.

Fury pulsed through her. "Don't placate me. I'm not a child. I don't know what kind of relationship we can have if you don't respect me enough to tell me the truth."

He was silent for several seconds. "Okay," he said. "You're right."

"Thank you." They both stayed on the line. "Now, do you want to tell me how long you've been seeing Helga for?"

He let out a gust of breath that was part guffaw. "*Seeing* Helga? What on Earth gives you that idea?"

"Either that or you've started wearing lipstick the color of boiled shrimp."

He chuckled. "You're a good detective, Pen. But remember: two sources. Her name is Cynthia. We met at the club. It's a recent development. Boiled shrimp, eh? Yes, I suppose I can sort of see that."

They said their goodbyes and hung up. That was on Tuesday.

Something hit Pen on the shoulder. A green wine gum fell onto the bench beside her. She looked up in time for another one to graze her cheek.

"Hi Fergus," she said.

He poked his head out the window of Hugo's car. "Oh, hello Pen. I didn't see you there."

Fergus came over and sat beside her. He offered her a wine gum from his roll. She declined.

"You're such an intellectual." Fergus took the book from her and examined it. The cover featured a shapely bum with white jodhpurs stretched over it and a hand gripping its jaunty cheeks. He held the book's cracked spine in his palm, letting the pages fall open seemingly at random. He scanned the spread and smiled.

"I knew it. Did Jo give this to you? It's my copy."

"How can you tell?"

"Magic."

Pen peered down at the passage it had opened on:

> For a small, slight man, Jake was sexually well endowed, but he spent enough time fingering a spot that Tory afterward discovered was—

He lifted an eyebrow and handed it back to her.

"Thanks," Pen said. Fergus stayed put.

"Do you forgive me?" he asked.

"For what, exactly?"

Fergus offered her the last wine gum. She shook her head. He chewed it thoughtfully.

"For telling everyone that you were a cock-tease who'd dipped her pen in the faculty ink."

She closed the book. "And for writing pervy limericks about me and putting them on the internet?"

"Also, yes."

"And for leaving porn magazines outside my door?"

"They weren't all from me."

"That's worse."

"I know. I'm sorry." He bowed his head in a show of contrition.

"I'm sorry, too," she said.

"You are? Why?"

"For using you."

"You did?" Fergus looked genuinely surprised.

"A bit."

He considered this. "That's all right. I forgive you."

They sat in comfortable silence for a moment. A sparrow trilled overhead.

"How are things with Flossie?"

"Tickety-boo."

"What?"

"Fine. Wizard. Excellent. Mum likes her now. Says she's got a great seat."

"I'm happy for you."

"And you? Seeing someone?"

"Not sure yet," she said.

He knelt down abruptly. For a disquieting moment, Pen imagined what it would be like to be married to Fergus. She pictured a procession of white-blond children on ponies, all with his long legs and world-weary eyes. On one knee among the discarded cigarette butts, using the bunny ears method, Fergus tied her shoelace.

Then he stood and brushed off his pant legs. "Teatime. Toodle-pip."

Fergus strode back to the car, leaving his empty candy wrapper on the bench beside her. Pen smoothed it out and used it as a bookmark.

⌒

After hanging up with Ted on Tuesday evening, Pen had called her mother. Anna picked up on the second ring.

"How long have you known?" Pen asked.

"Hello to you, too, my darling." Anna was boiling beets for a salad. She had just come in from a walk and her hands were still cold, even after she had washed them in hot water. Unlike Ted, who had received a phone call from Margot, no one had warned her what was coming. She did not have any context for this conversation. "Known what?"

"I found the letter. From Margot. In your notebook pocket."

"Oh." Anna sat down hard at the kitchen table. Olive, who was sprawled underneath, harrumphed.

Anna had understood in her bones almost from the beginning that Ted could not love her in the way she needed him to. But she'd disregarded this instinct and countered it with images of eternal togetherness, a fusion of selves. Because Ted had told her he loved her. He'd been the first person in her life to speak those words. He's reserved, she'd reassured herself. And then: He's preoccupied. He has to prove himself. And later, with mounting certainty, the old drumbeat of self-hatred: It's me. I'm defective.

As much as Marie-Helene had wanted to love the little girl she'd volunteered to take in, she had not even been able to like her. Marie-Helene had always believed that Anna's birth mother's "weakness" was implanted in Anna, and she'd seen it as her job to drive it out. Anna's reading, her imaginativeness, her high spirits: all were dangerous to Marie-Helene. All would lead to ruin. After Anna had gotten away, Ted had seemed like a safe haven. His stable family, their traditions, their loyalty to one another, and even, yes, initially, their ease, their air of belonging to something different, more solid, built of sturdy red brick, not peeling vinyl siding. Something durable. But Ted had not known what to do with her pain. While Anna had suffered, he had receded further. He had built walls of success, of money and false laughter. And then Gregory had died, so suddenly she had not been able to say goodbye. Quiet Gregory, who may not quite have loved her, but whom she had loved, and from whom she had sensed affection, perhaps even pride. She'd gone "home" for the funeral, to help Marie-Helene, protected by her hope. There, in the only bathroom of the sad house, she'd lost that hope. Marie-Helene had told her that God did not want her to have a child, and Anna had believed her.

Years later, when Pen had come, Anna had brought herself back. She'd found the young woman she'd buried alive, the one who had wanted to share with other lonely souls the stories that had meant so much to her, and she had resuscitated her. Anna had finished her doctorate while Pen was in elementary school. She'd even brought Pen to visit Marie-Helene, as if to repay a debt, or perhaps to show her *I'm better than you think I am. I, at least, am able to love.* A mistake.

By the time Pen was in grade five, Anna had begun teaching.

And then, one summer, Ted had returned from London behaving in a distant way that was chillingly familiar.

"It took me a long time to face what should have been obvious," Anna said, after a silence.

"Were you ever in love with him?"

"I was," Anna said. "I believed I was. Which is the same thing, isn't it?"

"No," said Pen.

Anna spoke slowly, trying to find the right words. "I just mean that there's no real way to tell when you have nothing to measure it against. I loved my impression of Ted. I loved how responsible he was. How well he treated his mother. I could see he would be a good father. What I wanted more than anything was a family."

"Well, that didn't work," Pen said. She hung up. It was the cruelest thing she had ever said to her mother.

Anna looked at the phone in her hand. She understood how hard it was to separate people from ideas of people. She did not know if her early memories were real, but she clung to them: strong arms around her, lips pressed to her forehead. A finger running the length of her nose. She had tried to become the mother she had invented for herself, the one who held her child close and made her feel safe, like she belonged somewhere. To become that woman, to fill the void she had left, had been her deepest wish. She dialed, pushing carefully on the keys.

Pen opened her window with a shaking hand. Her phone buzzed, and she answered it.

"You have every right to be angry," Anna said. "But I wouldn't change a single decision that led to you."

Pen swiped at her dripping nose. "What did you face that should have been obvious?"

Her mother exhaled. Pen pictured her standing by the mug cupboard in the kitchen, winding the cord of the old phone around her fingers, Olive sprawled at her feet. It was early afternoon there. They would have just come in from a walk.

"That we didn't know each other. How could we? We hardly knew ourselves."

Pen didn't answer. Anna tried again. "It takes courage to be known. You have to show yourself to the other person. He couldn't, and after a while I realized that neither could I. Without that . . . compassion, for lack of a better word, love can be hard to find, some days. And marriage becomes like a three-legged race with a stranger. We stumbled along, out of balance, for years."

Pen could hear her mother's soft breathing. It made her want to climb through time and space and crawl into bed with her. To feel the warmth of her mother's breath on the back of her neck.

When the camp bus had pulled into the mall parking lot and Pen had seen Tilda, not her mother, through the bus window, she had felt a coldness pass through her. No one had ever used the words "major depressive disorder" or "attempted suicide" with Pen, but she knew. *She did it* was her first thought.

Anna had not done it, though. It was true that she'd had a bad time, that August. Ted had gone away early in the month and taken with him the women's watch she'd found in his drawer, gift wrapped in a pretty box. Old feelings of rejection, of being worthless, of being lied to. She'd been having trouble sleeping. She'd wanted to be well rested for Pen's return. She'd taken her pills twice, doubling her usual medications as well as the sedative her pharmacologist had just prescribed for insomnia. An accident. Sleep had overcome her in the bath. Ted had come home late and found her unconscious in the cooling water. The hospital had kept her for forty-eight hours and then sent her home, deeming the incident insufficiently serious for a longer period of supervision.

Still, they had sent her away, "just to be sure." She had not resisted. A private place, the same one as before. Tilda had moved in. Pen had turned thirteen without her mother. Tilda's primary concern had been to ensure that no one found out, not even Pen. "Your mother has a mild case of pneumonia," she'd said briskly. "She just needs some rest."

It wasn't until several somnambulant months later, on Boxing Day, that Anna had learned the truth. The jewelry store, the damning receipt with Ted's purchase history accidentally revealed, the piercing of her fog. She'd called Helga, kind Helga, who had told her the truth. But it was not the truth Anna had expected. It wasn't one woman in London; it was two. Confronted with evidence, Ted had cracked like an egg. He'd produced, from somewhere in his office, that letter in the blue envelope that she had not even realized she'd kept. He had tried to explain why he hadn't told her sooner. With a strange feeling of release—it wasn't her; it had never been her—Anna had ended the false marriage.

"Pen, I need you to understand something," Anna said. The water was boiling over on the stove, but she did not notice. "I think you know this. I was afraid of scaring you, but I think I scared you more by making you mistrust what you sensed. It's a terrible thing to do to someone. I'm sorry."

She was speaking distinctly, her voice strained by the effort to make herself understood.

"There were two moments in my life, both before you were born, when the pain was too much, and I wanted it to end. But since you were born I have never—I would *never*—" Anna drew a sharp breath and forced herself to continue. "My mother left me, and I *will not* do the same to you. Do you understand?"

"Okay." Pen's voice had gone small. It was hard not to go straight back to her mother's darkened bedroom with the heavy curtains pulled across the windows, and the feeling she'd had then and for a long time afterward, of trying to hold Anna in place, to keep her from drifting up into nothingness.

"Do you believe me?"

"Yes."

"I'm sorry for what I put you through. It wasn't fair."

"It's not your fault. Don't apologize."

"Pen?"

"Mmhmm."

"I love you."

"I know. I love you, too."

"Are you all right over there? Edinburgh seems very far away, suddenly."

"It does. But I'm fine."

"Are you sure?"

"I'm sure."

That's enough, you're done, Pen told herself as she lay in bed that night. *Now you know. And they survived. Make your own life, however you want it.* It was a good pep talk. She fell asleep and did not remember her dreams.

45

After her conversation with Fergus on the bench, Pen went up to her room to get ready. She considered a dress but instead put on jeans, her favorite sweater, her polar bear necklace, and, hearing her mother's voice in her head, a jacket.

The sun was still high in the sky. Already, the nights that had fallen at four were a distant memory. By June, when they were celebrating the end of exams, the sun wouldn't set until after ten, and it would often rise before they had made it to bed. But this was April.

Dalkeith Road turned to St. Leonard. Pen cut in toward George Square, turned right on Nicholson Street, and continued past the mosque kitchen, where you could get a vegetarian lunch for two pounds to eat in the garden of the Pear Tree, past the Festival Theatre where Alice would play a terrifying modern-day Clytemnestra in August, and past the Blackwell's bookstore across from Old College, where you could take your purchases into the attached café and read undisturbed for hours.

Nicholson became South Bridge and then North Bridge, with Waverley station squatting, troll-like, beneath it. Princes Street, the thorough-fare that divided Old Town from New, was named for the sons of King George III, who, despite his long reign, was mainly remembered by British schoolchildren as the mad king who lost America. Reputation may not be everything, Pen thought, smiling for Tilda, but it was something.

Beyond Princes Street, on a curving, downward-sloping street called Broughton, was the "smart" stationery shop where Jo would work that summer. It was so smart that few people shopped there, and Sylvia, who would return to Edinburgh in August to "take in the festival," would come by often to test the merchandise. They would, in the relative privacy of a city whose summer population did not know them, experiment with being a couple.

She turned right, away from the clock-towered Balmoral Hotel, and crossed Princes Street and Waterloo Place to Calton Hill. The gently sloping hill, ascended first by stair and then along a generous walkway, was crowded with monuments: to the philosopher and mathematician Dugald Stewart, to the naval commander Admiral Lord Horatio Nelson, to the soldiers and sailors who perished in the Napoleonic Wars. The last and largest of these, the National Monument, was left unfinished. With twelve Doric columns arranged in the shape of a square bracket, it had been modeled after the Parthenon in Athens.

Sasha, who would in two months graduate from St Andrews with a first in history and several offers of employment, including one at a well-known London museum, which he would accept, was standing high up on the monument's platform, between two of the columns, looking out over the city. To the west stood the neighborhood of Stockbridge, where Pen would live the following year; to the southeast was Holyrood Park, Arthur's Seat, and Pollock Halls; and straight ahead, over the edge of Leith, lay the Firth of Forth, the estuary of the River Forth, flowing into the North Sea.

The base of the platform was taller than Pen was. Grateful to be wearing jeans, she found a foothold and hoisted herself up until she was standing beside him.

"Did you know that it took seventy men and twelve horses to carry each of these columns up the hill?" Sasha did not lean in to kiss her, not even on the cheek.

"Really," she said, breathing hard from the climb. She placed her palm against the ridged, cold stone.

"They ran out of money," said Sasha. "Now it's known as Edinburgh's Disgrace. Which, come to think of it, would be quite a good name for you." He was trying to sound light, she thought, but there was a raw edge to his voice, and his face was unshaven.

"So they told you?"

He nodded. "I was worried you'd left because of something I'd done. They took pity." He was wearing the sweater with the moth hole. It brought out the moss-colored flecks in his eyes.

"You minded?"

"Being run out on in the middle of the night and then ignored for a week? Yes. I minded."

"It wasn't a week. Just five days."

"You're right, that's much kinder."

"You stopped calling after two."

"Your voicemail was full. And I know when I'm not wanted."

"That makes one of us."

They considered each other in silence.

"What do you mean?" he asked.

"That weekend when you invited me up just to ignore me."

He winced, as if she had slapped him.

"I know you apologized. But why did you act like that? The Freddie situation doesn't fully explain it. My best guess is that it has to do with Charlotte."

Pen drew in a deep breath and tried to let it out slowly. Sasha was avoiding her eyes, looking instead at the water. She wondered if he was going to disconnect himself again and keep looking past her. Even if he did, she knew she would not regret this.

He lifted his eyes to hers. "I asked you to come because I liked you," he said. His voice was serious. It was not a voice of persuasion. "I've liked you from the beginning. Your intensity and complete lack of artifice. The way you look at people like you can see into their souls. And then you started making the strangest jokes and recommending books to Dad. Who, by the way, has actually been reading them. That first night, and the next morning after Kevin bolted on you, and then again upstairs, it was all I could do to stop myself from trying to kiss you. But you're a good three years younger than I am, and I didn't want to assume—"

"You could tell I liked you, too," she interrupted. His words were having too strong an effect on her. She could not let his praise, or her reaction to it, stop her from finding out what she needed to find out.

"Yes," he admitted. "And whatever you saw in me, it was not what most people see. You brought out a part of me I'd mostly forgotten about. It felt good to remember, but it also scared me. It was not at all convenient."

He broke eye contact for a moment, then found it again and soldiered on.

"What was convenient was what I had with Charlotte. We've known each other a long time, and we've gone through various phases, the most recent of which involved sleeping together every now and then."

Pen felt jealousy flare in her.

"The man she wanted to be with had ended things, although she and I both knew they would eventually get back together, and we both found ourselves unattached," Sasha continued. "We get on well, but we don't make a good couple, we've tried it, so there was no danger of mis-aligned expectations on either side. It seemed like a good arrangement. Until I realized I was more interested in sitting at home on my computer talking to you. I told her we had to stop, right before I asked you up for the weekend. Then Mum rang me with the news that Freddie was in trouble. I should have messaged you right away to postpone your visit. But I didn't, I put it off. After Mum and I got off the phone, I was a bit shaken up. I went out for some air and ran into Charlotte. St Andrews is very small, you see. And then—"

"You got drunk together, had amazing sex all night long, and in-vented a convoluted polo-related excuse?"

He began to smile, presumably at her undisguised jealousy, but stopped himself and went on with his story. "The match wasn't an invention; it took them ages to call it off. I should never have bothered with it, though. I should have gone up directly. Knowing what I was putting you through, and Mum, when she had so much on her mind, made me feel even more ill than I already did. You're right, I was incredibly hungover. When I arrived that afternoon, stewed in self-loathing, there you were all bright-eyed and rosy-cheeked. I still fancied you horribly, and I knew with com-plete certainty that I would disappoint you. And that the longer I waited to do it the worse it would be. I thought it would be better for you to stop feeling anything for me as soon as possible. That's pretty patroniz-ing now that I think of it. I'm sorry."

She considered this new information.

"It is a bit condescending. I'm not some ill-informed novice who needs to be protected from the facts of life. If you had just told me then, I wouldn't have thought differently of you," she said. "I'd have been jealous of Charlotte, I'm jealous of her now, but it's not like we were together. I assumed you were sleeping with other people. Why shouldn't you have been? Even I had a thing with someone." His look of surprise was gratifying, under the circumstances. "It was the being jerked around and lied to part that made me want to hate you."

"And did you? Hate me?" he asked.

"No. But not for lack of trying."

He shook his head, smiling in earnest now. "Do you forgive me for behaving like a jerk?"

She took his face between her hands. His chin was rough, and his lips were very red. She kissed him. He made a low noise of appreciation, or of desire, and pulled her to him.

"Why did you say *Jesus* like that when you came to pick me up?" she asked when they stopped to breathe.

"Did I?"

"You did."

"Probably because developing an all-consuming crush on a first year when you're about to graduate is objectively a terrible idea," he said into her hair. She turned to face him. He looked self-conscious. As if to mask his reaction, he kissed her again.

Joy crashed over her, painful in the way pleasure can be. It didn't announce itself as joy, only as a feeling as strong as any she had known. It didn't originate in her mind, but in her body. She felt the wave, and then the yank of the undertow. It was like forgetting yourself in the ocean and getting pulled under, where there was no air, with no idea which way was up, spiraling, dancing toward the unknown, afraid, impressed. She stopped fighting it.

46

The next time Pen went with Sasha to Talmòrach, it was May. The air smelled of rich mud and was full of sunlight and bird chatter, and the lawns, shrubs, and leaves were a luminous green.

They parked in the usual place by the stables. While Sasha carried their bags, heavy with the exam notes Pen had envisioned them spending hours poring over, up to the turret, Pen walked the long way around the house, admiring its springtime incarnation, and descended the terrace steps to the gardens. She found Christina kneeling in a flower bed, planting begonias.

Seeing Pen, Christina jumped to her feet. "Darling!" she said, pulling off her gloves and hugging her close.

"I had a feeling I might find you here," Pen said. The gardens had been remarkable even in the fall and winter, but now they were so full of life and beauty that she hardly knew where to look.

"Funny," said Christina, resuming her previous position amid the white and pink buds that looked like roses, but without the thorns. "I used to hate gardening."

"Really?" To Pen, Christina seemed thoroughly at peace. "Why?"

"I was hopeless at it. Murdered every plant I touched," said Christina, surveying the neat row she had planted. "I cannot describe to you how I despised, when I was your age, getting things wrong." She looked up at Pen. "Perhaps I don't need to."

Pen knelt beside Christina in the cool, damp earth. She picked up the trowel and dug a hole, as Christina had been doing, and then dropped one of the seedlings into it, and covered it over, patting the soft soil.

"I can't imagine what you must make of us," Christina said, after a while. "It was strange, not telling you. But we truly did think it would be best for you to hear it from your father."

"I don't blame you," said Pen, digging another hole. "It was Margot I heard it from, in the end."

"I gathered as much. I suppose she shared some of her insights from the sea?"

Pen turned to face Christina. She was relieved to hear her make light of Margot's theory.

"I'm not the martyr she imagines me to be," Christina said. "Although I'll admit that I did throw myself into managing this place for the wrong reasons, at first. To prove wrong those who said I couldn't, to show myself that I could. Mastery was its own game to me, in those days. And of course, I was in love." She snuck a look at Pen, who was busy with her next seedling. "But I soon learned that there was meaningful work to be done. As there is almost anywhere, if you look closely. With the estate run poorly, without repairs to the cottages or working equipment for the farms, without services for families who had to travel to Stonehaven for every little thing, there was not much hope for the future. The people who lived here had little chance of making a success of their own hard work. With the estate run well, there was money to invest in the land, the village, the school. We've built a real community. Not everyone would be suited to the life I chose. But I chose it freely; it's mine. Getting to choose for oneself is a gift so vanishingly rare that one must never squander it."

In the silence that followed, Christina considered whether to tell Pen about the decision she and Elliot and Margot had lately reached, about the future of the estate. Talmòrach would not hang over her sons and George. It would be turned over, when they could no longer manage it, to the National Trust. They had jointly created an endowment for its upkeep, so her work would continue. Their children's futures would not be limited by the dictates of the past. *No*, she thought. *That's a conversation for another day.* Christina knew how unusual it was, that her own first love had stuck the way it had. She did not expect, or even hope, that the same would be true for her son. Much as she liked Pen, or perhaps because of how much she liked her, Christina hoped that she would live widely, would experience as much as she could, before narrowing her freedom. This, after all, was only the beginning.

"So you don't believe a mother has to choose between being a selfish monster and being eaten alive?" Pen asked.

"Heavens." Christina laughed. "Margot does have a flair for the dramatic." She looked thoughtful for a moment. "Do you know why the female octopus dies when she does?" she asked.

Pen did not even try to guess. Marine biology was, for now, part of her vast body of ignorance. "No," she said.

"It's so that she doesn't compete with her children for food," said Christina. "Or eat them by mistake. Or otherwise get in the way of progress. It's common enough, in nature, this stepping aside after reproducing. The parents have had their turn, they've lived their lives, and their death gives the next generation a fighting chance to survive. The hatchlings have everything they need by that point. The lessons of the past are in them already. It's time for their stories to begin, unencumbered by guilt or duty or expectations." Christina gave Pen her self-aware smile. "I'm not saying we should follow their lead. Human children are too vulnerable. Parents don't become redundant right away. But we do become so, eventually, if we've done our jobs at all well."

Sasha came down the steps into the gardens, with Nellie on his heels. He kissed his mother's cheek in greeting. "I'm going to take Pen away from you now, Mum," he said. "She's my guest this weekend."

"Oh, how good of you to remember," Christina said. She squeezed Pen's hand. "Away with you."

They entered the house through the boot room. Sasha turned her around, so they were face-to-face. She tilted her head up, but instead of kissing her he drew her to him and wrapped his arms around her lower back, pressing his cheek against her hair. They stood there for a while, amid the rows of boots and coats, feeling one another's hearts racing.

Later, while Sasha was in the kitchen taking charge of lunch, Pen slipped through the swinging door to the dining room. It was bright with daylight. She stood in front of the small, unsigned painting between the doorway and the old-fashioned bellpull. In it, a furious sea, rocked by waves, unbound by horizon, confronted the sky.

August

The young couple held hands. Her glossy hair was pinned up. Her shoulders were bare, and her pale arms looked vulnerable, exposed by her milky gown, which hugged her figure and dipped into a V at the back. He wore a kilt of red and green tartan, and his knee socks matched her dress. A third stood down below, facing them.

The bride leaned into her betrothed, whispered something in his ear. He lifted her veil and kissed her delicately, as if afraid to smudge her lipstick. Standing on the base of the National Monument, they looked like figurines atop a calcified, half-eaten wedding cake.

Pen watched them. Prosecco and quiche were laid out on a picnic blanket, and voices collided in midair; everyone else had already forgotten the couple. They were backlit, she noticed, as the photographer adjusted his camera. She hoped he would soon get them to turn around.

"Excuse me?" the groom had said a minute or two before. Pen noticed there was a pimple between his eyebrows that had been covered up with makeup a shade too orange for his skin, and that he had a small tattoo of a bird on the inside of his forearm. "Could you lads give us a hand?"

Charlie had been the first to notice them. "Of course," he said, nudging Sasha's elbow.

"Ta, mate," the groom said, as Charlie and Sasha stood to help hoist the bride up onto the stone platform.

Sasha and Pen had come up for the weekend to see Alice's play. Everyone was camping out in the flat on Dublin Street that Pen, Alice, and Jo would share for their second year. The flat had high ceilings and a large kitchen with windows that opened wide. Wooden beams on a pulley system let them suspend their laundry above the farm table, where it would dry over their heads while they talked into the night.

Pen had found a job in London for the summer. Not at a news magazine of great editorial distinction, but at a small, scruffy one with a literary bent and offices on the second floor of a walk-up in Dalston. Pen was hardly paid enough to cover her Oyster card, but the work suited her: she went through every story, word by word, to check the facts. She was staying in George and Rosh's spare room and, in lieu of rent, she took Danny for long walks every morning and played with him in the evenings so George could sleep, work, or just be alone.

Pen was still watching the couple and wishing them luck in her mind. "They're so young," she said, noticing that Alice was looking at them, too. "I hope they've thought this through."

Alice took a last bite of quiche and threw her empty paper plate at Pen like a frisbee.

"Don't be a downer," she said. "If not, they can always cheat on each other and get divorced like everyone else, it's not the end of the world."

Charlie put an arm around Alice's shoulders and looked at her, his face lit up like a Christmas tree. He'd begun looking at her that way the morning she'd learned she would be playing Clytemnestra in the Festival. She'd run up to his room and banged on his door, nonverbal with excitement. His congratulatory kiss, he claimed when they finally came up for air two days later, had gotten away from him. It was clear that nothing had gotten away from either of them.

When Sasha's fourth-year exams were over, after he'd been pelted with eggs and flour and silly string and then washed it all off and recovered, he'd once again appeared at Pen's door.

This time, they did not talk. She backed up to let him in, he stepped forward to lift her into his arms, and with impressive agility he had the door closed and her up against it within seconds, their breath mingling, his hands in her hair, his mouth pressing down on hers. It was a revelation, this heedlessness. They did not pause to close the flameproof curtains or to turn on music to cover the sounds they were making or to consider whether it was a good idea, whether it would last.

Later, he helped her pack up her room in Lee House. They loaded her dictionaries, anthologies, and paperbacks into boxes. She stood on the bed, untacked the relics from the bulletin board, and slid them into one of the folders she used for her coursework. Sasha sat at her desk and wrote on the tab in small, deliberate letters, "Pen: First Year."

While he loaded the car, she took a final look around the room. It felt alien. Satisfied that she had forgotten nothing important, she closed the door.

Now

You look up at me in the darkness. Your eyes are the grayish-blue of sea and sky, almond shaped, watchful. You hold my gaze, and I hold yours. "Good morning, my love," I say, my voice rough with hours of silence, and you smile.

I lift you up, warm from dreams, and settle you in my arms. Outside, the grass is buried in snow. I can feel the breath of winter through the edges of the windowpanes. In here, in our quiet corner where the tenses merge, we are snug.

You burrow into me, hedgehog-like, searching. My nipple shrieks as you latch. Still, better milk than limbs. In so many ways, we humans have it easy.

I was your home for a while, I think, as I hold your head in the palm of my hand. And I will be your harbor for a long time yet. But not forever.

When your turn comes, is there something I'll whisper in your ear as

I leave you in a new room, without me? Something like *It takes courage to be known*, or *The only way is to make peace with yourself*? Probably not. Probably I'll just pretend I'm not crying and put some old stories into your bedside drawer for you to find. In case you should ever go looking for them.

Acknowledgments

No mothers were eaten alive during the writing of this book, but there were some close calls.

I owe an immense debt of gratitude to Samantha Haywood and Laura Cameron for bravely taking this story (and me) on in 2022, for gently preventing me from giving it a dull title, and for being unfailingly generous with their time, intelligence, and confidence ever since. Thank you, too, to the wonderful Transatlantic Agency team members who have supported this book, including Evan Brown, Eva Oakes, and Megan Philipp.

It takes a flying leap of faith and a great deal of hard work by many to bring a first novel into the world. To everyone at Pamela Dorman Books, Viking, Penguin US, Penguin Canada, and Quercus UK, who invested energy in this book and loaned me their genius, I am so honored and grateful. Profound thanks to Laura Dosky and Nicole Winstanley in Canada, to Pamela Dorman and Marie Michels in the US, and to Katherine Burdon in the UK, for being the wise and thoughtful voices in my head, and for laboring alongside me, fortifying walls, vacuuming under rugs, and de-cobwebbing corners to make this story fit for habitation.

In the US I am deeply thankful to Brian Tart, Andrea Schulz, Patrick Nolan, Kate Stark, Mary Stone, Rebecca Marsh, Tess Espinoza, Nicole Celli, Tricia Conley, Diandra Alvarado, Jason Ramirez, Lynn Buckley, Becca Stevenson, Anna Brill, Molly Fessenden, Andy Dudley, Rachel Obenschain, Kelly Danver, and to every member of the Penguin Publishing Group sales team. Special thanks to Janine Barlow, Lauren Riebs, and Chelsea Cohen for lending their exceptional eyes to this text and for keeping me from making the kinds of mistakes that would haunt me for the rest of my days; to Catherine Nolin for her stunning jacket painting; to Claire Vaccaro, Meighan Cavanaugh, Jason Ramirez, and Lynn Buckley for doing such a beautiful job of designing this book; and to Natalie Grant and Jane Glaser for being a pleasure to work with.

Here in Canada, oceanic thanks to Kristin Cochrane, Emma Ingram, Beth Cockeram, Sabrina Papas, Jasmin Shin, Bonnie Maitland, Alanna McMullen, Brittany Larkin, and the incredible team at Penguin Canada. Thank you for welcoming my unusual path and for the many years' worth of kindness you have shown me.

In the UK, thank you ever so much to Emily Patience, Alex Haywood, Andrew Smith, Ellie Walker, and the whole excellent Quercus Fiction team.

For finding time to read this in manuscript form, for their generous words, and for their moral support and community, I am beyond grateful to Ashley Audrain and Carley Fortune.

Thank you to my dear friend and mentor Sarah MacLachlan, without whom I would still be muttering to myself while moving commas around in my bedroom.

Thank you to Christina Gordon for always understanding what I mean and for helping me stay the course.

Thank you to Heather Reisman for her love of books and for her invaluable encouragement.

A very special thanks to Monica de La Villardière (formerly Mokes, née Ainley) for reading the first ten chapters of this on her phone in the dead of night, for scrambling up the National Monument in a miniskirt, and for countless other acts of friendship dating back to a church basement in 1990. To the great sorrow of tutors everywhere she is not The Real Alice Diamond, but without her I surely could not have written what I view as the central love story of this book.

I am thankful for everyone who made my years in Edinburgh worth writing home about, including Kate Fish, Georgina Barstow, Jessie Thomas, Rebecca Connell, Lucy Russell-Hills, Tom Cabot, Rollo Gwyn-Jones, Will Wells, Ludo Shaw Stewart, and every person who showed warmth to Snow Yanks in the mid-to-late 2000s. This is far from an exhaustive list, and all blunders and mistakes are, naturally, those of my characters or my own. To Ellie Metrick, Sam Taylor, Sophie Green, Iza Dezon, Karen Wookey, and all early readers who offered notes and enthusiasm, thank you. To Claire Battershill, Sarah Polley, and Nathan Englander, thank you for Wednesdays.

I can't imagine how I could have written this, let alone brushed my teeth and put on socks, without the generosity, love, support, and example of Don and Denyse Green, who have taught me so much about building a world. For the practical and moral support of Sophie, Matt, Deeva, and Lee, I am so appreciative (and one lucky in-law). Thank you to Molly Knight, whose vision for me is far grander than my vision for myself, and whose friendship I can't fathom living without. For the patience, kindness, and care of Rosemarie Dulay, who understands the sacrifices a mother makes far better than I do, I am thankful every day. I am deeply grateful for the constancy, advice, and multiple close readings of Shelley Ambrose.

To my parents, Doug Knight and Colleen Flood, who were early, repeated, incisive, and eagle-eyed readers of this manuscript, and whose love of books (and love in general!) made me who I am, thank you and thank you.

To Esmé and Frida, the greatest gifts of my life, thank you for asking me to tell stories, and for understanding that I need to do it.

And to Anthony, my person, my partner in everything for eighteen years and counting, thank you from the bottom of my heart for knowing me better than anyone else, for making it possible for me to face my fears, and for lighting me up. I love you. I love you both so much.